"I would prefer our conversation to take place when I'm at least covered," she said in a tart voice that gave him hope.

A saucy Genevieve he could take. A beaten-down, frightened Genevieve made his stomach knot.

"I'll turn my back and allow you to leave the water so you don't grow chilled," he offered.

When he didn't immediately proffer his back, she frowned and made a circling motion with her hand.

Smothering a smile that surprised him by twitching at his lips, he swiftly turned his back and stared at the keep looming in the distance.

Damn it but he didn't want to be soft toward her. He didn't want her to make him smile—or anything else. But he was a liar if he suggested such. He could tell himself all he wanted, but there was something about the lass that was compelling.

His body and mind were not in accord on this matter, and his body was fast winning the battle.

By Maya Banks

In Bed with a Highlander
Seduction of a Highland Lass
Never Love a Highlander
Never Seduce a Scot
Highlander Most Wanted

Highlander Most Wanted

MAYA BANKS

BALLANTINE BOOKS • NEW YORK

A Ballantine Books Mass Market Original

Copyright © 2013 by Maya Banks

Published in the United States by Ballantine Books, an imprint of The Random House Publishing Group, a division of Random House, Inc., New York.

BALLANTINE and colophon are registered trademarks of Random House, Inc.

ISBN 978-0-345-53324-1
eBook ISBN 978-0-345-53889-5

Cover design: Lynn Andreozzi
Cover illustration: Alan Ayers

Printed in the United States of America

www.ballantinebooks.com

9 8 7 6 5 4 3 2 1

Ballantine Books mass market edition: March 2013

For Kate Collins, a wonderful editor and champion.
And to Gina Wachtel and Linda Marrow,
whom I love to pieces.

Highlander
Most Wanted

CHAPTER 1

"Do you ever wish but for a moment to go back in time?" Genevieve McInnis whispered as she stood in the window of the tiny tower room that had been appointed to her more than a year past.

The summer sun was high and showed no signs of lowering in the sky, and yet she could sense darkness. Knew it was coming. The Montgomerys would not allow the injustice done to one of their own, and now the whole of the McHugh clan—or what was left of it— would pay the price for Ian McHugh's daring.

She should be afraid, but she'd long ago accepted her fate. Her possible mortality. She didn't fear it as she once may have. There were worse things than death, as she'd discovered. Sometimes living took far more courage. Facing another day. Enduring. *Those* things took strength. Far more than dying.

The wind picked up, blowing cool on her face, relieving the sting of the sun. Her question whispered softly in her ears, as if the wind had gathered it up and carried it back on its wings.

If only she'd never met Ian McHugh. If only she'd stayed in her chamber that fateful day when he'd arrived at court and had become instantly obsessed with her.

But his obsession hadn't been limited to her. He collected things. Women. They were objects he viewed as possessions. He was like a petulant child guarding his favorite toys. If he couldn't have her, then no man would.

It was the same with Eveline Montgomery, a woman who, like Genevieve, had spurned Ian's advances. This time, however, he'd crossed the wrong clan, and he'd paid for it with his life. Graeme Montgomery had righted the wrong done against his wife and had spitted Ian on his sword in front of the whole of the McHugh clan.

And now the entire clan waited with anxious worry for the return of the Montgomerys. Ian's father, Patrick, the laird—as laughable as that thought was—had fled only this morn, because he bore the knowledge that Graeme Montgomery would return to avenge his wife. As Genevieve had prayed that he would.

Finally. *Finally*, she would have at least a *hope* of freedom.

Patrick was no laird. Ian had run roughshod over his father from a very early age. Ian made the decisions. Ian bullied his father. Ian had ruled in Patrick's stead for years now. All that was left for it was for Patrick to step aside and name Ian as his successor.

Only now the clan lay in ruins. Many had fled, avoiding the inevitable bloodbath that would surely occur. Others had stayed only because there was no place for them to go.

Such was the case with Genevieve.

Where would she go?

To her family, she was dead. Believed killed in an ambush as her party made the journey to her betrothed. Ian McHugh had swept in, slaughtering every last man and woman accompanying her to her intended husband's holding. He'd borne Genevieve back to his own keep, vowing that no man save he would ever possess her.

It was a vow he'd kept.

She raised her hand to touch the scar marring her left cheek. She closed her eyes to prevent the sting of tears. There was naught crying did for the matter. She was long past the stage of tears and self-pity.

When she'd rebuffed Ian's advances after her capture, as she'd done the first time they were introduced at court, his rage had known no bounds. He'd slashed her face with his knife, swearing before God that no man would ever again look upon her with desire.

He was right. No man could look upon her now with anything but horror. She'd witnessed too many times the instant recoil when she turned her head and the scar came into view.

And in the end it hadn't mattered that she'd refused Ian's advances, because he'd taken what he wanted, over and over, until she had no defense against him. No strength. No power. Just numb resignation.

She hated herself for that. Shame and humiliation were her constant companions, and now that he was dead she wanted only to be free of this place.

But where would she go?

Indeed, where would she go?

She closed her eyes, willing her anxious heart to stop tightening in her chest. Dread was squeezing her breathless, and she knew she was on borrowed time. Her fate—and judgment—awaited her.

The door to the tiny prison that had served as her chamber flew open, and Taliesan limped heavily toward her, her face a grimace of pain and fright.

"Whatever are we to do?" Taliesan whispered. "Surely we are doomed. The Montgomery laird will never have mercy on us. Not after what Ian and his father did to the Montgomery lass."

Taliesan was cousin to the McHugh laird's late wife. The entire McHugh clan consisted of distant relations and a band of misfits that had been pulled into the clan after being cast out of their own. She was the only friendly face in a sea of animosity that emanated from the other clansmen.

Genevieve never understood what she'd done to encourage such hatred toward her. She certainly wasn't here of her own volition. And the rest of the clan well knew it. She'd done no harm to a single McHugh, though the same could not be said for her.

She winced as the words *whore* and *harlot* echoed in her ears. The insults were hurled at her on a regular basis, and she'd hardened herself to the pain and humiliation they caused.

She was what Ian McHugh had made her. Nothing more. She wouldn't bear the blame for the actions of another. Nor could she spend the rest of her life languishing in regret for what hadn't been her choosing.

"Have you heard of their approach?" she asked Taliesan.

Taliesan nodded, her eyes darkening further in dread. "Aye, I have. The watchman bore word barely five minutes ago. The Montgomery army approaches, but 'tis worse than we could have imagined, for the Armstrong army accompanies them. They come *united*."

"Sweet Jesu," Genevieve whispered in horror. "They mean to kill us all."

'Twas the last thing Genevieve had ever wanted. Aye, she'd dreamed of Ian's death. A long, horrible death, and she'd been cheated of that when Graeme Montgomery ran Ian through with his sword. His death was far too quick and merciful for the manner of man he was.

She whispered a heartfelt prayer that her sins wouldn't be the death of them all. All she wanted was a chance. An opportunity to be free. She wanted to live instead of existing in a constant state of fear and humiliation. 'Twas not so much to ask for, was it?

"What do we do, Genevieve?" Taliesan asked in a voice hoarse with fear.

Genevieve squared her shoulders, her spine stiffening with resolve. And pride. "We must see to the women and the children. The men will have to face the consequences of the laird's foolhardiness. 'Tis naught to be done about it except throw ourselves on the mercy of the Montgomerys and Armstrongs and pray they are indeed merciful."

Genevieve swept past Taliesan, and when she stepped just outside the door she turned, her voice cracking like a whip.

"Come, now. Let us gather the others. If we are to face our doom, let it be with pride. Pride that Ian and his father failed to demonstrate. If the men of this clan won't do justice to their name, then 'tis left to the women to stand up."

Taliesan's own features tightened and her chin notched upward. "Aye, you are right."

Genevieve slowed her pace to match Taliesan's awkward gait and pulled the hood of her cloak over her head to hide her face.

She would gather the women and children of the clan into one chamber, and then she would appeal to the sensibilities of the Montgomery leader.

It occurred to her that she owed this clan nothing. That, even now, she should be fleeing and taking advantage of her only chance for the one thing that had been denied her.

Freedom.

But she had no place to go. No sanctuary. No coin or food on which to survive.

Mayhap . . . Mayhap the Montgomery laird would be merciful and perchance would place her in an abbey where she could peacefully live out her days, free of the rule of a man who'd been bent on destroying her.

CHAPTER 2

Bowen Montgomery spurred his horse to a gallop as he charged up the last rise that obscured the view of the McHugh keep. Beside him rode his brother, Teague, and they were both flanked, bafflingly enough, by Aiden and Brodie Armstrong.

Many a Montgomery and an Armstrong were turning over in their grave at the idea of the two clans allying with one another to take up a cause. But it wasn't just any cause. It was one involving a woman who was dear to both sides.

Eveline Montgomery. Wife of Graeme Montgomery but daughter to Tavis Armstrong, laird of the Armstrong clan and, until days earlier, the Montgomerys' blood enemy.

Bowen still didn't know what to make of it all. He'd have rather taken up the matter of Patrick McHugh himself and claimed the holding until such time as Graeme determined its fate. It was a task he and Teague easily could have handled themselves, without interference from the Armstrong whelps, but the last thing Bowen had wanted was to start a war when Eveline was in such a fragile state after her ordeal.

His sister by marriage was stalwart, but even the fiercest of lasses would be staggered by her treatment at a monster's hands.

"Have you a plan?" Teague shouted above the pounding of hooves.

Bowen gave a short nod but kept his gaze trained forward as they topped the hill overlooking the McHugh keep. 'Twas an easy enough plan. Kill Patrick, avenge Eveline, take control of the keep, and eliminate those who rebelled under Bowen's command.

"And do you care to elaborate on your plan?" Teague asked in exasperation.

Bowen pulled up, his horse dancing sideways along the edge of the steep rise. Beside him, Teague, Aiden, and Brodie reined in their horses and stared at the keep below.

"I plan to run Patrick through with my sword," Bowen said calmly. " 'Tis offensive that he still breathes our air. He is a liar and a coward."

"Aye," Brodie said with a dark scowl. "He looked me in the eye and said he had no knowledge of my sister while he knew she lay below in the dungeon, sorely abused by his bastard of a son."

Aiden's brows drew together and he gestured below as the rest of the Montgomery and Armstrong soldiers ascended the rise and made an impressive line atop the hillside.

Their armor glinted in the sun, bounced, and reflected a dazzling array of flashing beams. To those below, it must look like hell about to descend. The Montgomery army alone was an impressive enough sight to make the most hardened warrior flee in terror. But add the might of the Armstrong soldiers and it was a fighting force unrivaled by even the king's army.

Never before had two such powerful clans allied. It would likely never happen again.

"Is that a white flag draped from their guard tower?" Aiden asked in disbelief.

Bowen's gaze sharpened and honed in on the banner fluttering in the wind.

"It looks like a bed linen," he muttered.

"Aye," Teague agreed.

"There are two of them!" Brodie exclaimed, pointing at the twin tower on the other side of the gate.

Sure enough, another linen was unfurled, catching the breeze and fluttering wildly from the wide window cut into the stone tower.

"They're giving up without a fight?" Aiden asked in disbelief.

Bowen frowned. "Perhaps 'tis a trick."

"If so, 'tis a stupid trick," Brodie growled. "They're vastly outnumbered, and even if the odds were even they would be no match for us. Even if they were able to take a few of us by surprise, they would be quickly annihilated."

"There's only one way to find out," Teague said with a shrug.

He drew his sword and urged his horse forward.

Bowen dug his heels into his horse's flanks and hurried to catch up to his brother.

Behind him, Brodie and Aiden let out a shout that was caught and echoed through the ranks of their men until the entire hillside roared with their battle cry.

When they were a short distance from the wide-open gate to the courtyard, a young lad stumbled outside the walls clutching a sword that was much too big for his small frame, and attached to the end was a crudely made white flag.

There was no need for him to wave it, because his hands shook so badly that the swatch of material flapped madly in the wind.

Bowen reined in his horse in disgust and stared in disbelief at the lad, who couldn't have been more than six or seven years old.

"They send a child to confront an approaching army?" he roared.

Teague was without words as he stared, dumbfounded, at the sight before him. Aiden and Brodie looked to Bowen, shaking their heads the entire time.

"Cowards," Brodie spat. " 'Tis naught I despise more than a coward."

"Please, do not harm us," the child said, his teeth chattering as if he were in the dead of winter. " 'Tis a flag of surrender we fly. We bear no arms against you."

"Where is your laird?" Bowen coldly demanded.

"G-g-gone," the lad stammered.

"Gone?" Aiden echoed.

The lad nodded vigorously. "Aye, this morning. My mum says he fled because he knew he was going to die for his sins."

"Your mum was right," Teague muttered.

Fear flashed in the lad's eyes. "Many are gone. There aren't so many of us left. We don't want war and would pray that you are merciful in your dealings."

He kept his gaze averted, his head bowed in a subservient manner, but Bowen could see the lad's hands trembling and it angered him that this child would be sent into harm's way.

"Ansel! Ansel!"

A woman's voice rang strongly through the courtyard. It resonated with anger—and fear. And then a slight figure adorned in a cape that completely obscured her features from sight appeared through the gates.

She ran to the child and grasped his arm, quickly pulling him into the folds of her cape until he was hidden from view. Only his feet stuck out.

"Who sent you on this fool's errand?" she demanded, looking down in the direction of the child's head.

It was a question Bowen would very much have liked to know the answer to as well.

"Corwen," the child said, his voice muffled by her cloak.

The only thing visible on the lass were her hands peeking from the long sleeves of the cape. Bowen studied them with interest as they gripped the child so tightly that they went white at the tips.

Young hands. Smooth. Nary a wrinkle in sight. The nails were elegantly fashioned and rounded at the tips, and the fingers were long and slender, pale, as if they hadn't ever been kissed by the sun.

'Twas evident this was not one who worked in the fields. Or in the keep cleaning, either.

"Cowardly bastard," she spat, startling all four of the men with her vehemence—and the base language. Not that any disagreed with her assessment.

"'Tis the lass who directed us to the dungeon where Eveline was being held," Brodie said in a low enough voice not to be overheard.

The hairs at Bowen's nape prickled and stood on end. Aye, 'twas so. When Graeme had despaired of uncovering his wife's whereabouts, the shadowy, caped figure had appeared at the stairs and directed them below, where they'd indeed discovered where Eveline was being held prisoner.

"Is what the lad saying true?" Bowen directed at the lass. "Has Patrick McHugh fled, leaving his clan and his keep to fall as they may?"

The lass went still, her hands leaving the lad to curl into tight fists at her sides. If her body language was any indication, she was furious.

"Aye," she said coldly. "All that is left are the women and children, those who are old and cannot travel, and the warriors who have wives and children they refused to leave. The others left at dawn."

"And where are those who remained?" Brodie persisted.

"Inside the keep. Huddled in the great hall, wondering if each breath will be their last," she said in a disdainful voice.

Bowen

Something about the lass's tone rubbed Brodie the wrong way, and it irritated him fully that she was hiding her face from him.

"Remove the hood, lass," he ordered. "I'd know who it is I speak with."

She froze, her hands lowering to her sides until they pressed against the skirts of her dress. Did she dare openly defy him in front of his men and the Armstrongs as well?

His expression darkened and his lips thinned. "Do as I have ordered," he snapped.

With shaking hands, she pushed the lad behind her and then slowly lifted her fingers to the edges of the hood. She was turned so that her right side was presented to him and his men, and as she lowered the hood from over her head a gasp went up behind Brodie.

Jesu, but the woman was beautiful. Perhaps the most beautiful woman he'd ever seen in his life. Her features were rendered with perfection.

Long brown hair fell in waves over her shoulders. There were varying shades mixed in and, with the sunlight beating down on her, the different colors were highlighted in a dazzling array. He'd thought the lass had raven hair the first time he'd seen her. She'd been in the darkness of the keep and only the barest strands had peeked from her cape. But here, in the full glory of the sun, it was evident that her hair was not simply plain black. Nay, it was a magnificent mane of hair that seemed to change color depending on the way she moved and the source of light.

Her bone structure was small and delicate, her cheek high and her jawline firm, leading to a perfect bow of a mouth. A dark eyebrow arched, and long eyelashes heavily fringed the vivid wash of green.

It felt as though someone had punched him solidly in the gut, for he could not draw breath. His men were no less affected as they gaped at the sheer perfection before them.

Why on earth had she taken such pains to hide her beauty?

Then she turned to face him, her mouth set into a firm line, her eyes wounded and guarded, as though preparing herself for further reaction.

Another gasp—this time of horror—echoed harshly through the air. Bowen recoiled, as though he'd been struck and he hadn't been prepared for the blow.

The other side of the lass's face was . . . *ruined*.

A jagged scar ran the length of her face, starting at her temple and ending at the corner of her mouth. 'Twas obvious no care had been taken in the stitching of it. There was no smoothness to the scar and it was equally obvious that the wound had not been inflicted so very long ago.

He saw her flinch at the reaction of his men—at his own reaction—and it shamed him. But close on the heels of regret came . . . rage. Already furious at the turn of events and all that he'd learned since his arrival, he grew even angrier as he stared upon the lass.

"What the hell happened to your face, lass?" he demanded.

CHAPTER 3

Color suffused the side of her face that wasn't scarred. Humiliation dulled her eyes, and Bowen felt a twinge of regret for so baldly stating his demand for information.

She was quite possibly the most fascinating female Bowen had ever laid eyes on. One side of her face was impossibly perfect. The other was a complete tragedy.

Curiosity burned in his veins, making him impatient and edgy. He wanted to demand the whole of it. Whether it was an accident or done apurpose. The shame in her eyes hinted at something as dark and sinister as the scar itself, and it made him all the more determined to ferret out the truth.

"By what name are you called?" Bowen asked, switching tactics when it became obvious that no reply was forthcoming.

'Twas obvious that she wasn't comfortable on the topic of her scar, and there was plenty more information he needed in light of the developments within the McHugh clan.

"Genevieve," she answered softly.

It was as beautiful a name as the one side of her face was. A name to match the woman she surely must have been before the other side of her face was flayed open by a blade.

"Genevieve McHugh?"

Her chin came up, her eyes glazing over, becoming unreadable.

"Just Genevieve. Who I was is of no import, for I am that woman no longer."

Teague's eyebrows went up at the cryptic statement. Brodie and Aiden were equally taken aback.

"Well then Genevieve, it would appear as though you are acting as the spokesman for your clan. Take us within to meet the remainder of the McHugh clan, so I can decide what is to be done with them."

Genevieve's lips twisted in scorn, her eyes sparking with anger.

"Your arrogance is misplaced, good sir. These people had naught to do with the mistreatment of Eveline Montgomery. They are as much a victim of Ian's and Patrick's cowardice as Eveline herself."

Brodie stepped forward, his lips curled into a snarl. "I doubt they were imprisoned in a dungeon and tormented with their fate. My sister was ill-used by Ian McHugh for years. He has long acted as her tormentor."

Genevieve eyed Brodie with a level gaze. "There are many kinds of torment, sir. Nay, the clansmen were not imprisoned in a dungeon. Nay, they weren't threatened or subjected to the kind of abuse Eveline was. I am sorry for her. I would not wish Ian McHugh on my worst enemy."

Her face flashed with pain and a sorrow so deep and gut-wrenching that it bathed Bowen with discomfort. Her distress radiated like a beacon, and it was instinctive to comfort her in some way.

He extended his hand, his intention to touch her arm, but she shied instantly away and stared warily at him as she put careful distance between herself and him.

"Never think they have not suffered, though," Genevieve continued. "They have long endured without a strong leader. Patrick was laird in name only. Ian was a bully who thrived on making others fear him. His own father feared him. Anyone who dared to speak out or disagree with Ian suffered dearly for the perceived slight."

"Aye, I believe it," Teague said grimly. "'Tis not a pretty picture that has been painted over the last while. We learned of his character from Eveline. Anyone who would torment a sweet, young lass at such a tender age is a monster who should be consigned to hell."

"I have every confidence that is where he resides even now," Genevieve said with quiet conviction.

"Take us to the others," Bowen cut in, impatient to be done with the matter. "After meeting with your kin, I'll decide what is to be done."

"They are not my kin," she said softly. "But I would see them treated fairly all the same."

Perplexed by the mystery of Genevieve—*just Genevieve*—Bowen gestured toward the courtyard, indicating that Genevieve should proceed.

Ansel fled from Genevieve's skirts and didn't stop, disappearing into the keep up the steps from the courtyard.

Genevieve walked in a measured, unhurried pace, head held high, her dignity gathered round her like a cloak in winter. There was a serenity to her stance that seemed far too practiced, as though this were a defense mechanism, one with which she was well acquainted.

She was too calm, considering that she was facing an enemy army with vengeance and the thirst for blood on their minds. Most women—and men—would be terrified and likely pleading for mercy.

Not this woman.

She was regal and poised, almost as if she were the one granting them a favor by escorting them within. Bowen couldn't detect a single quiver. Was she truly so unaffected, or was she merely a master at masking her emotions? Had her injury so numbed her to the judgment and reactions of others that she simply didn't register all that went on around her?

Nay, he'd seen her initial response when he and his men had reacted to the shock of her scarred face. Though she'd quickly masked it, she'd been hurt and embarrassed by the collective horror that had arced through the assembled men.

It shamed him that he and his men had demonstrated such disrespect for a woman who was obviously gently born and bred. But the damage was done, and he couldn't call back the reactions of himself or Teague and Eveline's brothers.

The courtyard was barren. No sounds could be heard, not even in the distance. The wind kicked up, blowing cool where the sun had beat down on their heads.

When they mounted the steps into the keep, a nervous buzz could be heard from within. There was quiet weeping, and the low rumble of masculine voices offering words of comfort. But there was an edge, even in the men's words, that couldn't be mistaken.

They all awaited their fate.

Bowen stepped into the hall behind Genevieve, his expression grim and a sense of sadness gripping him. He had no desire to visit death and destruction upon the innocent. For the first time in a history steeped in violence, the future looked peaceful.

The Montgomerys had achieved at least a temporary truce with the Armstrongs—a genuine truce—sealed by Graeme's marriage, and his love for Eveline Armstrong.

And the truth of it was that Bowen could find no fault with the Armstrongs for wanting only to protect Eveline. Tavis Armstrong seemed a fair, just man, as much as it pained Bowen to admit such.

When the McHugh clansmen caught sight of Genevieve, and then of the four men who strode in behind her, there was an instant barrage of noise. Babbling, the weeping intensified. Dark scowls adorned the men's faces, and there were accusing glares from some of the women.

All directed at . . . Genevieve?

Bowen frowned in puzzlement, but before he could say anything two women launched a harsh accusation in Genevieve's direction.

"How you must be gloating now," one hissed. "Are you here to witness our murder? Did you offer to whore yourself to the enemy so that your position would be secure?"

"How could you?" the other demanded. "There are children here. Aye, mostly women and children and our husbands who remained behind, knowing their lives would surely be forfeit."

More stepped forward as if to add their own condemnation, but Bowen took his own step forward, planting himself between Genevieve and the others.

Teague's brows drew together and he moved to Genevieve's side, but she seemed unruffled by the animosity directed at her. Her expression was passive and unreadable. No emotion shone in her eyes, and she stared ahead, her features set in stone.

Was the woman inhuman? No man or woman alive could stand by and suffer the insults thrown her way without some reaction. And yet Genevieve seemed impervious to it all.

"Careful how you malign your champion," Bowen said, his voice cracking like a whip over the hall.

The crowd went utterly silent.

Aiden and Brodie stepped forward, their gazes sweeping over the gathered McHughs. They looked unimpressed. Bowen couldn't fault their assessment. A more sorry lot of misfits he had never seen.

"Champion?" one woman asked, finally breaking the silence.

She looked terrified, but she stepped forward, her gaze going inquisitively to Genevieve.

"Is it true you championed us, Genevieve?"

Genevieve didn't respond. Her gaze met the other woman's unflinchingly, but she didn't say aye or nay one way or another.

"No one could fault you if you had only saved yourself," the woman added softly.

Then her eyes found Bowen's and though she trembled, her hands quickly diving into her skirts to disguise how badly they shook, she met his gaze with courage.

"I know not what your plans are, sir, but I would ask two things of you."

Bowen studied the young lass with interest. She was a brave slip of a thing, barely meeting his shoulder. He couldn't discern her age, though she looked only on the cusp of womanhood. No doubt, given time, she would be a stunning lass, made only more so by her courage and fire.

Her hair was the color of wheat washed in moonlight. And her eyes were an arresting shade of blue-green that reminded him of the sea on a bright, sunlit day.

She took another step forward, and it was then he noticed that she walked with a limp. A grimace twisted her lips before she quickly forced it away. Her hand went to one of her clansmen, and he was quick to steady her so that she didn't fall.

"What is your name, lass?" Bowen asked kindly, not wanting to reward her bravery by frightening the wits out of her.

"Taliesan," she murmured, dipping into a curtsy that made Bowen afraid that she'd take a tumble.

He would have stepped forward in case she indeed teetered, but her clansman once more steadied her with his firm grip. Bowen nodded his approval to the older man, mentally making note of the man's appearance.

Bowen never forgot a good deed, and later he'd ensure that he and the man spoke privately.

A lot could be known of a man by observing his treatment of others. It was something Bowen's father had taught him from a very early age. Robert Montgomery had always said that the words of a man were meaningless. But actions spoke volumes, and it was always through deeds that the true measure of a man could be ascertained.

"And what two things would you ask of me, Taliesan?" Bowen asked.

Taliesan's cheeks colored, and Bowen could tell that she fought not to duck her head. Her hand gripped her clansman's arm, but she firmed her lips and then stated her request.

"I would ask that you have mercy on my clansmen. 'Tis true that Ian and his father, our laird, acted without honor. And 'tis also true that an innocent woman suffered greatly at their hands. Ian is dead, by Graeme Montgomery's own hand, and now Patrick has fled, leaving his clan to the fate that should be his."

Taliesan turned her head, sweeping her gaze over the men, women, and children stuffed into the great hall.

"We have no place to go. We have no other home than here. We would serve you and your laird well."

Teague, Aiden, and Brodie were no less affected by her eloquent plea than Bowen himself. But it angered him that, so far, the only people who'd had courage enough to confront him had been a mere lad and two fragile lasses. What manner of clan was this to allow their women and children to fight their battles for them? The women and children should be cherished above all else and protected fiercely. It appalled him that so little value was placed on their position in the clan.

"And what other thing would you ask, lass?" Bowen asked, hoping to give himself some time for the flames of anger to die down. He wanted to haul every last man into the courtyard and beat them all soundly.

Taliesan licked her lips and, after a nervous glance at her clansmen, directed her gaze at Genevieve.

"I would ask that Genevieve bear no ill treatment at your hands. She has suffered enough."

Genevieve's features tightened in horror, the first sign of emotion she'd displayed since they'd entered the hall.

"Talie, no!" Genevieve whispered harshly. "Please, do not! I beg you!"

Bowen's brows lifted, surprised that this proud lass would beg anything after the courage and haughtiness she'd demonstrated. What could she possibly not want Taliesan to relate?

Taliesan glanced unhappily at Genevieve, but she did as Genevieve asked and fell silent.

There were disapproving looks cast Taliesan's way. Lips curled. Nostrils flared. Hostile glares were directed at Genevieve.

Bowen wasn't even sure how to respond to such a slight, though he was sure that Taliesan had intended no offense. Not only had his honor been called into question, but he was extremely curious as to what Taliesan had meant by her cryptic statement. Genevieve looked so mortified, however, that he couldn't bring himself to demand an explanation, even if it was what he felt compelled to do. There would be plenty of time to sort out this mystery later. First, he had to make it clear that he wasn't some monster lusting after the blood of the innocent.

"I assure you, I have no intention of mistreating Genevieve or anyone else under my care," Bowen said, the reprimand clear in his voice.

Taliesan flushed and dropped her gaze, but she offered no apology, and, oddly, Bowen respected her all the more for it.

"Then what do you mean to do with us?"

Bowen's eyebrow arched in surprise, as, finally, one of the McHugh men found his cods and spoke up.

"And here I thought the McHugh clan depended on their women and children to go to battle for them," Bowen said, disgust evident in his words.

The men in the room bristled and stiffened. Some of their faces went red with anger, but others darkened with shame, and they averted their eyes. They well knew what Bowen meant.

" 'Tis a disgrace to send a lad waving a flag of surrender," Teague growled, speaking up for the first time. He was positively seething with anger and disgust, and now that Bowen had addressed the issue, Teague was only too eager to voice his dissatisfaction as well.

Aiden and Brodie both nodded, their arms crossed menacingly over their chests. Brodie, especially, looked furious. For a moment, Bowen truly worried that he and Teague would have to intervene, because Brodie looked as though he wanted to take on every McHugh man gathered in the hall and bathe in their blood.

"And your women do all the talking on your behalf," Brodie added. "Why are they not better protected? Why are they left to confront your enemy? 'Tis disgraceful. What measure of man not only allows such a thing but *encourages* it?"

The man who'd posed the question as to their fate took a step forward, his expression grim and ashamed. But he met the gazes of Bowen, Teague, Aiden, and Brodie unflinchingly, his chin lifted as if to convey that he'd take their censure and whatever retaliation they wished to mete out.

"We worried that if a warrior met you at the gates it would be seen as a challenge, and we had no wish to wage war against you. We know we're outnumbered and outmanned. Patrick McHugh was not a man well versed in training. And Ian—"

He broke off, clearing his throat in obvious discomfort.

"I would speak freely if I may, good sir. 'Tis not respectful, what I have to say, but 'tis the truth all the same."

Bowen nodded. "By all means. I would have your honesty. By what name are you called?"

"Tearlach McHugh."

"Carry on, then, Tearlach."

"Ian was a dishonorable man. Not only for his treatment of those weaker than himself, but for his tactics in warfare. He'd stab a man in his back rather than ever face him in a fair fight. We aren't trained, Montgomery. 'Tis readily apparent enough. We wouldn't have stood a chance against you, and so those of us who remained behind decided to place our fate in your hands and that of your laird's. 'Twas our only choice. We have wives and children, and we have no wish to die and leave them uncared for and unprotected, even though you think we do neither."

It was a sincere speech, one that impressed Bowen for its honesty. It was apparent that he had no liking for speaking ill of his laird's dead son, but he stated the truth matter-of-factly.

"I appreciate your candor, and I'll return the favor by being just as straightforward," Bowen said, sweeping over the assembled crowd with his gaze.

Genevieve hadn't moved. She stood stock-still, her hands folded rigidly in front of her. And her eyes looked so far away that Bowen doubted she had any idea of what went on around her. It was as if, just for a time, she'd taken herself to another place.

Her scarred cheek was turned away from him, and he marveled at how beautiful she was with her profile presented. Never had he seen a woman to rival her, and yet when both sides of her face were visible it was startling how that beauty was transformed into something pitiable.

There were so many questions he wanted to ask, but none were appropriate to the occasion. He couldn't afford to become distracted from his goal. His brother had tasked him with this duty, and Bowen would fulfill it at all cost.

"My brother, Laird Montgomery, is with his wife, Eveline, whom Ian captured and sorely abused. He will remain at her side until he's satisfied that she has fully recovered and is safe from any and all threats. Patrick McHugh is a threat to Eveline and to both the Montgomery and the Armstrong clans. And we do not tolerate any threat."

The people tightly grouped together in the hall began to grow nervous. Their agitation was evident as they began to fidget and exchange fearful glances.

"I claim this holding and all that belongs to Patrick McHugh for my laird until such time as he decides what is to be done with the land, the keep . . . and the people."

Bowen held up a hand when everyone began talking at once.

"My brother is a fair and just man. Give me, and him, no reason to call you enemy and you will fare well. For the interim, I will act as laird and my brother will assist me in compiling a full report as to the workings of this keep and land so that I may pass it to Laird Montgomery and he may determine what is to be done. If you work hard and give me no cause to doubt your loyalty, there will be no issues. If you betray my trust, you will be dealt with swiftly and severely. There will be no second chances. Are we understood?"

There were murmurs of "Aye" and grim expressions

all around. Some were fearful. Some were resentful. Some were angry. But not a single McHugh voiced their disagreement.

Bowen glanced at Taliesan, as well as Genevieve, to gauge their reaction to his strong words, but neither lass was so much as looking in his direction.

Taliesan had retreated behind the older man who'd supported her when she would have fallen, and Genevieve stood rigidly a short distance away. She resembled a statue. Cold and imposing, as if she felt nothing at all. But Bowen knew that to be untrue. He'd seen the flash of emotion in her eyes in that one unguarded moment. He had the feeling that beneath the icy façade she presented to the world was a fiery, passionate woman who seethed with tightly held emotion.

Shaking off his thoughts and the distraction posed by Genevieve, he turned to Teague, Aiden, and Brodie. "We must assess the situation with all haste. I do not like leaving my brother and his wife nor your family," he said to Brodie and Aiden, "without adequate protection, and we have the might of our combined armies here. We have no need of so many."

Teague nodded his agreement. Then he glanced back at the McHughs, who were still watching the four men fearfully.

"Let us go back to our men and discuss what it is we will do," Teague said. "I do not want every McHugh privy to our conversation."

CHAPTER 4

As soon as the Montgomery warrior quit the room, Genevieve's shoulders sagged, and for the first time she allowed her gaze to sweep over the gathered McHughs.

If she expected there to be any remorse in their eyes for their misjudgment of her, she was sorely mistaken. There was the usual mixture of disgust, disapproval, outright sneers, pity—yes, pity from a few—and confusion, because many of the McHughs had yet to determine why she hadn't tried to murder them all in their sleep.

There was only one McHugh she'd dreamed of making suffer a long, drawn-out death. She'd actually been disappointed when Graeme Montgomery had ended Ian McHugh's life so quickly. It hadn't been bloody enough. Or painful enough. Ian deserved to suffer because he was a horrifying human being who deserved no mercy and no leniency.

Pity that Graeme had been concerned only with hying his wife to safety and so had dispatched Ian with ruthless precision so that he would no longer be a bane to anyone's existence.

One day Genevieve would like to thank the laird in person, but there would be too many questions she had no intention of answering were she to do something so unladylike and unbecoming a gently bred lass as to offer her grave thanks for the killing of another man.

"Genevieve?"

Genevieve broke from her bloodthirsty thoughts and blinked rapidly to bring her focus back to the present. Taliesan stood in front of her, her delicate features pulled tight with concern.

Genevieve sighed. Taliesan was the closest thing to a friend that she had—not for lack of trying on Genevieve's part to remain aloof and distant. The very last thing Genevieve had wanted was any kinship with these people.

Nay, they weren't to blame for the actions of Ian McHugh, but Genevieve was resentful of the situation that had been forced upon her, and every slight she suffered at the hands of the McHughs had only compounded her determination never to form a bond. She wanted to be gone from this place. Someplace where she could be alone, and then maybe she could forget the last year of her existence and she could find peace.

Such an elusive creature. Peace and happiness were things she'd long taken for granted, sheltered in the loving bosom of her family.

Even now, just remembering them made her chest ache fiercely. Sorrow weighed down on her, as if she carried a load of rocks on her back.

A year ago, she'd been so happy. So very naïve, convinced that nothing bad could ever befall her. Ian McHugh had proved her wrong, and had changed her, irrevocably, from a starry-eyed young lass ready to take on life's challenges with a smile and a laugh to a mere shell of her former self. A person she could never hope to regain.

"What is it, Taliesan?" Genevieve asked gently, not allowing her rage to bleed into her voice.

Taliesan was a sweet lass who'd dealt with adversity and remained as good as an angel despite her lameness.

"I worry for you, Genevieve," Taliesan said in a low

voice. "We have no idea what manner of man this Bowen Montgomery is. The Montgomery laird is said to be a fair man. 'Tis obvious he has great affection for his wife. 'Tis also said that he treats her with great respect and demands the same from everyone around him. In his hands, I'd not worry over the fate you would suffer."

Genevieve reached to touch the other woman on the arm. " 'Tis not your concern, Talie."

"But it is," Taliesan said fiercely. "My clan has wronged you grievously. What you have suffered at Ian's hands makes me want to weep. Think you I don't know all he has done to you? All he has made you suffer? And my clan is no better, because they know. They *know*, and yet they turn their backs because they know they did nothing to stop Ian. Just as Patrick did nothing to stop his son. And so they scorn you instead, because to acknowledge that you are a victim would be to acknowledge that they allowed you to be so."

Genevieve's cheeks bloomed with heat, and she felt ill hearing it so clearly outlined how evident was all that Ian had subjected her to. She hadn't thought her humiliation could be any deeper. She was wrong.

That everyone knew sickened her. That Taliesan so clearly pitied her was more than Genevieve could bear. She longed to be away. Where she could be someone else. So that Genevieve McInnis could quietly die as she was believed to have done a year past.

"Do not interfere," Genevieve said firmly. " 'Tis best if you concentrate on you and your kin. Do not concern yourself with me. I've survived the worst. Naught can be done that is more than I've endured at Ian's hands."

"I cannot turn my back on you," Taliesan said, her voice thick with emotion. "I won't ignore your plight as others have done."

"Talie, please," Genevieve pleaded softly. "I pray that Bowen Montgomery is as fair as his brother is reported to be, and that he will allow me to travel to an abbey where I may seek refuge and seclusion."

"Oh Genevieve, no!" Taliesan said in a shocked whisper. "What of your family? You're young and you've your entire life ahead of you."

Genevieve shook her head, sadness tugging relentlessly at her heart.

" 'Tis better that my family believe I am dead, as was reported a year ago. I could never face them. I could never shame them thus. No man would ever want me, Ian McHugh's whore. I would never gain an advantageous marriage. I would be a burden to my father and mother all the rest of their days. My mother's heart would be broken, and they could never hold their heads up at court. Nay, 'tis better this way, for they have already mourned me and I died with honor. I would prefer that over living in shame and bringing dishonor to my family."

Tears filled Taliesan's eyes. "I hate him for what he did to you."

Genevieve's nostrils flared. "I hate him too, but 'tis a wasted emotion, for now he is dead and can never hurt one weaker than himself again. 'Tis time to pull together the pieces that remain and, hopefully, find . . . peace."

"I will not rest until you are happy and well placed," Taliesan ground out.

Genevieve smiled and laced her fingers through Taliesan's and squeezed the other woman's hand.

"I think we would have made great friends," Genevieve said sadly. "Aye, I would count myself fortunate to have a friend such as you."

Taliesan's lips formed a tight, mutinous line. "I *am* your friend."

Genevieve shook her head. "Nay, 'tis better this way. I would not have you suffer the condemnation of your clan because you associated yourself with me. You know not the importance of such things. It takes only a few well-placed words to destroy a lass's reputation and ruin her chances of marriage, children, or any sort of future. Heed my words, Talie. Beware whom you ally yourself with."

"You speak of dishonor and of dying with honor over living with shame. There is no greater dishonor than choosing loyalty based on what it loses or gains me. If marriage, a husband, children, a secure future are my forfeit for choosing a friendship with a woman with more honor in her soul than the mightiest warrior, then I have no desire for those things."

Genevieve's eyes widened at the determination and utter sincerity in Taliesan's impassioned speech. She had no response. What could she possibly say?

"I thank you then," Genevieve said softly, emotion crowding her words. "I would be honored to call you friend for as long as I remain on these lands."

Taliesan smiled and shook her head. "Nay, Genevieve. We are friends no matter where you go from here. 'Tis the way friendship works."

Impulsively, Genevieve pulled Taliesan into a fierce hug. She closed her eyes, savoring the contact with the other woman. It had been so long since she'd had the comfort of another. Something as simple as a hug. The support of friendship. Unwavering support—and loyalty.

All the things she'd thought long lost to her.

For an entire year, Genevieve had known only brutality in the touch of another. Ian hadn't allowed anyone other than himself to touch her, unless it was to cause her pain or humiliation. He guarded her jealously, like a prized plaything only he was allowed to indulge in. It had been the loneliest year of Genevieve's life. It had changed her, and she didn't like the person he'd made her into.

Genevieve slowly let go of Taliesan, reluctant to sever the bond, no matter how momentary it had been. She was starved for the simplest of things. Human touch. Laughter. A smile. The smallest moment of happiness. Affection. Camaraderie. All the things she'd enjoyed growing up in the arms of her loving family.

Taliesan caught Genevieve's hands and squeezed. "What will become of us, you think?"

"I know not," Genevieve said honestly. "Their anger is directed at Ian and your laird. Ian is now dead, and the laird is long gone from this place. 'Tis doubtful he'll return. It would serve no purpose to vent their ire on the McHugh clansmen. They know well who was responsible for the injustice heaped upon Eveline Montgomery."

Many McHughs had stopped to listen to Genevieve's careful explanation, and though they would never acknowledge her, she could see the relief in their eyes as they reasoned that her words made sense. Hope replaced the fear.

There were a few who were more outspoken, and determined that Genevieve not be spared even a moment's humiliation.

"What does a whore know about the way a man thinks?" Claudia McHugh sneered.

One of the McHugh men who stood close to Claudia chuckled. "She knows their thinking in one regard. 'Tis a well-known fact she spread her legs for Ian and whoever else was present."

Claudia and two other women snickered. "Aye, you have the right of it there. But whoring is all the lass knows. If Graeme Montgomery's brothers want to be pleasured, the lass will spread her legs quick enough. For the Armstrongs, too, I wager."

"With a face like that, a lass has to compensate in other areas. If she's good enough on her back, 'tis no matter what her face looks like. A man can close his eyes."

More laughter rang out, and Genevieve died a little more. Inch by inch, they chipped away until soon there would be nothing left to salvage.

Then a sound behind Genevieve made her turn, and the blood leeched from her face when she saw that Bowen Montgomery stood just a short distance away, flanked by his brother and the two Armstrong brothers as well.

It was equally obvious that all four men had heard Claudia's assessment, as well as the words of the McHugh man.

Despair filled her heart and threatened to burst right out of her chest. She wanted to weep, but her tears had long since been spent, and they did no good. They never had.

Never had she wished harder for the floor to open and swallow her whole. Never had she wished so hard that she had been murdered in the raiding party that had taken the rest of her escort.

To the world, Genevieve McInnis was long dead, and now she wished with all her heart that it were true. Only then would she be able to escape the hell that was her daily existence.

CHAPTER 5

Bowen's nostrils flared and his lips twitched as he stared at Genevieve, watching as the life literally left her body, her eyes, her very soul.

Never before had he seen death in the gaze of someone who wasn't mortally wounded. But her eyes *were* wounded. The death blow was figurative rather than literal, but it had inflicted just as much damage.

All the color fled her face. She was dangerously pale, and she swayed like a sapling in the wind.

Tears filled her eyes, and he could see her biting into the inside of her cheek in an effort to call them back. Her hand went to her face, covering the scar, almost as if she sought to hide from the view and judgment of others.

Here was a woman who despised being weak before others, and yet a line had been crossed that even she couldn't pretend indifference to.

Teague's jaw twitched, and he glared a hole through the McHughs who'd been so loose with their tongues.

Bowen waited, fully expecting Genevieve to defend herself, and perhaps he wanted to know what it was she would say. She didn't strike him as a woman who had any issue with stating her mind. She'd certainly done so with him.

Instead, she walked stiffly past him, her gait slow and

painful, as if it took everything she possessed just to remain standing. It was the shuffle of a much older woman, one wizened with age, the weight of an entire lifetime bearing down on her.

Teague stared at the offending McHughs in disbelief. Brodie and Aiden both frowned, and then Brodie made a move toward Genevieve, but she glanced up, and when she saw Brodie take that step forward, she stiffened further and hurried at a faster pace out of the hall.

Bowen shook his head, still unable to believe the overt animosity directed at a woman who should inspire pity in others. Not such hatred.

The scar had been so vivid against skin so pale that, indeed, she'd looked more dead than alive.

"What the hell was all that about?" Brodie demanded, his jaw stiff with rage.

He advanced toward Taliesan, and she backed up so quickly that her lame leg buckled. Her limbs got tangled and she went down hard.

"Brodie," Bowen said sharply. "You're frightening the wits out of the lass."

Brodie scowled harder, but he stopped his advance and then, to Taliesan's obvious befuddlement, he reached down and scooped her up, setting her upright once more.

"Are you hurt?" Brodie demanded. "My apologies, mistress. 'Twas not my intention to frighten you. I am angered by what I just witnessed, and I'm puzzled as to why no one put a stop to it."

Taliesan swallowed with visible effort, her eyes flashing nervously among the four men standing before her.

Behind Taliesan, Genevieve's tormentors scooted discreetly in the opposite direction, but Bowen called them down.

"You'll not leave this hall without my by-your-leave,"

he said in an icy tone. "And I'll not give it until I have an explanation for the disparagement of the lass."

The McHugh man's lips curled, and anger lit up the woman's eyes. She fairly seethed, and her hands went to her hips.

" 'Tis not disparagement if 'tis the truth," the woman said in a haughty tone.

"And yet she championed you," Bowen said softly. "I wonder why she bothered."

The woman flushed, her cheeks growing red. Her eyes lowered in shame, and the man shifted uncomfortably beside her.

"She is naught but Ian's whore," the man muttered.

Bowen exchanged glances with Teague, Brodie, and Aiden. Then his gaze settled on Taliesan. It was obvious he would find no answers here. None that would satisfy him at any rate.

"Where would Genevieve have gone?" Bowen asked.

His brother looked surprised. Brodie looked puzzled by Bowen's question, and Bowen supposed he could understand their confusion. He had very abruptly turned the topic of conversation. But the truth was, he couldn't stomach standing in front of Genevieve's tormentors. What measure of person would seek to humiliate another in such a fashion?

They had the matter of the McHugh holding to determine, as well as the fate of the clansmen, and yet he was inquiring as to the lass's whereabouts. He wasn't even sure himself why he'd asked, but the look in her eyes, the absolute desolation that had washed the color right out of her face, still haunted him.

"She oft spends her time alone," Taliesan whispered. "Usually in her chamber."

"And where is her chamber?" Bowen asked patiently.

" 'Tis up the stairs," Taliesan stammered. "All the way

to the end of the hall. In the tower. Next to Ian's chamber."

Bowen noted the hesitation in her voice, saw the way her gaze skittered sideways when she mentioned the proximity to Ian's chamber.

He wondered how much truth there was in the taunts of the others. The idea that this woman had been Ian's mistress turned his stomach. How could she give herself willingly to an abuser of women? She well knew what had happened to Eveline. She'd been the one to point Graeme to the dungeon. And yet she'd willingly give her body to such a monster?

His disgust nearly choked him.

He glanced at Teague. "Have Taliesan give you a tour of the holding. Ensure that she suffers no pain or injury."

Taliesan flushed, her eyes cloudy with embarrassment over Bowen's matter-of-fact reference to her damaged leg.

To Bowen and Aiden he said, "'Tis a good idea for you to accompany Teague. We will meet in the courtyard after you've viewed all there is to see. Call the clansmen together so that we may address everyone in residence."

"And where are you going?" Teague asked, his brows drawn together as he stared at his older brother.

"I have matters to discuss with Genevieve," Bowen said.

Genevieve sat rigidly on the small mat that served as her bed. She hadn't bothered lighting a candle or pulling the furs far enough from the window to fully bathe the room in light.

She was finally breaking, and she marveled that it hadn't happened before. The horror of last year would have broken even the strongest person, and yet she'd been determined that she would never crack in front of Ian.

It had infuriated him. He wanted to break her, had become obsessed with coming up with more ways to humiliate her, to hurt her, to demean and debase her.

She'd become immune to the remarks of others, and Ian had allowed them to speak to her and *of* her as they liked. They could look, but not touch. They could torment her, but she was Ian's possession—obsessively coveted to the point of madness.

She existed in a world that had become her public and private hell. In the first months, she'd spent an inordinate amount of time questioning. Why? Why was this being done to her? She was obsessed with knowing what sin she'd committed to merit such treatment. Animals were treated with better regard than she.

Every word, every comment, every dig, she'd taken to heart. Until the day she'd become numb to it all. It worried her on a distant level that she'd become so . . . inhuman. Like a thing. A ghost with no feelings, no emotions. Her body remained, but her spirit had long since departed.

But how else was she to survive? Moreover, why was she so determined *to* survive? It seemed so silly that her pride wouldn't allow Ian to fully break her. She wouldn't give him or his clan the satisfaction of knowing they'd completely destroyed her. Nay, she'd survive this, and after she left this place? Then she could die or not die. Survive or not survive. It mattered not, because no one would know.

She sucked in several breaths as they jerkily left her body in ragged spurts. She'd very nearly lost control of her emotions there in the hall, in front of everyone.

Her humiliation had been so great that she'd been tempted to tears. To let it all unravel there and finally let go.

Thank God she hadn't. Thank God she'd kept it together just long enough to seek solace in the tiny chamber that was her only sanctuary. If only she could bar her door against the world, but Ian had allowed her no bolt, no lock, no loops in which to place a slat of wood to secure the door shut.

She had no privacy save that afforded by others. She had no rights, no privileges, not even the basest, most inconsequential things that others took for granted.

The mat was hard and uncomfortable. Her leg was prickly and numb from the awkward position in which she sat, so she drew her knees upward until she hugged them to her chest and hunched over to rest her cheek over the tops.

She closed her eyes and wondered what bargain she could strike with Bowen Montgomery that would gain her the freedom she craved above all else.

There was only one skill she possessed that a man like Bowen Montgomery might be interested in—if one could even call it a skill. And the idea of whoring herself *willingly* sickened her to the point that her stomach rebelled and protested vehemently.

But what else was she to do? What else did she have to offer?

Nothing.

What was one more coupling compared with gaining her freedom? Surely Bowen could not be as brutal as Ian. There was kindness in his eyes. She hadn't imagined it. Perhaps he would be gentle with her, or, at least, not as sadistic as Ian.

It was a hope that she clung to when there was nothing else to hold on to.

Fear struck her as she remembered Bowen's brother and the two Armstrong warriors who'd accompanied Bowen on his quest. What if they demanded her services as well? What if Bowen wanted to share her with them?

A low moan escaped her. It was a pitiful sound that came out as more of a soulless wail. She clamped her mouth shut, refusing to give in to the abject despair that clawed at her.

She wouldn't give up. Not now. Not when she'd survived so much.

She had hope, no matter how unlikely it might be. It was more than she'd had in the past. Ian was dead. He couldn't hurt her, couldn't control her, any longer. Now she just had to trust that not all men were as evil as Ian. And pray to God they didn't prove her wrong.

CHAPTER 6

Bowen stood in the doorway of Genevieve's room, staring through the three-inch opening to where she sat on a shabby sleeping mat.

Her legs were drawn protectively to her chest, and he wondered if she had any idea how vulnerable such a position made her look.

Then she let out a low wail that was so filled with despair that it clutched at his throat, squeezing until it was difficult to draw breath.

He hesitated, his earlier determination to speak to her waning. She was suffering. Privately. Away from prying eyes and the disparagement of others. He should walk away and not let on that he'd been here at all.

But he couldn't. It made no sense to him that he was fascinated by this particular lass. She intrigued him. She was a mystery he was determined to solve.

And he owed her a debt for the aid she'd given his brother in finding Eveline. Aye, he did, and he left no debt unpaid.

He pushed her door open wider and took a step forward. When she didn't stir, he cleared his throat, alerting her to his presence.

Her head snapped up, her eyes flashing in alarm. Her stance was immediately defensive, and so automatic that it seemed she'd had much practice in defending herself. That thought made him frown.

"Why do you take it from them?" he asked bluntly, because there was no subtle way for him to ask what he wanted to know.

Her eyes widened, as though she couldn't believe that he'd been so forthright.

"Why do you suffer their abuse and allow their words to go unchecked. You don't strike me as an overly meek lass."

She lifted one shoulder in a delicate shrug that shrouded her in a look of utter defeat. Exhaustion swam in her eyes and there was such resignation that it made him flinch.

Never had he witnessed such expressive eyes, and he wasn't sure he liked it. Every emotion was there to see in the aqua-green pools. Her early stoicism was gone, and now he realized how hard she'd had to work at keeping her face expressionless. The façade had crumbled. One had only to look closely to know exactly what she was feeling. She'd never make a warrior. She gave away entirely too much.

"They only speak the truth," she said in a brittle voice. "Should I rail at them for daring to say what is true?"

Bowen frowned, his stomach revolting at the thought. And yet he still couldn't quite accept it.

"You were Ian McHugh's whore?"

She flinched at the baldness of the question, but Bowen had never been one to mince words. Graeme was far superior with honeyed words. Bowen had the disconcerting habit of speaking his mind.

Then she raised her gaze to meet his, and he blinked at the dullness that had replaced the wash of emotion. It was as though someone had doused a lit candle, plunging a room into darkness.

"Aye, I was Ian McHugh's whore," she said bitterly.

"'Tis common enough knowledge. Ask anyone in the keep. They'll tell you the way of it."

He couldn't help his expression or the distaste that crept into his mouth. He shook his head, unable to comprehend why.

She pushed herself from the mat and paced a few feet away before turning, her arms securely folded over her chest. Again, he noted the protectiveness of her stance. It was as if every movement were for the sole purpose of self-preservation.

"I would speak to you on a personal matter," she said in a careful tone.

Perplexed by the abrupt change of topic, he merely nodded, curious as to what the lass would say to him.

"I do not wish to remain here any longer," she said. "I have nowhere to go. No family to aid me. The McHughs are not my kin and they will not care what happens to me. I cannot depend on their generosity to provide for me."

Bowen started to interrupt her, to say that the McHughs had little say in what happened at this keep, but Genevieve continued in a trembling voice, the only hint of how unsettled she was.

"Please, good sir, pray let me continue before my courage leaves me."

Bowen nodded his agreement, and Genevieve took in a deep breath. She turned her face away, so that the scarred cheek was hidden from view. He didn't know if she did it apurpose or if it was purely instinctive to hide that part of herself.

"I should like to seek refuge in an abbey, but I would need transport and . . . coin . . . neither of which I possess," she whispered. "I aided your brother, and though it was not why I did such a thing, I would be ever appreciative if you would see fit to provide for my entry into the abbey."

His brows drew together as he stared at her in disbelief. It was the very last thing he imagined her requesting.

Her hands fluttered nervously and she rubbed self-consciously over her scarred cheek before pulling her hair forward to hide the deformity.

"I would be willing to stay for as long as you need assistance in assuming leadership over the McHugh clan. I can give you information. I can also give you . . . ease."

Her cheek colored and her gaze fell. She wiped her hands down the skirts of her dress over and over as she waited.

"Ease?" he echoed, not at all sure what she'd just offered. He had an inkling, but surely not.

"I would act as your leman," she blurted. "For as long as you want or need, provided at the end of our . . . liaison . . . you would escort me to an abbey so that I may seek entrance."

He gaped incredulously at her. And then he laughed, because what else was there to do? She spoke of entering an abbey and in the next breath offered to act the whore for him.

Perhaps he hadn't fully believed the truth of what she was to Ian until now. She bargained with her body like a seasoned whore, and he was disgusted by the idea that she would sell herself to him, bartering as if this were a common exchange of goods and services.

More color stained her cheeks, and her eyes flashed with . . . hurt? How could she possibly be hurt? Nothing about this woman made any sense to him, and he had the idea that he'd never fully know the whole of her. It would likely infuriate him to ever try to understand the inner workings of her mind.

"I know I am naught to look at," she said quietly. "I do not blame you for your disgust. 'Tis said I have skill in . . . bed."

She choked out the last word as if it were suffocating her. The color had fled from her face, and she looked ill.

Jesu, but this became messier all the time. Now the lass was convinced that his disgust was over the scar on her face.

He sighed, angered by the whole of it. And more than a little appalled that she'd offered herself without care. She hadn't displayed even a modicum of self-respect.

Aye, it didn't just make him angry. It made him bloody well furious.

"Do you not have more pride?" he demanded. "Do you offer yourself to every man who crosses your path, or is it because you find yourself without a protector now that your lover is dead. Would any man do?"

She went utterly white. "Protector?"

A hoarse, dry laugh escaped her, and the sound was guttural and ugly in the silence. He thought that she would say more, but she clamped her mouth shut and leveled a stare at him.

Her eyes were cold, unfeeling. The façade was back. No emotion reflected whatsoever. It was like looking across the waters of a loch in winter.

"What say you, Bowen Montgomery? Will you accept my proposition? Do we have an agreement or nay?"

He shook his head, distaste foul in his mouth. "I have no desire for Ian McHugh's leavings."

He spun on his heel and stalked from the room, but not before he saw the flash of anguish replace the coldness in her eyes.

CHAPTER 7

Bowen strode through the keep and into the courtyard. The hall was devoid of people and eerily quiet. They'd all been summoned by Teague to hear their fate.

It was a damnable mess. There wasn't even that much to claim. Patrick had fled and taken all that was in the coffers, leaving his clansmen to fend for themselves.

The cowardly act was incomprehensible, for when a man took the position of laird to his clan he made a vow to provide for and to protect every last person under his leadership.

What was Bowen even to do with the McHugh people and what was left of the keep? He would have to petition Graeme for supplies and coin in order to care for those who remained.

He stepped into the sunlight and surveyed the assembled clansmen. As soon as his presence was detected, all eyes went to him. There were more McHughs than Bowen had originally thought. Not as many had fled with Patrick as assumed, and perhaps they'd known better.

But their wealth was gone. Most of the horses and livestock had been taken. And now Bowen was left with a mess to clean up.

He found Teague, Aiden, and Brodie, who stood by

the steps leading into the keep. He put his hand on Teague's shoulder so he could address his brother.

"I would send you to Graeme with an accounting of what has occurred. We have need of supplies, coin, food. Graeme will need to know exactly what has happened here and make a decision on the matter. I will voice my recommendation through you, but, 'tis ultimately his choice. The king will also have need to know what has occurred. Rumors will circulate rapidly through the Highlands, and I'd rather Graeme and our king know firsthand what is the truth."

Teague nodded his agreement, but then he frowned and turned to Aiden and Brodie.

"We discussed that you would return to your father's lands and take back your soldiers. I will be returning part of our army to my brother so that our clan is not left unprotected."

Brodie nodded.

Teague glanced back at Bowen, and then again at the Armstrong brothers.

" 'Tis something I never thought would happen, but I have a boon to ask."

Brodie's eyebrows went up, and he and his brother exchanged quick glances of surprise.

"If I am to journey back to Montgomery Keep with the majority of our men, and you are to return to your father's keep with the whole of your army, Bowen will be left in a vulnerable position here."

Bowen frowned and started to deny any such thing, but Teague swept his hand up to silence his older brother.

"Before, the plan was simple. Patrick was to have been eliminated and, with him, any possible threat. 'Tis not the case now. We have no idea where Patrick is, whom he may have allied himself with, if anyone, and he could very well be a problem."

Aiden and Brodie both nodded their agreement.

" 'Tis true," Aiden said. "We hadn't counted on Patrick being gone. We'd intended to deal with the matter in a concise manner and then go on our way, leaving a few men behind to claim the holding and care for the surviving clan members."

"The thing I ask is for one of you to remain behind with Bowen while I travel back to our lands to consult with Graeme and apprise him of the situation," Teague said.

"I'll stay," Brodie said. "I'll keep a dozen of our men and send the rest back with Aiden. Combined with the Montgomery warriors who remain behind, 'tis more than enough of a fighting force to defend the keep."

"You have my thanks," Bowen said in a sincere voice.

Nay, it wasn't necessary for one of the Armstrongs to remain behind, but Bowen appreciated that Brodie was willing to do so when their families had been at war for so many years.

"You have my thanks as well," Teague said. "I do not like leaving my brother when I'm not certain of his protection."

Brodie nodded. "You took very good care of my sister. You offered her protection and . . . acceptance. My family owes you a debt of gratitude for that. Many would have scorned her and forever labeled her the enemy's daughter. 'Tis a small thing you ask, and I am glad to do it."

Bowen offered his arm to Brodie and Aiden in turn, clasping hands in a warrior's shake and show of respect. Then he nodded at Teague.

"Let us speak now to the McHugh people so they'll know their fate."

The four men turned to face the assembled clansmen, and Bowen took in the tense undercurrent that rippled through the air.

"Patrick McHugh now has a bounty on his head,"

Bowen said loudly, inciting a cascade of shocked gasps and a torrent of whispers.

"Any who ride or ally with Patrick McHugh also have a bounty. He committed a great sin against the Montgomery and the Armstrong clans. He will not go unpunished."

"What will happen to us, sir?" a young lad blurted from the crowd.

Bowen let out his breath in a long puff. "As of today, this keep and all that is contained within belongs to the Montgomery clan."

There were murmurs, protests, angry outbursts, and, from some, amusement.

"There's nothing to claim!" one of the men yelled out. "The laird took everything of value save a few head of sheep and the older workhorses that aren't able to ride long distances."

Bowen held up his hands. "Be silent until I am finished."

The angry buzz quieted.

"Now, as I said, the keep, the lands, the sheep, and the workhorses . . . They all belong to Graeme Montgomery and I, as his brother, am his steward and will oversee the running of this keep until such time as he decides on the matter."

He paused a moment and swept his gaze over the crowd.

"You can accept it or don't accept it. 'Tis solely up to you. You can stay or not stay. 'Tis your decision. But know this. If you decide to stay, under no circumstances will rebellion or disrespect be tolerated. You'll continue to work this keep and do your duties as before. My brother is journeying to Montgomery Keep for supplies and food so that we can adequately care for ourselves."

There were instant murmurs of surprise and shock. Many shook their heads in bewildered disbelief. Had they expected to be turned away or slaughtered on the spot? Perhaps 'tis what would have happened if Ian or Patrick were in this situation. Perhaps it was what the McHugh people had come to expect from the men who led them.

"But who are we, sir?" a woman called out, her expression solemn.

Bowen frowned. "I do not understand your question, mistress."

"We are McHughs, led by the McHugh laird. Whether it be a proud leadership or not is not what is in question. Regardless of the circumstances that led us to where we are this day, we're all McHughs. Now we're told that we belong to the Montgomery clan and that a Montgomery laird will assume leadership of us. What does that make us? Are we still McHughs, or are we forced to be Montgomerys?"

Several others joined in, taking up the question until a raucous furor swept through the courtyard. Again Bowen held up his hands, and this time Brodie stepped forward with a roar that silenced everyone on the spot.

"Thanks," Bowen said dryly as the big man took a step back, a fierce, intimidating scowl on his face.

Having Brodie Armstrong here with him might not be a bad thing at all. The man could intimidate even the fiercest warrior with his booming voice and dark scowl.

" 'Tis no worry of mine what you call yourself," Bowen said, when calm had once more been restored. "If the McHugh name is one you're proud to wear and is something you want to preserve for your children, then 'tis your right to do so."

"In time, will Graeme Montgomery allow us to elect our own laird? One that bears our name?" one of the older McHugh men asked.

"I cannot speak as to what my brother will decide," Bowen said. "Right now, I am your laird and 'tis me you'll obey or suffer the consequences. Later, Graeme may well decide on a McHugh to be laird of this clan, but 'tis too early to be thinking of such things."

There were a few grumbles from the crowd, but most of the clansmen nodded and Bowen heard murmurs of " 'Tis fair enough."

Bowen squared his shoulders in preparation for a busy afternoon.

"I'll be coming around to each of you to discuss your current tasks and your role in this clan. I have no desire to upend your lives any more than necessary. My task was to avenge my laird's wife, and now that Patrick McHugh has removed himself from this keep I see no reason for his clan to suffer for his sins."

Again there were looks of surprise and appreciation on the faces of the McHughs. It was obvious they'd expected much worse, and, in truth, had Patrick stayed behind, things likely *would* have been made much worse.

Patrick was a coward of the worst sort, but in this matter he'd spared his clan much grief by slinking away like a dog with his tail betwixt his legs.

As soon as Bowen settled matters with the McHugh clan, there was still the matter of Patrick to deal with. Graeme wouldn't be satisfied to allow the man to simply escape. Bowen would need to consult with his brother and determine their course. Patrick would need to be hunted and held accountable for his actions. And for the theft of his clan's riches.

It surprised him that there wasn't more animosity from the McHugh clan over their laird's defection. In their place, Bowen would have led the hunt to bring Patrick back to face punishment from his own clansmen.

"Be excused to go about your duties," Bowen said, waving his hand in dismissal. "I'll be around to meet individually with you as soon as matters are settled with my brother and our men."

Bowen, Teague, Brodie, and Aiden stood back as the McHugh people slowly filtered from the courtyard, their expressions dubious as they considered their fate.

"'Tis more than we bargained for," Teague said in a low voice.

Bowen nodded. "Aye. But we cannot leave them to fend for themselves. It would invite attack from another clan seeking to add to their land and power. As soon as word gets out that Patrick has deserted his clan, the vultures will start circling. 'Tis important that we establish a strong presence here."

"I will be glad to remain behind with you and help in this matter," Brodie said, anticipation gleaming in his eyes.

The oldest Armstrong son seemed to savor the challenge, and if Bowen was honest he, too, was keen to exert his authority and leadership here, away from his own keep, where he served his brother.

Not that he wasn't being dutiful to his brother by serving him in this capacity. Graeme was his laird, and Bowen owed both Graeme and Eveline his absolute loyalty. But this was an opportunity that he looked forward to. No situation here was beyond his abilities or those of his men.

"I'll be glad to have your aid," Bowen said with genuine warmth.

It was a new dawn in the history of both the Montgomery and the Armstrong clans. One made possible by the marriage of Graeme and Eveline, a marriage once viewed with hostility and resentment on both sides.

Never before had the clans worked together or even tolerated each other's presence. And yet now they were allying in the common goal of eliminating the threat to both their clans.

CHAPTER 8

Bowen listened patiently, Brodie at his side, as two elder McHugh men explained their duties and the holes that had been left by those who'd chosen to leave either with Patrick or after his departure to seek their own way.

It was clear in their voices the disdain felt for both their former laird and for the clansmen who'd departed willingly.

Bowen had toured the keep, speaking with men and women alike as he analyzed their needs as well as what duties needed to be performed.

Not many women had left. A few had gone with their husbands and children, perhaps to seek refuge with kin in other clans. But most had remained, and there would be no issue of having adequate cleaning, clothes washing, and cooking for the clan.

There were also enough younger men who hadn't yet achieved warrior status within the clan to do the hunting and tend to the remaining livestock. Horses would be needed, because there weren't enough mounts for working or traveling.

" 'Tis obvious you have vast knowledge of the workings of the keep," Bowen said to the two older men.

Peter McHugh puffed out his chest, his pride stoked by the compliment. Hiram nodded. "Aye, we do, Laird."

It still took Bowen aback to be addressed as Laird. He wasn't sure how he felt about it, though if he were truthful, it gave him great satisfaction.

"I need good men who know the workings of the keep. I need men who will be loyal to me while working for the good of the clan."

Peter nodded solemnly. "You'll find no more loyal men. Our concern is for the clan, not one man. Patrick McHugh turned his back on the clan. For that, he does not deserve our loyalty or our regard."

Bowen exchanged looks with Brodie, who nodded his agreement to Bowen's suggestion.

"Then the two of you will be in charge of your clan and you'll act as my go-between with your kin. 'Tis important that they have a face they are familiar with and that they trust. They'll not accept or embrace me straightaway. You'll take my orders to your clan and you'll ensure that those orders are carried out, as well as bear any concerns or problems that arise directly to me."

Both men nodded.

"It will be our honor and pleasure, Laird," Hiram said gravely.

"Laird! Laird!"

Bowen and Brodie swiveled with a frown as the feminine cry of distress reached them.

Taliesan was doing her best to hurry toward them, but she was hampered by her lame leg and nearly stumbled.

Bowen and Brodie both rushed forward, not wanting her to injure herself. It was obvious that she was highly agitated.

Brodie caught her by the arm just in time to prevent her from sprawling forward.

"You need to have a care," Brodie said, a frown darkening his features.

Ignoring Brodie's reprimand, Taliesan turned her pleading stare on Bowen.

"You must stop her, Laird. Please, she's distraught. She has nowhere to go. I dare not imagine what fate will befall her out on her own."

She wrung her hands, tears clouding her blue eyes.

Bowen held up his hand to stifle the endless babble of words.

"What do you speak of, Taliesan?" he asked. "Who are you talking about, and what has happened?"

"Genevieve," Taliesan burst out.

Bowen's lips formed a tight line, and then he sighed. "What has she done?"

"She's left the keep. On foot. She has nothing. Nowhere to go. No one to care for her."

Bowen blew out his breath in irritation. "I have no time for feminine tricks and manipulation."

Taliesan's eyes burned with sudden anger. "Think you that she's doing this for attention? To tug at your heartstrings or to gain a boon? Sir, you don't know Genevieve. You can't hope to know all that she has suffered. She told no one of her plan. But I saw her as she was departing. There was no life in her eyes. No hope. Nothing but death and despair, and 'tis a sight I hope never to see again. There is nothing for her here and she well knows it, yet there is nothing for her outside this keep, either."

"I think 'tis time we spoke frankly," Bowen said in a grim voice. "I would know all there is to know of Genevieve's situation before I take the time away from my duties to chase after a woman fool enough to strike out on foot on her own."

Taliesan sent Bowen and Brodie an unhappy look, indecision clearly reflected in her eyes.

"Come and sit before you fall," Brodie said, gently leading her toward the benches outside the bathhouse.

Bowen waited patiently as Brodie seated Taliesan, and then he stood before the younger lass and fixed her with a determined stare.

"You do not betray Genevieve by telling me her situation. I can't help her if I don't know the whole of it. My conversation with her has not painted her in a positive light. I would know if I've formed the wrong impression of her."

Anger tightened Taliesan's features.

"I can assure you that whatever impression you may have formed of Genevieve is indeed very wrong."

"Then correct my assumption," Bowen said patiently.

Taliesan sucked in a deep breath, grief once more swamping her eyes.

"I know of no other woman who has suffered as Genevieve has suffered," she said quietly. "Her clan name is McInnis and she hails from the Lowlands, close to the English border."

Brodie's eyes widened and he arched one eyebrow in Bowen's direction.

Bowen shook his head. "Wait a moment. She is a McInnis?"

Taliesan nodded. "Aye, she is—or rather, she was."

"The McInnis clan has strong ties to the Crown," Brodie murmured. "The laird is a longtime friend, and the McInnis clan wields much influence and power. The king is oft in residence as a guest of the McInnis laird."

"She is the laird's daughter," Taliesan softly interjected.

"That makes no sense!" Bowen exclaimed. "The daughter of the McInnis laird no more than Ian McHugh's whore?"

Taliesan flinched at the insult and her eyes blazed with fury.

"'Twas not of her doing!"

Taliesan yelled the words, startling Bowen with her vehemence.

"Tell us all, Taliesan," Brodie urged.

"I don't know all," she said in frustration. "Genevieve has never confided in me. 'Tis not something she would do, for she is intensely private and she has so little pride left that she maintains what she can."

"What *do* you know?" Bowen asked. "Was she truly Ian's whore?"

Taliesan flinched again, the color high in her cheeks. Brodie shot him a reprimanding look for offending the lass yet another time, but Bowen was only growing more impatient.

"Ian brought her here. She did not come willingly. This I know. I saw firsthand the manner in which he treated her. It was worse for her because she resisted— or she tried to."

"Jesu," Bowen muttered. "And yet naught surprises me when it comes to Ian."

"He was like a petulant child denied his favorite toy," Taliesan said. "He brought Genevieve here and vowed that no man would ever look upon her with desire again. He . . . he cut her face," Taliesan choked out. "Apurpose. He scarred her so she would not gain the attention of other men. He vowed that no one save him would ever possess her."

"He did that to her face?" Bowen asked hoarsely.

Taliesan nodded. "Aye, but that wasn't the worst of it."

"Not the worst?" Brodie asked incredulously.

"Nay," Taliesan whispered. "He made her his whore. His unwilling whore. He was obsessed with her and jealously possessive. No one could touch her or so much as look her way or she was punished severely. He *broke* her, Laird. Her family thinks her dead, and in a way she is, for she is no longer the Genevieve McInnis she once was."

Disgust swirled like sour ale in Bowen's belly. The conversation in her chamber replayed over and over in his mind, and he was gutted by his own disdain for the lass. He'd judged her and found her lacking. He'd acted as though she were beneath him, and he'd ignored her plea for help.

"Sweet mother of God," he muttered.

"You have no idea the depths of his depravity," Taliesan finished in a whisper.

Bowen was speechless as he took in all she had to say. Brodie wore a dark scowl and his eyes gleamed with a murderous light.

"His death was too quick," Brodie snarled. "Graeme had far too much mercy. He should have been made to suffer for all he has inflicted on innocent women."

"How long?" Bowen asked hoarsely. "How long has Genevieve been his captive?"

"An entire year, Laird," Taliesan said quietly. "If you think Genevieve is being dramatic or that she seeks to manipulate you or others by taking out on foot, you're *wrong*. She has no expectation that anyone will come after her or care enough to worry over her fate. Quite simply, she doesn't care what happens to her. She only wants to be free and to enjoy a moment's peace. She would feel deeply betrayed by all that I've confided in you. It brings me no pride that I have done so. But I would not have her mistreated any longer."

Bowen reached to take Taliesan's hand in his. "You did right, lass. And you needn't worry that Genevieve will be mistreated any longer."

Taliesan's gaze was hopeful as she stared back at Bowen. "Then you'll go after her?"

Bowen's lips formed a grim line of determination as he rose. "I'll not return without her."

CHAPTER 9

Genevieve stared at the rolling hillside dotted with rock outcroppings that spanned as far as the eye could see. A feeling of hopelessness weakened her with its intensity, and she tried valiantly to shake it off.

It mattered naught where she was. Walking out of the keep had been freeing in a manner she hadn't expected. As soon as she'd ventured beyond the walls, the oppressive weight bearing down on her had lifted.

No matter what happened to her from now on, she was no longer a helpless victim. Ian McHugh couldn't use or debase her ever again. No more would the McHugh clan mock and revile her.

She pulled the cape closer around her face, though there was no one to see her. There wasn't a single person or animal that she could see in any direction.

The keep had long since faded behind a hillside as she put more distance between her and her prison of a year.

Someone would help her. Someone would direct her to an abbey. She had to have faith, because at this point she simply couldn't fathom any more cruelty in the world around her.

There were good people in this world. She knew it firsthand. Her family were the best kind of people. They would die if they knew of her circumstances, and that was why *she'd* die before ever divulging her fate. It was kinder to let them think she'd been killed than to have them know the truth.

Her kin were loyal to their bones and fiercely protective of everyone they called friend or clansmen. Though court was rife with deception and greed, Genevieve had never experienced these things herself. Everyone had been kind and courteous to her. Everyone save Ian McHugh.

She froze as a distant sound reached her ears. Faint vibrations tingled her feet. A horse's hooves. Someone was close, and riding closer still.

She fled toward a small grove of trees nestled in the valley of two hills. A stream flowed through the middle, and congregated close to the banks were trees and other greenery. She all but dived into the bushes, praying that she hadn't been spotted.

The sound grew closer and then it stopped. She held her breath and peeked through the branches to see the body of a horse on the path she'd been walking. She couldn't see who was astride the horse because the foliage obscured her view.

Then the horse started forward again, and Genevieve sighed in relief. Still, she waited several long moments before extricating herself from the bushes and making her way back to the path.

The climb over the next hillside took more of a toll than the others. It was steeper and the rise was higher. When she topped the hillside and began her descent, she halted so suddenly that she nearly tripped and went tumbling down the incline.

Astride his horse just a short distance away was Bowen Montgomery. He was facing in her direction, calmly surveying her, almost as if he'd been waiting for her.

She had no idea what to do. No idea why he was here. Her first instinct was to flee, but she'd done nothing wrong. Whatever sins Ian committed had nothing to do with her, and she'd be damned if she was going to pay for them.

Pulling calm around her like a warrior's armor, she walked stiffly on, her head down. She was past Bowen when she heard him sigh. Then the soft thud of his feet hitting the ground as he dismounted his horse.

It took everything she had not to panic and run.

"Damn it, Genevieve."

Bowen's soft curse reached her ears mere seconds before his hand curled around her arm and he pulled her to a halt, turning her so she faced him.

It was instinctive to ward him off with her hands, to put a protective barrier between herself and the much bigger warrior.

But the action sparked anger in his eyes. His jaw tightened with fury, and fear scuttled up her spine.

"Don't look at me that way," he growled. "I'm not going to hurt you. I'd never hurt you. I'm angry because you thought you had to defend yourself from *me*. No one is going to hurt you, Genevieve. If you believe nothing else, believe that."

She stared at him in bewilderment, wondering where this outburst had come from. For that matter, what was he doing here and why had he stopped her?

She finally found her voice—and her courage.

"What are you doing here?" she queried. "Why have you come after me?"

He cursed again, making her flinch with the vehemence of his blasphemies.

"Think you I'm going to let you walk out of that keep alone, unprotected, with no clothing, coin, or food? How do you expect that you would last even a day? A lone female with no protector? You'd be easy prey for any man who happened along, and no one would ever be the wiser."

The blood drained from her face, because that was precisely what had happened with Ian. He'd slaughtered her escort and whisked her away to a life of captivity and depravity. No one had been the wiser. To this day, no one knew.

Genevieve McInnis was dead.

"I will not stay there any longer," she said in as firm a voice as she could muster. But it lacked conviction. She was afraid, and it was obvious to Bowen that she was afraid. Any fool could hear the quiver in her voice and see that her hands shook. "I already humiliated myself when I swore never to allow myself that kind of humiliation again. There's naught left but for me to go before I sacrifice what little dignity I have left."

Bowen put his hand on her arm. She tried to shrug away, but he persisted, drawing her closer to him with firm but gentle hands. It was obvious he made a concerted effort not to hurt her in any way. His palms smoothed up her arms to rest at her shoulders and he gave each a reassuring squeeze.

"I won't allow you to go."

She couldn't help the dismay that overcame her. Disappointment—and gut-wrenching fear—choked her, robbing her of breath. How cruel was the promise of freedom only to have it yanked away.

He sighed, and his features softened. There was a hint of sorrow—and regret—in his eyes, and that puzzled her.

"You'll not remain as a prisoner, Genevieve. Never that. You'll be well cared for and will be treated as an honored guest. No one will harm you. You answer to no one save me. I'll send word to your family, but until they arrive you'll be given the utmost regard. I'll have the head of anyone who dares cross me on this matter."

"Nay!" she shouted hoarsely, ripping her arms from his grasp. "Nay, do not!"

His brows furrowed and he stared at her in clear confusion. "I do not understand."

Her breath sputtered erratically from frozen lips. She was so panicked that she could barely force the words from her throat.

"You'll not send word to my family."

There was a note of hysteria in her voice that even she was cognizant of.

"Why the hell not?" Bowen demanded. "They must be sick with worry."

Genevieve shook her head, tears filling her eyes. A sob welled in her throat, and she couldn't call back the tears as they slid down her cheeks. It made her furious that this man could bring her to tears when Ian McHugh had never done so. She'd never allowed it. Wouldn't give him the satisfaction.

"They believe me dead. That I perished with the rest of my escort a year ago."

Bowen stared agape at her. "Then surely you would want to send word to them at once so they don't linger under such a misapprehension any longer."

She shook her head even more vehemently, and felt the frayed threads holding her together start to break. Perhaps she was finally going mad.

"'Tis better that they think me dead. If they knew all . . ."

She broke off, shaking her head and turning away, no longer able to look Bowen in the eye.

She dare not admit everything to him. She didn't think she could bear to see the pity and disgust in his eyes. Nor could she bear to hear the cold recitation of the facts from her own lips.

"'Tis better this way," she said again. "I would never have them know the whole of it. My shame is too great for them to bear. I would forever be a burden to them. There would be naught for me to do save return home and live in seclusion under my father's care for the rest of my days, and for my family to bear my shame for all time."

Bowen's lips tightened. She knew that he likely thought her daft. Or extremely selfish. 'Twas not her pride preventing her from sending word to her family. She had none left. The knowledge of what had happened to Genevieve would destroy her mother and the rest of her kin. She could never live with herself for causing them so much pain. She would die before bringing dishonor to her father's name.

"I have already brought dishonor to my clan," she said in a quiet, pained voice. "I despise myself for what I approached you with earlier. Only a person without hope or honor would do such a thing, and 'tis clear I have neither. How could my clan ever welcome me back with open arms when I've done so much to bring shame to the people who loved me most?"

Bowen stepped forward, his hand pushing away the hood of her cloak to cup her scarred cheek. The action startled her so much that she stood frozen, staring at him wide-eyed.

He caressed the mangled flesh, her distress increasing with every second his fingers touched her with such gentleness.

"I propose that we both forget about what occurred in your chamber earlier. I acted reprehensibly."

She shook her head, trying to free her cheek from his hand, but he palmed her jaw, holding his hand firmly in position.

"You reacted in disgust, as you should have. Who could blame you? What does a woman like me have to offer a man such as you? You're beautiful," she blurted out. "You could have any lass you crooked your finger at."

Aye, 'twas true. The man was simply divine to look at.

Not a single imperfection marred his body—or at least, what she could see of it. He was so beautiful to look at that she was sure many a lass had sighed upon setting eyes on him.

"I was once fair to look upon," she whispered. "And now I am ruined." She touched her face just above where his fingers rested and then offered a hoarse laugh that was abrasive in the still air. "Ruined in more ways than one. No part of me has survived Ian McHugh's possession. I'll never be whole again."

There was blackness in Bowen's expression that should have frightened her. Perhaps if she had anything left to lose, she would have been more afraid. As it was, she looked at him bleakly, resignation whispering through her veins.

"'Tis not your dishonor you wear," he said darkly. "'Tis no shame for bearing what is done to you and working to preserve your dignity."

She laughed again, the sound harsh and abrasive. "Dignity? I have none. None was allowed me. I proved that none remains when I offered to whore myself to you."

She closed her eyes against a fresh surge of tears, humiliation chanting an awful litany in her head.

"You can't imagine how it feels to have no other choice or to believe that all you're worth is what you can offer a man through your body. I used to think I'd reached my absolute lowest point, and that I couldn't possibly debase myself any more than I already had. I was wrong. 'Tis when I willingly offered my . . . s-s-services . . . to you that I realized I'd sunk as low as was possible. And yet I was so desperate for freedom that I was willing to debase myself, to face you with no shame or pride. I hate myself for that."

She choked out the words, her anger and grief swelling with every passing second. She wanted to rage against the world. Wanted to scream at the helplessness of her situation and the unfairness of it all.

Bowen's eyes glittered. He was furious. She couldn't blame him.

"I wish with all my heart and soul that my brother hadn't killed Ian McHugh," Bowen growled.

Her eyes widened and her lips quivered. "Why would you want him to live?"

He pulled her close, until she was pressed to his body, his heat wrapping around her like the warmest fur in winter. He caressed her scarred cheek with a touch so tender that it was a physical ache in her soul.

His head lowered until his mouth was but mere inches from hers. His eyes were fierce, yet when he spoke his voice was quiet and resolute.

"So that I could kill him now for all he has done to you."

Another tear crept over her eyelid and slipped unchecked down her cheek. He thumbed it gently away.

"Do not cry, Genevieve. 'Tis more than I can bear to see your tears."

She bowed her head, staring downward, but he eased his palm down to cup her chin and then he carefully nudged upward so she was forced to meet his gaze again.

"I'm taking you back to the keep," he said, his voice firm, brooking no argument. "You'll be assigned a new chamber. I want your promise that you'll not venture out alone again. I will not allow you to be ill-treated ever again, Genevieve. That is the promise I make to you."

She couldn't draw breath. She stared into Bowen Montgomery's eyes, looking for any sign of deceit or treachery. All she saw was burning sincerity—and rage. Rage *for* her. Not *at* her, but on her behalf. It baffled her. He was a complete stranger. He owed her nothing. He had every reason to despise Ian McHugh and his whore.

It would be so easy to lay siege to the keep and use her in any manner he saw fit. And yet he treated her gently.

The most unlikely of champions, and the most unlikely woman to inspire a man to champion her cause. She was naught but a scarred whore, and he was so handsome that he turned heads wherever he went. He was brother to one of the mightiest lairds in the Highlands, and he wielded much wealth and power.

It was absolutely true what she'd said earlier. This was a man who could have any woman he desired in all of Scotland.

And yet he seemed determined, whether she wished it or not, to see to her needs and . . . protect . . . her.

No one since her father and brothers had protected or sheltered her. No one had protected her against Ian, and Ian hadn't protected her from the words and actions of his own clan.

She was so overcome that she couldn't even put to words all that she was thinking.

"And when you leave?" she asked, fear already clutching her throat. "When you leave this place and I am naught but a memory, what then will happen to me?"

"I'll not leave you to this fate," he said in a quiet, firm voice. "If you have not changed your mind about sending word to your kin, then you'll either be placed with my clan and offered the protection that extends to all Montgomerys or I'll do as you asked and see you well placed at an abbey."

Relief was sweet and swift. She sagged, her shoulders drooping, and closed her eyes to savor the promise of sanctuary.

Such a wondrous thing. Hope. Something she'd been so long without. And yet now it bloomed, like the first blossom in spring, spreading its petals to seek the sun.

It was overpowering in its intensity, and she welcomed it, savoring it like a lost friend.

Hope was the sweetest gift. It made her look to the future, not in dread or despair but with new eyes.

"Thank you," she choked out.

Her fingers pressed into his muscular arms, her grip tight. She feared if she let go she would awake from a dream and find none of this was real.

"There is naught to thank me for. Now come. Let us return to the keep so that we may partake of the evening meal. You must be exhausted from your worries and the walk from the keep."

"You are an angel sent from God at last," she whispered. "I prayed for so long for one. I thought He had forgotten me, surely."

Bowen's features tightened and darkened. "I come too late. I have saved you from none of your misery. Would that I had known of your plight earlier. I would have come, Genevieve. I would have saved you."

She put her hand on his forearm, noting the paleness of her skin against his much darker flesh. " 'Tis not true. Your kindness is a beacon on the darkest night. I had forgotten that goodness exists."

He seemed discomfited by her praise, but she met his gaze, never once looking away, so that her sincerity could not be questioned.

Then he slid an arm around her waist and guided her toward his horse a few feet away.

"Come. You ride with me. Let us return before the others become worried."

Genevieve went gladly, marveling that she'd ever be happy about returning to McHugh Keep, a place that had been her hell for an entire year.

And she held his promise close to her heart, hugging it with every fiber of her being.

CHAPTER 10

When Bowen rode into the courtyard with Genevieve, he was treated to several knowing looks, which annoyed him. There were smirks from the McHugh clansmen, outright expressions of disdain from the McHugh women, and even his brother and the two Armstrong brothers raised their eyebrows.

Still, Teague, ever the gentleman, came forward to assist Genevieve from Bowen's horse so that Bowen could dismount. Genevieve was wary of Teague and immediately put distance between them. Teague frowned at her as if she gave him insult for fearing he would harm her.

Taliesan limped heavily into the courtyard, her gait far too fast for a woman with a lame leg. He started to call out a warning to her when she stumbled.

Acting quickly, Brodie caught her before she went down. She came up, her face scarlet with embarrassment, but she didn't allow it to deter her from her goal.

After murmuring a quick thank-you and a curtsy to Brodie, she continued on her way, at a more sedate but no less determined pace toward Genevieve.

"I would speak to you before I depart on the morrow," Teague whispered so only Bowen could hear.

Bowen nodded his agreement. "After the evening meal."

Teague stepped away and motioned for one of the Montgomery men to tend to Bowen's horse.

Taliesan finally made her way to Genevieve and grasped both of Genevieve's hands, her face reflecting her obvious relief.

"Thank God you've returned," Taliesan said.

Then, as if realizing the absurdity of what she'd said, she flushed and clutched Genevieve's hands harder.

"I sent Bowen after you. Please don't be angry with me. 'Tis no place for a woman alone, out on her own with no protection. I know you are unhappy here, but 'tis my hope that this will change under the Montgomerys' direction."

Bowen watched Genevieve closely, hoping she wouldn't hurt the lass's feelings, particularly when Taliesan had been so worried for her. Her heart had been in the right place, and she'd been genuinely concerned over Genevieve's fate.

He needn't have worried. Genevieve managed a half smile and she returned Taliesan's squeeze. "I thank you for your concern, Talie. 'Tis true enough that Bowen fetched me back, and for now 'tis glad I am to be here."

But Bowen saw the uncertainty and fear in her gaze as she surveyed the McHughs who dotted the courtyard and beyond, watching from the steps to the keep. There was scorn and derision in their stares that Genevieve would have to be a simpleton to miss.

She notched her chin upward, her face becoming bland and indecipherable. It was her mask, one he had quickly identified as her way of blocking out the shame and humiliation she experienced at the hands of others.

The lass may have said she no longer had pride, but she was dead wrong. She possessed more determination than most warriors of his acquaintance. She'd so perfected the "you can't hurt me" shield that she resembled an ice princess whose features were implacable.

After hearing of all that Ian McHugh had done to her—and he was sure he hadn't heard the whole of it—he wouldn't blame the lass if she had no spirit or will left. But she did, and he couldn't fathom how.

He would keep his promise to her to see her protected by his clan or well placed in the abbey of her choosing. But first he would attempt to change her mind about her family, because a lass needed her family above all else. He couldn't imagine Eveline without the support of her family, as well as that of the clan she'd married into.

And, he realized, he wanted Genevieve to be happy, because when he looked at her he saw a sadness and resignation so deep that it weighed heavy in his chest. 'Twas not a comfortable sensation.

Her fate could have been Eveline's. He'd grown to like his sister by marriage very much. She'd gained his respect and affection. Were it not for her resourcefulness, she would even now be wed to Ian McHugh.

The thought struck him that if Eveline had been married to Ian some years ago, as she was poised to do, it was likely Ian would never have met Genevieve. Never have become obsessed with her. Never have abducted and abused her for an entire year.

It was a sobering realization, and he felt guilt over his relief that Eveline had escaped unscathed.

"'Tis past time to be eating," Bowen announced loudly.

Genevieve regarded him hesitantly and hung back, watching as he started toward the entrance to the keep. But he stopped beside her and extended his arm, waiting patiently as she surveyed him nervously.

Finally, she slipped her hand over the top of his arm, resting it delicately, as was proper, and then he started forward, escorting her into the hall.

When he glanced back, he was satisfied to see that Brodie had waited patiently for Taliesan to make her way and shadowed her every step, watching carefully that she didn't fall.

Taliesan was a good lass, earnest and perhaps too trusting and good-hearted. Time had made Bowen cynical, and he knew it wasn't a falsehood that Taliesan would eventually be hardened by her experiences with others.

He sighed, because it would be a sad day indeed for a lass such as Taliesan to learn such a hard lesson. It was one that Eveline had learned firsthand from his own clan. It shamed him to admit, but his clan had been horrid to her when she'd first come to them.

Bowen seated himself at the high table and placed Genevieve on his right, while Teague took the seat on his left. Aiden and Brodie sat across from each other, and Brodie positioned Taliesan next to Genevieve. Bowen nodded approvingly at Brodie for placing a friendly ally beside Genevieve.

The serving women began to bring out food, and Bowen frowned as he sampled the fare. It was cold. Not at all appetizing, and it tasted old. A glance around the room signaled that no one else seemed to have issue, but one look at his own table told a different story.

Teague nearly choked on the first bite of his food. Aiden didn't even bother disguising his reaction, and promptly spat a mouthful onto the floor. Brodie swallowed with much difficulty, while Taliesan shoved the food around with her spoon.

Genevieve simply stared down at her plate, her face pale, her mouth set into firm lines. She reached for her goblet and took several swallows of the water she'd requested instead of ale.

She instantly choked and sputtered, water nearly spewing from her mouth. She bent her head and coughed harshly into her skirts. Her eyes watered and she couldn't seem to gain her breath.

"Genevieve, is aught amiss?" Bowen demanded. "Is the water bad?"

"Just went down wrong," she said, eyes still streaming. " 'Tis nothing to concern yourself over."

Suspicious, Bowen snatched the goblet before she could move it and took a cautious sip. He immediately grimaced, and he'd taken only the barest amount into his mouth. It was brine, so heavily salted that no one could possibly drink it.

His blood boiled at the insult leveled against Genevieve, and his fist pounded down on the table, causing several of the nearby serving women to jump and glance nervously his way.

"Bring me fresh water," he roared.

A woman scurried to do his bidding, and he was careful to taste the water himself before handing it to Genevieve. She looked shocked, and slowly took it from his hand, raising it to her lips.

She gulped down several swallows and then eased the goblet down onto the table.

Salt was a precious and expensive commodity and that it would be wasted on a malicious prank when the clan had so little angered Bowen as much as the slight itself.

"Is the food always thus?" Bowen asked Genevieve and Taliesan.

Genevieve's face flushed with color and she looked down, refusing to meet Bowen's gaze.

" 'Tis usual fare," Taliesan said, seemingly confused by Bowen's question.

But Bowen was focused more on Genevieve and her reaction.

"Genevieve? Do you not have an opinion on the matter?"

"I wouldn't know, Laird," she said quietly. "I was never allowed to eat in the hall. 'Tis the first time I've done so since my arrival here. I was always brought bread or cheese in my chamber. Sometimes gruel or an oatcake. The better fare was reserved for the clan."

He was sorry he'd asked, because now he seethed with anger. Genevieve had been treated like an *animal*. A captive beast shown no regard or caring. It enraged him that any woman should be treated this way.

"Better fare?" Teague snorted. "'Tis more likely you had the better of it."

Disdain was clear in his voice.

"I'll be sure to bring staples," Teague muttered. "Perhaps 'tis a good idea for you to lead a hunt while I'm gone. This meat tastes as though it was harvested months ago."

Bowen nodded his agreement. One of his first priorities had to be stocking the larders.

"We had better," Taliesan blurted.

Her face went dark red and she lowered her head.

"What mean you, lass?" Brodie asked in a gentle voice.

"'Tis disloyal of me to say," she murmured.

"Speak freely. There's no one to gainsay you here," Bowen pointed out.

Still, she was reluctant as she raised her head. "The laird took most of the fresh stores, leaving the older meat behind. He packed two horses with meat from recent hunts. There was stag, boar, and lamb. He took it all."

Teague scowled. "As soon as I've apprised Graeme of the situation, we lead a hunting party for Patrick McHugh. He has much to answer to."

Again Bowen nodded. "'Tis true he is a priority, but our foremost concern is the care of the people of this clan. We cannot allow them to starve or be without adequate protection while we seek revenge on a coward who has fled."

Aiden inclined his head. " 'Tis true enough and you've the right of it, Bowen. 'Tis a good leader who thinks first of the clan."

"I only do as I know Graeme would do if he were present," Bowen said matter-of-factly.

He turned to Genevieve, who'd yet to touch her serving of food. She seemed afraid to try it after the water debacle. He couldn't say he blamed her.

"What would you like, lass?" he asked in a low voice. "The fare they served the rest of us is not good. I can ask for bread and cheese if 'tis what you prefer."

"I would like that," she said quietly. "If 'tis not too much trouble. I do not want to cause strife."

"And I care not," Bowen said calmly. "They will obey without question or pay the consequences. They will offer you their respect and cease the childish jests against you. I will not be crossed in this manner."

Her eyes warmed and a hint of a smile curved her plump lips upward until he was fascinated by the twinkle in her gaze. In that moment, she was beautiful. 'Twas easy to forget the scar that marred the other side of her cheek, for the rest of her face was smooth and silky, and so beautiful that it made him ache.

Her courage and resilience gave her beauty that physical attributes—or the lack thereof—could never touch. She made such an effort to hide her deformity from him and the world that it was easy to forget it entirely, and it was always a shock when he was confronted with it.

More serving women came by the table, smiling shyly, some boldly in his direction, as they served him more ale and freshened his plate with warmer food. Not that he thought it would help.

He was surprised by the daring of a few. They coquettishly propositioned him with subtle hints—some less so than others. It wasn't that he wasn't used to lasses making overtures. Graeme teased him about having more than his fair share of women, and Graeme and Teague both jested that Bowen would throw up the skirt of any willing woman.

It wasn't entirely true, though he didn't argue with their assumption. 'Twas no use when their minds were made up and their view of him had been sealed.

But he did gain a lot of female attention wherever he went, and while some men would welcome it, he found it inconvenient. Particularly when the women were married and he had to worry about irate husbands.

Genevieve's lips grew tighter and tighter as the meal wore on. She looked pale, as though she were ready to retire before she dropped on the floor.

"Is aught amiss?" Bowen whispered, leaning forward so he could converse quietly with Genevieve.

"They are such hypocrites," she bit out, every word laced with fury.

Taken aback by her vehemence, he lifted an eyebrow in question as he stared at her.

"Don't pretend you don't know precisely what they want from you," she hissed. "And yet they would judge me and find me lacking for something that wasn't my choice when they offer their bodies to you *freely*. 'Tis ridiculous."

Her point was well taken, but Bowen also knew that nothing would change their opinions. Pointing out their blatant hypocrisy would only enrage them further and turn them even more solidly against Genevieve. If that were possible.

Genevieve gave an audible sigh of relief when the serving women began collecting the trenchers, signaling the end of the evening meal.

"I should like to go up to my chamber, Laird," she said in a demure voice that didn't quite fit the Genevieve he knew.

"You have been moved to the one adjoining mine,"

Bowen said firmly. Let the clansmen make of that what they wanted, but they wouldn't dare to speak out against him within his hearing or they would suffer the consequences. "You may go up as long as Taliesan accompanies you. I've moved her also, to the chamber on the other side of you."

Taliesan looked surprise. "But, Laird, I've always resided in a cottage outside the keep. I've never been afforded the privilege of remaining inside."

"Now you have," Brodie said with a scowl. "You and Genevieve will reside in adjoining rooms."

Taliesan clapped her hands together in excitement. " 'Tis wonderful, Genevieve! No longer will you have to worry about unwelcome visits. You'll have Bowen on one side of you and me on the other."

Brodie was unsmiling as he said his next words, and yet there was something odd in his voice. "I will be across the hall from both of you. If you have need of anything, I expect you to come to me."

"Or me," Bowen said.

Taliesan smiled, her cheeks turning pink and her eyes sparkling with warmth. "We will."

CHAPTER 11

Genevieve sagged onto the bed and placed her palms down on the soft mattress, caressing the linens in an absent manner. A bed was a luxury she hadn't enjoyed in a year. Not since leaving her own chamber in her father's keep.

She'd been spoiled. Shamelessly so. Her every need was seen to. She'd been loved, pampered, and doted on.

Sorrow plagued her, and she tried her best to shake it from her chest and heart.

The only time she'd been allowed on a real bed was when Ian was using her. She'd grown to dread such a thing as a mattress, for as long as she was on the hard floor with the thin mat she slept on, she was safe from his attentions.

Bowen had seen to her comfort by having someone light a fire in the hearth and leave a jug of water by the washbasin near the window. The furs had been tightly drawn and secured, and candles had been strategically placed and lit around the room, so that it was softly illuminated by the warm glow from the small flames.

She should crave the isolation. She should be relieved and grateful that no one would bother her. And yet she felt hopelessly alone. Fearful and edgy.

In all honesty, she had no idea what to do with herself. She sat utterly still and absorbed the change in the direction of her thoughts. Her plans. Everything had been sorted out in her mind, and then Bowen Montgomery had changed it all with his bold directive.

It should chafe her that he ordered her to stay within the keep. For an entire year she'd been subjected to the authority and rule of a man who had no care for her other than the misery he could cause her. And yet something about Bowen Montgomery made her stupidly . . . hopeful.

Ah, that word again. *Hope*. How sweet it was.

A knock sounded at her door, and she frowned. But before she could rise to answer the summons the door opened and Taliesan stuck her head inside.

"May I come in?"

Genevieve relaxed and motioned for Taliesan to enter.

The other woman carefully navigated her way into the room and limped heavily toward the bed where Genevieve sat.

"Is aught amiss?" Genevieve asked in concern.

Taliesan sank heavily onto the edge of the bed, rubbing her thigh through her skirts. "Nay. I was too excited to sleep, and the room is quite beautiful. 'Tis nearly as large as the entire cottage where I lived with my kin."

Genevieve took in the tightness of Taliesan's lips, despite the fact that nothing else in her demeanor suggested that anything was wrong. "Your leg is paining you, aye?"

Taliesan grimaced and looked down to where the heel of her palm was planted into her thigh. "Aye, but 'tis nothing I haven't dealt with before. 'Tis the way of things and naught to do about it."

"I'm sorry," Genevieve said softly.

Taliesan sent her a startled look. "Whatever for?"

"That you suffer pain. I wouldn't wish such a thing on anyone."

"You've a good heart, Genevieve McInnis," Taliesan said. " 'Tis glad I am that we are friends."

It was still an odd sensation to think of having an actual friend among the McHughs. It made little sense. The McHugh clan represented everything that was evil in the world. 'Twas true enough that Ian was but one man and that she couldn't hold the rest of his clan responsible for his actions, but no one had stepped forward to help her. No one had said this isn't right.

It was foolish of her to expend any anger or resentment over the matter. What, really, could any of the clansmen have done?

But simmering in the back of her mind was the memory of how they'd treated her. With such disdain and venom when they'd known full well that she was a victim. And that was what she couldn't forgive.

They could have shown her compassion. Even if they couldn't go against their laird and his son, they could at least have looked kindly upon her.

She wanted to hate them all and be done with this place, yet she couldn't conjure any dislike of Taliesan— nor could she ignore Bowen's edict that she remain.

And so here she was, treated as an honored guest in the very keep that had been her hell.

Taliesan tentatively touched Genevieve's arm, and it was then that Genevieve realized that Taliesan had been speaking to her while she'd been lost in her thoughts. She blinked rapidly and turned her attention to the other woman.

"What will you do now, Genevieve?" Taliesan asked softly. "I'm sorry for sending Bowen after you."

She shook her head and withdrew her hand from Genevieve's arm to twine it with her other hand in her lap. Her voice was so low that Genevieve nearly couldn't hear her.

"Nay, that's not truthful. I'm *not* sorry, because I worried greatly for you when you left alone and on foot. I know it was not my place to intervene, but I couldn't let something happen to you like what happened a year ago."

Taliesan glanced up, her eyes awash in earnestness.

"Pray forgive me, Genevieve, for truly, I had only your best interests at heart."

Genevieve sighed. "'Twas a foolish thing for me to attempt. I wasn't thinking clearly and had no plan or means to travel to my destination. I only wanted away."

"I know it's been horrible for you here," Taliesan said in a low voice. "But no longer do you have to suffer. Bowen has championed you. He and his kin seem like good men. Nothing like Ian."

Genevieve shuddered in revulsion. "Nay, not like Ian. At least, not yet."

Taliesan's gaze was sharp, her eyes narrowing as she stared hard at Genevieve. "Think you 'tis a trick?"

"I know not what to think," Genevieve said truthfully. "But 'twould be foolhardy of me to blindly put my faith in Bowen Montgomery—or any other man. He seems to be genuine and fair, but then Ian could be charming and convincing when he wanted."

The pain in her voice couldn't be disguised and she looked away, afraid that her composure would break and humiliate her in front of the other woman.

Unexpectedly, she found herself pulled into Taliesan's arms and hugged tightly. It was a surprising sensation. For so long she'd been bereft of touch, affection . . . comfort. How long had she gone without the basest of emotional needs?

She went stiff at first, unsure of what she should do. But Taliesan held on, her arms wrapped tightly around Genevieve. Gradually, Genevieve's own arms circled Taliesan's slender waist and the two women hugged fiercely as they sat on Genevieve's bed.

"I vow to be a good and loyal friend to you, Genevieve," Taliesan whispered.

The words settled into Genevieve's heart like a soothing spring rain. She was warmed through by the kindness Taliesan extended, and by the genuine offer of friendship.

"I will be a good friend to you as well," Genevieve promised.

Taliesan pulled away and smiled broadly. "Good. 'Tis settled then."

With her future so uncertain, Genevieve wasn't sure anything was settled at all, but she wasn't going to borrow trouble by dwelling on what tomorrow might bring. For now, she was content to have a friendly face amid a sea of animosity, and a warrior as her champion and protector.

With Bowen and Taliesan both at her side, the coming days might not be so difficult after all.

CHAPTER 12

Bowen answered the knock at his chamber door and admitted his brother, closing the door behind them.

"You're settling in well," Teague observed.

Bowen surveyed the sparsely furnished chamber and shrugged. He'd refused to take over the chamber of either Patrick or Ian, instead relegating those chambers to his brother, Brodie, and Aiden.

"You have need to speak with me?" Bowen asked, pushing matters to the point.

Teague nodded grimly before settling into one of the chairs by the open window. "'Tis not an easy matter I bring before you. It could be nothing, but I would be remiss if I didn't bring it to your attention."

Bowen frowned and took a seat across from his brother. "Say what is on your mind."

Teague took in a deep breath. "The story, as I've heard it, is that Genevieve convinced Ian to abduct Eveline."

Bowen's brows drew together and he reared his head back in surprise. "That doesn't even make sense. What on earth would she have to gain, and, furthermore, Ian doesn't strike me as the kind to take direction from a woman."

Teague held up his hand. "There's more. Let me explain all I've heard."

Bowen's lips curled in distaste. "Gossip. 'Tis obvious

none here have any love for Genevieve. They're hardly objective when it comes to the lass."

"That may well be the case," Teague said calmly. "But 'tis a story I've heard from numerous sources, and the facts don't change in the telling."

Bowen's mouth drew into a fine line, but he nodded for his brother to continue.

"'Tis said that when Ian received knowledge of Eveline's marriage to Graeme, and that when he heard the lass had perpetuated a grand deception to prevent her marriage to Ian, his ire was raised and Genevieve prodded him, stoking the flames of his anger and telling him that he should not allow a mere lass to make such a fool of a man like him. 'Twas also said that she was the mastermind behind his plan to find those among our clan who would ally themselves with Ian and play the spy, and that it was her idea for Eveline to be abducted and brought back as prisoner."

"How certain are you of this information?" Bowen asked.

"I'm not saying I'm certain or not certain," Teague admitted. "I've not made any judgment. I'm only relating all I've heard."

"But you think there is credibility to this story," Bowen pressed.

Teague hesitated a moment and then finally nodded. "Aye, the telling of it has been convincing. 'Tis not from people who are overtly hostile toward Genevieve. They do not trust her, and while no one denies that Ian abducted Genevieve and imprisoned her here, 'tis widely thought that she wielded much influence over him and that she used that influence for her own gain."

Bowen shook his head. "It doesn't make sense. What gain was there for her in Eveline being abducted? Spite? Resentment? It does not add up."

"Perhaps she is a consummate actress," Teague said in a grim voice. "She plays the role of the victim easily. Who, indeed, would assign any blame to a woman who has supposedly endured so much?"

Bowen's mouth opened wordlessly. "Think you it is all a ruse? That she's manipulating us?"

Teague shrugged. " 'Tis not my place to say. But I would not leave this place without giving you the information I discovered. 'Tis your choice to do with it as you wish, but I'd not have you unaware of what is being said or of the possibility that she is deceiving you—and others."

Bowen sat back, anger and disgust knotting his chest. He didn't like to think that the lass could be so calculating. But he couldn't discount the possibility. It would make him ineffective as a leader of this clan.

Now he wondered what the truth was. There was no question that the lass had been abducted and sorely abused. At least, in the beginning. But the question was whether the captor had turned captive and whether she'd been able to wield influence with Ian as time passed.

And could he blame her if she had managed to claim the upper hand with a man such as Ian? Had she merely done what was necessary to survive? Others would condemn a lass for using whatever means necessary to survive, but Bowen could admire such strength. Except that she had placed his sister by marriage in terrible danger.

Why would she plant such an idea in Ian's head? What purpose could it possibly serve for Eveline to be threatened in such a manner?

"Just have a care, Bowen," Teague said in a low voice. "There are vipers everywhere. You know not where Patrick is or what threat he may pose. Keep your eyes open and don't trust anyone. I'll return with supplies as soon as I've apprised Graeme of the situation. Perhaps the best thing is to take care of the McHughs' needs as quickly as possible and address the leadership of their clan so that we may wash our hands of the entire bloody mess."

Only, Bowen had promised Genevieve protection. He'd offered her sanctuary. Jesu, he'd even offered her a place in the Montgomery clan.

How could he possibly go to his brother with the woman responsible for endangering his wife?

"I'll see to the matter," Bowen said brusquely. "I'll not form my opinion until I've heard all there is on the subject."

Teague nodded. "Aye, 'tis best to do just that. If you have need of me before I return, simply send word. I'll come immediately."

" 'Tis odd," Bowen murmured.

Teague lifted one brow. "What's odd?"

"Us being parted. We've always worked as one. The three of us. Graeme as laird. Us always at his back. 'Tis strange now to be away from home. In a clan that is not our own."

"I don't doubt your leadership abilities," Teague said. "The McHughs will thrive with you as their laird, no matter how temporary."

Bowen rose. "I thank you for that. Go and return quickly. I prefer your company and am more comfortable with you as my right hand."

Teague clasped arms with Bowen. "Be safe, Bowen."

"And you," Bowen returned.

Teague left Bowen's chamber and Bowen turned to the window, staring broodingly into the night.

What an enigma Genevieve McInnis was proving to be. Bowen knew he had no right to be angry until he uncovered whether Teague's report was true. But he couldn't help the tight curl of rage at the idea that she'd somehow been responsible for the attack on Eveline.

He shook his head. Nay. It was not right to take that leap before he had proof. He would discover the truth soon enough. And he knew just the person he would go to for answers.

CHAPTER 13

Bowen was up at dawn to see his brother and Aiden off on their journey to return to their respective keeps. It was strange to have Brodie Armstrong remain behind as a source of support, but Bowen was glad of his presence. The McHughs were a hostile, stubborn lot, and the task before him was not an easy one.

When the Montgomery and Armstrong warriors filed out of the courtyard and toward the distant rise, Bowen went in search of Taliesan.

To his consternation, she was not to be found. It was likely she was with Genevieve, and if that was the case he didn't want to question her in Genevieve's hearing. He would simply have to wait for the right opportunity.

He broke his fast with Brodie in the great hall, and both men grimaced at the meal, which wasn't an improvement from the night before. It would be a miracle if either man survived long enough for Teague to return with food and goods.

"Have you seen Taliesan yet this morn?" Bowen asked.

Brodie frowned. "Nay, why do you seek her?"

"I have need to discuss a matter with her."

"'Tis early still. Perhaps she's still abed."

A look around told him 'twas not likely when the rest

of the clan was already up and moving. But then he hadn't yet spied Genevieve either.

He forced the rest of his food down and immediately set his mind to forming a hunting party. The idea of freshly roasted meat made his mouth water and his stomach rumble.

On his way through the courtyard, he spotted Taliesan carefully making her way from the row of cottages on the hillside just outside the stone skirt surrounding the keep. He paused and waited as she popped out of sight only to reappear at the gateway leading into the keep.

"Taliesan, I would speak to you," Bowen called as she neared.

She looked instantly nervous and bobbled a bit as she regained her footing.

"Of course, Laird. Is aught amiss?"

"I would speak to you privately," Bowen said, casting a glance around at the others milling about.

The worry in her eyes deepened, but she nodded hesitantly and awaited Bowen's directive.

He led her through the great hall, annoyance biting at him when he saw no place where people weren't congregated. He stepped outside the back of the keep, where, finally, he spied an area near the bathhouses, where it was quiet and private.

"Is something troubling you, Laird?" Taliesan asked, a tremble to her voice.

"Aye," he said bluntly. "I seek information, Taliesan, and I demand honesty from you."

She went pale and her eyes widened, but she nodded vigorously. "Of course, Laird. I do not lie. 'Tis not in my nature."

"Do you know anything of Genevieve influencing Ian's plan to abduct Eveline Montgomery from her clan?"

If possible, the lass went even whiter. Every bit of

blood drained from her face, leaving her to look as though she'd topple over in a dead faint.

The stricken look in her eyes told him more than she could possibly voice. It was all there for him to see.

God's teeth, but this wasn't what he'd wanted to hear. Or see, as it was.

"Taliesan?" he prompted.

He needed—wanted—the whole of it. He wanted there to be no guessing. No speculation.

"Do not make me say what I know," she begged. "I would not betray Genevieve in such a fashion."

"But you would betray me and my kin," he bit out. "A defenseless, innocent woman who's never done wrong to anyone."

"She is not the only one to have suffered!" Taliesan snapped.

Bowen's lips curled. "Nay, she is not. But neither has she been the one responsible for others' suffering. Can Genevieve say the same? Can she, Taliesan? You said you do not lie. So tell me the truth. What do you know?"

Tears glittered in Taliesan's eyes, and he felt like a complete bastard for being so forceful with the lass. But he had to know if he could trust Genevieve. If she had wronged his kin, Graeme would never accept her into their clan.

"I heard her say to Ian that he should not accept such humiliation from Eveline," Taliesan whispered, tears slipping down her cheeks. "She told him that only a weak fool would stand back and not retaliate."

Bowen's jaw clenched. The deceitful bitch had turned Ian McHugh's ire on Eveline. She'd been the cause of Eveline's imprisonment and her terror. He would *never* forgive her that. And neither would Graeme.

He turned to stalk away, but Taliesan's soft plea stopped him.

"*Please,* Laird, do not punish her. She's been punished enough."

Bowen stood a long moment, his back to Taliesan. Then he slowly turned, hating the distress in the lass's eyes.

"Where is she now?" he demanded.

Panic flared across Taliesan's face. "Do not hurt her!" Rage suffused her face, and she actually took a step toward Bowen as if to threaten him. "You are no better than him if you abuse her," she spat.

Bowen blinked in surprise at her vehemence. Then he frowned, because he'd just been handed a grievous insult.

"You think I'd *abuse* her?"

She flushed a dull red, but her eyes still shot sparks of anger.

"I know not what you think to do, Laird. You're angry. You feel you and your kin have been wronged. I *vow* you have not been wronged as much as Genevieve McInnis has."

Bowen heaved a deep breath and then sighed. "I'll not explain myself to you or anyone else. I am laird. However, if you think I'd abuse her or any lass, you couldn't be more wrong. I don't appreciate the insult, Taliesan. I won't tolerate such from you again."

Her lips quivered and fresh tears shone in her eyes.

"What the hell is going on here, Bowen?" Brodie demanded.

Bowen turned to see a scowling Brodie advancing toward him and Taliesan, his mouth drawn into a menacing line.

"Taliesan and I were reaching an agreement on a few things," Bowen said in a mild tone.

"Then why is she crying?"

Brodie sounded so horrified that it nearly amused Bowen.

"Because he is a brute and he frightens me," Taliesan blurted out. "And he's going to hurt Genevieve. I know it. I do not trust such smooth words and promises. Ian offered them time and time again. Pretty words from fair-of-face men. No thank you."

She ended on a shudder that had both Bowen and Brodie frowning with puzzlement. An uneasy sensation gripped Bowen's midsection and, judging by Brodie's black scowl, he was likely thinking along the same lines.

"What did he do to you, lass?" Bowen asked quietly.

She flinched as though he'd slapped her. It was an involuntary action brought on by the shock of his question. It was clear that she'd expected no such topic to arise, and she looked dumbfounded as to how to answer.

"N-nothing," she stammered.

"You said you never lie," he chided gently.

"That bastard did something to you?" Brodie all but roared.

She shrank back, and it was clear she wanted to be as far away from the two men as possible. He couldn't blame her. They were overwhelming presences. One alone would frighten a lass senseless. But the two of them together?

"'Tis nothing I cannot bear," she said in a regal tone laced with strength and acceptance. It made Bowen admire her spirit and ferocity even more. He could respect her loyalty and her protection of Genevieve. Even if he wasn't entirely certain the lass deserved such devotion from Taliesan.

"Where is Genevieve?" Bowen asked one last time, his stare leveled directly at Taliesan. He pinned her with his most forceful look and refused to look away until she was all but fidgeting beneath his gaze.

"She does not like to bathe in front of the other women," Taliesan said in a low voice. "They ridicule and mock her. She prefers to bathe alone, in the stream beyond the bathhouses. 'Tis the same stream that feeds the bathhouses. When Ian was alive, he forced his men to go with her, and they were allowed to look their fill. Sometimes she would go days without being clean because she couldn't bear their cruelty."

Bowen felt himself softening toward the lass when it was the last thing he could afford to do. There was too much about her that he didn't understand and didn't know. Little about her made sense to him, and the more he learned, the more intrigued he became.

"Take Taliesan to break her fast," Bowen directed. "I have need to speak to Genevieve."

Taliesan's eyes were stricken. "I beg you, Laird. Be merciful with her. She's so fragile that she could break at any moment. I don't know how she's managed to remain so stalwart for so long."

"I'll do my best, but, Taliesan, what you must realize is that if she's a traitor to my people, she will have to be dealt with accordingly."

Taliesan's face crumbled and she looked away, her hands wringing in obvious distress. Brodie touched her arm and guided her back toward the keep.

Bowen sucked in a deep breath and turned in the direction of the stream that snaked through the back of the keep beyond the protective stone walls. It was foolhardy for a woman alone to venture out to bathe in the stream. Anyone could happen upon her and either abuse her on the spot or spirit her away and she'd never be seen or heard from again.

But then if she'd had to endure constant escort from Ian's men, he could well understand why she'd seek privacy to wash herself. He paused a moment, guilt overtaking him at the idea of intruding on her. He could wait until she finished, could he not?

Then he stalked forward again, angered that he was

allowing this slip of a lass to rule his thoughts and actions. She was a manipulative deceiver and he would not be taken in by her sad eyes any longer.

When he topped the slight rise that looked over the stream, he was not prepared for the sight before him, even though he well knew what he might encounter.

Genevieve was rinsing soap from her hair, and Jesu, she looked like a goddess. Her right side was turned toward him, her face arched into the sun as she poured water over her head from a clay jug.

There was such contentment, a visible sigh puffing from her lips, and the sun shone over her features, illuminating every beautiful line of her face and body.

She was small and delicate, her features tiny but lush. A gently curved waist, plump buttocks, rounded hips, and her breasts . . . A hot flush traveled through Bowen's body and his breath came in ragged spurts as he took in the sight before him.

She was stunning. So beautiful that his cods ached. His hands fair itched to touch her, to caress her sleek flesh and coax sounds of pleasure from her lips.

The moment she turned her face and he saw the ravages of all that had been done to her, he went cold, and guilt surged through his veins.

He was acting no better than Ian McHugh, staring at her with lust in his eyes and heart. Thinking that she was no better than a vessel for his pleasure. He should not be here, intruding on her privacy. There was no honor in making a woman feel unsafe.

Before he could retreat, she looked up, as if feeling his gaze on her body. Her eyes were startled, and yet she didn't move. Perhaps she saw the foolishness of trying to hide now when she was in plain view.

Heat crawled over his cheeks. It brought him shame that he stood staring at her even once his presence was known. And yet he drank his fill of the vision before him. Aye, her face was scarred, but somehow it didn't matter. The lass's beauty could not be denied.

Or maybe it was her calm courage. The way she faced him, unwilling to flinch or play the shy maiden. She utterly fascinated him, and that was troublesome given his doubts about her.

'Twas true the lasses always paid him extra attention. His brothers teased him about his looks and his charm. He knew women found him comely and were eager to invite him to their beds.

He was used to the attention and could shake it off when there were more serious matters to attend to. But he did enjoy a warm, willing lass in his bed, and he'd never had to go without when he desired one.

But Genevieve didn't look at him with lust or a teasing glint to her eyes. There were no coy mannerisms or come-hither looks.

She merely stared back at him, as if unwilling to be the first to blink in their silent standoff. There was false bravado in her expression, as if she'd steeled herself for whatever was to come. Almost as if she fully expected pain or humiliation from him.

It made what he'd come to confront her over even more distasteful, and a pang of unwanted guilt nagged at him. He hadn't realized until now how much he wanted to be wrong. . . .

Finally, he started down the incline, breaking the visible tension between them. The lass was likely freezing, standing there hip-deep in the water.

He tried very hard not to let his gaze wander, but he was inexorably drawn to her breasts and down the flat line of her belly to where the dark curls of her womanhood were barely visible above the waterline.

Jesu, but he was breaking into a sweat and the morning air still had a decided chill to it.

Her body was perfect, and simply made for a man's

hands to appreciate. Her breasts were plump but not too much so. Just enough to fill his palm . . . and his mouth.

And ah but he could well imagine cradling her luscious backside in his hands as he stroked in and out of her.

As he neared the water's edge, Genevieve lowered herself in the water, her eyes hooded and wary.

"I would speak to you, Genevieve," Bowen said, his voice graver than he intended.

"I would prefer our conversation to take place when I'm at least covered," she said in a tart voice that gave him hope.

A saucy Genevieve he could take. A beaten-down, frightened Genevieve made his stomach knot.

"I'll turn my back and allow you to leave the water so you don't grow chilled," he offered.

When he didn't immediately proffer his back, she frowned and made a circling motion with her hand.

Smothering a smile that surprised him by twitching at his lips, he swiftly turned his back and stared at the keep looming in the distance.

Damn it but he didn't want to be soft toward her. He didn't want her to make him smile—or anything else. But he was a liar if he suggested such. He could tell himself all he wanted, but there was something about the lass that was compelling.

His body and mind were not in accord on this matter, and his body was fast winning the battle.

Soft splashing sounds reached his ears, and a shiver stole down his spine at the idea that she was rising from the water. Rivulets would be sliding down her sleek body and, even now, chill bumps would dot her torso, hardening her nipples, and water would cling to the damp curls between her legs. Hiding all that warm, moist womanly flesh that he ached to explore.

A blistering curse burned his lips. It was absurd for him to carry on like a lad who hadn't yet reached manhood. He stood there fidgeting like a nervous boy who'd just laid eyes on his first naked woman.

"You can turn around now."

Genevieve's voice was soft and sweet, and he spun immediately, eager to drink in her appearance again.

She was wrapped in a drying blanket. It covered every inch of her skin. Only her head poked out. Her wet hair lay limply over her head and was arranged to cover her scarred cheek.

He wanted to tell her that she needn't hide her disfigurement from him. It certainly didn't make him want her less. It had been Ian's intention to ruin her for any other man, but Ian was a bloody fool for ever thinking that scarring the lass's face would make her any less desirable.

His fingers curled in anger at the thought of Ian holding her down and flaying open her cheek with a knife.

She cleared her throat awkwardly at his prolonged silence.

"Laird? You wanted to speak with me?"

He let out his breath as she settled on one of the large boulders that lined the river. Her blanket was pulled even tighter around her as she huddled behind its protection.

The right thing to do would be to allow her to dress and return to the keep, but he didn't want anyone to overhear their conversation.

Deciding to sit across from her on the banks of the stream rather than to continue looming over her, he settled down and then met her gaze.

"I would ask you a question, and I'd like an honest answer."

Her eyes narrowed at the slight and she pursed her lips, but she remained silent. Then she merely nodded.

"Did you have anything to do with Eveline Montgomery's abduction?" he asked bluntly.

She froze. Went completely still. Where before she'd fidgeted nervously in the folds of the blanket, now she didn't so much as move a muscle. Her jaw tightened and fear crawled, ugly and dark, into her eyes.

She gripped the blanket so hard the tips of her fingers went white and the blood drained from her face.

Nay, the lass would never make a warrior, as he'd observed before. There was no way for her to disguise her actions. It was all there to see in her eyes.

However much he tried to control his anger, it crept over him, itchy and hot, until he was no longer able to remain sitting there.

As soon as he stood, she flinched back, becoming a much smaller target. There was such desolation in her eyes that it froze him from the inside out. 'Twas like looking over the most barren winter landscape. Cold and haunted.

"Tell me you didn't do this thing," he whispered.

"I can't do that," she said, her voice cracking like dry wood.

"Sweet Jesu, *why*?" he thundered. "How could you do such a thing, *especially* knowing the manner of man Ian McHugh was?"

He came across more forcefully than he wanted, but he was near to exploding.

"Genevieve? I expect an answer."

She looked so stricken, her eyes wide. Her mouth opened, but she swallowed and then closed it again.

They both jumped and turned toward the keep when shouts went up in the distance. Bowen strained to hear what the noise was about, and when he finally heard the distinct call his blood went cold.

"To arms! We're under attack!"

CHAPTER 14

Bowen made a grab for Genevieve, hauling her up beside him and then urging her back toward the keep.

"Run!" he urged. "Make haste."

Genevieve scrambled over the rocky terrain in her bare feet, the blanket still wrapped tightly around her body. Her clothing still lay on the bank of the river, and Bowen gave her no time to retrieve it.

He ran as fast as he was able with Genevieve in tow, until they reached the back entrance through the skirt. He ducked inside, his hands still firmly wrapped around Genevieve's arm.

"Go inside," he ordered. "Take cover in your chamber."

He nudged her forward and then broke into a run, unsheathing his sword as he went. When he reached the courtyard, it was chaotic.

The McHugh warriors looked bewildered, while the few remaining Montgomery and Armstrong soldiers were preparing for battle.

Bowen found Brodie in the crowd and shouted to him. Brodie looked up and then stalked a determined line over to where Bowen stood.

"What is happening? Who called the men to arms?"

"I did," Brodie said, his features grim and his eyes dark with the promise of battle. "The McHugh idiots were set to welcome their laird home. 'Tis not a welcome he seeks!"

"Patrick McHugh rides against us?" Bowen asked incredulously. Could they be so fortunate as to have the jackal come to them? "It will certainly save us time hunting him down."

"He's not alone," Brodie bit out. "He's found an ally in the McGrieves. They ride side by side with him, and they bring their army."

Bowen swore. "How many?"

"I don't know. They are but a fifteen-minute ride from the keep. The McHugh watchmen came in bearing the news that their laird returned. I had to tell the fools to prepare for war."

Bowen ground his teeth together until they nearly snapped under the pressure. "Spread word that McHugh comes to battle his own kin. Remind them of all he has stolen from them, and of the dishonor that he bestowed on their name. Tell them he has a bounty, and that any who side with him are enemy not only to the Montgomerys and Armstrongs but to the Crown as well. Look out for any traitors—and watch your back, my friend."

Brodie caught his arm as they clasped hands in a warrior's shake. "Aye, and you as well."

Bowen broke away and shouted harshly to his men to ready themselves. Then he called up to the tower watchman.

"Do you see them yet?"

"Aye, Laird!" the man called down. "They are topping the last rise to the keep, coming from the north."

Bowen turned, sword in hand, raising it above his head as he stared at the assembled troops.

"No mercy!"

"No mercy!" they roared back.

* * *

Genevieve frantically pulled on a simple day dress, not bothering with any underclothing. Her hands and knees shook until she was a clumsy mess and she wanted to scream in frustration.

"Genevieve, we are under attack!"

Taliesan's fearful cry from Genevieve's chamber door gave Genevieve a start. She whirled around, nearly tripping as she attempted to fasten her dress.

"Aye, I know it. Help me," she said grimly, offering her back to Taliesan.

Taliesan's fingers shook as she fastened the dress. As soon as she was done, Genevieve broke away and went to the small trunk positioned close to her pallet. She'd managed to keep so few of her things. Ian had taunted her with the gifts from her parents. Not many had survived, but what did remain, she cherished greatly. He'd taken great pleasure in breaking or ruining an object when he perceived she needed punishing.

She opened the trunk and pulled out the bow and the quiver of arrows fashioned especially for her smaller frame by her father. She slung the quiver over her shoulder as Taliesan looked on, mouth wide open.

When she started past Taliesan, the other woman put her hand out, gripping Genevieve's arm.

"Where are you going? What do you think to do?"

Genevieve squared her shoulders and looked Taliesan directly in the eye. "Listen to me. Go and seek refuge in one of the tower chambers. Make sure it's a room with no windows—and bar the door. Seek as many of the women and children as possible, and encourage them to do the same. Do not allow anyone inside who is not known to you."

"And you?" Taliesan asked fearfully. "What of you, Genevieve?"

"I will not be imprisoned again," Genevieve said fiercely. "The Montgomery men are all who stand between me and the McHugh Laird bearing down, seeking to reclaim his keep. I'll either aid the Montgomerys in defending their position or I'll die trying. I'll never again be subjected to the whims of a single McHugh."

"Have a care, Genevieve. I beg you. Do not do anything foolish."

Genevieve snorted. "I would hardly call killing a few McHughs foolish."

"God be with you," Taliesan said, pulling Genevieve into a fierce hug.

"And you," Genevieve returned. "Now go and seek shelter in the tower."

She swept past Taliesan and hurried down the hall to the stairs. As she descended, the sounds of battle could be heard echoing through the courtyard. The clash of swords and shields. The roars of rage and cries of pain.

As she stepped through the doorway, the smell of sweat and blood tainted the air and was oppressive in her nostrils.

The courtyard was a sea of chaos. It was hard to discern who fought whom. Her gaze sought out the now familiar Montgomery and Armstrong warriors, though their numbers were smaller than just a day before.

Patrick, being the coward he was, likely had set a watch on the keep and had attacked the moment the bulk of the Montgomery and Armstrong forces departed.

Her gaze halted when she found Bowen in the midst of a fierce battle with two of the McHughs who had departed with Patrick. He was holding his own, though, and didn't need her aid.

She searched farther, looking for Patrick, though she didn't expect him to be in front leading the attack. Nay, he'd be on the fringes, avoiding confrontation.

Finally, she found him and, as she suspected, he was lurking on the perimeter, sword in hand, but he wasn't engaged, and two of his warriors were solidly in front of him.

Rage suffused her as she stared at the source of her torment for the last year. Nay, he may not have taken an active part in her abuse, but he turned a blind eye to Ian. He never once called his son down for his actions. Never said to him he was being dishonorable.

He'd stood by while she'd been repeatedly used, a means for Ian to slake his twisted desires. He hadn't cared that she'd been broken numerous times. That, at times, she'd wanted to die. Or that her very soul had been forfeit to demons she could never hope to escape.

She reached over her shoulder to grasp one of the arrows by the fletching and quickly notched it. She raised the bow and set her sights on the man in front of Patrick. She would have to act quickly. Once Patrick sensed danger, he'd slink away like a rat in the darkness.

Rapidly taking aim, she let the first arrow fly. Savage satisfaction coursed through her veins when the warrior just in front of Patrick clutched his chest and toppled forward, her arrow embedded deeply in the area just above where his chain mail protected his vulnerable areas.

Patrick sent a panicked look, desperately searching for the source of the attack. He instantly hunkered down, cowering behind his shield, all the while hoarsely yelling for someone to come to his aid.

Her lips curling into a snarl, she notched another arrow and took aim, waiting patiently for the right opportunity.

Sweat beaded and rolled down her back. Her entire focus was on her target. Her arm ached from the strain of holding the bow at full draw, but she'd wait forever if that was what it took.

Revenge was sweet on her tongue. She didn't spare a moment's regret for killing another person in cold blood.

It was nothing less than she'd done in her dreams time and time again. It was all that had sustained her over the last months. Dreaming of vengeance.

Her arm was starting to shake when Patrick made his move. He'd evidently decided that he was in too vulnerable a position and shot upward, holding his shield to guard his upper body. He fled toward the back of the keep, where less fighting was taking place.

Calmly, she took aim at his leg, knowing it would slow him and it would also likely afford her a kill shot when he was forced to drop his shield.

She shot the arrow and was rewarded by the sight of him stumbling and dropping to his knees, his cry of agony rising above the din of battle. It struck him just above the ankle and rendered him incapable of walking. She notched another arrow, never removing her gaze from his fallen figure. She drew and waited, and, as she'd hoped, his shield dropped. Just enough . . .

She let the arrow fly.

It struck him in the side of the neck, going all the way through to the fletching. His eyes wide and glassy with death, he pitched to the side, sagging pitifully, wilting like a flower too long in the sun.

For a long moment, she stood, bow held high, staring as the life faded from his body. Then, slowly, she lowered her bow, calm pervading her mind.

It was done. She may not have been the one to deal Ian his death blow, but she'd exacted vengeance against his weakling of a father. If she was supposed to feel guilt over the taking of a life, it was too bad. She wouldn't spend a single moment being remorseful that Patrick McHugh had met such a violent end.

The continued sounds of battle seeped into her consciousness, and she turned, anxiously seeking the fate of the Montgomery and Armstrong forces.

Brodie was leading a group of Armstrong warriors,

and they were steadily slashing a bloody path through the McHugh and McGrieve combatants.

Her gaze swung rapidly around the courtyard to determine Bowen's fate. Her heart lurched when she saw him in the distance, engaged in a fierce sword battle with a huge warrior who could only be from the McGrieve clan. It was not someone she recognized.

But what made her chest tight was the McHugh man behind Bowen. He was not one of the ones who'd left the clan with Patrick. He had stayed behind and had since sworn allegiance to Bowen and the Montgomerys.

He was a traitor.

Clutched tightly in his hand was a dagger, and he was advancing warily toward Bowen's back. The loathsome coward was going to plunge the knife into Bowen's back, attacking him in the most dishonorable fashion.

It was a distant shot, and one she couldn't be assured of making with perfect accuracy. This was too important to miss or fall short.

Kicking up her skirts, she notched an arrow and bolted across the courtyard, praying she would make the shot in time to save Bowen.

CHAPTER 15

Bowen ignored the pain radiating from his side and his shoulder and fought with more savagery. This was his toughest opponent thus far, and the man showed no signs of tiring. Bowen would have to end it quickly or all his reserves would be used up, and he was already injured from his previous battles.

Their swords hissed and clanged, the sun bouncing off the blades in a rapid dance. Bowen drove him back, but then the bigger man charged, swinging like a crazed person, bellowing the entire way.

Bowen retreated but managed to slice his opponent's upper arm, drawing blood and momentarily halting his progress. As the other man warily stepped back, pivoting to ensure Bowen didn't gain position, movement caught Bowen's eye and he glanced beyond his opponent to see Genevieve a short distance away, holding, of all things, a bow with an arrow notched. And she was pointing it directly at him!

Before he could react or think to avoid the coming arrow, she let fly. His snarl of fury over the betrayal roared from his throat just as the arrow sailed past him. A cry of pain sounded behind him.

Thrusting his sword upward to ward off the coming blow, he drove forward, determined to end the fight here and now. His mind was ablaze, and he was confused as hell as to what Genevieve had done.

He never had the chance. Before he could deal the killing blow, Genevieve notched another arrow and sent one into the back of his opponent's neck. The arrow plunged directly through his Adam's apple, coated in bright red blood.

An odd, sucking noise gurgled from the McGrieve warrior, and blood seeped from his mouth just before he toppled forward like a felled tree.

Bowen instantly spun to see that a McHugh clansman—one who had not fled the keep with Patrick—held a dagger in his hand and it was obvious that he'd planned to plunge it into Bowen's back.

Genevieve's arrow had struck him through the forehead—an impossible target at best—and yet she'd made not one but two lethal shots with her bow.

The McHugh betrayer was suspended in air for the longest time, his eyes glazed and gray, until finally he sagged and folded like a dropped blanket, the knife slipping from his grasp just before he hit the ground.

The earth shifted beneath Bowen's feet and he swayed precariously, his head spinning. And then Genevieve was at his side, shouting for aid.

She drove her shoulder forcefully under his, fitting it into his armpit as she valiantly kept him from tumbling to the ground. Jesu, but he must have lost more blood than he'd imagined.

He nearly toppled them both, but her stubbornness prevailed. He heard her muttered oaths and smiled at the lass's colorful language. She had quite the saucy mouth.

"Give aid to your laird!" she bellowed in a voice that carried across the courtyard.

One of his eyebrows went up at her forceful command. The lass would do well leading troops in battle.

A man would have to be a fool to gainsay a woman with a growl like hers.

"Ah hell, Bowen, you've gone and managed to injure yourself."

Brodie's aggrieved voice echoed close to Bowen's ears, but he lacked the energy to look up and find Brodie's position.

"The lass saved me," he said faintly, thinking that if he were to die Genevieve should at least be credited with prolonging his life a few more minutes.

"You'll not die," Genevieve snapped. " 'Tis a paltry wound at best."

"Now she mocks my pain," Bowen said mildly.

Brodie's face appeared in front of Bowen, worried, his eyes crinkled with concern. "You're not making any sense. Babbling about like a drunken sot. And you're bleeding like a slaughtered pig."

"Am I?"

He looked down, surprised to see the entire front of his tunic turned scarlet. Then he tightened his jaw, bracing himself against the pain.

"I'll not rest until every last McHugh is driven from this place," Bowen vowed.

"They are retreating," Brodie assured. "We suffered minimal losses. When 'twas obvious we were well represented, despite our smaller numbers, the McHughs and McGrieves beat a hasty retreat. Our men are pursuing them to our borders now."

The matter-of-fact accounting soothed Bowen's agitation and pain. The world was spinning with increasing frequency, and he feared losing consciousness before he could ask the most pressing question.

He opened his mouth, but it had gone dry. He licked his cracked lips, sudden thirst gripping him.

"Patrick," he said hoarsely. "What of Patrick?"

Before there was any response, his knees buckled and

he heard Genevieve's cry of alarm just before the entire world went dark.

Genevieve made a grab for Bowen, but he was far too heavy for her to prevent him from falling to the ground. Brodie lunged and managed to save Bowen from eating dirt, hauling him up to hang Bowen's arm over his shoulder.

"Take him inside the keep to his chamber," Genevieve ordered briskly. "Post a man you trust to guard his door at all times. There are vipers in our midst. A McHugh tried to kill Bowen after swearing allegiance to him."

Brodie gawked at Genevieve, his eyes narrowing.

"Go!" she directed. "He is losing more blood and his wounds must be tended. I must send word to his brother. We are in a perilous position, and now, with him wounded, we are even more weakened."

Brodie nodded tightly. It was apparent he had no love of taking orders from a lass, but her commands were logical. This much she knew. He could hardly argue with her when Bowen's life's blood was seeping onto the ground.

Hauling Bowen over his broad shoulders, Brodie staggered slightly before gaining his footing and hastening toward the entrance to the keep. Genevieve looked warily around, ensuring no danger posed a threat, and then she went to seek out one of the senior Montgomery soldiers she knew to be trusted by both Bowen and Teague.

"You sir, by what name are you called?" Genevieve demanded as she strode up.

The hulking man frowned down at her, seemingly puzzled by the fact she carried a bow and a quiver half-full of arrows.

"I am called Adwen," he said gruffly.

"You must ride to intercept Teague Montgomery with

all haste. If you do not overtake him before he arrives on Montgomery land, you must go to their keep and apprise Graeme and Teague Montgomery of all that has occurred. We are vulnerable to continued attack from the McGrieves and the remaining McHughs. You may also tell the Montgomerys that Patrick McHugh is dead," she said flatly. "We need reinforcements as badly as we need food and supplies. Bowen has been injured in the battle and 'tis unknown what his condition will be. Give his brothers a full accounting."

Adwen straightened and then motioned for two others to join him. Then he glanced back at Genevieve with something that resembled respect gleaming in his eyes.

Almost too late, she realized that she was uncloaked. She hadn't given care to anything but quitting her chamber as quickly as possible. There was no hiding her disfigurement.

She turned quickly, presenting her unmarred cheek as heat rose up her neck and suffused her jaw. The urge to rub her hand over the rough, puckered skin was strong, but instead she curled her fingers into a tight fist, determined not to give in.

It mattered naught what these warriors thought of her. She wanted no man anyway. What did it matter if none desired her or looked kindly upon her?

Bleakness assailed her, because though it shouldn't matter, what lass didn't want to be looked upon with favor? What lass didn't want to feel beautiful?

"I will depart at once, mistress," Adwen said, his tone still respectful. "I'll give report just as you've outlined it to me."

"Then go with God, and a safe return to you and your men," she said.

He inclined his head and then turned sharply on his heel, barking an order to the two men accompanying him. They were bloody and looked battle-weary, but they didn't flinch at their duty and Genevieve respected them for that. They hadn't questioned her word.

She hurried toward the keep entrance, anxious to see how Bowen fared. The blood worried her, but she knew not where he'd been injured.

She stopped first in her chamber to put the bow and arrows away. She slid a finger lovingly along the worn wood bends and then solemnly closed the trunk, pushing herself upward to her feet once more.

Swaying precariously, she closed her eyes momentarily and steeled herself against the inevitable reaction setting in. She'd not spend a single moment regretting her actions. Nor would she allow Patrick McHugh to cast a pall over her. He was dead. No longer a threat. Vengeance was *finally* hers.

Her eyes popped open as she remembered Taliesan, sequestered in the tower, likely terrified and wondering the fate of the keep and clan.

Gathering her composure and breathing deeply to reinvigorate herself, she hurried out of her chamber and traveled to the far end of the hall, where once she'd been imprisoned, and where she'd existed for an entire year.

She beat soundly on the door, calling to Taliesan to open. A few moments later, there was much scuffling heard and then the door creaked open, only the dim glow of a few candles emanating from within.

"Genevieve!" Taliesan cried.

She was enfolded in Taliesan's hug. Beyond Taliesan, many of the women and children huddled inside the small room, their gazes anxious as they stared at the two women embracing.

Against her will, Genevieve's heart softened a bit at the fear so clearly written on the faces of the women of the clan. And the children. Eyes so big and wide. Their lives had been turned upside down by the selfish actions of an inept laird.

She didn't want to feel anything for these people. They'd all been a party to her misery and humiliation. They deserved nothing from her, and yet she couldn't turn her back on them, even if it was what she wished to do.

"What has happened?" Taliesan asked, pulling away. "Are we safe?"

The other women leaned forward, eager to hear. For once, there were no disparaging looks, no insults hurled, no name-calling. They all looked . . . vulnerable.

It was a feeling Genevieve was well acquainted with.

"Patrick attacked the keep with the aid of the Mc-Grieves," she said without emotion.

There were shocked gasps all around the small chamber.

"Did he mean to kill us all?" one of the women demanded.

Her tone was angry, and a quick look around showed Genevieve that there was anger on more than one face.

Genevieve shrugged. "He is without care for his kin or his duty as laird. 'Tis difficult to say how the mind of a coward works. He is dead now," she said in a dispassionate voice. "He is no longer a threat, but I have sent word to the Montgomerys, because now that Patrick is dead, we've sustained one attack and our numbers are lower than necessary to defend the keep from a larger attack. The McGrieves might very well decide to ally themselves with yet another clan in order to take over the McHugh holding."

There were cries of distress, a series of murmurs, whispers, and louder objections that echoed down the hall.

"You did right, Genevieve," Taliesan said, crushing Genevieve's hand with her own. "You have my thanks for looking after our interests so well."

None of the other women went as far as to express

gratitude. Several still looked at Genevieve with consternation in their eyes, as if they were loath even to consider the possibility that she was the one who'd been wronged.

"Where is the new laird in all of this?" one of the women asked, suspicion heavy in her voice.

"He lies injured in his chamber, under tight guard. One of the McHugh men who swore allegiance to the new laird attempted to cowardly attack him from behind. He is also dead, and the laird will remain under guard by those he trusts until he is well enough to be up on his own."

"Nay!" several whispered. "Who is dead? Who killed him? Who was it, Genevieve? You must tell us if it was one of our husbands."

The questions peppered her from all directions. Genevieve knew there was no easy way to relate the news. She raised her gaze, seeking out the woman she knew to be the wife of the McHugh man who betrayed Bowen.

"'Twas your husband, Maggie," Genevieve said quietly.

"You lie!" Maggie hissed. "He would never do something so dishonorable."

Genevieve steeled herself for such a response. It wasn't unexpected. Who, after all, wanted to believe such of their husband?

"I saw him with my own eyes," Genevieve added gently.

Maggie stared at her with obvious scorn. "And we're to believe the word of a whore?"

Genevieve flinched and took an immediate step back.

Taliesan rounded on the woman, her face flushed with fury. "You will cease your insults! Genevieve has done much for us, and I struggle to understand why. She should have washed her hands of us. She should have welcomed our deaths, and yet she saw us all to safety.

Even now she has sent word because we are in danger of another attack, and all you can think to do is heap petty, childish insults on her. Enough, I say! Act the adult you claim to be and cease acting like a child. The children of the keep behave better than the women of this clan ever have."

Several of the women had the grace to look abashed, but others regarded Genevieve with open hostility. She knew she'd gained instant enemies the moment she named the betrayer. But she would not lie. Not to save feelings. Not when the dishonorable person merited no respect or goodwill.

"I must go now," Genevieve said in a low voice to Taliesan. "I must see to the laird. I know not how seriously he was injured. There is much to be done below. The men will be hungry from their battles, and they must bury the dead. We will mourn our losses this eve, when an accounting is given."

"You're a brave and giving lass," Taliesan said, a ghost of a smile on her lips. "I know not how you manage it when Ian tried every conceivable way to crush your spirit. Your resilience is inspiring. I hope one day to be as you are."

Genevieve's response came out more as a sob. "Nay, Taliesan. Never pray for my fate. I wouldn't wish it on my worst enemy."

CHAPTER 16

Genevieve hesitated at Bowen's chamber door. It was closed, and she wondered if she would even be permitted entrance. Brodie had looked at her with suspicion, but surely he didn't believe she had anything to do with Bowen's injuries.

Thrusting her chin up and scolding herself for being the coward she so easily labeled Patrick, she knocked softly at the door. There was a long moment of waiting, and she was debating whether to knock again when it opened the barest crack and Brodie stood frowning at her.

She thought to explain her presence, when he swung the door wider and motioned her inside.

"Have you any skill at healing?" Brodie asked as she stepped through the doorway.

She paused, blowing out her breath. "It depends on what he has need of. I've never done any stitching, and I have no knowledge of poultices or drams."

Brodie's lips pressed together in consternation. "He has need of stitching for one of his wounds, certainly, and I would give him something to make him less restless, to ease his pain so the stitching can be done, but I do not trust a McHugh healer with his life."

Her hand went automatically to rub at the ragged scar on her face. "Nay," she agreed quietly. "I'd not have the McHugh healer stitch him, either."

As she spoke, she moved toward the bed, where another Montgomery soldier stood guard. Bowen lay there, eyes closed, but he fidgeted even in unconsciousness. His tunic had been removed, and she could see a ragged cut to his chest. The flesh lay open and was still bleeding, though the soldier wiped at it with cloths.

"Think you are up to the task?" Brodie asked. "Your hands are smaller and you would perhaps be more adept at a needle and thread than I or one of the other men."

She swallowed hard, still staring at the open wound. Then she squared her shoulders. "Aye, I have skill with a needle and thread. Surely 'tis not more difficult than laying stitch to material. I can sew a tight seam. But I dare not sink needle into his flesh if he's had nothing to calm him."

"I'll have the materials you need fetched to the chamber. If we give him enough ale, it will dull his senses enough for you to do the task."

Genevieve wasn't as convinced as Brodie was, but she didn't argue. She didn't want to anger the warrior, and if he saw no use for her, 'twas likely he'd bar her from Bowen's chamber.

Brodie pulled a chair from the window and positioned it directly beside the bed before motioning for Genevieve to sit. He gave terse instructions to the warrior attending Bowen, and then quit the room abruptly.

Genevieve leaned forward, her hand going to Bowen's forehead in an automatic gesture of comfort. He shifted beneath her touch and then quieted, rubbing against her palm.

"Bowen, are you feeling any pain?" she asked.

"He's remained unconscious, mistress," the warrior explained.

Genevieve turned her gaze on the warrior. "Aye, I know it. I'm trying to determine if he's aware of anything happening around him."

The warrior fell silent, abashed by her response.

She took the cloth that lay on Bowen's chest and gently wiped at the blood still seeping from the wound. Upon further inspection, she found a long gash in his upper arm, though it wasn't as deep or flayed open as the one on his chest.

Remembering the chain mail covering Bowen's chest, she realized that the sword must have sliced through armor and flesh. Thank God he'd been somewhat protected. With a cut this deep, the blow would most certainly have been fatal were it not for the protective covering that was sliced through.

"Has the wound been washed?" she asked, taking note of the dry cloth stained only with blood.

The warrior looked uncomfortable. "Nay, mistress. We were concerned only with halting the bleeding."

She nodded. "'Tis good, that. But fetch me water from the basin so that I may cleanse it before we set needle to flesh. It will help to remove any dirt or part of the armor that is embedded."

Looking relieved to be assigned a duty other than standing within Genevieve's view, the warrior hastened to fetch the pitcher by the window.

A moment later, he returned with a fresh cloth. He plunged it inside the clay jug and wrung it out, extending it toward Genevieve.

"By what name are you called, warrior?" she asked as she carefully began to cleanse the inside of the wound.

"Geoffrey, mistress."

"My thanks for your aid, Geoffrey."

He looked surprised by her thank-you, and he nodded solemnly.

Before long, Brodie returned with one of the Armstrong warriors. They both carried supplies in their hands, and Geoffrey scrambled to make way for them.

"I brought needle and strong thread, suitable for

stitching. Deaglan prepared a dram for Brodie, so that he's not combative when you apply the needle."

Genevieve sent Brodie a grateful look. She knew well the threat a man could pose when he was in his right head. One delirious with pain and only half conscious wasn't someone she wanted to risk placing herself in the path of.

She rose to allow the two men access to Bowen and hovered on the perimeter while they coaxed the potion down Bowen's throat.

When Brodie was satisfied that Bowen had taken all that he would, he took a step back and directed his attention to Genevieve.

"Give it a few moments to take effect before you set yourself to your task. Geoffrey, Deaglan, and I will remain to ensure that Bowen is still for the entirety of you tending the wound."

"You are kind," Genevieve said quietly.

Brodie stared at her a long moment. "And you are unused to such, are you not?"

She flushed and turned away, refusing to voice her agreement, though he well knew the answer to his own question.

"I know that Bowen champions you," Brodie continued. "You needn't worry that while he is recovering I'll allow any harm to come to you."

Guilt gripped her chest, tightening until it was hard to breathe. Bowen must not have discussed his concerns with Brodie, or the Armstrong warrior would not be so gallant toward her. What would he do once he learned the terrible truth that Bowen had discovered just minutes before the attack?

"Thank you," she managed to choke out, praying that her guilt wasn't clearly written on her face.

He gestured for her to take her seat next to Bowen, but cautioned her to wait a moment longer, until he was certain Bowen had succumbed to the effects of the potion.

She settled down, wondering how she'd ever control the shaking of her hands. Fear, such a constant companion, had risen sharply at the thought of discovery. Brodie Armstrong would loathe the very sight of her. He'd likely think she deserved whatever fate befell her at the hands of the McHughs—if he didn't decide to exact justice for his sister on his own.

She gripped her hands tightly together in her lap, concentrating her entire will on calming her scattered nerves.

After a time, Bowen quieted and ceased his restless fidgeting and turning. His breathing became shallow and his head lolled to the side, his body going lax.

Brodie leaned over, pushing at Bowen, attempting to rouse a response, and when Bowen remained still and silent he nodded at Genevieve.

She sucked in a deep breath and took up the needle and thread held out to her by Deaglan. After making certain a sturdy knot was at the end of the thread, she tentatively put the needle to the middle of the wound and pinched the flesh together with her free hand.

Warily, she watched for any reaction from Bowen and then, holding her breath, she plunged the needle into his flesh, pushing it through to the other side of the wound.

She breathed a sigh of relief when he didn't so much as flinch.

Leaning forward, she focused intently on her task, setting stitches close together to effectively seal the wound. She barely even breathed the entire time she sewed together one side. By the time she reached the edge, sweat rolled down her temples and dampened the tendrils of hair at her nape.

She tied off the knot at the end, making several loops

so it would hold, and then she rethreaded the needle to begin again where she'd started at the center.

It was long, painstaking work. Not a word was spoken as she diligently concentrated on each stitch. Blood oozed from the end as she neared the other edge, and Brodie reached over to dab it away so she could quickly seal the rest.

When she finished, she sat back with a deep sigh. Her shoulders ached from the effort and her neck was stiff. Her fingers shook as she finished tying the last knot. Then she severed the thread, the arduous task at last completed.

"'Tis a fine job you've done, mistress," Deaglan praised.

She nodded, too tired to speak. For a long moment, she stared at Bowen's still closed eyes, and then she finally turned to Brodie.

"I'll have need of binding to wrap his arm. 'Tis not deep enough to require stitching, but if 'tis not bound tightly enough, the flesh will not heal properly."

Brodie quickly handed her several long strips of linen, and Geoffrey lifted Bowen's arm so she could wind them around the wound.

When the bandaging had been completed, Genevieve sat back with a satisfied sigh. "'Tis done. Now it is up to him to heal. Perhaps 'tis best to prepare more of the dram so that he can rest comfortably in the coming hours."

"Aye, I'll see it done," Deaglan said.

"Now, 'tis time for you to rest, Genevieve," Brodie said. "I'll escort you to your chamber and post a man outside if it makes you feel more secure."

She hesitated, glancing back at Bowen. She had no right to ask what she was about to, but that did not deter her.

"I would prefer to remain here if 'tis permissible. I

would see him through the night and ensure that he does naught to tear his stitching. If he takes a fever, he'll need constant care."

Brodie frowned a moment, as he and the other warriors exchanged glances. Then, as if reaching a decision, he nodded.

"Aye, if that is your wish, then you may remain in Bowen's chamber. Deaglan and Geoffrey will remain close in case you have need of anything. You only have to call out. I'll oft check in on his progress, but now I have matters of the clan to attend to. There are dead to bury and traitors to ferret out."

She glanced up in alarm. "There are more?"

"I know not," Brodie said grimly. "You spoke of one who tried to plunge his dirk into Bowen's back. If there was one, there may well be others."

She nodded her understanding even as dread gripped her heart. McHugh Keep was already hostile enough for her. She'd named Bowen's betrayer, and if more were uncovered, she'd likely receive the blame for the consequences.

CHAPTER 17

It was late into the night and Genevieve sat awkwardly by Bowen's bed. She had rearranged herself countless times in the wooden chair where she'd taken position for the past hours, and still her muscles ached and stiffness had worked its way into her back and neck until they were screaming in protest.

And yet she hadn't moved. She kept watch as Bowen slept, silently transfixed by the image he posed on the bed. She drank in the sight of him, allowing her gaze to boldly roam over his torso and up to his perfect, unmarred features.

Here was a man, though scarred in body, whose face was utterly unblemished by so much as a mark. No crooked nose. No bump to signify a break during battle. The rest of his body was weathered, yet still beautiful in its imperfection, but his face was simply perfect.

Never before had she come into contact with a man to rival Bowen Montgomery in looks, and she'd seen many a fair face at court. She'd seen men who'd never seen the light of battle and had never sullied their hands in such a fashion.

Bowen's hands and fingers were rough and callused. He was well used to hard work and fighting. He was a man unafraid to do labor, and yet, at a glance, he looked superior to those men who'd never stepped onto a battlefield.

But it wasn't his looks that compelled her. It wasn't his face that fascinated her. Perhaps it was his gentleness from the onset. Before he'd learned of her sinful deed. She didn't expect him to ever understand her motivation. How could he? She'd been responsible for much wrong done to his kin and clan. He was ever loyal to his brother. That much was evident in his every word and action, and just as evident was the fact that the same loyalty extended to his sister by marriage.

He stirred for the first time since he'd received the first draft. He turned his face, a low moan escaping his dry lips. Instinctively, she lay her hand on his face in a soothing manner, and as she stroked, she murmured in a low voice that all was well and for him to rest.

She had no idea if he was cognizant of her words or if they had any impact, but he stilled nonetheless and settled back into sleep, his breathing slowing as his body relaxed.

Leaning forward in her chair, she grew bolder, sliding her fingers toward the thick long hair that hung past his shoulders. He was so beautiful it was hard not to touch him, and what harm would it do? No one was there to look on. Bowen would never remember that she'd offered him comfort while he rested.

It brought her solace she couldn't explain. Simply being able to touch someone without being forced. To offer something of herself that wasn't demanded of her. Having a deeper contact with another human being after being treated little better than an animal for so many months.

As soon as her hand left his face, he stirred again, a frown marring his face. His brow drew into a wrinkled line and he mumbled something indecipherable. She hesitated, her hand still in the air, and he turned his head first one way and then the other. His breathing sped up, and he seemed to grow more agitated by the second.

Taking a chance, she laid her hand on his forehead again, smoothing the lines away with gentle fingers. He instantly relaxed, and his breathing slowed.

'Twas like soothing a savage beast. He seemed to like her touch, though she was sure any who touched him would receive the same response. It was fanciful of her to think even for an instant that he would welcome her hand if he knew who offered him solace.

But for now she could pretend and enjoy a fleeting moment of peace.

She leaned forward in her chair, seeking to alleviate the awkwardness of her position. Her limbs ached and the muscles in her back protested every movement.

Leaving her hand in place, she gingerly stood, biting back the moan that threatened to escape when her body creaked and spasmed. So many hours in one position on a hard chair had taken its toll.

She glanced around, but seeing no remedy, she grappled with herself over whether to be so presumptuous as to take position next to Bowen on the bed. What if he awakened and found her there? What would his reaction be? Would he even remember that she'd saved him, or would his sole memory be of his confrontation with her on the banks of the river?

She perched on the edge of the bed, facing Bowen and sliding her bottom just so that she could enjoy the softness of the bed. She bumped up against his side and held her breath, praying she wouldn't awaken him from his slumber.

When he didn't move, she relaxed and then fidgeted until she found a comfortable position. Then she resumed stroking his forehead, every once in a while straying to his hair to delve into its thickness.

He gave a deep sigh and mumbled once again before

turning into her palm, nuzzling against the inside of her hand.

The simple action invoked a powerful response within her, one she hadn't thought she was capable of after a year in Ian McHugh's hands.

She began to imagine how it would be to have a warrior such as Bowen Montgomery touch her in the way she was touching him. With such aching gentleness. With respect for her pleasure and wishes. Would he be content with simply holding her and stroking her in a comforting manner, or would he be intent solely on his own pleasure?

Not having the experience to know the difference between Ian McHugh and any other man, she couldn't say. She simply couldn't fathom such kindness from a male, because she hadn't experienced it in so long.

But it was a nice thought. One that brought her immense pleasure. More so than she would have ever dreamed. And it was best she left it precisely there. In her dreams. Leaving herself vulnerable and open to the kind of treatment she'd been subjected to would make her the worst sort of fool. A man couldn't well abuse her if she never gave him the chance.

She rebelled at the thought that Bowen could be like Ian. There was nothing to say that she had any real knowledge of the man Bowen was, but it dismayed her to think she could be so wrong. She certainly hadn't been wrong about Ian. She'd known from their very first meeting that he was a man to avoid, and she'd done so until he'd forced her hand by raiding her escort to her future husband.

With shock, she realized she'd given no thought to her betrothed in many a month. She'd not tortured herself by thinking on matters she couldn't change. Even trying to imagine what her life would have been like married to a Highland chieftain was to open herself up to more hurt.

Was he married to another even now? 'Twas likely he was. Hers had been an arranged marriage. There was no affection involved. She'd only met the man once, when he'd come to formally offer for her hand on her father's lands. The accord had been reached between him and her father. Her introduction to him had been a mere formality, and an afterthought once the agreement had been struck.

By now she could have had a child of her own. A wee bairn to fuss over and spoil shamelessly. Her mother would have visited often, and perchance her husband would have been agreeable to her visiting her father's keep on occasion.

Grief overwhelmed her, and she quickly shut the door on old memories as they rushed to the surface. It was true enough that thinking on things she could not change was the fastest way to heartbreak.

But she still ached for what could have been, and perhaps it was why she had such fascination for Bowen Montgomery. He reminded her of the way things could have possibly been. Marriage to a man such as he, one with honor and loyalty, would have been appealing.

She absently stroked his cheek, sadness clinging to her like the most stubborn vine. Nay, those dreams were gone. Her life would be very different now. It was doubtful Bowen's offer of a place in his clan, firmly under the Montgomerys' protection, was still in place, but perhaps he would see fit to place her in an abbey as she'd first requested.

Making the best of less than desirable circumstances had become a way of life for her. She'd been forced to do it this last year, and she could do it again.

CHAPTER 18

Genevieve woke from a deep sleep with a start. Her eyes opened to darkness, and for a moment she was completely disoriented. All she knew was that she wasn't in her chamber, and it took her several long moments to place herself as the day's events came crashing back.

She scrambled out of bed, horrified that she'd fallen asleep and, worse, she'd been curled up right next to Bowen in the small space between him and the edge of the bed.

She sat up, wiping the sleep from her eyes and pushing her hair back from her face. The strands were in disarray, billowing wildly about her head.

What if someone had come in? What if someone had discovered her boldly sleeping next to the laird? She'd taken great liberties, and it had been a stupid risk.

She pushed up from the bed, desperate to put distance between her and Bowen. Stumbling in the darkness, she reached blindly for the candle that had been burning beside the bed only to find it nearly burnt to the wick.

In the hearth there were faintly glowing coals, not much left of the roaring fire that had burned hours earlier when she'd stitched Bowen's wounds.

Sleep and disorientation still clinging fiercely, she set about lighting a few of the extinguished candles and then built the fire back up so that a respectable blaze burned. Then she turned back to Bowen, hoping beyond hope that he hadn't been disturbed by her activities.

To her relief, he was still asleep.

She all but sagged back into the chair, reprimanding herself soundly for the urge that had overtaken her to be closer to the laird. If she'd learned nothing else, it had been to be cautious in all things, and yet the laird inspired her to idiocy.

Her eyes burned with the need to return to sleep, but she dared not allow herself to do so. Who knew what other foolishness she might embark on?

She yawned broadly, her jaw nearly cracking with the effort. Eyes watering, she focused her attention on Bowen, his face softly illuminated by candlelight.

He stirred, and again she breathed a sigh of relief that she'd awakened when she had. She wouldn't have wanted the laird to awaken with her curled up next to him like a satisfied kitten.

He began to thrash about, his head twisting from side to side, until she feared he'd toss himself right out of the bed. She rose, instantly leaning over him, trying the method of touching his face, but this time he would not be calmed.

A ragged moan escaped his throat, and she realized that he must be in pain again. It had been quite some time since the earlier dram, but she'd require the help of one of the men to force another down his throat.

Hurrying to the door, she hoped that either Geoffrey or Deaglan would be outside, as Brodie had assured her. When she opened it, she breathed a sigh of relief to see that, indeed, both men were at their posts—one beside the door and the other on the other side of the hall, sitting on the floor, his back against the wall for support.

When they saw her, they rose to their feet, any sign of fatigue quickly wiped away.

"I have need of your aid," she whispered. "The laird

is in pain and 'tis time for another potion. I cannot do it myself."

"Of course, mistress," Geoffrey said. "Deaglan and I will see to the matter."

The men followed her back inside, and Deaglan collected the small cup that held the mixture he'd concocted. With Geoffrey's help, they held Bowen's head and shoulders up enough that they could tilt the cup into his mouth.

Bowen coughed and sputtered, but most of the liquid went down.

They settled Bowen back onto the bed and then turned to Genevieve.

"He should rest easy for the next several hours," Deaglan said. "If you have need to return to your chamber, we will keep watch until you return."

She wasn't sure what to make of that. Whether it was an offer for her to rest or a suggestion because she stank of blood and sweat from the earlier battle. Either way, she must look a mess and, truth be told, she would appreciate the opportunity to wash.

"I should like to take a moment to change my clothing and rid myself of the smell of blood," she said with a faint smile. "I shall return in a short while."

Both men nodded, and she quickly retreated from the chamber to go next door to her own.

Stripping out of her clothing, she went to the small basin along the wall and poured water from the pitcher into the washing bowl. She'd love a full bath—it might take two to scrub the blood, dirt, and smell of death from her body—but she dare not risk venturing outside the keep, not only because of the dangers presented by a possible attack but from the McHughs themselves.

She had no way of gauging the current mood of the clan, or if Brodie had indeed uncovered more traitors than the one who had tried to murder Bowen. It was a sure bet that by now word would have spread as to her part in Meagan's husband's death and that she'd singled him out as a betrayer.

Having intelligence didn't signal being a coward. A smart lass knew when to stay out of direct fire, and she had no intention of braving the McHugh clan until she was certain as to what occurred after the attack on the keep.

She brushed her hair and took a washing cloth to the long strands, scrubbing as best she could the dirt and matted blood from her tresses. When she was reasonably satisfied with the result, she donned a clean dress and then sank onto her bed. A bed that she still marveled was her own. That she didn't have to share with anyone or fear that she would have unwanted bodies there.

She lay her head down and closed her eyes, enjoying the comfort of her pillow. It was heaven. And yet she'd slept so soundly next to Bowen. It was an oddity she wasn't sure she understood.

Never did she sleep too soundly. Too many times she had awakened to Ian's abuse, and she'd learned to always be prepared—even in sleep—for the worst. But the entire keep could have been laid siege to over the last hours and she wouldn't have known.

Surely it was because she was exhausted from the stress of the day, as well as from the mind-numbing task of stitching Bowen's wounds.

It had been no easy feat, and there had been extraordinary pressure for her to seal the wound properly. One misstep could have earned her serious reprimand and censure. She shuddered to think what her punishment might have been.

One of the ties securing the furs over the window had loosened, and a light breeze lifted the end, allowing the first faint shades of dawn into the room. Soon the keep would be alive with activity, though she was uneasy about the sort of goings-on that would be initiated.

'Twould be best if she remained here or in Bowen's room until such time as she was forced out. She had no desire to face what awaited her. She was delaying the inevitable, but at the moment, she cared not. She was more concerned with her self-preservation than with anything else.

When a knock sounded at her door, her dread immediately intensified. She scolded herself for being so quick to draw conclusions. It could simply be one of Bowen's men, seeking a report on his condition. Or Brodie himself come to ask how Bowen had fared through the night.

As she was attempting to right herself enough so that she could rise from the bed, the door swung open and she frowned at the breach of her privacy. Not that she'd been guaranteed any such thing. But she'd assumed, and she should have learned better by now.

Relief was instant when she saw it was Taliesan poking her head through the door. Genevieve immediately smiled in welcome, happy to see a friendly face.

"Oh, 'tis good you're awake. I much wanted to speak to you regarding the laird's condition and what is happening within the clan," Taliesan said. "May I enter?"

"Of course," Genevieve said, motioning her forward.

She patted the edge of the bed encouragingly, aware that she'd never been so openly inviting to another person in all her time here.

Taliesan seemed delighted with the overture and limped over, her gait much quicker and smoother this morn. Genevieve hoped that meant Taliesan's leg wasn't paining her as much as usual.

Taliesan settled on the bed next to Genevieve and impulsively reached over to hug her.

"What was that for?" Genevieve asked in bewilderment. But she found she didn't mind the affectionate gesture at all. It made her feel . . . wanted. *Liked.*

"You just looked as though you needed it," Taliesan said kindly.

"I did, and thank you," Genevieve said with a smile.

Taliesan's expression sobered. "What goes on, Genevieve? The Armstrongs and Montgomerys alike are being close-lipped about the laird's condition, which has fueled gossip that he lies dying in his chamber. There is much worry as to what our fate will be if that happens. 'Tis widely known that Patrick instigated the attack, and that some of the men who swore allegiance to the laird turned betrayer."

"How many?" Genevieve asked sharply.

Taliesan's eyes widened. "You do not know?"

Genevieve grimaced. "I know not anything. I spent the night tending the laird's wounds and watching for any sign of fever. I've only just come to my chamber a short time ago."

"Then 'tis sorry I am for disturbing you. You should be resting."

Genevieve shook her head. "I am well rested," she lied. "I would know what is occurring within the clan. Brodie left Bowen's chamber last eve to determine if there were more traitors in our midst."

Taliesan sighed, her mouth turning down in an unhappy frown. "'Tis a sad and disgraceful tale I bring you. There were three other McHugh warriors who remained behind and made a vow to support Bowen Montgomery. 'Twas discovered that they played a part in the killings of two men. One a Montgomery and one an Armstrong. They are to be executed, and the clan is in uproar over it."

"'Tis not less than they deserve," Genevieve spat. "They follow in the old laird's footsteps. A path steeped in treachery and dishonor. They bring shame to your clan's name. The clan should be first to want justice to be served."

"But they are husbands and fathers to our clan's women and children," Taliesan said quietly. "'Tis not such a simple matter when wives and children will be left without a husband and father."

"Aye, I know it, but they should have given the matter due consideration. The consequences of their actions were spelled out long before they chose to travel the path they trod."

"When will it end?" Taliesan asked softly. "Our clan is bathed in blood, betrayal, and treachery. All because of Ian McHugh."

"Nay," Genevieve said fiercely. "He carries not the full blame. Patrick McHugh allowed his son free rein. Patrick was laird, not Ian. He was too weak and dishonorable to stand up to his son and correct the wrongs that have brought this clan low. 'Tis on him *and* Ian that the clan should turn their ire. Not me. Not the Montgomerys or the Armstrongs. They set in motion all that has occurred when they made the choices they made."

"You are right, of course," Taliesan murmured. "But 'tis still sad that brother is pitted against brother. Father against son. Wife against husband. 'Tis no position for any clansman to be in. We are family. If we don't stand together, how can we stand for anything else?"

Genevieve grasped Taliesan's hand. "Aye, 'tis sad indeed, but there is naught you and I can do to change it. 'Tis their decisions. Their choices. They must live with the consequences."

Taliesan sighed. "I know you are right, but I still have no love of the entire sordid mess. It makes me fear for the future of our clan—our bloodline. Already we have a Montgomery laird. How long will it be before there are none of us left and we are but spoils of war, scattered to the winds, our name naught but a black memory carried to generations after us."

"You take far too much on your shoulders, Taliesan," Genevieve said gently. "You are wise for one so young, and you think deeper on matters than your kinsmen. You can only take responsibility for your own actions and act with honor in every encounter."

"I know you are right. 'Tis not me who is wise, Genevieve, but you."

"If I was wise, I would have found a way to kill Ian McHugh long ago and save us all the misery of his actions," Genevieve said, her voice so cold it sent a shiver down her own spine.

And 'twas true enough. Killing Ian would surely have meant her own death sentence, and yet that would have been preferable to the life she'd endured. But she'd stubbornly clung to her existence, refusing to be beaten down. Her damnable pride would not allow her to concede defeat to Ian or any other McHugh, most especially not Patrick McHugh. She would not have given him the satisfaction of ordering her death. And that was supposing that she would have even been killed. Just as easily she could have been consigned a fate as bad as the one Ian had heaped upon her. Given to the McHugh men to play the unwilling whore. Passed from one to the other and perhaps given as bounty to another clan.

Nay, as long as she had hope of one day regaining control over her destiny, she had silently endured, knowing that one day . . . one day she would be in a position to seek justice. That time had come the day before, when Patrick had been in her sights and she'd let the arrow fly.

"How is the clan taking the news of Patrick's death? Is it known who did the killing?"

Genevieve held her breath, feeling guilty over deceiving Taliesan. But if it was known that she had killed Patrick, the clan would only harbor more animosity toward her. She cared not if anyone ever discovered the truth.

"The clan is divided. There are those who are angry about Patrick's betrayal, and they believe the Montgomerys and Armstrongs acted accordingly. He was buried this morn, but the Montgomery and Armstrong men bore his body beyond our borders, not affording him the honor of being laid to rest on McHugh land. There are others who, while confused and bitter about Patrick's defection, still believe he should have been given the honor of being buried on his lands."

That Taliesan hadn't given voice to the fact that Genevieve had been the one who'd felled Patrick bolstered Genevieve's spirits. It was one less thing the clan would blame her for—not that they needed other reasons.

Genevieve reached over to squeeze Taliesan's hand. "I go to see how the laird fares. His injuries required stitching, and 'twas I who set needle to his flesh. 'Tis God's truth my hand has never shaken as much as it did last night. I must now watch for signs of fever and pray that he recovers quickly."

"If you have need of anything, summon me at once," Taliesan said, her voice sincere. "I will be happy to give you aid."

"Thank you, Taliesan. I never imagined finding a true friend among so many hostile faces, but 'tis glad I am to have you."

Taliesan smiled, her entire face lighting up so sweetly that it made Genevieve instantly warm all the way through. She stood, pushing herself up awkwardly from the bed, and smoothed her skirts.

"You must be starved. I will send up food for you to the laird's chamber so that you may eat while you watch over his recovery."

Genevieve's stomach cramped, and she realized that it

had been a long while since she'd partaken of any food. She smiled gratefully up at Taliesan.

"My thanks. If you would, have water warmed and brought up in a basin so that I may wash the laird's wounds and see to the dressings."

"I'll do it at once."

Taliesan started toward the door, but then she hesitated and turned, her fingers gripping the edge.

"Things will be better now, Genevieve. You'll see. No longer will you be forced to suffer such injustice. Bowen Montgomery seems a good and just man. He'll do what is right."

Genevieve nodded faintly, her stomach knotting not from hunger but from the knowledge that when the laird awakened he would demand an accounting from her. And what she told him could well mean that the Montgomerys and Armstrongs would be no safe refuge for her.

CHAPTER 19

Genevieve knocked at Bowen's door, and while she waited for the summons to enter she very nearly turned and fled back to her chamber. Only the thought that if Geoffrey and Deaglan had given the laird another potion he would be insensible awhile longer gave her the courage to stand her ground.

The door opened and Deaglan stood there, large and imposing. He took a step back and motioned for Genevieve to enter.

"He drank nearly all of the dram we gave him," Deaglan reported. "He is resting more comfortably now. I see no sign of fever. 'Tis to your credit and speed in stitching him up that he seems to be faring so well."

Warmth suffused Genevieve's cheeks at the unexpected praise. Kind words were foreign to her of late.

"'Tis good he is resting," she said as she made her way to the chair still positioned next to Bowen's bed.

She glanced at the sleeping laird and, indeed, he looked at peace. His brow wasn't creased in pain, and he seemed utterly relaxed.

Another knock sounded, and Deaglan frowned as he hurried to answer. A moment later, he came back in carrying food. Taliesan appeared behind him, her eyes large in her face. She seemed intimidated by the presence of the two guards.

Genevieve rose, offering a smile of welcome to Talie-san. Then she turned to Geoffrey and Deaglan. "Taliesan has brought food. Have either of you eaten since the laird was attacked?"

Geoffrey frowned, his brow knitted in concentration. "Nay, mistress. 'Tis the truth we have not."

"Then partake of what is offered," Genevieve said, waving her hand toward the food.

"Nay," Deaglan objected. " 'Tis your meal we take, mistress. You were at the laird's side since yesterday and have more need of sustenance than we do."

Genevieve rolled her eyes and stared at the mound of food carried by both Deaglan and Taliesan. "There is more than enough for all to share. You'll concentrate harder on your task of protecting the laird if your belly is full. Now eat. It would be a shame for it to go to waste. I'll not eat all of it, to be sure."

"Our thanks, mistress," Deaglan said gravely. " 'Tis most appreciated. We would not leave the laird's chamber door even to go below and break our fast."

"I'll see that food is brought to you at all meals," Taliesan said in a soft, shy voice.

Both men smiled at Taliesan, but then who wouldn't? The lass was sweet and good-hearted to her bones. She had a positive effect on everyone who came into contact with her.

"Thank you," Deaglan offered solemnly. "I appreciate your generosity."

Taliesan blushed pink, dipped a curtsy, and then limped from the room, closing the door behind her.

Genevieve plated a small portion of the food that Taliesan had brought to the chamber. Even though she was hungry, she knew she wouldn't eat much. Her stomach was too unsettled. She was too worried—and terrified—of what was to come.

The two men set upon the remainder of the food, and

it was evident they were indeed quite hungry as they dug into their offerings.

She returned to the chair at Bowen's bedside and picked nervously at the food. It was tasteless—probably a blessing—but she forced herself to swallow each bite, washing it down with water.

She was nearly done with her portion when the door opened. She swung around to see who had entered without so much as a by-your-leave, only to see Brodie looming in the doorway.

He nodded at Geoffrey and Deaglan, exchanging a few low words that she couldn't hear—although Brodie kept gifting her with the strangest looks.

When he was done with his brief conversation, he walked toward the bed. There was a peculiar light in his eyes, one she wanted to question him about, but she stifled the urge. There were some things she'd rather not know.

"How does he fare?" Brodie asked in a low voice.

Genevieve set her plate aside on the small table by Bowen's bed.

"He has settled. Geoffrey and Deaglan gave him another potion after he became agitated. 'Twas obvious he was in pain."

"And fever?"

She shook her head. "Nay, he is still cool to the touch. My hope is that the next time he awakens the pain will have subsided enough that he doesn't require further sedation. If God is willing, he'll pull through and be back on his feet in a short time."

Brodie nodded, his features easing. He looked tired. As though he'd not slept the night before, and 'twas likely he hadn't, given all she'd heard from Taliesan. She bit her lip to prevent the inevitable questions from bursting out. She wanted to ask him about the McHugh traitors. What the mood of the McHugh clan was, and if he feared another attack. And, most important, would he and the remaining warriors from the Montgomery and Armstrong clans be capable of fending off yet another attempt to reclaim the keep?

"You did a fine job, Genevieve. Bowen will owe you a debt of gratitude."

"Nay," she refuted softly. She knew better.

"I have matters to attend, and 'tis important we keep careful watch on the borders," Brodie said. "Summon me when he awakens and alert me if his condition worsens."

"Aye, I will."

He touched her shoulder briefly with his hand, and then he was gone before she could react to his gesture.

She sagged when Brodie departed the chamber. What a fraud she was, playing savior, making herself important.

Though none would likely believe it, she had no ulterior motive for helping Bowen Montgomery. She knew that she would answer for her actions, regardless of her role in keeping Bowen alive.

Despite all the wrong that had been done to her, she still had a burning sense of right and wrong. Perhaps her view was not shared by others, but it was what she thought that mattered to her. She could only control her own actions, and, if she could help it, she would not act with dishonor, for to do so would make her no better than Ian or Patrick, or the countless others who'd made the choice to sell their loyalty.

Deaglan and Geoffrey rose from their places by the fire. Deaglan stood by Bowen's bed long enough to offer his and Geoffrey's services should they be needed, and the two quit the room to resume their posts outside the door.

The chamber was once again blanketed in silence, and Genevieve sat staring at Bowen as he rested with ease.

Tentatively, she slid her fingers over Bowen's warm hand that was palm down on the mattress.

"I know you sleep, Laird," she whispered. "But 'tis my wish for you to recover even though I must answer for my actions when you awaken. You are the only hope for this clan. For me. I would have you live so that you may see this clan through the coming days. I do not want Ian and Patrick to win, though they are both dead and lie in cold graves."

She left her hand covering his, enjoying something so simple as an innocent touch. Completely harmless. His warmth bled into her cold hand, warming all the way into her arm.

He moved her in a way that was unfamiliar to her. She felt none of the loathing, fear, or disgust that she felt with Ian or the others with whom he tortured her.

He left her hungry, for what she couldn't be certain, but he instilled an ache deep within her soul, for no matter what he decided her fate to be, she knew him to be an honorable man.

Aye, she would be at peace whatever his edict. She deserved his anger and censure. She had done the terrible thing he'd accused her of, and yet he hadn't come to her in rage, making threats, and neither had he abused her.

He simply asked her if what he'd learned was true. And when had anyone questioned her before rendering judgment?

For that he had her respect. She only hated that she couldn't deny his claims.

Having forgotten the warm water she'd requested, she hurried to the fire, where the pitcher had been placed, hoping it hadn't chilled too much.

After dipping a finger into it and finding it still warm, she dipped several cloths into it and then laid them by the fire so they would be comfortable on Bowen's skin.

When she returned to Bowen's bedside, she carefully unwound the linen strips from his arm and examined the cut. She then cleaned it with the warm cloths, watching all the while for signs that he'd awakened.

After cleaning the wound to her satisfaction, she wrapped it in clean dressings and directed her attention to the stitches on his chest.

She wiped away crusted blood and placed a heated compress over the length of the cut.

Appeased that she'd done everything in her power to ensure his comfort, she settled back in her chair, weariness assailing her.

She would stand guard by his bedside, her prayers lifting to heaven for his quick recovery. Until she was forced away, she would remain here, Bowen's own guardian.

She'd prayed often enough for a champion of her own, and until now, her prayers had remained unanswered. Although it was likely Bowen would no longer champion her cause, she would hold dear the memory of the gentle warrior and his careful treatment of her for the rest of her days.

CHAPTER 20

It was late in the evening when Bowen began to stir. Genevieve sat up straight, her anxious gaze traveling immediately to Bowen's face as his eyelids fluttered and struggled to open.

Her first instinct was to bolt from the room, but she had to ascertain his fitness. All through the day she'd stood vigil by his bedside, watching closely for any sign of a fever.

Even now, her hand went automatically to his forehead and down to his cheek, testing for abnormal warmth.

He uttered a sigh as her hand glided over his face, and, while his face felt cool to her touch, his words had her wondering if he had indeed been overtaken by illness.

"Such a beautiful lass," he murmured.

She yanked her hand away, stepping back into the shadows cast by the burning candles. Though he had no apparent fever, 'twas obvious he was not fully awake, because he certainly wasn't referencing her with his remark.

She took this opportunity to slip away, heading to the door to alert the others. 'Twas time for her to take to her own chamber. The laird was awakening and, by all accounts, he was well and seemingly pain free.

Hearing no protest from the bed, she quietly opened

the door, slipping into the hall, where Geoffrey and Deaglan stood guard.

"The laird is awakening," she said.

She swayed precariously, fatigue sapping what little strength she had left. Deaglan put a hand out to steady her, but she quickly stepped to the side.

"He hasn't taken a fever and he isn't thrashing about in pain. Perhaps he'll be lucid now and aware of his surroundings."

"We'll see to him immediately and send word to Brodie," Deaglan said. "Now, go to your chamber, mistress, and seek your bed. You've remained at his side for two full days. You have need of your rest."

She nodded, only too willing to remove herself from Bowen's chamber before he fully awakened. Oh, aye, sooner or later she would receive her reckoning, but it would be after she'd enjoyed a full night's rest and could better face her judgment.

She went into her chamber, but even though she was weary to her bones, she couldn't sleep. She was too agitated, and paced her chamber restlessly.

Needing the coolness of the night air, she pulled the furs away from her window and leaned from the sill, breathing deeply of the chill.

It was a beautiful night, stars scattered like jewels across the sky. It was clear, with no cloud in sight and nothing to hide the near-full moon from view.

It glistened off the river that snaked around the keep and softly illuminated the landscape, making it glow with an eerie light.

She rested her arms on the narrow ledge and stared longingly toward the horizon. Below, the courtyard was mostly silent. Torches blazed along the tops of the stone wall, and she could see motion from the night guards as they manned their posts.

But the land was blanketed in silence. Deceptively

peaceful. There was no sign that, just two days prior, a bloody battle had been waged. Lives were lost. Women and children mourned husbands and fathers. Lives were irrevocably changed.

Sadness gripped her. 'Twas such a useless thing. And so unnecessary. Many had suffered for the actions of a few. Wasn't that always the way of things? The collective suffered for the actions of an inept, ineffectual leader.

She closed her eyes and allowed the cool wind to blow over her face, ruffling her hair until finally a chill skated down her spine.

A shout below broke her from her reverie and she quickly looked down to see several men scrambling to open the gate into the courtyard. When she looked beyond, she saw dozens of men on horseback riding toward the keep, two torches in the lead.

Her heart leaped into her throat until she heard someone shout, "The Montgomerys have returned!"

Relief took over. Teague was back. The messenger had been successful in overtaking him. Reinforcements had arrived, and they would be safe from attack.

But with the arrival of Bowen's brother came the fear that, surely, once Bowen had explained all, she would be an outcast. The kindness and understanding they'd shown her would be replaced by anger and thoughts of revenge.

She turned away from the window, agitation taking hold once more. For the first time, she didn't want to be alone. The isolation of her chamber—something she once longed for more than anything—was stifling and overwhelming. But she had no desire to return to Bowen's chamber, where even now her fate could be in discussion.

On impulse, she cracked open her chamber door,

peeking out to see if Geoffrey and Deaglan were outside Bowen's chamber. But nay, they *must still be inside*.

Quickly, she darted to Taliesan's door and knocked. The entire time she waited, she jittered from head to toe, not wanting to be discovered lurking in the halls when she was supposed to be in her own chamber, resting.

Finally Taliesan opened the door, and when she saw Genevieve she instantly swung it wide for her to enter.

"Is aught amiss, Genevieve?"

Concern radiated from Taliesan and Genevieve hastened to assure her.

"Nay. I could not sleep and was . . . lonely. And restless. I saw below my window that the Montgomery forces have arrived, and knew I wouldn't rest for the remainder of the night."

Taliesan shut the door and turned, her eyes wide. Relief shone in their depths.

"Oh, 'tis good news you bring. We need no longer worry about having to fend off an attack when we are sorely undermanned."

Genevieve wished she could be so relieved over the news. Worry was about to eat a hole in her stomach.

"Sit, Genevieve. Do you have need of anything?"

Genevieve settled on the edge of Taliesan's bed and shook her head. "Nay, just your company."

Taliesan, clad in only her nightdress, sat on the bed, dragging her lame leg up so that it didn't dangle over the side.

" 'Tis glad I am for your company. Things are so tense within the clan. I finally sought refuge in my chamber, because everywhere I turned there was naught but worry, anger, fear, and stress. The clan has no idea what to think or how they should feel. Many are resentful of the Montgomerys' and Armstrongs' intrusion, even as they realize the sins committed by Ian and Patrick and weigh this against the loyalty they feel they should have toward their own kin, regardless of their transgressions."

"I suppose we'll wait it out in your chamber together," Genevieve offered faintly.

"Why don't you try to sleep, Genevieve. You look exhausted. You can share the bed with me. No one will bother you here."

Genevieve glanced at the pillow and then stifled a yawn.

"Come. I have a nightdress you can change into. No need to go back to your chamber. I'll help you out of your dress, and then we'll both have a long sleep."

CHAPTER 21

Bowen let out a groan and then pushed himself up in the bed, surprised when pain set fire to his chest. He sagged back, all his breath leaving him in an excruciating rush. What the bloody hell?

His head hit the pillow and he reopened his eyes to see Brodie Armstrong looming over his bed.

"What are you doing here?" Bowen grumbled.

"Seeing how you fare. How do you feel?"

It was an odd question, but it gave him pause, because the fuzz was starting to clear from his mind, and the more it cleared the more the ache in his skull increased.

He felt as though he'd been thrown from his horse, dragged through the mud, and then stepped on repeatedly.

"I've felt worse." And it was true enough.

He struggled to make sense of why he was lying abed with Brodie in his chamber. Beyond Brodie he saw Geoffrey and one of Brodie's men, Deaglan, standing at the end of the bed.

It was a regular gathering in his chamber, apparently.

When he tried to maneuver onto his side, at least, his chest protested and it felt as though someone had driven a thousand tiny needles into his flesh. He glanced down to see a fresh wound, jaggedly cut across his chest.

It was stitched tightly and looked clean. The stitches

were close together and had sealed the flesh completely closed. Whoever had performed the task had done an excellent job.

"What happened?" Bowen asked, still rubbing bleary eyes.

His head was a vast void of nothingness, and trying to think only made it ache more vilely. His mouth was overdry, and his tongue felt large and thick. Almost as if he'd consumed far too much ale and suffered in the aftermath. Only, he knew he had done no such thing.

Brodie frowned. "We were attacked. Do you not remember?"

Rapid images flashed in Bowen's mind. It all came in one giant bombardment until he was dizzy.

"Tell me all," Bowen said curtly. "I want a full report. How long have I been abed? What of the rest of the clan. Did we suffer losses?"

Brodie held up his hand. "Your brother has arrived. It would be far simpler if I only give an accounting once, and he'll want to hear the whole of it."

"Teague? What the hell is he doing here?"

"Genevieve sent for him," Brodie said evenly. "The lass roared the order, in fact. She sent three of your men to intercept your brother. But I'll explain all when Teague arrives. I expect him at any moment. He was dismounting just moments ago."

Bowen simmered with impatience, but he fell silent, nodding his agreement that they would discuss all when Teague was present.

He remembered his confrontation with Genevieve on the bank of the river. He certainly remembered seeing her bathing, and how stunningly breathtaking she was. He also remembered well how pale she'd gone when he'd asked her if all he'd heard about her involvement in Eveline's abduction was true. The lass hadn't needed to say a word to confirm his suspicions. It was all there to see on her face and in her eyes.

But then he also remembered staring at her in the heat of battle and being convinced she was about to fell him with an arrow, only for her to take out a McHugh warrior behind him who'd been prepared to plunge a dagger into his back. And then she'd rushed to his side, refusing to let him fall to the ground.

After that, everything was a blank. He had no recollection of any of the events that had followed. And he still didn't know long he'd been in bed out of his senses.

"How long has it been since the battle took place?" Bowen demanded.

"Two full days," Brodie said.

Bowen swore. 'Twas certainly long enough to be abed with an injury as paltry as his.

The corners of Brodie's mouth turned up into a slight smile. "If it makes you feel any better, you were abed for so long because we held you down and forced a sleeping draft down your throat."

Only a little mollified, Bowen leaned back and then pushed himself upward to a sitting position.

They didn't have long to wait, as Brodie had suspected. Only moments later, Bowen's chamber door burst open and Teague strode in, his face drawn into grim, worried lines.

His expression lightened when he cast eyes on Bowen, and he hurried to his brother's bedside.

"Are you all right?" Teague demanded. "I came as fast as I could. We were nearly to Montgomery Keep when your men overtook me."

"Aye, I am well. 'Tis a paltry wound. Not worthy of two days abed. I'll be up on the morrow."

Teague turned to Brodie. "What in God's name happened?"

Brodie pulled up a chair, turned it backward, and then straddled the seat, resting his arms along the back.

"Patrick McHugh attacked, along with the McGrieves. We beat them back, but not before Bowen was injured. There was an attempt by a McHugh who'd remained behind and sworn allegiance to the Montgomerys. He snuck up on him and nearly stabbed him in the back as he did battle with another warrior."

Teague quirked up an eyebrow. "And yet he didn't."

Brodie shook his head. "Nay. Genevieve felled him with an arrow."

Teague did an instant double take. "Wait. Genevieve did *what*?"

"She put an arrow straight through the man's forehead, and then she finished off the soldier Bowen had been doing battle with. The lass was fierce in battle. And she has good aim."

Teague glanced at Bowen, his eyebrows drawn together. "What say you about this, Bowen? And what of the matter we discussed before I left?"

Bowen sent Teague a look that instantly silenced his younger brother.

"I'm more interested in the fate of Patrick McHugh. I saw him not in the heat of battle. Is he still lurking out there, hiding in some dark hole? And what of the other members of the McHugh clan. There was one traitor. Were there others?"

Brodie grimaced. "Aye. We found at least three. They were executed at dawn. They aided Patrick and the McGrieves, as well as their kin who rode with Patrick."

"And Patrick?" Teague asked. "What of him?"

Brodie took in a deep breath. "This is rather interesting. Patrick is dead."

"Dead? How? And who killed him? Find me the name of the soldier who ended Patrick's life so he can be handsomely rewarded," Bowen said.

"Well, that's the thing," Brodie hedged. "We found two arrows in Patrick McHugh. One in his leg and one right through his neck. Both arrows belong to Genevieve."

Bowen and Teague gaped at Brodie and then looked at each other in astonishment.

"Are you certain it was the *lass* who killed him?" Teague asked skeptically.

"I saw her shoot the two men in defense of Bowen. It's not a stretch for me to believe she felled Patrick as well. The lass is calm under pressure. And she's lethal with that bow of hers."

"What happened after I blacked out?" Bowen asked.

He wanted to know all, because he was haunted by strange sensations. He could swear that Genevieve was at his side, her hand touching his face. It was a soothing balm to his pain, and he hadn't wanted her to leave. Only, when he'd awakened Geoffrey and Deaglan were present and there was no sign of Genevieve.

"Genevieve propped you up so you didn't plant your face in the ground," Brodie said with thinly veiled amusement. "Then she started barking orders like a seasoned commander. 'Twas she who sent riders to fetch Teague. She was concerned that we might suffer another attack, and with Bowen hurt and losses during battle we were considerably weakened."

Bowen shook his head, utterly perplexed by the lass. He should be angry—nay, furious—with her for her part in Eveline's abduction, and yet he couldn't muster any enthusiasm for administering any sort of punishment for her crime.

At least, not until he heard her reasoning.

"She guarded you as fiercely as a wolf bitch with her pups," Brodie said, admiration clear in his voice. "She stitched your wound and then stood vigil by your bedside for two days. I came in to find her sleeping next to you during the night. The lass had exhausted herself and had fallen asleep. I left before I could disturb her, but she remained in that chair by your bed for two days straight, barely eating or sleeping the entire time."

Teague was frowning harder by the moment, and Bowen could see that he battled to remain silent. Bowen shot him a warning look before turning his attention back to Brodie.

"How many losses did we suffer?"

"Not many, but with a force as small as what we had after the departure of Aiden and Teague with the bulk of our soldiers, even a few is too many. I lost one of my men, and two Montgomery warriors were killed in battle."

Bowen swore. "I should not have sent Teague away."

Brodie shrugged. "'Twas necessary. We had need of supplies. Food. This clan has little, and if they are to survive, they need aid. Even with fewer men, we were superior on the battlefield. The men with Patrick and the McGrieves outnumbered us, but their losses are far greater than ours."

Bowen looked to his brother. "Did you arrive at Montgomery Keep, and were you able to tell Graeme all before you received the summons?"

"Nay," Teague replied. "We were not far from our borders. I sent half the men to give report to Graeme and to tell him of all that had occurred. I brought the remainder with me as reinforcements in case another attack is launched."

"He was watching," Bowen muttered. "He was hiding like a thief and awaiting his opportunity to attack in an effort to regain the keep."

"He was a fool," Brodie said bluntly. "And he paid for it with his life."

"Think you the McGrieves will rally support and seek to take McHugh Keep by force?" Teague asked.

Bowen's lips curled. "Only a fool would have attacked in the first place. So, aye, I count the McGrieves as fools, and I think they see an opportunity to add to their lands."

"I would send word to my own father," Brodie spoke up. "I would apprise him of the events so that he too may render aid to us. I will need to inform him of the man we lost, and he'll likely send reinforcements along with food and goods."

It was on the tip of Bowen's tongue to refute that he needed anything from the Armstrongs, but he must remember now that the two clans were now allies, bonded by marriage.

Teague didn't look any happier about it, but he too remained silent. He'd already humbled himself enough by asking that Brodie remain behind to help Bowen.

"I will stay on until support from Graeme arrives and we receive his directive. He'd not want me to leave you when you're injured and in danger of another attack."

Bowen nodded at his brother. Then he turned back to Brodie. "Your father, as well as Graeme, will likely send immediate word to the king. Such an upheaval will surely reach his ears, and he'll not like the clans warring when he went to such lengths to end the fighting between the Montgomerys and Armstrongs. He's determined to bring peace to the Highlands now that his truce with England has been reached."

Brodie scowled. "As long as our king doesn't interfere. His meddling has become a nuisance."

It was obvious that Brodie still had not forgiven their king for ordering the marriage between Graeme and Eveline, even if the end result had achieved precisely what the king had wanted and the marriage had resulted in a happy union for both Graeme and Eveline.

Bowen couldn't say he blamed him. He'd not liked the

edict any more than the Armstrong clan had when it had first been rendered.

Brodie rose from his chair, swinging his leg over before pushing the chair back against the wall.

"'Tis time I seek my bed. Rest easy and heal, Bowen. There is still much to accomplish."

Bowen nodded at Brodie. Teague offered his good night, and then the two brothers were left alone.

As soon as the door closed, Teague turned to Bowen, his brow wrinkled in consternation.

"What of Genevieve? Did you not confront her? What was her part in Eveline's abduction?"

"I have not had the opportunity to discuss the matter with her," Bowen said in a low voice.

It was a lie, and he had no love of deceiving his brother. But he knew if he told Teague the truth, the lass would be condemned in Teague's eyes, and Bowen wasn't ready to have judgment rendered on Genevieve. Not yet. Not when he had yet to discover why she would do such a thing.

He was still mulling over all that Brodie had related. If Brodie was to be believed, Genevieve had saved Bowen's life. And she'd killed Patrick McHugh—a feat neither he nor his warriors had managed in the mayhem.

She was a perplexing puzzle, and one he had every intention of deciphering. He wanted time to do so before he made a rash and hasty decision on her fate. If he confided what he knew to Teague, Graeme would most assuredly find out, as would Brodie and the rest of the Armstrongs. They'd want to seek vengeance, and the idea of more pain being heaped on Genevieve turned his stomach.

"I thought you were going to seek her out," Teague said, still not satisfied with Bowen's words.

"Aye, and I did. I found her bathing in the river. I was set to discuss the matter, but the call to arms was sounded. I took Genevieve to the keep and ordered her to seek refuge within."

"An order she clearly obeyed," Teague said dryly.

" 'Tis glad I am she didn't. Mayhap I would not be alive if she had."

Teague fell silent. Then he shifted in his chair, his lips pressed into a tight line. "Aye, if Brodie is to be believed, you indeed owe your life to the lass. If she killed Patrick McHugh, the Montgomerys and Armstrongs alike owe her a debt."

Bowen could tell that Teague had no love for that admission. He was set against the lass, and Bowen couldn't entirely blame him. She had betrayed Eveline. She'd endangered both Montgomerys and Armstrongs with her treachery.

Still, Bowen couldn't help but think that he didn't have the whole of the story, and, until he did, he refused to condemn her to the rest of his clan. Or Brodie's.

Teague's sharp gaze found Bowen. There was something akin to fear in his brother's eyes, and Bowen's brow furrowed as he stared back.

"How bad is it, really, Bowen?" Teague asked softly.

Perplexed, he answered, "What do you speak of?"

"Your wound. 'Tis the truth that my heart nearly stopped when we were chased down by the riders and told that the keep had been attacked and that you'd been injured. They knew nothing of your condition, and I feared to find you dead when I arrived."

" 'Tis naught but a scratch," Bowen said.

Teague uttered a *hmmmph*. "A scratch that required extensive stitching, from what I can see. You scared me, Bowen. I'd not lose you. Especially not in a cause such as this. I'd rather lay waste to the entire clan and those who oppose us than have you struck down by a cowardly act."

Bowen smiled. "Rest easy, brother. I'm harder to kill

than that. It would seem the lass was determined that I not go down that day. Though, even if I had suffered a dagger in my back, 'tis just as likely I would have survived."

"I'd rather not chance it if 'tis all the same to you."

Bowen nodded wearily. "Aye, neither would I. 'Tis the truth this paltry cut pains me greatly, but I'll not say anything lest I have another potion poured down my throat. I've been insensible for two days from that poison they keep feeding me."

"I'll leave you to rest," Teague said, rising to his feet. "On the morrow, I'll meet with Brodie to determine if more needs be done to ensure the safety of the keep. If it's not too much trouble, perhaps you could remain abed and out of trouble."

Bowen grinned and raised his arm to clasp his brother's. "I'm glad you returned, even if I have no liking for the circumstance that prompted it."

Teague grasped Bowen's arm in his firm grip. "Well, don't be surprised if Graeme himself makes an appearance after he's heard all there is to hear."

Bowen groaned. "God help us."

CHAPTER 22

The next morning, Bowen slowly attempted to rise from his bed. Movement stretched the flesh sewn together, and he winced as he righted himself.

He pressed a hand to his chest, feeling the wound and testing to see how tender it was.

While he certainly wouldn't be back on the battlefield this day, he could at least take himself from the bed before he became a permanent part of it.

He staggered to the washbasin and cleaned his face. What he needed was a good bath. He still smelled of sweat and blood. There was a layer of grime on him that only a good scrubbing would take away.

Throwing a tunic on over his head, he searched for a clean pair of leggings and decided not to bother with boots. He'd retrieve them after he'd washed.

Geoffrey was alone in the hall, and he stood at attention the moment Bowen stuck his head out.

"Do you have need of aid, Laird?"

Bowen shook his head. "Nay, I'm going to bathe."

Geoffrey fell into step behind him and the two went down the stairs to find the hall empty, not yet alive with the day's activities.

Bowen continued out the back of the keep, deciding that he'd make use of Genevieve's stream.

The chill would certainly wash away the remnants of sleep, and his head needed a good clearing.

The brisk morning air hit him as soon as he stepped outside. He inhaled deeply, enjoying the lavender-painted sky that heralded the coming sun.

He'd nearly forgotten that Geoffrey was just a few steps behind when he topped the slight hill overlooking the stream. The sight that greeted him halted him in his tracks.

Genevieve was in the stream, her hair pulled over her shoulders as she rinsed the strands.

He turned sharply to Geoffrey. "Return to the keep at once."

Geoffrey looked startled, but Bowen knew the moment he saw beyond to where Genevieve was bathing. The younger man's cheeks reddened and he looked hastily away.

"Of course, Laird," he mumbled, even as he backtracked as fast as he could.

Satisfied that Geoffrey could no longer see Genevieve, Bowen turned back to the river and pondered whether he should intrude yet again on her bath.

She was a lure too strong to ignore. He should be gallant and step quietly away, but instead he moved forward, his gaze never leaving her.

"It seems to be a habit, my finding you here," he said mildly when he was within hearing distance.

Genevieve's startled gaze shot up, and she immediately covered the upper portion of her body with her arms. The action made the soft mounds bulge upward, so that the pale globes were readily visible.

"What are you doing out of bed?" she demanded. "'Tis too soon for you to be moving about. What if you tear the stitches?"

"I have it on good authority that the person who set the stitches did an excellent job."

She stared cautiously at him, her eyes dark and wounded. She expected the worst and, in a way, he couldn't fault her for that. She'd only been given the worst thus far. Ian McHugh certainly hadn't shown her any kindness, and, from what he'd witnessed, neither had most of the McHugh clan.

" 'Tis freezing, lass. What are you doing in the river at this hour?"

"I needed to clean the dirt and blood from my hair," she said in a low voice. "I would do so in privacy, if you please."

"Well now. It would seem we have a bit of a problem, because I came here myself to wash."

"Turn your back then, please, so that I may leave the water and dress, and then I'll leave you to *your* privacy."

He did as she bade him and presented his back. He could hear the splash of water, and he imagined her naked, water glistening on her skin. His body hardened as desire lanced through him like quick fire. It caught him completely by surprise.

He willed himself to regain control, but his body clearly had other ideas. His mind was filled with images fired by his imagination. And he had a rather vivid imagination where Genevieve was concerned.

Still, it made no sense that he had such a strong reaction to her. She bore the mark of another man—a man who'd made her his whore. There was much for her to answer to in regard to his clan, and yet he found himself making excuses for her. His mind sought a reasonable explanation for her actions, when there was nothing reasonable about her placing Eveline in such grievous danger.

Aye, she was all wrong for him, and yet he was drawn to her like a moth to flame.

"You can look now," she said, annoyance still evident in her tone.

He swiveled around to see her perched on one of the boulders overlooking the water. She had a drying blanket wrapped fully around her, and he wondered if she'd bothered to dress or if she was unclothed underneath.

Her hair lay bedraggled over her shoulders, still wet from the washing and as yet uncombed. She looked like a nymph from the sea. A scarred nymph, with secrets swirling in her eyes.

Bowen moved toward the water's edge, pulling his tunic over his head as he went. Out of the corner of his eye, he saw Genevieve hastily look away. He'd planned to bathe in his leggings, but if she was going to afford him privacy, he'd fully strip and enjoy a good scrubbing.

When she started to move, the protest was out of his mouth before he could call it back.

"Nay," he said. "Don't go."

She glanced back with a startled expression, which quickly became wary as she studied him.

"I would leave you to bathe, Laird. 'Tis not seemly for me to be present."

"Aye, 'tis the truth—'tis probably not. But I would talk with you here, away from all the others."

His hands paused before pushing down his leggings, and he looked in her direction. "Look away lest you be offended by my nudity."

She nearly fell off the boulder, so hastily did she yank herself around. And yet, while he watched her as he removed the last of his clothing, she turned slightly to regard him over her shoulder.

He smiled, taking in the furtive glance. She looked shy, and he found it oddly endearing. Surely he would burn in hell for being so bold, all but inviting the lass to look at him. A better man would have walked away the moment he saw her bathing. But he wasn't a better man, because he wanted nothing more than to spend a few moments with Genevieve, away from the prying eyes of others. Away from the judgment that awaited, and away from his duty not only to this new clan but to his own. Always his own.

He owed absolute loyalty to Graeme as laird of the Montgomery clan. He was Graeme's representative, and he couldn't fail to seek justice for wrongs done to his clan.

But who had ever stood up for Genevieve? Who had sought vengeance for all the wrongs done to her?

He couldn't understand why the lass didn't want her family to know she was alive, but then he could hardly understand the depths of all she'd endured. He understood pride. He understood it all too well. Every time he looked at her, he was struck by the unflagging and almost stoic pride with which she carried herself. Like it was all that she had left and she refused to be stripped of it.

As much as he thought she should send word to her family, how could he take away that choice when, for the past year, all her choices had been taken away?

The water was bracing, and he flinched as he waded in and it crept up to his more sensitive regions. There was nothing like cold water to chill one's ardor. He shivered, and then plunged downward in order to have done with it.

As he hunkered down, he called to Genevieve. "You can look now, lass."

She turned carefully, seeking him with her gaze. She pulled the blanket tighter around herself, and he was struck by the picture she presented, perched on the boulder, long damp hair streaming down her body. A mermaid. She reminded him of the mythical being from the sea.

"This water is frigid. What possessed you to bathe so early in the morning when 'tis so cold?"

She lifted one shoulder in a shrug. "I didn't think any-one would be about so early."

Her avoidance of the others made sense. He couldn't fault her for wanting the one thing she'd been denied in the past year. Privacy and a moment's peace. And yet he'd felt no guilt over intruding on that privacy. Indeed, his blood had quickened the moment he realized that she was in the stream and it presented the perfect op-portunity to speak to her away from his kin or the Arm-strongs.

"It would appear that I am indebted to you," Bowen said.

She cocked her head to the side, her expression one of puzzlement. "For what, Laird?"

"What indeed," he said with a snort. "It would seem you were busy while I was in battle. Your arrows were found in four different men. One of them being Patrick McHugh."

She whitened as if all the blood had been leeched from her face. Her fingers gripped the ends of the blanket and she made herself even smaller, if possible.

"'Twas a brave thing you did," Bowen continued. "One might wonder why you bothered. You put your-self at great risk by not seeking refuge, as you were told to do."

The shock of the cold was beginning to wear off. He looked to see that the bar of soap he'd brought with him was still lying on the bank with his clothing.

He didn't want to shock the lass by striding out of the water to fetch it.

"Will you toss me the soap?" he asked.

Genevieve glanced down and frowned, then looked back up at him. Careful to keep the blanket securely wrapped around her, she hoisted herself off the rock and then bent to fetch the soap. She underhanded it to him, and he caught it in the air.

As he began to cleanse himself, he found her gaze again.

"So why did you do it?"

Her shoulders heaved as she expelled a sigh. "Because I hated Patrick McHugh as much as I hated his spawn of a son. 'Twas my right to kill him. I was denied the pleasure of killing Ian, but 'tis glad I am all the same that he met his end."

Bowen paused to rinse the soap from his arms. She was calm and unemotional about death and killing, something most lasses never had occasion to discuss, much less take part in.

"And why did you choose to intervene in my battle?"

Her eyes narrowed. "Is that a reprimand?"

He laughed at the instant fire in her eyes. The lass still had spirit.

"Nay. I can hardly reprimand you when I stand here whole and hearty instead of lying in a shallow, cold grave, now, can I?"

"It was the right thing to do," she muttered. " 'Twas a cowardly act to attack from behind."

"You have my thanks, and that of my clan."

She swallowed and her lips trembled as she spoke her next words. "We cannot pretend that our last conversation here in this same place did not happen."

Bowen sighed. "Nay, we can't."

Her chin lifted, and again he saw that unflagging pride. And determination not to be beaten down.

"Tell me my fate, Laird. 'Tis not comforting not to know."

Bowen sank into the water and tilted his head back to wet his hair. For a moment, he lost himself in the task of bathing, because the simple truth was he hadn't decided the matter of her fate. He had no idea what to say to her. Not yet.

As he righted himself, he saw Genevieve turn and

abruptly stand up. She began walking toward the keep, her pace determined, and he called out for her to stop.

She froze, still facing away, and then slowly turned, her eyes ablaze. "I'll not play this game," she said fiercely. "I'll not be taunted. I'll not have my fate dangled over my head like an axe about to drop. If you had any decency, you would not make me suffer so."

There was so much hurt in her voice that it made him flinch. And her eyes. Pools of green so sorrowful he could drown in them. Ah, but he was making a muck of this.

"Don't go, lass. 'Tis the truth I haven't spoken of your fate because I haven't decided it."

"Is that supposed to make me feel better?" she asked incredulously.

"Sit down, please. 'Tis likely the only place we can have a private moment to converse."

" 'Tis hardly an appropriate place," she said. "I should not be here watching as you bathe. If others knew of it, I would be painted a whore all over again. Only this time I would be the Montgomery laird's whore."

She was right, of course, and yet he didn't want her to walk away. He had a pressing need to get to the heart of the matter, for his own peace of mind. He didn't want to condemn her. He wanted . . . He wasn't sure what he wanted. He wanted her not to be guilty of what she was accused, but she hadn't denied what he'd confronted her with.

"Turn away so that I may fully rinse and dress. Then we'll discuss the matter."

For a moment he thought she might refuse him, but then she turned away and stood rigidly, waiting for him to finish.

He quickly rinsed the last of the soap from his body and then walked from the water. God's teeth but it was cold. Colder than normal for an early summer morning.

The sun was only just creeping its way over the horizon, a distant ball of orange painting the sky in shades of gold and amber.

He grabbed the drying blanket and quickly toweled off before dragging his leggings and tunic back on. At least his body was behaving normally now. His cock had shriveled to nothing as soon as he'd touched the water.

"You can turn around now," he said.

She took a cautious peek over her shoulder and, seeing him fully clothed, turned and went back to her rock. He sat on the one across from her and leveled an intent stare in her direction.

"Tell me why," he said simply.

Her eyes lowered, and she fidgeted with the ends of the blanket held firmly in her grip. "Does it matter why? I did a terrible thing. You and your clan rightfully deserve justice for my sins."

"Aye, it matters," he said in a low voice. "It matters to *me*, Genevieve. I would know what drove you to such."

She lifted her gaze and stared directly into his eyes, her voice earnest and passionate, almost as if she was pleading with him to understand.

"Because you were my only hope."

The faint whisper sounded loud in the calm of the morning. He didn't know what to say. How to respond. What could she mean? He shook his head in confusion.

"I do not understand."

Tears filled her eyes, and she clutched the blanket even tighter around her, as if it were all that protected her from grave harm.

"I knew if Ian were to take Eveline, his deed would not go unpunished. The Montgomerys and Armstrongs are two very powerful clans. They would never stand for such a wrong being done to one of their own, and Eveline was both Montgomery *and* Armstrong."

Bowen continued to stare at her as understanding

slowly dawned. He let out his breath in a long exhale, as he finally realized her scheme.

"You *wanted* us to come."

"Aye," she whispered. "I did not know if my fate would be any better at your hands, but it could not be worse than what I endured with Ian. It was a chance I had to take."

Bowen's head was swimming with all that she'd related. "I do not know whether to applaud your genius or condemn a plan that was so fraught with danger to an innocent woman."

Genevieve bit into her lip as if to stifle something she was about to say. Then she merely looked away, refusing to meet his gaze any longer.

"What is to be done with me?" she finally asked, her gaze still averted.

Her shoulders slumped in a posture that screamed defeat. Resignation. It pained him to see her so lifeless when he knew deep inside that there existed a passionate, vibrant woman.

He took in a deep breath, knowing his decision would be met with arguments from both his kin and the Armstrongs if Genevieve's part in Eveline's abduction was ever brought to light.

"I made you a promise, lass. One I intend to keep. I told you that I would either see you well placed within my own clan or I would see you entered into an abbey, as was your wish. 'Tis more likely that, given what you did, the abbey would be a better choice. I know not if my kin would ever forgive the wrong you did to Eveline."

A tear trailed down her perfect, unmarred cheek. The scarred side of her face was turned away, as was her habit, and she presented such an image of loveliness and tragedy that his breath caught in his throat.

He had the fiercest urge to pull her into his arms and

offer her comfort. He doubted the lass had experienced anything resembling comfort in all the time she'd been in captivity.

"I do not deserve for you to keep your promise, Laird. It was exacted when you knew not what I'd done. 'Tis perfectly understandable if you wish to go back on your word. I would not blame you."

"But I would blame myself," Bowen said. "I am not without sympathy for your plight. I cannot even say that your plan was not without merit. If 'twas any other woman than my brother's wife that we spoke of, I would not feel the anger that overcame me when I discovered what you'd done. 'Tis hard for me to be objective when I know Eveline and the gentleness of her spirit. And yet I cannot discount the desperation and necessity of your actions. I cannot find fault with a lass for only wanting to be free."

A choked sob ruptured from her throat. She put a balled fist to her mouth in an attempt to stifle the sound of her distress. When she spoke, her voice cracked from the strain of holding back her sobs, and yet her words were earnest and heartfelt.

"I would not wish harm on another, even to save myself. You have to believe that."

Bowen studied her a long moment, his heart aching with the need to touch her. "Aye, lass," he said. "I believe I do at that."

"I should go now," she said, rising with haste, the ends of the blanket flapping in the breeze. "The others will have risen, and I would not have them find me in a state of undress in your presence."

"Nay," he murmured. "You have suffered the opinions of others too much already."

He watched as she made her way back to the keep. She made a forlorn picture, barefoot, her hair wet from her bath, and the drying blanket wrapped around her. When she topped the rise, she paused for a brief moment and looked back at him, their gazes connecting across the distance. And then she turned toward the keep and slowly disappeared over the ridge.

CHAPTER 23

"Where on God's earth have you been?"

Such was Bowen's greeting when he entered the hall to find Brodie and Teague about to break their fast.

Bowen sat next to Teague and across from Brodie.

"A good morning to you, too," Bowen said dryly.

Teague frowned. "You shouldn't be out of bed, and what were you doing outside the keep? You had no one with you?"

Bowen chuckled. "When I need a keeper, I'll most assuredly come to you, little brother."

"Did you lose your shoes wherever it was you went?" Brodie asked mildly.

Bowen glanced down at his feet with a grimace. "I had no need of them for bathing."

"Why are you so bloody cheerful this morning anyway?" Teague asked suspiciously. "For a man who was wounded in battle, you don't seem too aggrieved over the matter."

Bowen rolled his eyes. "Would you prefer I stomp around and bellow, 'Off with their heads'?"

"Depends on whose heads you're demanding to be cut off," Brodie offered.

"I can think of one," Bowen said, looking pointedly at Teague.

"I'll tell you, if the Montgomerys don't arrive soon

with different fare to eat, my stomach may eat itself from the inside out," Brodie grumbled. " 'Tis impossible to coordinate a hunt when we're trapped at the keep for fear of attack."

Teague stared down at this morning's offering and poked at it with his knife. "I'm not even sure what this is supposed to be. 'Tis not even warm, and the taste isn't something I can identify."

Brodie leaned down and sniffed, his expression promptly turning sour. " 'Tis a wonder the McHughs have survived this long if this is what they eat on a daily basis."

"Perhaps we should inspect the larder," Bowen said. "Or perhaps 'tis better we never discover what's within."

Teague nodded his agreement and then pushed his food aside. "I have not the stomach for this today. I was dreaming of savory food back at Montgomery Keep when we were overtaken by the soldiers bearing us news that you were under attack."

Brodie's eyes gleamed with sudden light. "What say you we make a round of the borders. It could double as a hunt and, God willing, we'll bring back something that's actually fit for the table."

Teague brightened, his stomach already in agreement if the rumble was any indication.

"A pox on both of you," Bowen said sourly.

Teague grinned. "And nay, you aren't allowed to come with us. We'll be back before the evening meal. I'll set Geoffrey and Deaglan on you to ensure you don't over-tax yourself while we're away patrolling our borders."

"Patrolling my arse," Bowen grumbled.

Still, as restless as he felt, and as much as he resented being confined to the keep and unable to participate in the patrol or the hunt, he was eager for an opportunity to spend more time with Genevieve without having to offer explanations to Teague or Brodie.

Teague rose and clapped a hand on Bowen's shoulder. "We're off. Pray that we are successful. 'Tis no telling how long we'll have to wait for a decent meal otherwise."

Bowen watched as the two men departed the hall. Teague and Brodie seemed to have developed a liking for each other that went beyond mere tolerance. It was an odd thought, the idea of a Montgomery ever willingly embracing friendship with an Armstrong, but it would seem that Teague and Brodie had done just that.

The cold food in front of him held no appeal, and yet he was famished, not having eaten in two days' time. With a grimace, he forced himself to choke down a healthy portion of the food and he chased it with copious amounts of water.

When he was done, he rose, his stomach feeling as though it were filled with rocks. It may have been a better idea to have suffered hunger rather than actually partaking of what was masquerading as food.

He headed up to his chamber, though he had no desire to remain there. His chest did bother him, aye, but he had no intention of spending another day abed.

Once inside his chamber, he put on his boots and then combed out his long hair. He secured it at his nape with a leather tie, though it was still damp from washing.

His fingers positively itched for a sword. Some kind of activity to remove the clumsiness from his blood. Everything seemed to move in slow motion. He was slower to process and to react. A good battle would serve to wake him up.

After examining his stitching to ensure there were no tears or bleeding, he adjusted his tunic and then left his chamber once more. Surely someone would accommodate his need for exercise this morn. He was in the mood to beat someone into a pulp.

* * *

Genevieve had done an excellent job of avoiding situations where the McHugh clansmen would be present. It gave her no pride to admit that most of her time had been spent behind the closed door of her chamber.

Only by going to the stream in the wee hours of dawn had she been afforded the privacy in which to bathe, although the last two times she'd gone, Bowen Montgomery had made an appearance.

'Twas obvious it was a practice she was going to have to give up.

She paced the interior of her chamber, pausing ever so often to stare out her window to the distance. She'd seen Teague Montgomery and Brodie Armstrong depart with a few men accompanying them many hours past. It was well into the afternoon now, and she'd not eaten since Taliesan had brought cheese and bread to her chamber that morn.

Anxiously she awaited the signs that the rest of the keep had taken their afternoon respite. After the midday meal and the tasks of the day were completed, the clan was allowed a time to rest and do as they wished.

So far Bowen hadn't changed the practice, though she'd never seen him, his brother, or his men take part in a period of rest. They seemed always to be so focused.

Finally, the courtyard cleared and clansmen returned to the keep as well as to their cottages. Genevieve watched from her window as they walked toward their respective quarters.

This was a time when she could venture outside to breathe the fresh air. Being sequestered in her chamber was enough to drive her daft. Even a short walk to the river and back would be most welcome. But the tedium of being isolated had not been enough to make her risk confrontation with the McHughs—any of them. Especially as it was probably widespread by now that she'd been the one to kill Patrick.

Collecting her hooded cape and then gathering the hood tightly at her chin so her face was hidden from view, she left her chamber and hurried down the stairs.

Not wanting to risk going through the hall, she slipped through the door to the courtyard. She stayed close to the keep as she rounded the corner to head beyond the walls to the river.

Perhaps she'd merely sit on the hill overlooking the grassy section where sheep had once grazed. There was only one sheep and her lamb, left only because Patrick had likely been unable to catch them. But the grassy knoll was pleasing to the eye, and it brought her a measure of peace to soak in the beauty around her.

She sat with her back pressed to a huge rock outcropping so it would shield her from the view of anyone looking from the keep. Pulling her legs to her chest, she rested her chin on the tops of her knees and let out a deep sigh.

It was such a beautiful afternoon. The sun was still high, and only just leaning toward the horizon in its descent. The skies were painted a vivid blue, with not so much as a whisper of clouds to mar the perfect canvas.

She inhaled deeply, savoring the sweet-scented air. The sun's rays bathed her in warmth, caressing her skin and instilling a comfortable lethargy. A nap would be next to heaven. Just her stretched out under the Highland sky, with the sun dancing across her flesh while the wind whispered a soft melody in her ears.

Her eyes were closing, her muscles loosening as tension seeped from her body. She had nearly drifted off, her thoughts and dreams of forgotten places, when a sound rudely jerked her back to awareness.

Her eyes flew open and her head whipped up to see that there was an intruder on her solitude.

Fear and dismay gripped her throat and squeezed her stomach when she saw that Corwen McHugh stood only a short distance away, a belligerent look on his arrogant features.

Ice spread through her veins until she was numb. What was he doing here? His presence could mean nothing good. Not for her.

Instinctively, she scrambled to her feet, turning in the direction of the keep, looking for something . . . anything.

"Are you happy now that you've brought destruction on the whole of the McHugh clan?" Corwen barked, his voice angry and petulant, like a child deprived of having his way.

But he was no child. A chill snaked up her spine, and she shut her mind to the awful images that her memories conjured.

He had long been her tormentor, and she hated him for that.

"I've done naught that was undeserved," she gritted out.

Corwen's lips twisted into a sneer. "You're naught but a whore, and you were treated as such. 'Tis thanks to you that Ian and Patrick both are dead. Cursed female. You bring nothing but death and ill fortune."

Hatred took hold and she glared fiercely at him. "Aye, 'tis true enough. I am cursed. You'd do well to avoid me lest you suffer the same curse."

For a moment, she saw a spark of fear in his eyes, and she thought he might well simply turn from her and hasten away. But then his eyes darkened and his face twisted into something dark and evil. *Menacing.*

He advanced, too quickly for her to escape. She tried to back away but stumbled, and her arms flew out in an attempt to steady herself.

He caught both her wrists and yanked her up against his body. She opened her mouth to scream, but he tossed her around so that her back was pressed to his chest and he clamped a hand over her mouth.

She fought back, kicking, hitting, twisting her body frantically as she tried to escape his hold. She attempted to bite the hand covering her mouth and he yanked it away long enough to strike her with his balled fist.

She went down hard, sprawled on the ground, stunned by the blow he'd administered.

"Stay down, whore," he spat. "You're naught good for anything but spreading your legs. You'll give me ease or you'll receive a sound beating."

A strangled cry ripped from her throat, past already swollen lips. She tasted blood, her mouth split from his fist.

She tried to roll away and rise to her feet, prepared to run as she'd never run before. But he was on her, knocking her facedown to the ground, her breath torn from her chest.

His weight pressed her down, and she struggled to escape him to no avail. Not again. *Never* again. His was a face burned into her memory along with Ian's. If only she'd seen him in battle the day she'd sent an arrow through Patrick McHugh's neck. She would have surely killed him and not felt a moment's remorse.

He'd held her down while Ian had slashed open her cheek. He'd held her down while Ian had raped her, her blood smearing them both. And then he'd taken his own turn, forcing himself upon her repeatedly.

She closed her eyes and tried again to scream, but Corwen flipped her over and smashed his mouth to hers in a brutal kiss. 'Twas not a kiss. A kiss was something wonderful. Romantic. Something exchanged by two lovers. Playful. Passionate. But not punishing. Nay, this was not a kiss. It was something horrible and evil.

She bit into his tongue and was rewarded with another fist to her face. Her vision blurred and she shook her head, trying to clear the fuzz from her mind. Pain rocketed through her, and she was dimly aware of him tearing at the bodice of her dress.

Shock held her immobile. This couldn't be happening.

Was she never to be safe from the unwanted advances of men? Was she forever consigned to rape, and to men taking from her what they pleased, damn the damage done to her in the process?

How much more could she take? Her face, her body, her very soul had been ripped from her. Nothing was her own any longer. She'd become someone else, Genevieve McInnis dying, and in her stead a woman Genevieve hardly knew anymore.

No.

No!

The word screamed through her mind. Stuttered hoarsely past swollen, cracked lips. It echoed over and over until it became a litany. A denial that this could be happening.

Rough hands underneath her skirts. Painful between her legs. He grunted in satisfaction when he managed to rip most of her dress from her body. But her cape remained intact, spread wide as he tore her dress, baring her body to his view.

Coldness swept over her. A frightening numbness took hold. Acceptance that this was happening and there was nothing she could do to stop it.

Just like so many times before.

Something inside her turned off. Darkness crept in, a soothing balm to the fear and rage that blew through her. She could no longer feel his hands upon her. She couldn't feel anything at all.

Hatred and bleak realization were all she knew.

An ungodly roar sounded. It was unlike anything Genevieve had ever heard before. A moment later, Corwen was ripped from her body, and thrown a good distance.

With casual indifference, she watched him sail through the air and hit the ground with a thud that she felt as much as heard.

And then Bowen's voice, anxious and worried.

"Genevieve! Are you all right?"

CHAPTER 24

Bowen hovered anxiously over Genevieve, rage and worry blowing like a wildfire through his veins. She focused her stare on him, but it was a dead, lifeless stare, as if she had no awareness of her surroundings.

"Speak to me, Genevieve," he urged.

He was afraid to touch her for fear of hurting her. Blood trickled from her mouth. 'Twas obvious the bastard had dealt her at least one blow, but who knew how many more or what the extent of her injuries were?

He had been in time to prevent her from being raped, but the lass was still deeply traumatized.

"I'm all right," she said faintly.

It was enough to make him rise and turn his attention to the McHugh warrior, who lay on the ground a few feet away. Fresh anger smoldered within him. He was seething with fury that this man would dare to abuse Genevieve.

The warrior attempted to scramble to his feet, but Bowen leveled him, knocking him flat upon his back again. Bowen's chest protested, his wound fiery with pain, but he paid it no heed. His sole intent was to remove this man as a threat to Genevieve forever.

The warrior threw a punch in an effort to dislodge Bowen, but he was solidly pinned to the ground. Bowen doubled his fist and rammed it into the other man's face, and then before the warrior could respond, Bowen grasped the McHugh man's head and gave it a great yank, effectively breaking his neck in one swift motion.

'Twas the truth he'd rather make the bastard suffer, but his focus was on ending things quickly so he could attend to Genevieve.

Bowen dropped the warrior's head and it lolled to the side, his eyes glassy in death. He stood to his feet, staring down in disgust, before turning his attention once more to Genevieve.

He knelt at her side and gathered her gently in his arms.

"Speak to me, lass. Did he hurt you?"

She stared at him in shock, eyes wide. "Y-y-you k-killed him."

"Aye, I did," he said grimly. "He well deserved it."

Her gaze shifted sideways, toward the felled warrior, her mouth round. It was all too much for her to take in.

Bowen gently directed her gaze back to him.

"Do not look upon him, Genevieve. He is not worth your regard."

Her head snapped back and there was a fierce light in her eyes. "Nay. He is not."

Just as quickly, she seemed to realize that she was all but naked to Bowen's gaze. Shame filled her eyes and she made a grab for her cape, trying to shield her nudity.

Bowen carefully helped her arrange the cape to cover her as best he could, all the while holding her firmly in his embrace.

He could feel her heart beating frantically against his own chest.

But what nearly killed him was when he found her gaze again, her eyes were shiny with tears.

"Ah lass, do not cry," he said hoarsely. "He is not worth your tears."

She buried her face in his shoulder, and Bowen went

to his feet, bearing her slight weight with him. Mindful that she was properly covered, he began the walk back to the keep.

Fury beat at him. He was livid that she'd been attacked under his watch and care. That she would continue to suffer at the hands of the McHughs filled him with rage all over again.

The lass had endured enough. When would it end?

Her muffled sobs tore at him. He wanted nothing more than to bear her safely back to his own chamber, where he could be certain no one else would hurt her.

He ignored the looks and questions of others as he made his way through the hall to the stairs. He warded off his own men, determined not to stop until Genevieve was well out of the sight of others.

When Taliesan met him at his chamber door, her face stricken with worry, he gruffly told her to be off and to ensure no one came to his chamber door.

He knew the lass was only concerned about Genevieve, but he also knew that Genevieve would want to be away from the prying eyes of others, and he would fulfill that wish above all else.

As soon as he shouldered his chamber door closed, he placed Genevieve on his bed and seated himself at her side. He touched her swollen bottom lip and thumbed away a smear of blood.

"What did he do to you?" he demanded.

The fresh wave of tears nearly slayed him. 'Twas true enough he was a disaster around female tears. They made him feel helpless to fix whatever was the matter, and God only knew he'd do anything to remedy a lass in distress.

Her lips trembled and her voice was a near-whisper, so that he had to strain to hear her. "Naught that has not been done before."

As if it didn't matter. As if she were resigned to her fate.

It only infuriated him all the more. He wanted to go kill the bastard all over again. His death had not been long or painful enough.

His fingers curled into tight fists as he sought to control the rage working within him.

"You'll not suffer such again," he said fiercely. "I vow it, Genevieve. You will never be made to give anything but what you choose to give freely."

She turned her face away, but not before he saw a silver trail of tears leak from her eyes.

He lowered his head and pressed his lips to her temple. "I am sorry I was not there sooner."

She turned, her eyes a wash of vibrant green, shiny with moisture and a silent plea.

"Will you . . ."

She bit her lip and stifled whatever it was she was going to ask. He touched a finger to her unmarred cheek and let it trail downward in a comforting caress.

"What is it you ask, lass? You have to know if 'tis within my power I'll do it for you."

Faint color suffused her cheeks, and she looked suddenly nervous.

"Will you hold me?" she asked softly.

Instead of answering, he leaned forward, rolling onto his side next to her. He gathered her in his arms and pulled her in tight to his chest. He stroked her hair and pressed his lips to the crown of her head.

" 'Tis the truth I'd like nothing more."

She burrowed further into his chest as if seeking the warmth and comfort he offered. She clung tightly to him, and he was just as content to hold her just as tightly in return.

For the longest time, he lay there with her in his arms, her head tucked underneath his chin. Her breathing slowed and she seemed to relax, the tension and fear leaving tightly coiled muscles.

He knew there was still the matter of her injuries to attend to, but he was loath to break the intimacy that had bloomed between them.

No matter what the lass may have done in the past, he could not bring himself to hold any of it against her. She had done what was available to her in an effort to free herself from the reality of rape and abuse.

He'd consign no lass in such a situation to punishment or retribution. It pained him to imagine his own sister, Rorie, in such a predicament. He'd hope that any woman in Genevieve's position would be resourceful enough to think of a way out, just as she'd done. Even if the result had been Eveline's being abducted and terror-ized.

It was still an issue. Mayhap not for him, as his mind was already made up where the lass was concerned. But there was the problem of Graeme and the Armstrongs, neither of whom would have any love for Genevieve when it was revealed what she'd done.

But he'd not leave her to fight this battle alone. It may cause him a great deal of trouble with his kin and the newly forged alliance with the Armstrongs, but he'd not leave Genevieve to suffer alone.

She deserved a champion when one had long been de-nied. There was no one to stand up for the lass. Except him.

He stroked the soft tresses of her hair as tenderness overcame him. It pained him to imagine what her exis-tence had been for the last year, but if he had any say in the matter, she'd never suffer such again. Regardless of the consequences for him.

CHAPTER 25

Bowen's head came up as a loud knock sounded at his door. Genevieve stiffened and pulled away, her eyes wary.

In an effort to ease her nervousness, he put a gentle finger on her lips.

"'Tis naught for you to worry over," Bowen said. "I'll return in a moment."

He slipped from the bed, and she hastily pulled the cover to her chin. He needed to have proper clothing fetched from her chamber so that she wouldn't feel vulnerable in her torn dress and the cape that barely covered her nudity.

He unbarred the door and opened it a crack to see who was there. Teague and Brodie stood shoulder to shoulder, their expressions dark.

"We have a situation," Teague said bluntly. "Upon returning from our patrol, we found a man dead. His neck was broken. It could be a precursor to an attack."

Bowen shook his head. "I killed him."

Brodie's and Teague's eyes widened.

"You did what?" Brodie demanded.

Teague started to push forward. "You've a lot of explaining to do, Bowen."

Bowen warded Teague off, and he stepped back in surprise.

"Is there a reason we're not allowed inside your chamber?" Teague asked.

Bowen stepped farther from the doorway, and then quietly shut the door behind him.

"Genevieve is within."

Brodie's eyebrows shot up, while Teague frowned.

"The man you found dead attacked her earlier today. It's fortunate that I came upon them when I did or he would have raped her."

Brodie scowled and bit out a curse.

"The whole lot of them are little better than animals," Teague said in disgust. "Is the lass all right?"

"She was frightened, of course. I took her to my chamber to shield her from the other clansmen. 'Tis obvious she is not held in high regard here, and I would protect her from their venom as well as from any possible retaliation."

Teague blew out his breath. "They will not like hearing that you killed one of their men. It will seem as though we seek to destroy them after executing the ones who betrayed us. Now this."

Bowen's lips curled into a snarl. "I care not what they like or don't like. If they want to be treated fairly and decently, then 'tis upon them to act accordingly. I'd not tolerate such treatment of a lass, no matter who she was. 'Tis disgraceful."

"What then would you have us tell them?" Brodie asked. "The body was brought up to the courtyard, and 'tis widely assumed that the killing was part of a staged attack. They are all convinced that the McGrieves will lay siege to us at any moment."

Bowen had to take a breath to steady himself as anger gripped him all over again. Then he looked up at his brother and at Brodie. His voice was dangerously soft, and for those who knew him well it hinted that he was very near to losing any control he currently maintained.

"You tell them that *I* killed the man for his attack on Genevieve. You also tell them that the lass is under my protection, and that any slight to her is a slight to me, personally. One I will retaliate against. I will not tolerate any disrespect of her. Let the dead McHugh warrior serve as a warning to the others."

Teague looked troubled by the decree, but Brodie nodded his agreement. He didn't seem to be any happier than Bowen that Genevieve had been mistreated so.

Bowen stared at his brother, his lips pressed together in consternation.

"Tell me you agree with me on this, Teague."

Teague sighed. " 'Tis not that I don't agree. I'd not condone the lass being abused in any manner. She's sore in need of a champion, and 'tis obvious you're taking the reins. But I think you should have a care in how you handle the issue with the McHugh clan."

"Right now I wouldn't care if the lot of them fell into a deep hole and disappeared from the earth," Bowen spat.

"I understand your anger," Brodie said calmly. "But we need level heads in order to prevent utter chaos. They're angry. They're confused. They're afraid. They need leadership and a firm hand."

Bowen nodded. "Aye, they do. Right now I'm too furious to face them and attempt any effort to be placating. 'Tis a sin how they've treated the lass, and I'll not forget that."

The door opened just down the hall and Taliesan peeked her head out, staring cautiously at Bowen, Brodie, and Teague. She hesitated, as if afraid to voice her questions.

Bowen sighed and motioned for her to come forward. "Come, lass. Say what it is you want to say."

Brodie and Teague turned as Taliesan limped toward them, her gaze still worried.

Her hands were twined tightly together, and she stopped a foot away from Brodie and Teague. Brodie frowned and touched her arm to draw her closer.

"Forgive my impertinence, Laird, but I would inquire about Genevieve. I'm ever so worried. Can you tell me how she fares?" Taliesan asked anxiously.

Bowen softened at the lass's earnest words. 'Twas obvious Genevieve had a friend in Taliesan. Perhaps the only kind face in a sea of animosity and treachery.

"She fares well," he said quietly. "She suffered fright and a few bruises, but I intervened before more damage could be wrought."

Taliesan looked stricken. Tears shone in her bright eyes and her lips trembled.

"What happened to her, Laird? Who did this to her?"

Brodie put a comforting hand on Taliesan's shoulder. "'Tis all right, lass. Bowen has taken care of the matter."

"The man who attacked Genevieve is dead," Bowen said bluntly.

"Good!" she said in a fierce voice. "I hope you killed him."

"I did."

"And is Genevieve all right?" Taliesan asked, worry still bright in her eyes.

"'Tis the truth she was frightened and upset, but she is resting comfortably, and I've assured her that I'll not allow it to happen again."

"Thank you, Laird," Taliesan said. "Genevieve needs someone like you to stand up for her. No one has ever done so."

Bowen motioned Taliesan aside, pushing past his brother and Brodie. He drew the lass toward her own chamber and said in a low voice, "Can you bring me clothing for Genevieve? Her dress is torn and she has only her cape to cover herself."

Taliesan nodded vigorously. "Aye, Laird. I'll bring it at once."

"Give me a moment to finish conversing with my brother and Brodie, and then bring the clothing down."

"As you wish, Laird."

She turned away and went back to her chamber. Bowen turned back toward his own, eager to be back inside with Genevieve.

"Were you successful in the hunt?" he asked.

"Aye," Brodie said. "A dozen or more rabbits and a young stag. The meat will be tender and succulent."

Bowen's mouth watered at the mere thought of having fresh-cooked meat.

"Have one of my men bring food for Genevieve and myself. We'll eat in my chamber tonight."

Teague nodded. He started to retreat, but then he hesitated.

" 'Tis likely Graeme will be here soon."

Bowen understood it for the warning it was intended to be. "Aye, I know it," he said evenly.

"Think on your priorities between now and then," Teague said. " 'Tis not an easy path you've chosen in championing the lass."

"Nothing good is ever easy. Or worth it."

Brodie nodded his agreement. " 'Tis true, that."

Teague rested a hand on Bowen's shoulder. "You have my support, Bowen. No matter what. That extends to the lass as well. Even though I know not the whole of it."

Bowen extended his arm to overlap Teague's, clasping his shoulder in a like gesture. He stared into his brother's eyes, grateful that Teague had chosen not to condemn him for standing with Genevieve.

"You have my thanks, Teague. You and Brodie both."

Brodie quirked a lip and grinned his amusement. "Did

you ever imagine yourself saying such to an Armstrong? Did it leave a bad taste in your mouth?"

Bowen smiled. "I'll admit to being reminded of the meals I've suffered through of late."

Teague and Brodie laughed, then retreated down the hall with promises to send food up for Bowen and Genevieve as soon as the meat was prepared.

Bowen turned to go inside his chamber, but was stopped by Taliesan's soft call. Leaving the door open, he waited for the lass to approach and then took the soft bundle of clothing from her.

"My thanks, Taliesan. You are a good friend to Genevieve. I'll make sure she knows of your kindness."

Taliesan's cheeks colored and she dipped a curtsy. "Please tell Genevieve that if she has need of me I am but a few doors away."

Bowen nodded and then withdrew into the chamber, closing the door behind him.

Genevieve was sitting up in bed, the bed linens pulled to just underneath her chin. Blood had dried at the corner of her mouth and along her jawline, and her bottom lip was swollen.

"Taliesan brought you clothing," Bowen said as he approached the bed. "Let me build up the fire and then you can dress in front of the hearth. I'll not look. I promise."

She smiled faintly. "'Tis too late for modesty, I think. You've seen all."

He sat on the edge of the bed, her clothing on his lap. "'Tis not too late for respect," he said in a serious tone. "And 'tis respect that I give by offering you privacy in which to dress and make yourself more comfortable."

Damn if the lass's eyes didn't tear up again. It was like a fist to his gut, and suddenly it was hard for him to breathe.

He touched her cheek as if to ward off the tears.

"You've not had much to smile about, lass, but I plan to remedy that. I would give anything to make you happy again."

"You are a good man, Bowen Montgomery," she said hoarsely. "I was not wrong about you."

He took the clothing from his lap and laid it next to Genevieve on the bed. "Let me go add logs to the fire so you'll be warm. Your flesh is cold to the touch. When I am done, you can dress by the hearth."

He stood and strode toward the bin where the pieces of wood were stacked. When he glanced back at Genevieve, she presented a sight that affected him deeply.

Hair tousled. Vulnerability reflected in her eyes. Covers drawn up to her chin and knees hunched against her chest. But the look on her face as she stared back at him . . . It was a look filled with wonder. Gratitude. Of discovery. As if she were seeing him in a whole new light.

It was a look that men coveted from women. A look that said he was her champion and that there was no other man in the world for her.

He reprimanded himself for letting his thoughts grow so fanciful. Aye, Genevieve may be grateful, but it didn't mean she looked at him in any other way than that of gratitude. It was a look she would give to any man who'd defended her.

He busied himself building the flames, so that it became uncomfortably warm in the vicinity of the hearth. But he knew that she was chilled, that the traumatic event had given her the kind of bone-deep cold that was difficult to recover from. He'd see to her comfort even at the expense of his own.

When he was satisfied with his effort, he turned back to Genevieve and gently pried the linens from her tightly balled fists.

"Go and warm yourself by the fire, lass," he said in a

gentle voice. "I'll stand by the door with my back turned, or, if you prefer, I'll wait in the hall and you can summon me back inside when you're finished."

"You can stay," she murmured.

Keeping her cloak tightly against her breasts, she maneuvered out of bed and walked toward the fire. As promised, Bowen went to the door and crossed his arms over his chest as he faced away.

He could hear the light sounds of her dressing and he closed his eyes, imagining the sight behind him. Her nude figure outlined by the glow from the hearth. His breath caught in his throat and his body instantly hardened.

He chastened himself, berating himself for being no better than the bastard who'd tried to rape her. He should not be thinking on such things when the lass was recovering from the horror of being attacked.

But he wasn't thinking of what he could take from her. He thought only of what he could *give* her. Of how he could woo her with sweet kisses. Tell her how beautiful she was. Stroke and caress her body until she sighed with contentment.

He wanted to show her how it could be between a man and a woman. Take away all the pain and humiliation and shame and, in their place, give her something beautiful.

Ah, he ached to be the one to show her how good loving could be. But 'twas more than that, for he wanted her more fiercely than he'd ever wanted a lass and he couldn't even explain why. He cared not that she was scarred, that a man had marked her face so that no man would ever want her. If that had been Ian's goal, he'd failed miserably, because Bowen wanted her with a need that bordered on obsession.

"You can look now."

Her soft call tore him from his thoughts. He blinked

and willed his body to calm, for he didn't want to face her with the evidence of his arousal in plain sight.

Slowly he turned, positioning his body so that it wasn't so readily obvious.

She looked even more beautiful. Clad in a nightdress, she stood by the fire, her bare feet peeking from underneath the hem. Her hair tumbled over her shoulders in waves and her scarred cheek was turned away.

There was still the dried blood at her mouth, and he hadn't queried her about other injuries.

He strode forward, taking one of the cloths he used for cleaning and he dipped it into the basin of water by the window. When he neared her, he cupped her chin with one hand and then gently dabbed at the corner of her mouth with the cloth.

She flinched but remained where she was while he cleaned the blood from her swollen lip.

He frowned when he noticed that a bruise was already forming on her chin and lower jaw, where she'd been struck.

"Where else are you hurt, Genevieve?" he asked.

"Nowhere. He hit me twice, but 'tis all he had time to do. You arrived in time to prevent more."

His scowl deepened. "I should have been there to prevent him hitting you at all."

She slipped her hand over his arm, holding it in place as he cupped her chin in his firm grasp.

"You came. 'Tis all that is important. You kept it from happening again. For that you have my thanks."

His heart softened, and he rubbed his thumb over her cheek in a tender caress.

"I would that you never have to experience such again."

She closed her eyes and turned further into his caress, rubbing her scarred cheek over his palm. Then, as if realizing she drew attention to her defect, she froze and tried to shrink away.

"Nay," he protested. "Do not hide from me, Genevieve. Never hide from me. You have to know that the scar on your face matters not to me."

She swallowed, and he could feel that she trembled beneath his touch. She looked at him with such hope that it was painful for him to see. This was a woman who was afraid to hope anymore. Time and time again, her hopes had been crushed, and now she gazed at him as though she battled with herself over whether to allow that hope to take flight.

"Come," he whispered. " 'Tis time to seek our bed. I would have you warm and comfortable this night."

Her eyes widened, and she clutched at the hand covering her cheek.

"What will be said if I spend the night in your chamber, Laird?"

His lips curled, and his words were fierce. "I don't give one damn what is said. These people have neither my respect nor my loyalty. They'll not disparage you, for if they do they'll suffer my wrath. I've let it be known that I'll tolerate no insult to you. You have my protection, Genevieve. I'll not have you leave my chamber this night."

Though he meant every word he'd said, he also recognized the validity of her fear. It would be disrespectful of him to have her name bandied about as whore to him now that Ian was gone. He would give the clansmen no further opportunity to mock or demean her.

His voice softened as he gazed at her. "No one will know, lass. I will speak to Taliesan, who champions you fiercely, and it will be known that you rested this night in her chamber."

The relief was stark in her eyes. Her entire body seemed to sag. He lowered his hand, with hers still holding on to it, and pulled her toward the bed so they could seek their rest.

Another knock sounded, and Bowen wanted to growl his frustration at the constant interruptions. Then he remembered Teague's promise of food. His belly growled at the idea, and he sighed.

"Go on to the bed and make yourself comfortable. That will be food sent up, fresh from the hunt."

Genevieve brightened and slipped her hand from his, placing it over her belly. Then she grimaced.

" 'Tis the truth I'm near to starving."

"Then go and I'll bring the food inside to you. Fear not. I'll not allow anyone to enter while you are present."

The smile she gifted him with warmed him to his toes. Then she hurried by him and crawled into bed—*his* bed—and pulled the covers high around her.

Never had he seen a more wondrous or more beautiful sight than Genevieve McInnis snuggled sweetly in his bed, awaiting his attendance.

CHAPTER 26

Genevieve snuggled tighter into Bowen's embrace and sighed in utter contentment. Lazily, she opened her eyes only to discover that it was already past dawn.

Dismay filled her that the night was over. 'Twas the most beautiful night she'd ever spent. Never had she felt such peace, nor had she ever felt as safe as she had wrapped in Bowen Montgomery's arms.

"The lass has awakened."

Bowen's teasing voice slid like silk over her ears. She was reluctant even to answer for fear that he would immediately cast her from his chamber. She wanted this moment to last forever.

"Aye," she finally whispered, knowing she couldn't delay the inevitable.

But he didn't hurry her, nor did he tell her to return to her own room.

Instead, he stroked a hand up and down her back until she nearly moaned from the pleasure of it.

"How do you feel this morn, Genevieve?"

She rubbed her cheek against his chest, savoring the smell and feel of him. It seemed so odd to her that she felt no fear in Bowen's presence. She'd learned to fear all men. There was not one she trusted, and she'd been abused by many.

And yet Bowen was . . . different. From the very start

he'd been different. He'd treated her with kindness and gentleness, and he'd defended her.

"Better," she said, her words escaping on a sigh.

"'Tis good to hear. I hope your jaw isn't paining you too much."

She attempted to shake her head, because she was too content to speak.

His hand closed over her nape, massaging and caressing. Then he nudged her head upward, using his other hand to slide under her chin and prop her up as he examined her mouth.

He frowned a bit as he tilted her head left then right.

"There's a bruise. And your lip is still swollen."

His expression was murderous by the time he finished his perusal of her features. Then, to her surprise, he hauled her upward, so that she sprawled over his body, her face just inches from his own. His arms closed over her back so that he hugged her to him.

"Bowen, your wound!" she protested.

"'Tis naught but a scratch, and you did a fine job stitching it. It doesn't pain me at all."

She didn't entirely believe him, and it shamed her that she'd only just paid heed to his wound. He'd fought with her attacker when he was only a day from his sickbed.

"I should look at it," she said anxiously. "You could have torn the stitching in the confrontation yesterday."

He gave her an amused smile, his eyes alight with warmth.

"If it will put you at ease, I'll let you examine it."

She pushed back from his embrace and then positioned herself on her knees at his side.

He sat up and then tugged his tunic over his head, baring his muscled shoulders and chest to her view. Her gaze wandered over his torso, drawn inexorably to the expanse of male flesh.

Her fingers came out to trace the puckered line of the still sealed wound.

"Does it pain you?"

"Nay, lass. Not when you touch me so. I feel naught but the sweetest of pleasures."

Heat rushed to her cheeks and she nearly snatched her hand away, but he captured it and held it firmly against his chest.

"I like your touch," he said huskily. "I remember you touching me when I was insensible with the potion they gave me."

More embarrassed now than ever, she ducked her head. How bold he must think her. She should not have taken such liberties with his person, certainly not when he was barely conscious.

"Are the stitches to your satisfaction?" he asked.

"Aye," she whispered. "I see no sign of infection."

He tugged her back down to his bare chest. 'Twas like being touched by fire. His heat surrounded her and beckoned her closer still.

His hand feathered over her cheek and then delved into her hair, circling to her nape, and then, to her shock, he raised his head and pressed his lips ever so gently to hers.

She gasped against the fullness of his lips, but all tension fled her as she relaxed into his hold.

Oh, aye, *this* was a kiss.

He was exceedingly tender as he explored her mouth, his lips sliding over hers. His tongue brushed against her bottom lip, lapping at the cut in the corner of her mouth.

It was intoxicating, like drinking too much ale. She was drunk on his touch and the sensation of him against her. She experienced a rush such as she'd never felt before, and she never wanted it to end.

His other hand went to her scarred cheek, and when she would have pulled away, he caressed the damaged flesh and framed her face with both hands in order to deepen his kiss.

When she let out a breathy sigh, his tongue slid inside her mouth, soft and sensual and coaxing. Shyly, she met his tongue with her own, dancing and teasing the way he was doing with her.

He pulled back, his breath coming raggedly and his eyes half-lidded. The color in his cheeks was high, almost as if he had indeed taken a fever. But that look . . . He looked at her as if she was the most beautiful lass he'd ever laid eyes on. For a moment she was able to forget that her face was ruined, and that she bore the mark of another man's greed and lust. For in Bowen's eyes she saw herself as a beautiful, desirable woman.

"You taste just as sweet as I knew you would," he said in a husky voice laced with passion.

" 'Tis my first *true* kiss," she admitted.

His eyes softened. "And what think you of your first true kiss?"

He hadn't misunderstood her intent. Aye, she'd been kissed, but never with such sweetness or reverence. It made her want to weep for all that she'd missed.

" 'Twas wondrous. I've never experienced anything to match it," she said honestly.

" 'Tis glad I am to be the first."

He continued to stroke her cheek and he thumbed her bottom lip, which was now swollen for an entirely different reason.

Then he raised his head and softly captured her lips in another lingering kiss. This time when he pulled away there was regret in his eyes.

" 'Tis time for me to rise. I wish it were not so. 'Tis the truth I'd rather never leave this chamber, and I'd sell my soul to do nothing more than kiss you for the rest of my days. But I have matters to attend to and the issue of another dead McHugh. And we must take you to Taliesan's chamber so our story will be sealed."

Mentioning her attacker had the effect of being doused with cold water. She immediately withdrew, shame crowding her heart.

She was acting the wanton mere hours after another man had tried to rape her. What was wrong with her?

The McHugh clan didn't need prompting to cry her whore, and here she was in the laird's chamber. It was an open invitation for others to revile her more.

"Nay, don't look like that, lass," Bowen said in a quiet tone.

He sat up and reached for her, sliding his hand up her arm in a caress that made her shiver.

"You'll hold your head high, for you bear not the blame for what has happened. The man who attacked you received what he deserved, just as anyone else will should they dare to touch you."

"I am not worth such vehemence," she said, refusing to meet his gaze.

He captured her chin and forced her to look at him. His eyes were angry, and his lips were drawn into a tight line.

"You're worth it to *me*."

She knew not what to say. She stared back at him in befuddlement.

Leaning forward, he pressed a kiss to her forehead and rose from the bed.

"I'll see you to Taliesan's chamber and have her attend you. Perhaps 'tis best if you remain above stairs until I've made my case clear to the rest of the clan. You'll not remain a prisoner of your own chamber, though. You are free to come and go as you please, and 'tis something you should be able to do without fear of attack. I'll ensure that it is so."

"I know not why you do this for me," she said, her heart squeezing in her chest.

He extended his hand to help her from the bed.

"Because 'tis something that should have been done for you long ago."

CHAPTER 27

Bowen walked Genevieve to Taliesan's chamber door, but when she started to go within he grasped her hand and gently tugged her back.

Surprise flared in her eyes as he pulled her to him and lowered his head to sweep her mouth in another kiss.

It was like being set fire to. He felt more alive than he'd ever felt. God's bones, but he wanted nothing more than to sequester them both in a locked chamber where he could hold her and kiss her for the rest of the day.

Hellfire. Forever was more to his liking.

She gave the sweetest sigh, and it gave him even more pleasure that he was able to please her. 'Twas obvious the lass had never known a gentle hand, nor had she ever experienced the joys of loving.

It had angered and saddened him that she'd said his kiss was her first. Oh, he knew he hadn't been the first man ever to kiss her, but 'twas obvious her meaning. He'd been the only man ever to softly woo her with tender, passionate kisses.

He dragged himself reluctantly away and then bade her to go inside and close the chamber door. As he stood there, staring at the closed door, he was struck by the thought that he could well be in love with her.

It was such a stunning discovery that he could no

more than stand rigid as he was pelted with all the ramifications.

In love.

The more he played with the idea, the more he realized that it was truth. He well knew how a man looked and acted when he was in love. Graeme had certainly fallen hard for his wife, and now Bowen had done the same for a lass who was trouble. A *lot* of trouble.

He was torn between marching into Taliesan's chamber and telling Genevieve he loved her, and damn the consequences, and going below stairs to address the issue of her safety within the clan walls. And then he needed to configure a plan to remove her from here as soon as possible.

Only there were many problems with that.

One, he had to tread very carefully with Genevieve. She would not take his declaration well, and it might drive her away and any progress he'd made in gaining her trust would be gone.

The lass had been damaged by all that had been done to her. It wasn't something that was going to disappear from her memory overnight. She would require careful wooing and an extraordinary amount of patience on his part.

Two, he didn't want to be parted from her, so the idea of removing her from McHugh Keep with all haste left him with a dead sensation in his chest. He was needed here, and there was no timeline for how long. His brother needed his aid, and he would provide it, no matter what. But neither did he want Genevieve exposed to such venom on a daily basis.

'Twas a perplexing conundrum, to be sure. He wasn't at all sure he liked this matter of love.

Testy and irritable, he turned from Genevieve's door and put distance between it and him before he lost what measure of control he was maintaining and burst into her chamber like a lad declaring his love for the first woman he fell for.

By the time he reached the hall, he was gripped by agitation and he scowled at everyone who crossed his path.

'Twas enough to set to rumor that he was intent on killing someone again. His brother and Brodie hurried to him in the courtyard, their concern apparent as they approached.

"What ails you?" Teague asked warily. "I hear you're on another rampage."

Brodie stood silent, watching the interchange between the brothers as if he was loath to intervene in any way.

Bowen arched an eyebrow. "What makes you say such?"

"We were told you had plans to kill another McHugh. I wanted to see what sin had been committed this time."

Irritation bit sharply at Bowen. "You say that as if there was no sin committed before."

Teague's eyes narrowed and he suddenly became very serious. No longer were his words flippant or drawn out for effect.

"The lass's being attacked hardly constitutes no transgression." His brow was etched with anger and his eyes blazed. "'Twas not my intention to discount what the lass went through. 'Tis enough. She should suffer no more. No matter my feelings about her or the sins *she* has committed. No one deserves such treatment."

Bowen crossed his arms over his chest and nodded his satisfaction. "'Tis glad I am to hear you say so."

Teague scowled. "How could you think otherwise? I believe you've handed me great insult. When have I ever condoned the mistreatment of those weaker, especially a mere slip of a lass?"

"I'd rather not have to break up a fight between the two of you," Brodie said in a calm voice. "The word was spread that you entered the hall in a killing rage and that surely another McHugh life would be forfeit. Teague and I merely came to ascertain your demeanor for ourselves."

Bowen snorted. " 'Tis true enough I scowled at the lot of them, but I've not shed any more blood. Not yet. But the day is still young. I may have a need before 'tis over with."

Teague lifted his chin in Brodie's direction. "I say we don't allow him all the amusement."

Bowen chuckled and shook his head. "I aim to make my point loud and clear. Consequences will be outlined for disobeying my directive where Genevieve is concerned."

Teague stared at him a long moment and then lifted his gaze to Brodie. "Would you excuse us a moment, Brodie? I'd like to have a word alone with my brother."

Brodie nodded and slipped away, disappearing around the corner of the keep.

Bowen raised one inquiring eyebrow in Teague's direction.

"What are your plans for the lass?" Teague asked bluntly. "And I don't mean what do you intend to do with her as far as punishment or retribution. 'Tis obvious you have a keen interest in her. I'm more interested in your personal plans for her."

Bowen frowned. "I'd say 'tis none of your affair."

"Don't hand me that," Teague muttered. "Think on this, Bowen. Do not do this to the lass. You want to bed her. 'Tis plain as the nose on your face. She isn't a lass to be casually bedded, and you should well know this. I may have reservations where she is concerned, but she's been hurt enough. Don't take advantage of her in this manner."

Bowen stared in shock at his younger brother. "You insult me, brother. Who says I have any intention of casually bedding the lass? Moreover, 'tis none of your affair what my actions are toward Genevieve. You've made your judgment of her clear."

Teague shook his head. "Nay, I have not. I have eyes. I can see how tormented the lass is. I can see what has been done to her spirit. 'Tis enough to turn my stomach. You make a game of bedding lasses. You use wit and charm to woo them into your bed, and then you move on to another challenge. I'm merely telling you that you should have more respect for Genevieve than to simply make her another conquest."

Bowen's lips curled and he bared his teeth. They ground together until his jaw pained him. He advanced on his brother, a low growl emanating from his throat.

"I *love* her," he said fiercely. "She is not some passing amusement. The last thing I'm going to do is hurt her. I'll kill anyone who tries."

By saying it aloud, he thought perhaps it might seem silly to him. That perhaps he'd been swept up in the moment with Genevieve and that maybe he wasn't quite to the point of love yet.

But he was dead wrong. The words felt right on his lips. Saying them aloud only confirmed what his heart already knew. He was well and truly in love with the lass, and there was naught but contentment within him at the whole idea.

Teague's mouth dropped open and his eyes widened in shock. He continued to stare wordlessly at Bowen until finally Bowen shoved his hand through his hair in disgust.

"Hellfire, Teague. Stop gaping at me like a fish out of water."

Teague shook his head and then blew out his breath. "Have you lost your *mind*?"

" 'Tis clear I have," Bowen bit out. " 'Tis no fault of mine that I fell in love with the lass. Do you know how ridiculous it sounds? I fall in love with a woman made whore by another man. I fall in love with a woman whose face was ruined by a blade. I fall in love with a woman who betrayed my kin. Take your pick. 'Tis obvious I'm not in my right mind, but it does not change the fact of what is."

"What the hell are you going to do?" Teague asked.

"I know not," Bowen said wearily. " 'Tis true she set Ian on Eveline."

At Teague's instant scowl, Bowen broke off and held up his hand.

"The lass had sound reason," Bowen defended.

"You *are* out of your mind," Teague said in disgust.

"Just listen," Bowen snapped.

Bowen carefully explained Genevieve's reasoning in encouraging Ian to abduct Eveline. He was reaching and he knew it, but he was determined to win favor for Genevieve in some manner.

Teague sighed when Bowen finished his explanation. "Am I supposed to applaud the lass's ingenuity in angering the Montgomerys and Armstrongs alike so they attack the keep and she is rescued? What would have happened if Eveline had been raped or killed? Think you Graeme would look kindly on the woman responsible just because she acted in self-preservation?"

Bowen clenched his teeth even harder. "I'm asking you to consider for a moment if our sister was in Genevieve's place. Would you condemn her then? If she consigned a woman who was not our kin to a similar fate, would you be so quick to malign her? Or is it because 'tis Eveline we discuss and not some nameless, faceless woman?"

Teague hesitated, and Bowen knew he had him. It was all he could do not to smile his satisfaction.

" 'Tis not fair to make me imagine Rorie in Genevieve's position. I wouldn't care who Rorie had to condemn in order for her to escape such depravity."

"'Tis as I suspected," Bowen said.

"Curse it all, Bowen. Why could you not fall in love with a less complicated lass? Do you have any idea the problems she brings to the table? Assuming you can ever win Graeme over and he accepts the lass, the Armstrongs certainly won't be so forgiving, and when they find out all there is to find out we'll be lucky if we don't go to war with them after all."

"Then perhaps 'tis best they never find out," Bowen said quietly. "'Tis a private matter, and one that should not be openly discussed. Graeme will have to know the whole of it, aye. But he is the only one. He is my laird. Not the Armstrongs. They have no say in Genevieve's fate."

"I suppose you are right," Teague said wearily. "Still, 'tis not an easy path you've chosen."

"Aye, I know it. But 'tis also true that nothing easy is ever worth it. And Genevieve will be worth every effort I make on her behalf."

CHAPTER 28

Genevieve was exceedingly shy with Bowen after the night she slept in his arms. He found it endearing, and his heart melted a little more every time she ducked her head or smiled when she thought he wasn't looking.

He was working on the lass. He had no intention of suffering in the hell that was unrequited love. It was an interesting enough dilemma, given that many a woman had reportedly suffered such with him. It was also true that he'd never given it much consideration. Now he knew how those women must have felt when they reportedly pined for his attentions, because he found himself playing the love-sick fool vying for a crumb of attention or approval from Genevieve. Anything to make her smile. Make her *happy*. He'd give her the damn moon if that was what it took.

He also realized—not that he hadn't already known it—but it was driven home with more force that she'd never enjoyed a man's attentions. Had someone pay court to her. She'd never been wooed. Her marriage had been arranged, and on her way to her husband-to-be Ian had taken her and turned her life into a living hell.

Bowen was determined to give her all she'd never had, and so he set about courting her.

Teague and Brodie despaired of him. Teague routinely made Bowen the butt of his jests, and both men threatened to throw him into the river if he continued on his present course.

Bowen took it all in stride. Never before would he have tolerated the teasing and taunting, but he found he cared not. The way Genevieve's face lit up when he complimented her made every taunt well worth it.

He did, however, keep the verse that he'd memorized a strict secret. He felt uncomfortable enough whispering the words to Genevieve under the softness of moonlight, but when she looked at him, her eyes shining like twin suns, all discomfort disappeared.

In that moment he wouldn't have cared if the whole of the keep heard his recitation. The look on Genevieve's face was an image he'd long carry with him and treasure.

They walked slowly under the glow of the moon, the rays bouncing off the surface of the gurgling river. He laced his fingers through hers, enjoying something as simple as holding her hand.

His past associations with women shamed him. He didn't discuss such with Genevieve. They both bore shame, but for different reasons. Genevieve's had been forced upon her. But Bowen's had been solely of his own choosing.

He'd embraced his liaisons with women. He'd enjoyed loving. And what man didn't like a good tup? He and Teague used to tease Graeme for his monkish ways, but Bowen thought now that Graeme had the right of it for being more discerning in his bed partners.

Graeme had come to Eveline without having bedded every lass in the vicinity. Bowen certainly couldn't say the same, and just thinking on it made him wince.

What would Genevieve think if she knew of the casual way in which he'd divested lasses of their skirts? Would her opinion of him change? How could it not?

It wasn't that he didn't have great love for women.

Indeed, it was the opposite. But now he wondered at the lack of respect he'd shown them. It pained him to be lumped in the same category as Ian McHugh. While he'd certainly never forced himself on any woman, could he say he hadn't made them his whore?

He couldn't even think on it any longer, because he did not like the potential results.

Genevieve had fundamentally changed him. Maybe from the moment he'd laid eyes on her, but certainly the moment he'd heard her story and knew of her pain and her bravery.

He wanted to be a better man for her. He wanted to be someone worthy of her.

He wanted her to love him.

"What are you thinking on?" she asked softly.

He blinked in surprise and lowered his gaze to hers. Many days had passed since her attack and the night she'd spent in his arms, and each day he'd carefully wooed her, gaining her trust. And it hadn't been easy, because he'd vowed not to make her the brunt of clan gossip, and so every effort had been made in secret and it was taking a toll on them both.

What should be something wondrous was stressful, as they sought to hide from the prying eyes of others. But still, he looked forward to every stolen moment. Every opportunity to steal away and spend time in Genevieve's presence.

Never had he displayed so much patience and fore-thought with another woman. He was determined to win Genevieve's heart, no matter how long it took.

"You looked so deep in thought. I wondered what caused you to be so pensive."

Bowen smiled. "I was only thinking that 'tis a beauti-ful night made only more beautiful by the woman who walks beside me."

'Twas obvious she blushed, even in the glow cast by

the moon. It was in her mannerisms, the way her gaze skittered sideways and she ducked her head in that shy way.

But he also saw her smile. It was a sight that never failed to tighten his chest. It had never been brought home to him the fact that she never smiled until finally she did. And now he sought to make her do so at every opportunity, because it was a sight he savored.

"You've a silver tongue, Bowen Montgomery," she said, her teeth flashing with her smile. "A silver-tongued devil, you are."

"I'd prefer to use my tongue for other purposes," he murmured.

She paused, turning to face him as they topped the rise overlooking the river.

"And what purpose would that be?" she asked innocently.

The little imp was teasing him. It delighted him that she'd be so free with him. She'd always been so reserved and cautious. Careful never to make any overtures that could possibly be misconstrued.

Yet tonight she was looking at him with a devilish gleam in her own eyes. He may be silver-tongued, but she was developing one of her own and he loved it.

"I can think of several," he murmured as he lowered his lips to capture hers.

Her breath caught, as if she'd swallowed his. This time she boldly returned his kiss, almost as if she'd grabbed hold of her courage and put it all on the line.

He was content to allow her to dictate the kiss. His hands slid up her neck, to just beneath her ears, and his fingers splayed out, his palms gliding over her jaw.

Kissing her was something he'd never grow tired of. It was like drinking warm sunshine or licking the sugary sweetness of honey from a spoon.

Smooth, silky-soft, and delicate and ultra feminine.

She inspired possessiveness such that he all but screamed that she was his.

And the hell of it was she didn't even know it.

He hadn't told her.

Not one single word.

No "I love you." No soft entreaty for the words to be offered to him in turn.

It was a vow he'd made before God and on her behalf. He'd pressure her into nothing. He'd not demand a single thing she was unwilling to give.

He'd wait for bloody ever if that's what it took.

"Kissing is so very nice," she said with a breathy sigh. "I never thought so before now. I always thought it rather horrid."

She winced as if she regretted being so bold in her words. 'Twas likely she hated that she'd brought up a subject that was inherently shameful for her. But for Bowen, it was a signal that she was growing more comfortable with him, and so he embraced her willingness to discuss the terrible things that had happened to her.

" 'Tis because you were not kissing me," Bowen said smugly.

Genevieve laughed, and it was the most exquisite sound. It captivated him and made him want to pull it from her again and again.

"Mayhap you have the right of it," she said in a rueful tone. "You are very skilled at it."

He went quiet, not wanting to delve into the topic of why he was so skilled at kissing. 'Twas a dangerous topic. One he would be well rid of.

So he kissed her again, because he knew it would silence any further questions or comments. Besides, kissing her was no hardship.

They were deep into a breathless, bone-melting kiss when Bowen heard a shout in the distance. He immediately picked up his head, using one hand to shove Genevieve behind him while his other hand went to the hilt of his sword.

He strained to hear the voices while Genevieve clutched at his tunic, huddled against his back.

"Montgomerys arrive!"

The call was picked up and echoed through the watch-towers and around the perimeter of the keep. Bowen relaxed his grip on both Genevieve and his sword, and then pulled Genevieve back around to his side.

" 'Tis my kin," Bowen explained. "They bring supplies. Come. Let's return to the keep so that I may greet them."

CHAPTER 29

Genevieve's heart was in her throat the entire walk back to the keep. Bowen was solicitous, slowing to match her pace even though 'twas obvious he seethed with impatience to greet his kin.

She'd heard Teague laughingly say that he was certain Graeme would arrive himself once he learned that the keep had been attacked and Bowen had been injured. With all her heart, she hoped that he'd remained behind and had not accompanied his men to McHugh Keep.

Her time with Bowen had been nothing short of perfect. Aye, she was living on borrowed time. It couldn't last forever. She didn't expect it to. If Graeme had arrived, it would be over a lot sooner. He would learn of all she'd done, and he'd want retribution. How could he not?

She'd done harm to his wife. She'd endangered his entire clan. It wasn't something she expected to be forgiven for, even if Bowen had seemed willing to overlook her transgressions.

She clung tighter to Bowen's hand as they neared the courtyard, where the Montgomery soldiers were even now piling in. Then she yanked her hand back, realizing the intimacy of holding Bowen's hand and the fact that his clan would be looking on.

It was instinctive to reach for her hood and pull it over

her head. She'd relaxed around Bowen. Something about him made her feel comfortable. She didn't seek to hide from him.

Her cheek itched, and she lifted her hand to rub at the scar before gathering the neck of the hood and pulling it tight so the material was pressed against her face.

She wanted to flee. Duck in the back and escape to her chamber. The last thing she wanted was to stand before Bowen's kin as though she had the right to do so. She was nothing to Bowen and even less to his clan. She had no interest in being present when she was judged.

"Genevieve, 'tis all right," Bowen said in a soft voice as they neared the courtyard.

"Pray can I be excused, Laird?" she asked, her lips stiff from nerves.

He stopped in his tracks and gathered her hands in his, not caring who looked on. She wanted to pull her hands away before they were seen. Desperation gripped her. The last thing she wanted was to present a spectacle.

For a long moment he stared into her eyes, and then his gaze softened. He touched a hand to her face and gently pushed a tendril of hair from her cheek.

"Return then to your chamber. I'll see you later."

She all but fled across the terrain, making certain she circled the keep so she could enter through the back entrance to avoid any confrontation with Bowen's kin.

Her heart beat so wildly that she feared passing out as she became light-headed. At the top of the stairs, she nearly ran into Taliesan, and she was so grateful to see the other woman that she gripped Taliesan's hands.

"The Montgomery forces have arrived," Taliesan said. "I heard them arrive from my window. They bring food and supplies. We'll be safe from attack now, surely!"

"Aye," Genevieve said as she sought to catch her breath.

She glanced toward her chamber and turned, all but dragging Taliesan along with her.

"Keep me company," Genevieve urged. "I find I have no desire to be alone this night."

Taliesan good-naturedly complied and, with the door shut behind them, Taliesan sent a concerned frown in Genevieve's direction.

"You look as though you've suffered a fright, Genevieve. You're nervous, and your hands are shaking! Whatever is the matter?"

Genevieve sought to calm herself as she stood in front of the hearth. She debated setting a fire, but she wasn't sure her hands were steady enough for the task. Still, it would do her good to busy herself with something.

"I heard Teague say he would not be surprised if Graeme Montgomery himself arrived with the party bearing supplies."

Taliesan nodded. "Aye, I saw him below. He arrived with his men. Teague and Brodie went out to greet him." Then she frowned. "I did not see Bowen. Were you with him?"

Genevieve's face exploded with warmth and she turned her back to Taliesan as she set logs for the fire. She and Bowen had spent a great deal of time with each other of late, but they'd not done so in an obvious manner. Bowen had been careful to keep appearances, something for which Genevieve was grateful, even if she had no care for what the McHughs thought.

It wasn't so much what they thought as what they would do. They would take any opportunity to disparage Genevieve. Many held her accountable for Ian's death, and now Patrick's. With Bowen killing her attacker and issuing his warning to the entire clan that anyone doing harm to Genevieve would suffer the same fate, their animosity toward her had only intensified.

Bowen hadn't mentioned the abbey again. He hadn't mentioned her fate at all, which made her more uneasy with every passing day. She knew she was a fool to allow herself to dissolve into fancy where Bowen was concerned. She was nobody. She was dead.

"Genevieve?" Taliesan asked in a soft voice. "What is between you and Bowen? 'Tis forward of me to ask, I know, but I sense that he's infatuated with you. Do you return his feelings?"

Genevieve set fire to wood and then stood back, staring into the crackling flames. Then she slowly turned to face Taliesan.

"There is naught between me and Bowen Montgomery. He has been kind to me. Nothing else."

Taliesan sighed. "I see the way he looks at you. He fair eats you with his eyes."

Genevieve shook her head. "There is naught to look upon."

"You are still a beautiful lass, Genevieve. The mark Ian put on your face does not take that away."

Genevieve regretted that she'd been so impulsive in urging Taliesan to enter her chamber. Taliesan was a sweet and genuine lass, but right now Genevieve wanted only to be alone and away from Taliesan's innocent prying.

"I would go to bed now, Taliesan," Genevieve said quietly.

Taliesan shuffled awkwardly to Genevieve's side and suddenly Genevieve was enfolded in Taliesan's arms.

"I did not mean to hurt you."

Genevieve turned and hugged Taliesan to her. "I know you didn't. 'Tis my fault for being too sensitive. I'm just weary and nervous over the Montgomerys' arrival."

"I will leave you to rest. Would you like me to have food brought up to your chamber on the morrow?"

"'Tis kind of you to offer, but I will be fine. I cannot hide in my chamber forever."

Taliesan withdrew and, offering Genevieve a reassuring smile, limped slowly out the door, shutting it behind her.

Genevieve sagged onto the bed and flopped backward, staring at the ceiling. She closed her eyes and let her thoughts drift back over the many days spent in Bowen's company.

They'd been magical. She'd been filled with a longing that instilled an ache deep in her soul.

She didn't entirely understand it—she didn't understand Bowen or his seeming interest in her. Had she imagined it? Nay, he couldn't feign something like that, and what purpose would be served by deceiving her in such a fashion?

He acted as though he genuinely cared, which puzzled her because, given the sins she'd committed against his clan, he should be angry. He should want vengeance. Or, at least, for her to pay for those sins.

And there was the fact that she was no great beauty and Bowen was so beautiful to look at that it hurt.

She was damaged. The whore of another. She wore his stamp of possession on her cheek, and that would never change. Every time Bowen looked upon her scar he'd be reminded that another man had possessed her.

A sense of futility filled her heart until she could no longer bear the weight of it.

What would happen to her now that Bowen's brother had arrived? Would she be punished? Would she be sent away?

So many questions that she didn't have answers for. And she wasn't sure she was brave enough to demand them from Bowen or his brother, the laird.

If she was truthful, she'd admit that she wished with all her heart to go back in time and relive the past days over and over.

She was struck by the fact that, for the first time in a year, she'd been . . . *happy*. It was astounding, but it was true. She'd been content. She'd smiled. She'd laughed. And she'd been happy.

How long had it been since she'd enjoyed a moment in time? Precious minutes filled with contentment?

Not since she'd left the bosom of her family had she considered herself happy.

A warm tear leaked from the corner of her eye and trailed down her cheek.

Happiness seemed impossible. A lifetime ago. Something she'd thought never to experience again.

But, just for a moment, Bowen had given her that, only for her to have it cruelly snatched away by the encroachment of reality.

CHAPTER 30

"Graeme!" Bowen called as he strode across the courtyard to greet his brother.

Graeme turned from where he stood with Teague and Brodie, his eyebrows furrowed as he took in Bowen's appearance. As Bowen neared, Graeme pulled him into a hearty embrace and slapped him on the back.

"You look hale and hearty," Graeme observed. "From the report I received, I expected you to be abed convalescing."

Bowen smiled. " 'Twas greatly exaggerated, my injury. 'Twas naught but a scratch."

"That scratch required extensive stitching," Teague drawled.

Graeme's gaze sharpened. "Is this true?"

Bowen shrugged. "I am well. 'Tis all that matters."

"Aye," Graeme agreed. "Indeed, 'tis all that matters."

"How fares Eveline?" Bowen asked. "And Rorie? Did you leave them at the keep?"

Graeme shook his head. "Rorie stayed behind. She was distraught over missing her reading lessons. But I bore Eveline to her family at Armstrong Keep. I worry that she is not over the upset caused by her abduction."

"I just hope you brought us food," Teague grumbled. "I'm nigh to starving!"

"I would know all that has occurred here," Graeme said, ignoring Teague's outburst.

Bowen flinched inwardly, knowing that he would have to tell Graeme about Genevieve and the part she played in Eveline's abduction. 'Twas a task he didn't relish. The last thing he wanted was to be the one responsible for having more anger directed at the lass.

Already he was determined that, even though he had to tell Graeme all, he would bring his brother around on the matter of Genevieve. No matter what it took.

He hadn't set it in his mind exactly what his plans were regarding the lass. He knew only that he didn't want to be without her. And, in order to ensure that, he had to convince Graeme to offer her sanctuary within the very clan that Genevieve had betrayed.

That was assuming that Genevieve bore any affection at all for him.

It was a matter he had to drive from his mind, because the alternative didn't bear thinking about.

"Let us go within, where we may speak," Bowen said.

Graeme started to gesture toward Teague to accompany him and Bowen inside when Bowen put out his hand to stop his brother.

"Nay," Bowen said quietly. "What I have to say needs be said in private."

Teague's eyebrows rose and Graeme's eyes narrowed as he studied Bowen. After a moment's hesitation, he nodded.

"Very well. Then let us go and discuss what's on your mind."

Bowen issued an order for Graeme's horse to be attended to, and then he and Graeme left Teague and Brodie standing in the courtyard.

Forgoing the hall, where he should have offered his brother refreshment after his travels, he instead stopped a serving woman and issued a command for her to serve him and Graeme inside his chamber.

"Your secrecy is making me extremely curious," Graeme said as they mounted the stairs. "Is aught amiss?"

Bowen remained silent until they were behind the closed door of his chamber. He directed Graeme to make himself comfortable in one of the chairs by the fire.

Graeme shook the travel dust from his tunic before easing down to stretch his legs before the fire.

"You worried me, Bowen," Graeme began. " 'Tis the truth I suffered great fright when I received word that the keep had been attacked and you were injured. Eveline was distraught. 'Twas difficult to persuade her to remain behind under the protection of her kin."

Bowen grimaced. " 'Twas not a serious matter. Were it not for the fact that Brodie kept pouring a potion down my throat, I would have been up from my sickbed in much less than two days."

Graeme pursed his lips and studied Bowen. "How have things worked with the Armstrongs?"

"All is well. Aiden departed with Teague, but Brodie remained behind to lend his aid. 'Tis fortunate for me that he did. We may not have survived the attack and been able to drive them back were it not for the Armstrongs who elected to stay."

Graeme nodded his satisfaction. " 'Tis a good thing this alliance, then. Perhaps this will be a new dawn for the Montgomerys and the Armstrongs. Eveline has united us. 'Tis a fact that still mystifies me."

"Patrick McHugh is dead," Bowen said bluntly. "He was killed in battle."

Graeme's face twisted into a savage expression. "Good. I'd not suffer him to live a minute longer. Did you witness his killing firsthand?"

Bowen shook his head. "Nay, I did not."

" 'Tis a shame. I'd know whom to thank."

" 'Tis known who did the killing," Bowen said. " 'Twas a lass."

Graeme's head reared back. "A lass? In battle? What mean you?"

" 'Tis a long story, and one I have need to tell," Bowen said.

Graeme stared at him with narrowed eyes. A knock at the door interrupted whatever would be said next. Bowen went to admit the serving woman, and she nervously brought in the food for the two men.

When she finished setting out the food by the hearth, Bowen saw her to the door and in a low voice said, "See that Genevieve has food brought to her chamber this night. She will be hungry."

The serving woman dipped a curtsy, her lips pressed into a fine line.

"So tell me of this lass who felled Patrick McHugh," Graeme said as Bowen returned to the fire.

"I would tell you the whole if it," Bowen said. " 'Tis too important not to."

Graeme arched an eyebrow but fell silent.

"Do you remember the lass who directed us to where Eveline was being held in the dungeon? She wore a cape with a hood and her face was hidden from view."

Graeme frowned a moment, his brow creased in concentration. "Aye, I remember. I was frantic to find Eveline. 'Tis a shame. I never had the opportunity to thank the lass. Everything happened so quickly after that."

"Her name is Genevieve. Genevieve McInnis," Bowen said slowly.

"The lowland McInnises?" Graeme asked.

"Aye."

Graeme's frown deepened. "What's a McInnis lass doing in McHugh Keep? They are close with the king.

The laird's daughter was killed in an ambush on her way to wed her betrothed."

Bowen shook his head. "Nay. Genevieve lives still."

"Wait a moment. Are you saying Genevieve is the laird's daughter? And that she's not dead? And she is the one who directed us to Eveline?"

"Aye, but that is only part of the tale. I have much to say, so eat and listen."

Graeme fell silent and then motioned for Bowen to continue.

"Ian met Genevieve at court and became infatuated with her. He set upon her and her escort when she was traveling to meet her betrothed and killed every member of her party. 'Twas believed she too was killed."

Graeme started to say something, but Bowen held up his hand.

"Ian took her back to his keep, and when she refused his advances he cut her face so that no man would ever look upon her again with favor."

Graeme let out a curse. "The poor lass. And she is still here?"

"There is more," Bowen said quietly. "He raped her repeatedly, forcing her to become his unwilling leman. She has been prisoner here for a year."

"Have you sent word to her family? Are they coming to fetch her?"

Bowen blew out his breath. "Nay. She would not allow it."

"Why not?" Graeme demanded. He looked stunned.

" 'Tis better if I tell you the whole of it. 'Tis a complicated matter, and it only becomes more complicated."

Graeme's brows drew together, but he nodded. "Carry on, then."

"Genevieve is deeply shamed by all that has been done to her. She's permanently scarred. She bears the shame of what Ian forced upon her. She's determined not to bring dishonor to her family, and she doesn't want them to know what was done to her."

Bowen could see that Graeme itched to argue, so he continued on before Graeme could interrupt again.

"As I said, she is the one who directed us to Eveline."

He drifted off, reluctant to say the next. He knew it would condemn Genevieve in Graeme's eyes, and he'd do anything to spare the lass that censure. But he wouldn't lie to his brother. Graeme needed to know all so the slate was cleaned from the beginning.

"What you don't know is that Genevieve was responsible, indirectly, for Eveline's abduction."

"*What?*"

Graeme exploded, sitting forward, some of the food knocked from the plate. His jaw was clenched, then he wiped at his mouth and stared at Bowen in confusion.

"The lass was responsible for Eveline's abduction? I don't understand."

" 'Tis not necessary to go over every aspect," Bowen said in a low voice.

"Oh, aye, it is," Graeme said, cutting Bowen off before he could proceed. "It's very necessary. If this Genevieve had anything to do with Eveline's abduction, I want to know about it."

Bowen sighed. "She encouraged Ian to seek revenge. Word had drifted to Ian and Patrick of the deceit Eveline had perpetuated in order to escape her betrothal to Ian. Ian felt a fool and Genevieve took advantage of his anger and his fixation with the lass. She helped plot Eveline's abduction and goaded Ian to act."

"For God's sake *why*?" Graeme roared.

"Because we were her only hope of salvation," Bowen gritted out.

Graeme blinked and then shook his head. "You aren't making sense."

"I'm making perfect sense. The lass is smart. She knew

that the Montgomerys and the Armstrongs would not tolerate the taking of Eveline. One or both of the clans would be forced into action. Genevieve knew that we would come and we would seek revenge on Ian—and Patrick. It was her only hope of escaping the life that Ian had forced upon her."

Graeme's jaw bulged and he flexed it as he clamped his teeth together. 'Twas obvious he was battling his anger, and Bowen didn't want that anger to go unchecked.

"There's something else you should know, Graeme."

Graeme glanced up, meeting Bowen's determined gaze.

"I'm in love with her."

CHAPTER 31

Graeme's face grew stormy. His mouth worked up and down, but no words would come out. Then he shook his head. "She betrayed our clan—she betrayed *Eveline*—and you love her? Have you taken leave of your senses?"

Bowen's lips tightened. "She had good reason for what she did. I'm torn on my feelings over it, but she was in a desperate position and she did what she had to in order to survive. I cannot fault the lass for that. If Eveline was not your beloved wife, you would not see fault, either."

"Do not tell me what I would find fault in," Graeme said fiercely. "She purposely put another woman in harm's way for her own gain. I shudder to think of all that Eveline endured. 'Tis my greatest fear, even today, that she did not speak of all of it in an effort to spare me the pain of knowing. Have you any idea what it's like to worry that something that horrific has happened to someone you love with all your heart and soul?"

"That and more has happened to Genevieve. Repeatedly," Bowen said coldly.

Graeme exhaled and his expression eased. He looked weary and he rubbed at his forehead.

" 'Tis not something I can easily forgive, Bowen. You

have to understand that. You cannot expect me to accept this."

"I promised her that we would give her sanctuary within the Montgomery clan," Bowen said through a tight jaw. "I would give her that protection as my wife."

Graeme's jaw went slack, and his eyes darkened with anger. "You would marry a woman who has so wronged your clan? Your sister by marriage? Think of what you do, Bowen. She has you by the cods. 'Tis clear she is manipulating you."

Fury blew over Bowen. He'd not expected Graeme to be happy over the situation. He expected his anger. He'd not expected Graeme to take things this far and insult him in the process.

"I'll not grant my blessing for this," Graeme said, his voice laced with anger. "I'll not welcome her into the Montgomery clan."

Ice slid into his heart. Bowen was numb with the realization of the choice before him. And yet he knew without hesitation that it was the right choice. He could not leave Genevieve. He could not break his vow to see her protected. And loved.

She'd been dealt so much at such a young age. It was unconscionable to throw her to the wolves and walk away. He would not live without her. Even if it meant going his own way.

"I'll be with Genevieve with or without your blessing," Bowen said, his words dropping like stones in the silence of the room.

Graeme stared at him, mouth gaping. "You would really choose this woman over your own kin?"

Bowen stared back for a long moment, the silence growing ever more uncomfortable. "Tell me something, Graeme. Would you choose your kin over Eveline?"

Graeme seemed stunned by the question. His brows furrowed and he didn't open his mouth to respond.

Bowen's lip curled and he gazed at his brother in disgust. "I didn't think so."

He turned, only wanting to step away so that his anger could calm and he could think more rationally. When he put his hand out to open the door, he paused and turned back to Graeme, who was still sitting by the fire.

"You can rest in my chamber this night. I'll seek other accommodations."

He quietly left the room and shut the door behind him. It was instinctive to go to Genevieve's door. He hated to barge in without knocking, but neither did he want to remain in the hall long enough to be seen.

He opened the door and slipped inside. Genevieve was by the fire, her long hair unbound and streaming down her shoulders. She was perched in a chair, her knees to her chin and her heels resting on the edge of the seat.

He made a small sound so she'd be alerted to his presence, and she whirled around, her eyes wide with fright.

" 'Tis just me," he soothed.

She relaxed, but her eyes remained alert and searching.

He walked forward, realizing the presumption of his barging into her private quarters—a place he'd assured her that she would not be bothered. He stood a few feet away, unsure of what to do now that he was here and Genevieve sat before him, a vision of loveliness silhouetted by the fire.

"Would you like to sit?" she asked softly, gesturing toward the chair opposite her. "You look as though you have much on your mind."

He took the chair and leaned forward in it, his elbows resting on his knees.

"I wanted to see you," he said simply.

He'd not upset her by telling her of Graeme's reaction to his declaration. He hadn't even yet given her the words—his feelings. In truth, he was . . . afraid.

It amused him that a man well versed in the ways of women and confident in his own powers of seduction should be so uncertain over a lass. But Genevieve was different. She was important. He didn't want to mishandle the situation and ruin any chance he had of making her his.

She reached her hand across the distance and held it out to him. Such a simple gesture, yet it touched him deeply. He slid his fingers over her smooth palm and curled them around hers, enjoying the contact.

"Did you greet your brother?" she asked cautiously.

"Aye," he said grimly. "He is settled in my chamber for the night."

She frowned, her eyebrows drawing together. "Where then will you stay?"

He hesitated, not wanting to be overbold, and yet he wanted to be honest with her.

"I would like to stay here. With you."

Her eyes darkened, then widened in surprise. Her hand trembled inside his, and he squeezed to reassure her.

"I am not expecting anything you are not willing to give," he said in a low voice. "Your company is enough."

She shifted in her seat and then rose, her hand still grasped within his. Her hair fell down her back and the simple shift she wore tangled at her knees, baring her feet as she closed the distance between them.

She stood between his spread thighs and slowly lowered her mouth to his, touching softly and hesitantly. Her breath stuttered nervously over his lips as she shyly deepened the kiss.

"Ah, lass, what you do to me," Bowen whispered.

He pulled her down to perch on his lap and wrapped both arms around her, holding her against his chest as she tucked her head beneath his chin.

He rubbed one hand up and down her arm, just wanting to absorb the feel of her. His mind was alive with the choices before him and the repercussions for those choices. And yet the biggest consequence of all would be not to have her. Everything else he could face, but not a future without Genevieve.

She lifted her head, bumping into his chin as she pulled away. She stared at him with such dread in her eyes that it twisted his insides.

"Genevieve, what is amiss? You have to know I will never hurt you."

She shook her head, her eyes filling with tears—and shame. "I know you'll not hurt me, Bowen. There is something I must tell you. If you knew . . . You would not want me thus. And yet I must tell you, because I cannot allow things to progress between us if you don't know."

Fear took hold and wouldn't let go. He didn't like the tone of her voice. He didn't like the agony in her eyes.

He touched her face, his fingers shaking as he traced the scar on her cheek.

"What is it, lass?"

She closed her eyes and lowered her head so she wouldn't meet his gaze. Her voice was so low he had to strain to hear.

"I willingly took Ian to my bed."

Bowen was certain he could not have heard properly.

She opened her eyes and lifted her chin a notch, peeking at him from beneath her eyelashes.

"'Twas when Eveline was brought to the keep. Ian was set on h-h-having her. He intended to rape her. He was in such a state. He was triumphant, like a man drugged. Euphoric that he'd succeeded in spiriting Eveline away. He kept saying that the lass would not make a fool of him and that he'd punish her."

Her breath caught and held until finally it hiccupped softly from her throat.

"I could not allow it."

Her voice cracked and a low sob welled from her chest.

" 'Twas my doing that she was here, and I was so shamed. I knew that I could never be happy knowing that my freedom was bought by the suffering of another. So . . . so I invited him to my bed. I s-s-seduced him."

She broke off and turned her face away, her hands flying to cover her cheeks and the tears that fell.

Bowen stared at her in shock, and then anger assailed him. She flinched when she looked back and saw his reaction and immediately she tried to rise from his lap.

He caught her, holding her fiercely to him. He wrapped both of his arms around her and buried his face in her hair.

God, he was furious. Furious that she'd taken so much on her shoulders, that she bore so much weight. Guilt. Shame. And *none* of it did she deserve.

He was furious with himself for spending so much time being angry at her. And he was livid that Graeme had denounced the match between him and Genevieve because of all she'd supposedly done to Eveline.

There was nothing more he wanted to do than to march back to his chamber, confront Graeme, and tell him the whole sordid truth, but he'd not leave Genevieve to shoulder her grief alone.

He would show her this night how it could be with a man who loved her.

"I am not angry with you, lass," he said, his words muffled by her hair. "I'm shamed at how much time I spent being angry with you before."

"I was willing," she whispered. "I played the whore he made me that night. And the next. Oh God, I hated myself. 'Tis only then I contemplated the sin of suicide. Not before, when he raped me. When he had others hold me down and witness my humiliation. Not even when he let others h-hurt me. But then. Oh God, 'tis a sin to even admit this, but I was so broken by what I'd done that I wanted to throw myself from the tower."

"Oh, my love," Bowen whispered in a tortured voice.

He rocked back and forth, holding her in his arms as her tears wet his chest. He kissed her hair, her temple, then pulled her away long enough to kiss her cheeks, her nose, and her lips as he sought to comfort her.

She fused her lips to his hungrily, the heat and salt from her tears on his tongue. She clutched at his neck, holding him fiercely as she returned his kiss.

"If I should never be with another man again, I would want you to be the last," she whispered. "Show me, Bowen. Show me what it's like. Take away the memory of Ian."

"You'll not ever have to beg me for anything, my love. If you ask me for the moon, I'll fetch it for you."

Her eyes softened and the tears stopped as she stared back at him, her forehead pressed to his.

"Show me," she whispered again.

He rose from the chair, bearing her with him as he hefted her into his arms. He carried her to the bed and laid her gently atop the mattress.

Not wanting to ruin a single moment of what was to come, he leaned down, planting his palms on either side of her shoulders as he stared intently into her eyes.

"I'll be gentle, lass. I'll go slowly and woo you as sweetly as a lass ever deserved. But if I go too fast, if I do anything to frighten you, if you want me to stop for no other reason than you're afraid, you must tell me. I'd never do anything to hurt you. I'd cut off my right arm before ever making you suffer pain."

She smiled up at him, her eyes glowing like twin emeralds.

"I trust you, Bowen. Only you. Love me now. Make me forget all that is in the past."

He lowered his body to hers, his mouth pressing warmly to hers. "Aye, lass. Tonight all I want you to think on is the present."

CHAPTER 32

Genevieve absorbed Bowen's kiss hungrily. Such sweetness she'd never known. Never had a man been so tender and patient with her. Her heart was filled with such an ache that she was nearly overcome.

She knew not what her future would hold, but for tonight she wanted only this. To be in Bowen's arms. To know, just for a moment, what it felt like to be cherished and . . . *loved*.

She could pretend the past had never happened. That her face was unmarked and that sins hadn't been committed. That Bowen was her love—her only love—and that he was the first to ever touch her.

Instinctively, she pressed the scarred cheek into the mattress so that his lips danced across the unmarred flesh of her other cheek. But he wouldn't allow her to do so.

Gently, he turned her so that the scar was bared to him, and pressed tiny kisses over the rough line, leaving no part of the mark untouched.

"I would be content to do naught more than kiss you for the entire night," he murmured.

"And I you," she whispered back.

His hands delved into her hair. He ran his fingers through the long tresses, stroking and smoothing them from her face and forehead.

"Sit up, lass, so that I may attend you."

Her body trembled as she did his bidding. He positioned her on the edge of the bed and he began to slowly divest her of the shift she wore. His gaze held hers all the while, as if he were looking for any sign that she was unwilling or frightened.

'Twas true she was nervous. She didn't want to disappoint him. But she was not afraid. Not of him. Never of him.

She held her breath when he tugged the shift over her head and she slid her arms around her body, covering her breasts, as she was suddenly bare before him.

"Do not hide such loveliness from me," he chided gently.

He carefully pulled her arms away from her body. She was shocked to discover that his hands trembled against her. It was as though he was every bit as nervous as she.

Her heart clutched. She found it endearing that he was so sweet and gentle, and that he seemed unsure of himself.

She loosened her hold on herself and allowed him to pull her arms away so that he could view her nudity. The immediate look of satisfaction in his eyes bolstered her flagging courage.

She was no stranger to lust. Ian had looked upon her like a man determined not only to possess her but to own her, to insert himself into every part of her mind, body, and soul.

But the way Bowen gazed upon her was different. She soaked it up, holding it close and savoring every look, every touch.

"I would undress you as well," she said huskily, but she hesitated, because she didn't want to seem overbold.

He took her hands and guided them to his tunic, to the lacings securing the neck.

"Nothing would bring me more pleasure than to have your hands upon me."

Clumsily, she worked at the laces and then allowed her hands to glide down his muscled arms and to his taut abdomen, where she gathered the material and began to push upward.

He helped her tug it over his head, and her gaze settled on the stitched scar curving across his chest. As he had done with hers, she leaned forward and kissed every inch of the mark, her lips lingering over the puckered flesh.

His heart thundered against her mouth and his breath escaped his mouth in a long hiss.

"Do you have any idea how much I've dreamed of this?" he asked. "Your mouth on me, the sweetness of your kiss and caress. 'Tis more than I could possibly have ever wished for."

She ducked her head shyly, her cheeks heating at his fervent words.

He reached to cup her jaw, rubbing his thumb over her cheekbone as he gazed tenderly at her. "Ah, lass, your shyness is so endearing."

She rubbed her face into his palm, aching for more of his caress. Then he slowly rose, standing before her so that she had access to his leggings.

The ridge of his arousal was readily visible, and she swallowed nervously as she began to divest him of the last of his clothing. Finally his hands covered hers and he assisted her in pushing them down his legs, and he stepped free.

He was a magnificent sight standing before her. All male, hard, muscled, the ultimate warrior. Scars criss-crossed his body, some old and fading, some, like the one on his chest, much newer.

'Twas evident that this was a man who'd fought in

many a battle. He bore the marks of the most seasoned warrior, a testament to his strength and training.

From the dark hair at the juncture of his thighs, his erection jutted upward, thick and heavy. She'd learned to fear such a sight, because she knew it meant only pain and humiliation for her.

But this was a testament to his arousal and his need of her. *Her*. A scarred lass with nothing to offer him, her virtue long ago taken against her will.

It was hard not to shrink away in shame all over again, for she was not worthy of this man or of his regard.

Bowen eased down onto the bed again, taking in the instant change in her demeanor. He stroked her hair, allowing his hand to run the length of her tresses as he stared at her in question.

"Why that look? As though you would turn from me in shame?"

Her eyes were haunted. Sadness clung to them, drenching the pools with a wealth of unspoken emotion.

"Once I would have been worthy of you," Genevieve said in an anguished voice. "I was innocent and untouched. My parents were of noble birth, and I was fostered in the king's court. I attended the queen herself." She looked up, her face filled with sorrow and the knowledge of all that had been forced upon her. "Now I am no more than the lowliest whore. Certainly not fit for a warrior bearing the Montgomery name and kin to one of the mightiest lairds in all of Scotland."

Rage filled him. He was awash in it until it flamed his senses and burned through his veins. "Not worthy?" he said, his voice gruff and unyielding. " 'Tis *I* who say who is worthy, and there was never a woman more worthy of my regard than you."

A look of wonder slowly lit her face. Her eyes widened and then lightened. She stared at him as if he'd just single-handedly defeated an entire army on her behalf.

"Oh Bowen," she breathed.

He slid his arms underneath her legs and lifted and rotated so he could position her on the bed. He laid her out like a feast—and, indeed, she was. A feast for the eyes and the senses. He could hardly contain himself, so great was his need to touch her.

With trembling hands, he stroked up her soft belly, just above where the dark patch of hair shielded her most feminine flesh. It beckoned to him, and the urge to delve his fingers into her sweetness was strong, but he didn't want to rush. If it killed him, he was going to be exceedingly patient. And it very well might.

He caressed the satiny skin over her rib cage, and then up the valley of her breasts, as he gazed at the perfection of the plump mounds. Perfect, pink-tipped breasts. Her nipples were enticingly round and erect, inviting his mouth to suckle.

When he cupped one of the dainty globes in his palm, she went still, not even a breath escaping her lips. Her nipples puckered to rigid points, and tiny chill bumps broke out and raced across her chest.

"You are beautiful, Genevieve," he said hoarsely. "There is not a lass more beautiful."

For a moment, he thought he'd spoken wrongly. That he'd gone too far and that, in his effort to make her feel beautiful and womanly, he'd come across as insincere.

But then she looked at him and her eyes glowed with vibrant light. She looked . . . content. It was a look she hadn't worn until now, and he couldn't blame her. She'd had little to be happy about.

"You make me *feel* beautiful," she said, her lips trembling with emotion.

Her words hit him right in the chest, and he went weak all the way to his feet. He leaned over and brushed his mouth across hers, sipping at the nectar of her lips. " 'Tis glad I am of that, lass, for 'tis the truth that you are more beautiful to me than a thousand Highland sunsets."

He nibbled his way down her jaw to her ear, and then spent several long moments eliciting soft moans from her as he teased the delicate lobe. He licked and nipped until she fidgeted restlessly underneath his seeking hands.

He plucked her nipples to fullness, toying with them with his fingers. His mouth watered with the need to run his tongue over the tips. After leaving her ear, he made a line of bites down her neck to her shoulder. He grazed his teeth over the sensitive skin in the curve of her neck until she shivered beneath his mouth.

And then, finally, he allowed himself to slide his mouth downward. He left a hot, damp trail over her flesh, until at last he reached the lushness of her breasts.

He licked the tips of her nipples, and she gasped, arching her back. Her hands flew to his hair, her fingers dragging over his scalp as she pulled him closer, demanding more.

He toyed with her nipples, licking and teasing, and then he sucked a velvet tip into his mouth and tugged strongly as he suckled at her breast.

" 'Tis heaven," she sighed.

Her fingers loosened and she stroked his hair, caressing the long strands until he closed his eyes in pleasure.

Her touch was wondrous. He would be content to have her hands upon him all the days of his life.

"Aye, 'tis heaven," he agreed.

But he knew being inside her would be beyond heaven. The anticipation was killing him. He couldn't wait to slide into her velvety softness. He only prayed he wouldn't spend himself the moment he dived into her sweet heat.

He continued his downward path, pressing tender

kisses to her belly, and then he positioned himself over her, his arms pressed to the outsides of her thighs as he kissed his way to the wispy, dark hair between her legs.

Her eyes went wide and she lifted her head, a protest forming on her lips when he parted her thighs and pressed a kiss to the soft curls.

"Bowen, nay!"

He chuckled low. "Aye, lass. Lie back and let me love you."

He slid his fingers over the silken folds and found the taut nub of her woman's pleasure. As soon as he touched her, she jerked and let out a sharp cry.

He doubted any man had ever given a care for her pleasure. She'd been used as a vessel for the pleasure of others. Her needs and wants had never been considered. He was determined to change all of that tonight.

Lowering his head, he nuzzled through the warm, moist flesh and tasted the essence of her femininity. It was a heady sensation. She filled his senses. She overwhelmed him.

He ran his tongue over her entrance and upward until he lapped at the little nub of flesh above her opening. She shook uncontrollably, the muscles in her legs jumping and spasming as he continued to lavish attention on her woman's flesh.

"Bowen!" she cried out.

He glanced up to see her eyes wide and almost frightened. She was as taut as a bowstring, and her expression was a mixture of pain and intense pleasure.

"What's happening?" she asked, her voice bewildered.

"'Tis your woman's pleasure," he said gently. "Let me give it to you, Genevieve. Trust me. Just let go. Don't fight it. It will be wondrous."

She sighed and relaxed, her muscles going lax. He returned to his task, determined now more than ever to bring her the ultimate pleasure.

He wanted to ensure she would be prepared for him, because the last thing he wanted was to hurt her. He was a big man, and she was a tiny lass. He'd not use brute force and cause her pain.

As his mouth found the tiny bud and he gently suckled it, he slid a finger inside her opening, testing her wetness. She tensed around him, clamping down on his finger. She was small, her passageway narrow, and it sucked greedily at his finger.

He eased it deeper, plunging through plush, satin walls as he worked his tongue over her most sensitive parts.

She twitched uncontrollably. She sighed and moaned, becoming more verbal with each lap of his tongue. Her hips bucked upward and her hand slid over his hair as if she were begging for more.

He would take her to the very edge. He wanted her desperate for release. Then and only then would he take her and possess her. They would find satisfaction together.

He eased his finger from her passageway and then slid both hands under her rounded buttocks, lifting her so that he could feast more easily on her feminine flesh.

He savored every taste, every swipe of his tongue. He swirled the tip around her opening and then slid his tongue inside, delving as deeply as he could and then sealing his mouth over her entrance and sucking.

She let out a cry and clamped her thighs tightly around his head. She twitched beneath him, and he could tell she was close to release.

Anticipation licked up his spine. He was so eager to be inside her that his movements were clumsy as he eased her buttocks back to the mattress and removed his hands.

Parting her thighs, he positioned himself between them and maneuvered himself in place atop her. Their bodies were flush, a perfect fit, her softness a perfect foil for his hardness.

"I want to be inside you, lass. I ache to be inside you. Hold on to me and set your gaze on me. I want you with me the whole way. If you want me to stop, say the word. I'll stop even if it kills me."

She smiled, her eyes soft with something that looked like love. Maybe it was because he wanted it to be. Maybe he imagined it. But he embraced it and held it close, hoping beyond hope that she could grow to love him in time. He'd wait forever if that was what it took.

He would have to be patient, because first she had to trust, and it might take a long time for her to overcome all the betrayal she'd been handed.

Positioning himself at her small entrance, he pushed forward only enough to lodge himself just inside. There he paused, not wanting to rush and risk hurting or frightening her.

He had but one chance to make this perfect, and he was determined to do just that.

"Breathe, lass, and hold on to me tight. I'll be gentle and move slow. I want it to feel good."

Her hands slid up his arms to his shoulders, where her fingernails dug into his flesh, marking him with tiny claws.

He pushed forward, entering her inch by inch. Never had he taken it so slowly or been so careful. He watched her closely for any sign that she wasn't with him. She emitted a small sigh and fidgeted beneath him as if she were as impatient as he for him to seat himself all the way inside her.

She closed around him, all soft and sweet and lush. Absolutely lush and decadently sinful. Never had he felt such a rush of pleasure. Or contentment. 'Twas like coming home. As if he'd waited for her—and this moment—forever. And maybe he had.

She completed him in a way he'd never imagined a female completing him. He had kin, clan, his duties to his brother. Graeme, Teague, and Rorie had always come first. He placed their well-being and needs above his own. And now Genevieve had taken over. He'd move the sun if that's what it took to ensure her safety and happiness. Nothing was more important than her security. His focus was and had to be solely on her, for she had no other to champion her cause. If he didn't see to her happiness, who would?

Closing his eyes, he slid deeper, pushing inward until finally his hips met the backs of her thighs and the hair at his groin mingled with the baby-fine hair between her legs.

Her eyes were glazed. She looked as though she was overwhelmed, intoxicated. Her hands worked up and down his arms as if she couldn't remain still, and then she lifted them upward to dive into the hair that streamed over his shoulders.

He withdrew, and they both groaned with the exquisite pleasure that assailed them. He thrust forward, a gentle push. He glided wetly through the tight tissues, and sweat beaded his forehead as he fought for control.

"Bowen, I need . . ."

"What do you need, lass? Tell me. I will give it to you if 'tis within my power."

"I need . . . *you*," she said in a desperate voice. "'Tis clawing my insides, this need. I don't know what to do. 'Tis growing and growing until the pressure is an ache within me."

He eased back and then thrust a little more forcefully, setting a rhythm as he rocked against her. His hands wrapped around her hips, holding her steady as he pumped in and out of her tight clasp.

Sliding one hand to her groin, he eased his thumb low,

through the curls and into the V of her legs until he brushed over her quivering nub.

She tensed immediately, going so tight around him that he very nearly spent himself then and there. He groaned and halted, breathing rapidly to gain control.

Then he flicked his thumb over her again, eliciting another bone-deep shudder. She was close. Perilously close to finding her pleasure, and he wanted to take the plunge with her.

Pressing his thumb and then working in a sensual circle, he began to slide in and out, forcing himself deep. The friction was nearly unbearable. She was so tight that it was difficult to move with ease.

Her fingers dug into his arms. Her eyes squeezed shut and her mouth opened in a silent cry.

She went wet around him, suddenly easing his passage, and he thrust harder and faster. She arched high off the bed, and then she did cry out, the sound garbled as it ended in a gasp.

Like a wild thing, she bucked in his grasp, and he let her, riding her as she writhed beneath him. His release gathered in his cods, tightening every muscle in his body until it bordered on pain. It raced up his shaft and exploded in a tumultuous burst. He pulsed forcefully, planting himself deeply within her only to withdraw and push himself deep again.

Finally he paused, buried inside her, his body flush against hers as he quivered and emptied the last of his seed within her.

He gathered her in his arms, wanting only to have her as close as he could manage. She was limp and sated, her satisfied sigh purring over his ears.

For a long moment, he remained buried inside her tight clasp. He had no desire to leave. If it was up to him, he'd remain this way for as long as he could, a part of her, connected in the most intimate way possible.

He kissed her temple, nuzzling her skin, and murmured again that she was the most beautiful lass in the world. They weren't just words he offered. Platitudes he didn't mean. He cared not about the scar that marred her face. In *his* eyes, she was the most beautiful lass he'd ever known and nothing would change that. Not a scar. Not circumstances. She was his, and he didn't give one damn what others thought.

"I love you," he murmured against her hair. "I'll always love you, Genevieve."

But when he pulled away, he saw that she'd already drifted into a deep sleep, her mouth curved into the tiniest hint of a smile. She looked at ease, the lines on her forehead replaced by smooth skin.

He kissed her again and gently eased himself from the warm clasp of her body. Then he pulled the covers over the both of them and gathered her close so that she would sleep in the safety of his embrace.

CHAPTER 33

It was in the early hours of the predawn morning and Bowen lay in bed, Genevieve resting at his side, her head on his shoulder as he stroked the softness of her hair.

They'd both awakened but lay in the quiet, simply enjoying the intimacy and closeness of their embrace. Every once in a while, he pressed a kiss to her brow, because he was unable to keep from touching her and kissing her in even the smallest of ways.

Her hand idly rubbed his chest in an absent manner, but he liked her touching him. He never wanted her to stop.

"How did you become so skilled with a bow?" he asked, breaking the silence.

She lifted her head to look into his eyes, surprise wrinkling her brow.

"'Tis obvious you have great skill. You were able to fell four men in battle, and your aim is truer than that of any man I've witnessed."

"My father taught me," she said quietly. "He oft took me hunting with him. My mother despaired of him. She told him he was trying to make a lad out of me to compensate for the fact she never gave him the son he wanted."

She blew out her breath softly, a look of sadness clouding her eyes.

"I miss him," she admitted.

He squeezed her to him and pressed another kiss to her forehead.

"What will happen now, Bowen? Your brother is here."

Careful not to broach topics that would only anger him, he responded in a manner he knew to be truthful.

"I do not know. We did not speak overmuch on the matter. Today he'll tour the keep and will likely decide on the future of the McHugh clan."

"Promise me you won't allow me to be the cause of dissension between the two of you."

Bowen stiffened. Had she read more into his mood the night before than she'd let on? Was she more intuitive than he'd thought?

"Nay, lass, I won't."

That much was true. He refused to allow Genevieve to be a point of strife. Graeme had made himself clear, but Bowen had made himself equally clear. If Graeme could not accept her, then Bowen would take her away from the Montgomery clan. It hurt him to think of being separated from his kin—his brothers and his sister, Rorie. But it hurt even more to imagine being parted from Genevieve.

"Clan is important," she said, a note of grief in her voice. "I miss mine. I miss Mama and Papa with all my heart, but it soothes me to know that they'll never learn of my disgrace. It would hurt them deeply."

There was such sadness in Genevieve's words that it tugged at Bowen's heart. But, more than that, it gave him pause. Her words lay heavy on him, pricking at him.

It was an uncomfortable sensation, because he knew that 'twas a huge unresolved issue, her clan. He also knew that her solution was no solution at all, and yet if her parents knew that she was alive Bowen would lose her in an instant.

The thought discomforted him—nay, completely unsettled him—to the point of panic. He couldn't think of such. He gripped her tighter to him to assuage the unease that stole over him at the very idea of losing her.

"I want you to remain in your chamber this day, Genevieve," Bowen said in a grim voice. "There is much to be worked out, and 'tis best if you remain out of sight. I'd not have you hurt by the words or deeds of others."

He'd protect her from his brother's censure. In Graeme's current state, Bowen couldn't be certain that he would not confront Genevieve in his anger over what she'd done to Eveline. And if he ever did so, then brother would be pitted against brother, because Bowen would never allow Graeme to disparage Genevieve.

Sadness pricked at him and he shook it off, not willing to allow a shadow to be cast over him and Genevieve. He was determined to give her the love and happiness she deserved. Even if it meant choosing her over the people he loved and held close to his heart.

It was hard not to be angry at Graeme for forcing him to make that choice. He understood Graeme's feelings, but he went too far. He'd condemned a match between him and Genevieve without ever meeting the lass. And he hadn't really listened to her story. He'd reacted in anger, and now Bowen was forced to do the unthinkable.

The woman he loved or the clan he was fiercely loyal to.

It was a choice no man should ever have to make. And yet he faced it now.

God help him, but he could never forgive himself or live with himself or call himself a man if he turned away from Genevieve and left her to survive on her own. He wouldn't be able to sleep at night for wondering if she was happy, scared, alone, or hurt. And the simple truth was, he didn't want to be without her.

Nay, the lass had endured far more hurt than a lass should ever have to endure in one lifetime. If it was left to him, she'd never suffer another moment of unhappiness.

She leaned up and kissed him, her fingertips touching the side of his face. He captured her hand, holding it against his cheek as he returned her kiss.

His body leapt to life, already hungry for her again, and he'd had her over and over throughout the night. It would never be enough. He'd never have enough of her.

He hauled her into his arms, kissing her more aggressively. And then he rolled her underneath him, spreading her thighs with his knee.

"Again?" she whispered.

"Aye, lass, again."

CHAPTER 34

It was well past the hour when he usually rose that Bowen made his way from Genevieve's chamber and went in search of Graeme. Teague and Brodie weren't within the keep, and it was likely that they'd accompanied Graeme on his tour of the McHugh holding.

The night with Genevieve had put him at peace with his decision. It had calmed and centered him when before his emotions had been in turmoil after his confrontation with Graeme. This morning he was better able to discuss the matter with Graeme, and he hoped he could make his brother see reason.

As he entered the courtyard, Graeme rode in with Teague and Brodie and dismounted. His sharp gaze found Bowen, and his features tightened.

Bowen approached with a determined stride, stopping a few feet away from Graeme. Brodie and Teague were just dismounting and Bowen hastened to say what he wanted before they came within hearing distance.

"I would speak to you privately."

Graeme's lips thinned. "You've had much to say already."

"There is more. 'Tis information you should have before you set your mind on the matter."

Graeme hesitated a long moment before finally nodding, and then he turned to order his horse taken care of. After his directive, he looked back at Bowen. "Come. We'll walk to the hillside and speak there."

Side by side the two brothers walked around the stone wall guarding the keep and a good distance away from the keep and the cottages that surrounded it.

'Twas like old times. Bowen always at Graeme's side. Bowen always carrying out Graeme's wishes. He was plagued by sadness over the rift between them, but it was one he hoped to have sorted.

Graeme paused, his gaze taking in their surroundings. The wind whipped around them, sailing over the hillside.

"What's on your mind, Bowen? I assume you spent last night with Genevieve."

There was strong disapproval in Graeme's voice, but Bowen didn't react. He fixed his stare on the distant river as he gathered his thoughts.

"Genevieve set Ian on a path that she thought would bring about the most likely chance of his death—and her rescue."

"Aye, you told me. By encouraging his plan to abduct Eveline," he said in disgust.

"Apart from the fact that you place the blame on the wrong person, Genevieve did not carry out the plan. She was not the longtime tormentor of Eveline. 'Twas Ian, and you well know it. There is more you do not know. I've told you that she was abducted by Ian, her face ruined by his knife, and that he raped her repeatedly. He also invited his men to do the same."

Graeme's face twisted in disgust and he issued a rare blasphemy.

"What I learned only last night, and I learned it because the lass was in tears and sorely afraid to confide in me, is that she was *ashamed* because she invited Ian to her bed, not once but twice. Do you want to know why, Graeme?"

A look of discomfort crossed Graeme's face, but he didn't respond. Bowen pressed on.

"She invited the bastard to her bed because he was set on raping and abusing Eveline as retribution for sins he thought she'd committed against him. Namely, ever daring to refuse him. Just as Genevieve had once done at court. Only Genevieve was not so fortunate to escape his revenge. But she could save Eveline, and she did so by willingly taking Ian to her bed in order to spare your wife. And, because she did so, she considers herself unworthy of me, my regard. Or my *love*."

He finished the last fiercely, because he was gripped by rage all over again. He was furious that he'd misjudged her so, and that she still suffered the condemnation and judgment of his kin for wrongs she hadn't committed.

Graeme's lips formed a tight, resigned line. There was sorrow and regret in his eyes.

" 'Tis a mess. The whole of it is a sorry tale. 'Tis disgraceful that one man caused so much suffering and grief because he was but a spoiled child deprived of all he wanted. His father is as much to blame as he."

Bowen nodded. "Aye, he was. The lass put an arrow right through his neck. She sought retribution for the wrongs he allowed Ian to visit on others. She was full of hatred for them both."

" 'Tis not an easy matter before you, Bowen. Even if I grant my blessing and consent, there is the matter of her clan. You cannot hide the lass forever. 'Tis possible you'd even see them when you attend court. They would be hurt and furious if 'twas discovered that you'd kept the news of her being alive from them. They might even wage war with our clan over it."

Bowen took in Graeme's words, but they were not matters he hadn't already considered. He well remembered the look on the lass's face the night before, when she'd spoken of her family. How haunted her eyes had been. And the longing in her voice when she'd admitted she missed them.

And now Graeme was putting before him a very solid point. Bowen wanted to marry Genevieve. He wanted to take her to the Montgomery clan so she would be happy and well protected. But Graeme was right. He couldn't keep her hidden away forever. He didn't want to.

Never would he want her to think he was shamed by having her as his wife. He didn't give a damn what people thought of her disfigurement. She was beautiful and breathtaking to him. He'd take down anyone who said otherwise.

Dread filled his heart because he knew, but was loath to acknowledge, the path that lay before him. He knew what was right—what was best—and it filled him with desolation.

"I need some time to think on things," Bowen said in a low voice.

Graeme sighed. "If it makes things any easier for you, I will relent. I take back all that was said last night. I will welcome the lass into our clan if 'tis your wish. You are my brother, and I love you above all others. I want what is best for you, and I want you to be happy. If the lass makes you happy, then I will accept her."

Bowen nodded and clasped his brother's arm.

"I would meet the lass when you've had time to think on all that plagues you," Graeme said.

"Aye, you will. I'll introduce you myself."

"I'll leave you then."

Graeme clapped Bowen on the back and squeezed his shoulder in a gesture of comfort. Bowen offered a grim smile and turned back toward the river and made his way down the hill to the banks.

The same banks where he and Genevieve had conversed more than once. Where he'd seen her glowing like a sea nymph, her body wet and glistening.

Christ's bones, but the realization of what he had to do crippled him. He was paralyzed by the mere thought. Grief consumed him, but at the same time there was a peace slowly seeping into his consciousness.

'Twas the hardest thing he'd ever have to do, but it was the *right* thing.

CHAPTER 35

Genevieve left her chamber a few hours after Bowen departed, even though he'd told her to remain inside. Normally, she'd obey his dictate—she'd done so until now—but the tiny, cramped chamber was driving her daft and she needed but to stretch her legs a short while.

She paused outside Taliesan's door, tempted to see if she was within. Genevieve would feel better with the lass's company, but neither did she want to involve Taliesan if one of the McHughs came across Genevieve and hurled insults and accusations at her.

Genevieve had been very careful to avoid the majority of the McHugh clan ever since the battle, and she knew not if they had knowledge of her part in Patrick's killing. But even if they didn't, the fact that she'd been the reason for Corwen's death was enough for them to vent their anger on her.

Gathering her cape and hood around her, she rapidly descended the stairs, hesitating as she peeked into the hall. 'Twas time for the noonday meal, and many were gathered round the tables in the hall. She'd make her escape through the exit to the courtyard and pray that she passed unmolested.

Ducking her head, she hurried on her way, her stride rapid. The wind pulled at her cape when she stepped outside, and she shielded her eyes from the sand and grit kicked up by the gusts.

When she rounded the corner, she came face to face with a group of women who were returning from the river with their washing.

Their expressions turned to anger the moment they realized it was she. One woman dropped the basket of damp clothing and, without saying a word, picked up a rock and hurled it at Genevieve.

It struck her on the arm, and she flinched in pain. She turned to protect herself and, to her horror, the other women followed suit.

"Whore!" one spat as she threw a rock that sailed over Genevieve's head. Thank God.

"Murderer!"

The litany of names made Genevieve recoil. She took her hands from their protective barrier long enough to collect her skirts so she could run back toward the keep as fast as she could.

One of the rocks struck her square in the middle of her back, and she cried out in pain. Another grazed her temple, and she felt the warm trickle of blood slide slowly down her cheek.

But it was the one that hit her in the back of the head that felled her.

She went sprawling forward and nearly fell into the arms of Teague Montgomery as she rounded the corner to the courtyard.

She hit the ground with a painful thud, but she knew she couldn't remain down. They'd be on her like a pack of wolves, and she feared they wouldn't stop until they killed her.

"What the devil?" Teague demanded as he knelt on the ground beside her.

As he turned her over, she saw that Brodie Armstrong

was at his side, and his face was drawn into a fierce scowl.

Teague wiped his thumb over the blood on her face, his eyes narrowed. "Who did this to you?" he demanded.

"They're coming," she gasped.

Teague glanced up, and Genevieve could hear the shriek of the women as they rounded the corner, their thirst for blood—her blood—evident in their cries.

"Brodie," Teague barked. "See to it."

Teague gently gathered her in his arms, shielding her all the while with his own body. Brodie roared his order for the women to halt and then he laid into them for what they'd dared.

Genevieve huddled in Teague's arms, her head burrowed into his chest as he rapidly strode for the door to the keep. Her prayers were answered when he bypassed the hall and headed straight up the stairs to her chamber.

When he shouldered through her door, he plunked her down on her bed, and then immediately left her to wet a washcloth in the basin.

She lay there numbly, shock making her cold and insensible. She was vaguely aware of pain in her head and in other places, but all she could picture over and over was the rage and hatred on the faces of the women.

Oh God, she would never have a place here. She'd known it, but somehow having Bowen here had made her look beyond the intense dislike the McHughs had for her.

She closed her eyes as a tear squeezed from the corner of one and slid wetly down her cheek.

"Don't cry, lass," Teague said gruffly. "'Tis enough to make me panic."

Her eyelids fluttered open and he swam in her vision. He sat on the edge of the bed next to her and, with a frown of concentration, carefully wiped the blood from her scarred cheek.

She was mortified to have him in such close proximity performing such an intimate task. But he held her chin firmly with one hand so she couldn't turn away while he cleaned the wound with his other hand.

" 'Tis naught but a knick," he assured her as he pulled the cloth away. "It won't leave a permanent mark."

Her eyes watered again, and she had to call back the laughter that threatened to escape. "The last thing I'm concerned about is another mark on my face," she said with a sob.

Sympathy twisted his features. Then he rose, clearing his throat awkwardly. "Shall I fetch Taliesan for you?"

She shook her head. "Nay," she whispered. "I'd rather be alone right now."

Teague nodded and started for the door. "Summon me if you have need of anything. I'll make sure food is brought up for your meal."

"Thank you," she said gratefully. "And thank you for helping me."

Anger darkened his eyes. " 'Tis disgraceful how they abuse a mere lass. Bowen will be furious. Graeme will not tolerate such," he amended.

She lifted her fingers to touch the tender spot on her temple and moved it around to inspect the bump on her head.

"Are you all right?" Teague asked gently.

She took in a deep breath and dropped her hand into her lap to grip her other hand. She faced him bravely, determined not to allow him to see how affected she was by the blatant show of animosity.

"Aye, I'm fine," she said. "Thank you for your aid."

Teague nodded and left her chamber, closing the door behind him.

* * *

"You've been out here for hours," Graeme said dryly.

Bowen turned his head from where he sat on one of the rock outcroppings overlooking the river to see his brother standing a short distance away.

He sighed. "I've been thinking."

Graeme took a step forward until he was directly next to Bowen, his booted feet mere inches from the water lapping the bank.

"Aye, that much is obvious. You didn't even hear me approach. What is it that has you so occupied?"

"Genevieve."

"Ah. That explains much," Graeme said.

Graeme settled onto the rock next to Bowen and stared over the water as Bowen was doing.

"And what have you decided about the lass?"

Bowen closed his eyes, not wanting to voice his thoughts. His heart was filled with a piercing ache and he was overwhelmed with grief for what he must do.

"I have to let her go," he said, his voice breaking halfway through the words.

Graeme turned his stare on his brother.

"She'll never be happy unless she's been reunited with her family," Bowen said. "'Tis not fair to her or them for them to go on thinking she died. I heard the longing in her voice when she spoke of them. They love her and she loves them. She was very dear to them. Their only daughter. I cannot be selfish and take her away with me and keep her only unto myself. She's been denied choices for far too long. How can I be another force in her life that does the same? I want her. God, I want her. I love her. But I want her to be happy more than I want myself to be happy. And I cannot bear the thought that there would always be sorrow in her eyes were I to take her to Montgomery Keep and perpetuate this myth that she is no one. Not important."

Graeme slid his hand over Bowen's shoulder. "I think

you're doing the right thing. The lass has had nothing but heartache, and 'tis true she's been denied a choice in everything. I can only imagine the grief that her clan has endured thinking she is lost to them. You do a good thing reuniting her with her kin."

"She may hate me for it," Bowen said bleakly. "I speak of denying her choices, and yet I seek to go against her wishes by informing her family that she lives. She will not thank me for it."

"Sometimes the right thing is the most painful choice," Graeme said quietly.

"Aye, I know it."

Graeme's eyes were full of sympathy, and regret filled his face. "I am sorry for your grief, Bowen. I can't hope to understand the choices before you. I would be devastated if I ever had to face giving up my Eveline."

"I would bring more trouble upon my clan were the McInnises to discover that their daughter was alive and under my protection. But, most important, I don't think Genevieve will ever truly be happy if all is not resolved with her family. And I want her happiness more than I want my own."

Graeme put his hand on Bowen's shoulder again but remained silent as the two brothers gazed into the distance.

There was naught to say when Bowen was dying on the inside.

"Bowen!"

Bowen tensed at the distant call. He and Graeme both turned to see Teague approaching, a grim frown on his face.

"A group of McHugh women were doing their damnedest to stone Genevieve," Teague said without preamble.

Bowen shot to his feet. "*What?*"

"I came upon her fleeing back to the keep with a mob

of women on her heels hurling rocks at her. I took the lass back to her chamber and tended her wounds."

"How badly is she hurt?" Bowen demanded.

"I think she's just shaken up. She had one cut to her face, and she likely has bruises where the other rocks landed, but she was just frightened and upset. I told her to remain above stairs and not to come out."

Bowen swore violently, his fingers curling into tight fists. " 'Tis no way for her to live!"

He raked one of his hands through his hair and turned away, fury pumping through his veins.

"I cannot allow it to continue, Graeme. They've made the lass's life hell. They won't stop in their attempt to make her unwelcome here."

"I understand," Graeme said in a voice quiet with sympathy.

Bowen tried to collect his thoughts when his only thought was to go to her as quickly as possible. He turned to his brothers—both of them—his expression grim and determined.

"I cannot stay here with her. Even if I send word to her family. I cannot allow her to remain here another day. They hate her. 'Tis no way for Genevieve to live, and she cannot remain a prisoner in her chamber."

He glanced up at Teague and then looked between him and Graeme.

"Will you stay, Teague, and carry out Graeme's wishes as to the fate of the clan and the lands? I must return to Montgomery Keep and bear Genevieve with me so that she will be safe."

Teague looked surprised and glanced at Graeme to gauge his opinion.

"I'm agreeable if you are," Graeme said. " 'Tis a lot to ask, but no more than I asked of Bowen. You have a mess here. 'Tis no doubt on that matter. It's going to require a strong hand and much patience. What say you, Teague? Are you up to the task?"

Teague's expression was solemn, but he nodded. "I'll not tolerate the ridiculousness that Bowen has. 'Tis time someone took a much firmer hand with the lot of them."

Graeme's eyebrows rose. "I hardly call killing three of them having a light hand. Some might say he's been overly intolerant."

"They need to have the wits frightened from them," Teague muttered. "Their women are nothing more than shrewish harpies intent on making everyone around them miserable, and their men are cowardly weaklings."

Graeme turned to Bowen. "Perhaps 'tis best if you send word to Genevieve's family and direct them to Montgomery Keep. Tell them all, but allow them to meet her at our keep. Their anger will be high if they're forced to come to the clan responsible for all the harm done to their daughter. And, with the McHughs so hostile toward Genevieve, 'tis likely the McInnises will come ready to go to war. I wouldn't blame them if they wanted to wipe the earth clean of the McHughs' existence. If they ever did to a daughter of mine what they've done to Genevieve, I would not rest until I'd shed every drop of their blood."

"Aye, 'tis the best course. I would remove her from this place immediately," Bowen said. "If you'll transcribe my words to the McInnis laird, I'll send a messenger before we depart for Montgomery Keep."

Graeme nodded. "Of course. I'll write the message as you dictate it. I'll accompany you back to our keep. I've seen enough. It turns my stomach to remain here any longer."

"If you'll excuse me, I'll go to Genevieve to see if she is all right and also to tell her of our departure," Bowen said. "I'll dictate the letter to her kin, and we'll depart at dawn tomorrow."

CHAPTER 36

Genevieve stood by the fire, warming her still shaking, chilled hands. It wasn't hard for her to imagine harboring such intense hatred for another. She despised Ian and Patrick McHugh with all her heart. But it baffled her that the McHugh clan held such animosity for her over something that was clearly not her doing.

Were it not for the reckless, selfish acts of Ian McHugh, she would even now be married to another.

But it burned in the back of her mind that were she married to another, she would never have met Bowen and she would never have spent a precious night in his arms.

'Twas hard to say if she'd accept all that she'd endured in the past year for that one night, but the time spent loving him had gone a long way toward easing the pain and humiliation of Ian's abuse.

Her door opened and she turned to see Bowen burst in and stride across the room toward her. She was in his arms in but a moment, and he squeezed her so tightly she could barely breathe.

His hand went to her temple, grazing over the small cut, and then both hands swept over her hair, stroking, as if looking for any sign of injury. 'Twas obvious his brother had told him all.

"Are you all right?" he demanded anxiously. "Teague told me what happened. Are you badly hurt?"

She shook her head. "Nay. A slight ache to my head, but 'tis all. I was frightened, but Teague set the matter to rights."

He crushed her to his chest again and kissed the top of her head. "I'm taking you away from here."

She went completely still. She was sure she could not have heard him correctly. Was he finally placing her in an abbey as she'd requested?

"Genevieve?"

He carefully pulled her from his chest and stared intently at her, his gaze questioning.

"Do you not want to go?"

Her breath stuttered over clumsy lips and she tried to smile, knowing she failed miserably.

"Of course I do. 'Tis what I've said I wanted from the start. That you'll see me well placed in an abbey is more than I could have dreamed."

He frowned, his expression turning fierce. " 'Tis not an abbey I intend to see you to. You will ride with me to Montgomery Keep and we leave on the morrow."

Relief made her shaky. She was so overcome that for a moment she simply could not speak. Her hands flew to cover her face as she tried valiantly not to lose her composure.

Bowen grasped her shoulders, his fingers tight. "I am sorry, Genevieve. 'Tis something I should have done long before now. Selfishly, I wanted you here with me and I allowed you to suffer as a result. Teague and Brodie will remain here to see to the mess that is the McHugh clan. I'm taking you from this place, and you'll not be treated in this fashion again."

She threw her arms around his waist and hugged him. Her cheeks were wet, but she kept her face buried in his tunic so that he would not see the intensity of her reaction.

But he knew.

He hugged her just as fiercely, and then finally he pried her away and cupped her chin, his eyes sorrowful and full of regret.

"The joy in which you embrace this news shames me. I should have sent you from this place the moment I knew of your plight. I'm sorry, Genevieve. I'm sorry that I caused you more pain."

She leaned to kiss him and placed both hands on his face. " 'Tis glad I am you didn't send me away from you. The night spent in your arms is one I'll treasure forever."

"I would spend this one with you as well," he said gruffly, his eyes ablaze with desire.

A flutter worked deep in her chest. Her mouth went dry as he bristled, all delicious warrior male. And he wanted her.

It made no sense for a man such as he to want a woman scarred when he could have any woman he wanted at the crook of his finger.

She'd seen the looks the McHugh lasses had thrown his way. She'd heard the blatant invitations, the coy smiles, the boldness with which they made their desires known. And yet not once had he looked their way.

"I'd like that," she said softly as she rubbed her cheek along his chest.

He grasped her shoulders and lowered his head to capture her mouth in a breathtaking, smoldering kiss. There was more demand in his movements tonight. He wasn't as patient or tender as he'd been the previous night. It was as if he'd lost all ability to hold back and he wanted her with a desperation that overtook him.

Excitement coursed through her veins. Heat flushed her skin as her body responded to his demands.

"I want you," he rasped. "God, Genevieve, I want

you so. You're like a drug in my blood. An addiction I have no desire to ever conquer."

He picked her up as if she weighed naught and carried her to the bed, where he dropped her with a soft bounce.

He stood over her, looming, big and fierce, as he quickly divested himself of his clothing. He stripped his tunic over his head and she sucked in her breath at the expanse of muscles, the rock-solid breadth of his chest and his thick shoulders and arms.

So strong, able to protect, and yet capable of being exquisitely tender and loving. So very loving. There was nothing she delighted in more than lying surrounded by those huge arms, knowing that he'd allow nothing to harm her.

He pulled his leggings down and hastily pried his leather boots from his feet, tossing them across the room with no care.

He was magnificent, a study in a warrior's form. Beautiful. Scarred and beautiful.

Realization was stark and strong as it struck her that she was willing to forgive his scars and even considered them beautiful. A mark of who he was. What made him the person he was. Aye, they made him beautiful, and yet she was deeply shamed by the mark on her face. She'd never viewed it as a badge of honor, proof of her survival and the ability to overcome devastating odds. But she was willing to grant those attributes to Bowen, denying herself the same accord.

They both bore scars. They were both survivors. These were marks to be borne with heads held high. Could she ever accept that and stop hiding behind her shame and humiliation? It was a nice thought, but the deepest scars were those unseen, the ones on her heart and her soul and her mind. And those were the most difficult to overcome.

"I'm going to take your clothing piece by piece so that

I may enjoy seeing each part of you bared before me," he said in a husky, passion-laced voice. "And then I'm going to love you until dawn's rays reach through the window and signal our departure."

Her pulse leapt to life and she arched restlessly, impatient to feel his hands on her body, coaxing it to life.

Never had she known pleasure at a man's hand until now. Until Bowen.

He settled on the edge of the bed and began working at the lacings on her dress. With patience he'd not displayed while undressing himself, he worked at disrobing her, removing her clothes piece by piece, his gaze soaking in her body as it was bared.

"You are a sight to behold, lass," Bowen breathed as he divested her of the last remaining piece.

She lay naked on the bed, vulnerable and open to his look, his touch. Her nipples were achingly erect, anticipating his mouth and hands. And her most feminine flesh pulsed as she remembered his mouth and tongue stroking over sensitive points.

Never could she have imagined the act of coupling as being a give-and-take, an act of mutual pleasure on the part of the man and the woman. With Bowen it wasn't just him taking, her giving and being left with naught.

He gave all he received and often more. He was patient and exacting, ensuring that he gave her as much pleasure as she gave him.

For that reason, she wanted this night to be special. One that he'd long remember. Relying on her instincts—she'd never done more than lie and endure Ian's brutality—she levered herself up and smoothed her hands over Bowen's broad chest.

She kissed him, taking the lead, exhibiting a new boldness that was completely foreign to her. He groaned and melted into her touch, tilting precariously until she placed both hands on his chest to prevent him from coming down on top of her.

She maneuvered up to her knees so she would have position over him and then fused her mouth to his, hotly and as demanding as he'd been, and she bore him down to the bed.

He landed with a slight bounce, his eyes widening and darkening in the same breath. She kissed him deeply, taking her cue from the way he'd kissed her the night before.

Then she straddled him, taking him between her knees. His erection strained upward, resting against the sensitive skin of her belly, and she tentatively touched him, circling his girth with her fingers.

He flinched and she yanked her hands away, fearful that she'd hurt him in some way.

"God no, lass, touch me. Don't take your hands away," he groaned. "'Tis heaven, your fingers around me."

Relieved that he'd liked her boldness, she gently took him in her grasp again, exploring his length and the fascinating mix of steel and velvety softness.

He sighed and arched in her grasp. His entire body was taut, and she marveled at the idea that she could bring him such pleasure with something as simple as a few caresses.

Reveling in her newfound role as temptress, she allowed her hands free rein, gliding over the dips and curves of his rock-hard body. She explored every inch of his flesh, delighting in the power she had to make him shudder and moan.

She leaned down and pressed her mouth to the flat of his belly. She smiled when his muscles bunched and coiled and his hands curled into tight fists at his sides. He'd made no move to stop her sensual assault. He lay back, his jaw tight and his eyes half-lidded as he tracked her every movement.

Then she lifted her head and hesitated, unsure of how to voice the question that plagued her.

He put his fingers to her hair, gently pushing the tresses behind her ears as he stroked downward.

"What is it, lass? You have a look of worry in your eyes, and 'tis the last thing I want you thinking on when you pleasure me so with your lips and hands."

She took a deep breath, summoning her courage. "Do you remember last night when you put your mouth . . ." She blushed to the roots of her hair even thinking of verbalizing her thoughts.

"Where, lass?" he asked gently. "Do you mean when I kissed you betwixt your legs and put my tongue to your womanly parts?"

She nodded shyly. "Aye."

"Did you enjoy it when I kissed you there?"

She nodded again. "Aye, I did. I wondered . . ."

"Say what's on your mind, love. You have nothing to fear with me. There's no need to be shy, no matter how adorable you are when you're so hesitant. 'Tis the truth when you gift me with that shy smile I want nothing more than to press you to the bed and sink into you over and over."

Her face went warm with pleasure at his heated words. It was obvious he meant every one of them and they weren't pretty words meant to woo or distract her.

"I thought if 'twas so pleasurable for me to have your mouth . . . there . . . that perhaps you would find pleasure if I were to use my mouth . . . here," she whispered as her hands found his length once more.

He went absolutely still. His jaw was clenched and his eyes blazed with quiet intensity. His fingers curled and uncurled, gripping the sheets and pulling them tight.

Then he lifted his hands and cupped her breasts before gliding upward to feather over her face.

"I cannot imagine anything sweeter than your mouth around me, lass. But I do not want you to do such for me, only to please me. Just your hands upon me brings me greater pleasure than I ever dreamed."

She leaned forward again until their mouths were but a breath apart. Their gazes connected, soulful and wanting. She kissed him, savoring each second they were in contact.

" 'Tis the truth it would bring me as much pleasure to taste and explore you," she whispered.

He groaned and closed his eyes, almost as if he were doing everything in his power to keep his control tightly reined.

"I am ever your servant," he said hoarsely. "Do with me as you will. I'll never gainsay you. I am yours to do with as you wish."

Her confidence bolstered by the obvious approval in his eyes and his words, she kissed a path down his jaw to his neck, where she stopped to tease and nip.

She savored every moan, every quick intake of breath, every time his body tightened in obvious approval of her actions.

She worked her way down, pausing to pay special attention to the wound on his chest, kissing every inch of the puckered flesh. Then she made her way farther still, teasing a line to his navel.

He jerked when she slid her tongue around the shallow indention and then delved within. Chill bumps danced across his pelvis and his belly.

As she moved lower, his erection bumped her chin and she paused to curl her fingers around his massive length. She wasn't entirely certain as to what she was doing. It was new territory for her. But instincts made up for a lot, and she was confident enough to follow those instincts.

She kissed the base, just above the wiry hairs that covered the heavy sac between his legs. Tentatively, she cupped his cods and massaged gently as she worked her way to the very tip with her lips and tongue.

By the time she reached the head, Bowen was gasping and his back was bowed tight in an arch, his hips up off the bed.

Growing bolder, she took the flared tip into her mouth and swirled her tongue over the ridges and toward the back. Then she lowered her mouth, taking more of him inside.

A warm spurt of liquid took her by surprise. It seeped from the tip and fell onto her tongue. At first she thought he'd already found his release, but 'twas just a small amount and he grew even more rigid between her lips.

"You make me insensible," Bowen gasped. "Never has a woman driven me to the brink of madness thus."

Running her tongue up the back side of his shaft, she let the tip fall from her mouth and grasped the base with one hand as she positioned herself astride him.

She wasn't even sure such a thing was done, but she was fascinated by the idea of complete role reversal. If Bowen had used his mouth on her, then she would use her mouth on him. And if he'd been atop her, then she'd be atop him.

She watched him for any sign of disapproval or that he didn't want her taking such a presumptive position. But, if anything, he looked eager. Excited. She, in turn, was excited that she could inspire such a reaction from him.

"That's it, lass," Bowen purred. "Take me inside you. Ride astride me."

His fingers closed around her hips, easily spanning the width with his large hands. As she positioned him at her entrance, he held her in place, offering her support. When he slipped inside her the barest inch, he began to pull her down his erection, inch by exquisite inch.

She let out a breathy sigh as she threw back her head. His groan mixed with her sigh as he penetrated deeper. Her eyes widened when her bottom came to rest atop his legs as he reached maximum depth.

She was full, stretched impossibly tight around him. She didn't know how she'd managed to accommodate all of him, but there wasn't a part of him that wasn't inside her.

"If I died right now, I'd die the happiest of men," Bowen gasped. "Never have I felt such pleasure."

She looked at him in befuddlement, because now that she'd accomplished the task of taking him within her, she had no idea what to do next. Her expression must have made this clear, because he slipped his fingers underneath her behind and gently lifted, arching his hips upward as he worked her hips up and down to meet his thrusts.

Her body was taut and her desire heightened by the different position. Every time he pushed inside her, his pelvis pressed against her sensitive mound and sparks of pleasure shot through her body.

After a time, she learned the rhythm and was able to take over, riding astride him as she braced herself with her palms on his chest. He moved his hands from her hips and cupped her breasts, toying with the nipples as she moved atop him.

It was enough to spur her own desire, sending her into a dizzying spiral as she spun out of control.

Her cries mingled with Bowen's as her release rushed over her, spurring Bowen's own. She tightened around him, spasming as his hot seed filled her, reaching the very depths of her.

And then he pulled her down, holding her tightly

against his chest as it heaved with exertion. He stroked her hair, her back, let his hands glide over her bottom as she lay atop him, his shaft still buried deep within her, pulsing with the last of his release.

"Was I overbold?" she asked as she rested her cheek over his thudding heartbeat.

He chuckled, his chest rumbling with amusement. "I invite you to be as bold as you like and I'll not ever complain."

A smile played about her lips as she nuzzled up underneath his chin.

"I liked tasting you," she said shyly.

He groaned and swelled inside her, stretching her once more. She lifted her head and looked into his eyes in shock.

"Do not look at me with such surprise, lass," he said dryly. "How do you expect me to respond when you speak thusly?"

"But 'tis so soon!" she exclaimed. "Ian never . . ." She broke off, ashamed that she'd been about to make comment on Ian's actions in bed.

He touched her in an effort to soothe her distress. "You have that effect on me, lass. You do things to me I've never experienced. I'll want you always. I don't know that I'll ever have enough."

He wrapped his arms around her and rolled atop her so their positions were reversed. He pushed forward, stroking to the very heart of her so she could feel he was fully erect once more.

"As you can see, I'm very much ready to have you again," he murmured.

She lifted her head to kiss him. "Then have me, warrior. Have your fill. The night is young yet and we have until dawn."

CHAPTER 37

Genevieve didn't sleep the entire night. Even when Bowen had drifted into a contented slumber after spending many hours loving her, she'd remained awake, focused on the fact that in just a few hours she would be rid of this place once and for all.

Excitement bounded in her veins. She had no idea of Bowen's plans, but he was taking her away and 'twas enough to fill her heart with relief and joy.

No more would she suffer the taunts and abuse of others. No more would she be forced to live in a place that held nothing but memories of pain and humiliation.

It was the hour before dawn when she realized that she had not spoken to Taliesan of her departure. Taliesan was the only person she would miss, the only person who'd been friend and ally to her at McHugh Keep.

Genevieve slipped from the bed, leaving Bowen to sleep as she quietly dressed. Then she went next door to Taliesan's chamber and let herself in. It was dark within the chamber, with only a few dying coals in the hearth to give light.

She went to Taliesan's bed and touched the girl's shoulder in an effort to wake her.

"Taliesan. Taliesan," Genevieve whispered.

Taliesan stirred and turned over. "Genevieve? Is aught amiss?"

Her voice was groggy and heavy with sleep.

"Nay," Genevieve whispered back. "I came to say goodbye."

Taliesan sat straight up in bed, pushing the covers aside. Then she started to scramble up and Genevieve put out a hand to halt her.

"What is it you have need of?" Genevieve asked.

"I wanted to light a candle so that I may see your face," Taliesan said.

"Remain in bed. I'll light a candle and fetch it back to the bed."

Genevieve went to the fireplace and added logs so that the flames would begin anew. Once a steady flame licked over the wood, she lit a candle and brought it back to the bed where Taliesan sat, her brow etched with concern.

"What is happening, Genevieve? Tell me you aren't striking out on your own again. I worry for you so."

Genevieve smiled and reached to cover Taliesan's hand with her own. She gave it a gentle squeeze. "Your friendship means much to me, Talie. 'Tis the only bright spot in the year I've been imprisoned here. But I am a prisoner no more. Bowen is taking me away. We are traveling to Montgomery Keep. I am free."

Taliesan reached forward and pulled Genevieve tightly into her arms. Her hug was fierce, and Genevieve could feel the wetness of Taliesan's tears on her neck.

"I am so glad for you, Genevieve. You deserve happiness."

"I could not leave without first giving you my thanks and telling you goodbye. I will miss you, Talie. I will not miss anything of this place except for you."

Taliesan pulled away, her eyes wet with tears. "I will miss you as well, Genevieve, but 'tis glad I am that you are away from here."

"I wish I did not have to leave you," Genevieve said

unhappily. "'Tis not a happy place to be, and 'tis not known what the fate of the McHugh clan will be."

Taliesan shrugged. "They have made their fate. Now they—we—must face the consequences of all we have sown."

"God be with you, Talie. And may we one day meet again."

Taliesan hugged her again. "And God be with you, Genevieve. If we should never meet, I will long carry our friendship and cherish it."

Genevieve caught her hands and squeezed. "I must go back now. There is much to be done before dawn, and 'tis when we are leaving."

"I will be down to see you off," Taliesan promised.

Genevieve smiled warmly at her. "I would like that."

Genevieve leaned over to kiss Taliesan on the cheek and then hurried toward the door before sadness overwhelmed her. It made no sense to suffer any regret over her departure, but she would miss Taliesan. The lass had been a warm and welcoming face in a sea of hatred and animosity. Genevieve would never forget it, or the kindness that Taliesan had shown her.

When she let herself back into her chamber, Bowen was awake and dressing by the fire. He glanced up, relief lighting his eyes.

"I did not know where you'd gone," he said gruffly. "You worried me."

She went to him, hugging him fiercely. He seemed surprised by the spontaneous gesture and hugged her back, holding her to him for a long moment.

"I was but saying my farewell to Taliesan," she said quietly. "She is the only person I shall miss. She is the only person who has been kind to me during my sojourn here."

"She is a good lass, with a valiant heart," Bowen said. "Aye, 'tis true, that."

"We have a short time before we depart," Bowen advised. "Is there anything you wish to take with you?"

"Only the chest at the foot of the bed," she said in a low voice. "'Tis all that survived the attack on my escort. It has the bow my father gave me, and my wedding dress my mother sewed herself. Ian destroyed all else. I would take them if 'tis acceptable. They are all I have left of my parents."

He touched her cheek. "Of course, lass. 'Tis not too much of a burden for you to take your belongings. I will see that they are packed in a cart to bear back to Montgomery Keep. Pack anything else you wish to take with you inside the chest and I'll have my men bring it down."

"Thank you," she said, touching his cheek in kind. "I'm ever grateful to you, Bowen. No one has ever shown me such kindness. I'm overwhelmed."

He brought her palm to his lips and pressed a kiss to the soft flesh. "Your happiness means much to me," he said simply. "Now, let us go and prepare for our journey. Graeme will be anxious to return to Eveline, and I must say my farewells to Teague and Brodie."

CHAPTER 38

Genevieve waited nervously by the horse Bowen had selected for her to ride. Bowen was conversing with his two brothers and Brodie Armstrong a short distance away, and she knew once Bowen said his farewells to Teague, Graeme would come over, because Bowen said he wished to be introduced to her.

It was enough to make her break out into a cold sweat.

She knew that Bowen would have told his brother all about her situation, and it sickened her that others would know of her shame. She'd tried to wear her cape and hood, but Bowen had stoutly refused to allow her to hide behind it, stating that she had no reason to hide, no reason to be ashamed.

Still, she bore it in the sack tied to her saddlebag, because she could not bear the thought of facing Bowen's entire clan without the barrier of her hood.

To her surprise, Teague and Brodie both accompanied Graeme and Bowen over to where she stood. Brodie was the first to offer his farewell. He simply ruffled her hair in a gesture that astonished her. As if she were a beloved little sister that he teased mercilessly. It warmed her and made her feel that she had a place among these people.

"Be well and happy," Brodie offered.

"Thank you," she said, her voice heavy with emotion.

Teague pulled her into a hug and kissed her forehead in an affectionate manner.

She clung fiercely to him, hugging him in return. "Thank you for your aid," she whispered.

"I was glad to give it," he said sincerely. "Safe journey to you."

And then Teague and Brodie walked away, deep in conversation, and she was left alone with Bowen and his older brother, Graeme, the laird.

She licked her lips nervously and peeked up at Graeme. He was not as fierce as she'd imagined. He had a kind, thoughtful look that gave her hope. He was rumored to be a fair man, though he was fiercely loyal and protective of those he loved.

And 'twas well known he adored his wife.

"'Tis good to make your acquaintance, Genevieve," Graeme said in a gentle tone. "I've heard much about you and the trials you have suffered. I want to offer my assurance that no such thing will occur on Montgomery land. You will be afforded protection and respect during your stay with our clan."

She had to bite her lip to prevent the flow of tears. She blinked rapidly and performed a deep curtsy in front of Graeme, chiding herself not to become a weepy mess in front of him.

"I'm ever grateful, Laird," she said sincerely.

Graeme nodded, then turned to Bowen. "If your business here is complete, let us be on our way. I'd see my wife as soon as possible. I do not like being parted from her."

"We are ready," Bowen said in a voice that told her he was as ready to be done with McHugh Keep as she was.

He held out his hand to assist Genevieve onto her mount. He lifted her high, and she slid into place on the saddle, excitement and nervousness assailing her.

She was truly leaving this place.

She could barely contain herself as she waited for the men to mount and give the call to move out.

Such a beautiful day. Symbolic. There wasn't a cloud in the sky. No fog. The morning sun cast a glow over a pink-and-lavender sky. If ever there were a more perfect day to set out and put her past behind her, this was it.

Bowen rode up beside her and reached over to clasp her hand. He squeezed and gave her a smile that warmed her to her toes.

Ahead, Graeme gave the call to move ahead. The gate to the courtyard creaked open and the Montgomery warriors began to file out one by one. Graeme fell into line just ahead of Bowen and Genevieve, and Bowen motioned her forward so that she was between him and Graeme.

From the corner of her eye she saw Taliesan trying to hurry toward the gate, but she was hampered by her heavy limp. Genevieve gave a cry of alarm when Taliesan stumbled, but Brodie was suddenly there to steady her. Then, to Genevieve's surprise, Brodie scooped her up and strode at a fast clip toward the gate so that Taliesan would be there when Genevieve rode past.

Taliesan's cheeks were stained with color, but she held her head high and waved bravely despite the tears of grief in her eyes as Genevieve rode past.

Genevieve kissed her fingers and extended them in Taliesan's direction. Her one true friend—her only friend.

"Safe journey to you," Taliesan called. "Be happy, Genevieve. Be happy."

"Farewell," Genevieve called. Then to Brodie she said in a fierce voice, "Take care of her, Brodie. Look after her well."

Brodie gave Genevieve a salute and then she was past the gate, following behind the line of Montgomery warriors that extended to the nearby hillside.

When she reached the top of the hill, temptation was too great and she swiveled in the saddle, looking back at the keep in the distance.

For a place she knew to be filled with darkness and pain, it looked much like any other keep. Seemingly harmless. Not a place of such evilness.

"Do not look back, Genevieve," Bowen said in a quiet voice next to her. "There is nothing for you there."

"Nay," she agreed, taking one last glance at the symbol of her imprisonment. "There is naught for me there. I'll not look back ever again."

She turned as her horse rode on and she notched her chin up, determined not to give way to the overwhelming sadness eating at her soul.

She knew not what her future held. But she was free of her past. From here onward, her future was what she made it. Bowen had given her something long denied her. A choice. And she was determined not to make foolish choices.

She glanced sideways at Bowen, wondering how much of a role he would play in her future. He acted as though he cared for her, but she knew not if his feelings were driven by pity or something much deeper. He hadn't spoken of his feelings—or the future—other than to tell her that he was taking her away.

He'd once promised her a place within his clan, as a Montgomery. But what did that mean? Was she to be his leman, as she'd once offered? Or was she to be treated merely as a cousin or sister or clansman and once they were home the passion between them would cool and become a distant memory?

She tried not to dwell on all the what-ifs and unknowns because it would do naught but drive her to madness.

She had to focus on the fact that she was being given a chance to start anew. She was free of the horrifying abuse that Ian had subjected her to for an entire year. He was dead. Patrick was dead. No one could hurt her anymore. Bowen had sworn that he would protect her from any threat. He was an honorable man, and she took him at his word.

Somehow, someway, she'd find her place in a new clan. And she'd find a way to make it up to Eveline, Graeme's beloved wife, for the horror she'd put her through. And pray that Eveline could find it in her heart to forgive her.

"How far is it to your lands?" Genevieve asked Bowen.

" 'Tis a half day's ride if we go hard. 'Tis more likely we'll arrive in the late afternoon. I don't want to overtax you, and there's no urgency to our return other than Graeme's wanting to ride to Armstrong Keep to collect his wife."

"He must love her a lot," Genevieve said softly.

Bowen smiled, his eyes warming at the mention of his sister by marriage. "Aye, he does. He's a fool for her and does not mind it one bit. Eveline has him completely wrapped, but to her credit she loves him just as fiercely as he loves her."

"And she does not hear?"

Bowen shook his head. "Nay, she is deaf. She has the ability to read lips, though, so have a care when speaking around her. She didn't speak for three long years, but she's broken her silence and her speech improves the more she practices."

"She sounds like an amazing lass," Genevieve said. " 'Tis no wonder Graeme loves her so."

"I think the two of you have much in common," Bowen said quietly. "You've both survived difficult circumstances. You're both strong despite your fragile appearance."

Only, Eveline Montgomery hadn't been made a whore.

She hadn't been forced to spread her legs for Ian McHugh and any other man of his choosing. It was a fact Genevieve could never forget.

Graeme lagged back so that Genevieve and Bowen caught up and rode at his side.

"Up the way, I'm going to part ways and take half my men with me to Armstrong Keep so that I may retrieve Eveline. We'll arrive at Montgomery Keep on the morrow."

Bowen nodded.

"I must send word to our king to apprise him of all that has occurred and of the McGrieves' involvement in the attack against us. I still have not heard from him on the missive I sent regarding the action we took in claiming McHugh Keep and ridding the world of Ian and Patrick."

Graeme's gaze fell on Genevieve as he spoke.

"Bowen tells me I have you to thank for killing Patrick. 'Twas your arrow that felled him."

Genevieve shifted uncomfortably on the horse and ducked her head.

"Aye, 'twas her arrow," Bowen said proudly. "She felled more than one warrior in the course of battle. She's proved herself worthy of any soldier in our army."

" 'Tis impressive, and you have my thanks," Graeme said. "Not only for removing Patrick as a threat but for saving my brother during battle. He is important to me, and I'd not have him killed if I can help it."

Genevieve smiled. "I was happy to do it. I had no wish for Bowen to die, either."

"You'll like our clan, Genevieve. I have a feeling our sister, Rorie, will make a fast ally of you. You won't have a choice, I fear. Rorie tends to do things her own way and she doesn't take no for an answer. She'll pester you until she has your entire story."

A peculiar look crossed Bowen's face. Sadness dulled

his eyes for the briefest of moments, but before she could ask him about it he shook it off and joined Graeme in teasing about Rorie and her doggedness.

For the next hours, they rode in companionable silence, every once in a while speaking of mundane things. After a time, Graeme called a halt and took half his men and bade Bowen farewell, promising that he and Eveline would be along the next morning.

Bowen and Genevieve continued north with a contingent of Montgomery warriors, while Graeme headed west toward Armstrong land.

With each passing mile, Genevieve grew more nervous as they drew closer to the Montgomery border.

A shout went up in early afternoon as they crossed over onto Montgomery land. An hour later, the keep came into view and Genevieve leaned forward in the saddle, drinking in the sight of the distant fortress.

It was nestled close to the banks of a river and the hillsides were lush and green. A herd of grazing sheep covered one entire hillside, while horses dotted yet another. On either side of the keep were cottages, clean and sturdy, and more within the keep, lining the stone wall that surrounded the main building.

It was obvious the Montgomerys had done plenty to ensure the well-being of their clan. The keep was well fortified. Children played along one side of the keep as mothers kept close watch. Warriors trained within the courtyard walls while others went about their tasks. Women washed clothing in the river while others tended a plot of crops on the front side of the keep stretching as far as the eye could see.

This was a clan of wealth and power. They obviously feared no one, and they protected their own.

She'd been right to set Ian on a path to anger the Montgomerys, no matter how wrong she may have been to involve Eveline. The Montgomerys would suffer no wrong done to one of their own, and they'd done just as she hoped and come with a vengeance.

Thank God she was free. Thank God she was gone from that terrible place. She stared hard at Montgomery Keep, for now it was her future. She would become one of them, because Genevieve McInnis had died one long year ago.

CHAPTER 39

When Bowen and Genevieve rode into the courtyard of Montgomery Keep, Genevieve's gaze was drawn to a young lass, who looked remarkably like Bowen, standing on the steps of the keep with what appeared to be a young priest.

The lass had long dark hair and vibrant blue eyes. Just like Bowen's. She was small in stature, her bone structure delicate and feminine. Yet the lass didn't look as if she'd reached womanhood yet. There were no curves or softer flesh. She was lanky, which only added to the delicacy of her bone structure.

Even her face was constructed on a small scale, her eyes seemingly too large for such ethereal features.

"'Tis my sister, Rorie," Bowen said, following her gaze. "Beside her is Father Drummond, who is tasked with teaching the little hoyden how to read and write. She's quite determined on that score."

Genevieve's eyes widened. "She must be a smart lass."

Bowen chuckled. "I don't know if it's that she's smart or that she's just stubborn. 'Tis likely a bit of both."

As soon as Bowen reined in his horse, Rorie flew across the courtyard, and when he slid from the saddle she launched herself into his arms.

Bowen hugged her tightly and whirled her around in a circle.

" 'Tis good to see you, lass," he said, genuine affection brimming in his eyes.

"I've missed you, Bowen! You've been gone far too long."

Bowen set Rorie down and then immediately went to help Genevieve dismount from her horse. He kept hold of her hand and pulled her toward Rorie, whose curious stare fixed boldly on Genevieve.

Genevieve cursed the fact that she'd forgotten to pull out her cape and hood. She felt naked and vulnerable, with no way to hide her hideous scarring. Even now she could feel Rorie's intent gaze sweeping over her face, and she wanted the earth to open and swallow her up.

"Who have you brought with you, Bowen?" Rorie chirped.

The lass seemed unfazed by Genevieve's scars, but she was still watching Genevieve intently.

Bowen held out his arm to his sister to pull her in close, so that he held both women in his arms.

"Rorie, this is Genevieve McInnis. She will be staying with us. Genevieve, this is my sister, Rorie. She's the baby, coming far after Graeme, me, and Teague. She's quite the brat, so forgive any rudeness that comes from her mouth."

Rorie huffed and rolled her eyes. " 'Tis a pleasure to meet you, Genevieve. Eveline will be glad of another friendly face around here. She's still finding her way around our clan, though things are a bit better now that she got herself abducted and rescued. Fear has a way of mending fences within a clan. But then they were all likely afraid Graeme was going to have all their hides." She shrugged. "At any rate, the matter is done with."

Genevieve's eyes widened at Rorie's blunt, matter-of-fact manner. Bowen chuckled and shook his head.

"I did warn you, Genevieve."

Rorie reached forward and grabbed Genevieve's hand.

"Come. I'll show you above stairs. There's only one spare chamber, so it isn't a mystery where you'll be staying. 'Tis the room next to mine, so we'll be seeing a lot of each other. Bowen can ensure your things are brought up."

Genevieve glanced quickly at Bowen, but he smiled and waved her on. Hesitantly, she allowed Rorie to pull her toward the keep, where Father Drummond was still standing.

"Father, I have someone I want you to meet," Rorie called out. "This is Genevieve McInnis, and she'll be staying with us. I'm afraid we'll have to cancel this afternoon's lesson. I'm showing Genevieve to her room."

Father Drummond smiled, and Genevieve was warmed by the welcome in his eyes.

"'Tis good to make your acquaintance, Genevieve," Father Drummond said, his voice soft and kind. "I hope you'll find your accommodations to your liking, and that you'll enjoy your stay with the Montgomerys. A finer clan I have not found."

"I'm discovering that," Genevieve said quietly.

"Come, Genevieve. Time's a-wasting," Rorie said, pulling her toward the inside of the keep.

Genevieve allowed herself to be dragged through the hall and up the stairs to the third level, where a row of chambers lined the hall.

Rorie directed her to one in the middle, but she paused outside a door and put her hand on it. "This is my chamber. Bowen's is across the hall, and Graeme and Eveline's is at the very end. Teague has the one on the other side of you. If you ever have need of anything, just knock on my door. I don't bite. I promise."

Genevieve smiled. She couldn't help but like the younger lass. "Thank you. I will."

They went to the next door and Rorie opened it and pushed in, gesturing widely.

"This is your chamber. 'Tis bare at the moment, but we can remedy that. No one has occupied it in quite some time. It's used for honored guests, but we have few of those. I can help you soften it and make it not so harsh. 'Tis not fit for a woman as it stands. It could use some flowers and feminine objects."

"You're very kind," Genevieve said softly.

Rorie plopped onto the bed, bouncing as she landed. "So what's your story, Genevieve? I'm alive with curiosity. I've heard nothing about you. No word was sent ahead, and Bowen has never brought home a woman. He has no need to. They follow him wherever he goes."

Genevieve's eyes widened. "He's that popular with the lasses?"

Rorie snorted. "Have you looked at him? There's not a fairer face in all the Highlands. He's prettier than most women. They either want him or are jealous of him. He can't walk for tripping over a lass batting her eyes at him."

Genevieve automatically raised her hand to cover the scar on her cheek. Why then was he bothering with her? 'Twas obvious he could have any lass he wanted, and there were many far more comely than she. And not as damaged and *sullied*.

Rorie looked chagrined. "I'm sorry, Genevieve. 'Tis a well-known fact that my mouth becomes carried away and that I prattle on about things I should not. My brothers despair of me, but they love me, and so I escape their censure. Most of the time," she added hastily.

Genevieve couldn't help but smile. The lass was charming in her own way, and Genevieve couldn't help liking her.

There was a knock on the door, and Rorie hastened to open it.

"Oh, 'tis your trunk!" Rorie exclaimed.

Bowen appeared with two men bearing her trunk.

They brought it inside, and Genevieve directed them to put it at the end of her bed.

Bowen looked as though he wanted to say something, but Rorie immediately began shooing him from the chamber.

"Not now, Bowen. Genevieve and I are conversing. I'll bring her down for the evening meal when we are done."

Bowen suppressed a grin and looked helplessly at Genevieve. "You see what we all have to suffer."

Genevieve smiled, comforted by the feeling of family around her. 'Twas just as it had been with her own clan. Though she hadn't had siblings, there had been countless cousins and clansmen who bickered good-naturedly. And Sybil, her closest friend since childhood.

For a moment, Genevieve was saddened. It had been agreed that Sybil would come to Genevieve once Genevieve was married, and that Genevieve's husband would arrange a marriage for her through his clan so the two lasses would not be separated.

It had been months since Genevieve had thought on Sybil. She'd put her friend from her mind because it was too painful to think on her.

But the antics within the Montgomery clan had made her remember.

"You look sad," Rorie said bluntly as she closed the door.

Genevieve shook off the melancholy surrounding her and forced a smile. "I was only thinking of my own clan and how you and Bowen remind me of my kin and of my childhood friend Sybil. I miss them."

Rorie pulled Genevieve down onto the bed and leveled a determined stare at her. "Tell me, Genevieve. How does a McInnis lass find herself among McHughs, and why does your clan think you dead?"

Genevieve sighed. Apparently Rorie had been told of

her circumstances, or at least a cursory telling. It was to be expected. The lass would have been curious.

There was no good reason Genevieve should tell her anything at all. But there was something about Rorie that inspired Genevieve to unburden herself. The lass might be younger, but her mind was sharp and her heart was good. And perhaps it was the promise of having a confidante that enticed Genevieve the most. She wanted to fit in here. Wanted . . . friendship.

And so she found herself telling Rorie the entire tale, even the part she played in Eveline's abduction, because she didn't want Rorie finding out later and feeling betrayed or enraged that Genevieve had been less than honest. And it all would come out eventually. There was no way around it.

Rorie's mouth gaped open, and her expressions were almost comical as she reacted to Genevieve's story. By the time Genevieve brought things to the present, Rorie had grasped Genevieve's hands and held them tightly.

" 'Tis a terrible, heart-breaking tale," Rorie burst out. There were tears in her eyes, and Genevieve was shocked at the lass's reaction.

"I'm glad you killed them," Rorie said fiercely. " 'Tis no less than they deserved. They deserved to suffer far more. They should have been gutted and left for the buzzards to feed on their carcasses."

Genevieve laughed, some of the horrible tension leaving her chest. Her laughter ended in a low sob, and Rorie pulled her into her arms, hugging her until Genevieve thought she might smother.

It felt so good. Both the unburdening and the offer of comfort from the younger lass. Genevieve could feel some of the protective barriers she'd held for so long begin to unravel in the warmth of the Montgomery family.

"I am glad you are here," Rorie said when she finally pulled away. "You'll be happy with us, Genevieve."

Genevieve smiled wanly. "I only hope Eveline can be as understanding as you."

"Eveline has the biggest heart of any lass I know. You'll love her, and she'll love you. I don't think she has it within her to hate *anyone,* and if she doesn't hate my clan after all they put her through, I don't see her harboring ill will against you either."

Genevieve let out a sigh of relief. Maybe this would all work out. Maybe she'd finally found a . . . *home.* A safe harbor from all the pain of the last year.

"Come, let's unpack your trunk so that you can settle into your chamber and your new life here," Rorie said cheerfully. "Then we can go down for the evening meal together."

Genevieve allowed Rorie to dictate the pace as the two women unpacked the items from her trunk. Rorie kept up a lively chatter that made Genevieve's head spin.

In all the time Genevieve had spent at McHugh Keep, she'd never once unpacked her trunk, though so few of her belongings had survived Ian's spite. It would have been too much like admitting defeat. She'd left every item packed, hoping beyond hope that one day she'd leave that place.

Though she would never return home to her father's lands, already she felt at home here at Montgomery Keep. Hope flowed into her soul, something she'd thought never to feel again.

She was free, and with people who would not harm her. There was nothing sweeter than *finally* knowing peace.

CHAPTER 40

Genevieve did wear her cloak to the evening meal. She had no wish to be the object of so much scrutiny as soon as she arrived. She knew at some point all would know of her scars and it was something she would have to deal with, but until she became more comfortable in her surroundings she preferred obscurity.

Rorie accompanied her downstairs. The two lasses had remained above stairs, unpacking Genevieve's meager belongings and moving other objects into Genevieve's chamber in order to make it more inviting.

The finished product delighted Genevieve. Her chamber rivaled her own chamber at her father's keep. It was comfortable and lavish, fit for an important guest.

Rorie had changed the bedding and added furs to the flooring and in front of the hearth. Large candles were placed around the room to lend brightness to the interior. Comfortable chairs had been moved within. Not a single detail had been overlooked. Genevieve could hardly believe it. She felt like a pampered princess when she'd spent the last year as the lowliest whore.

And when Rorie had seen the few dresses that Genevieve owned, she'd instantly vowed to set the women of the keep to sewing more for Genevieve.

Rorie urged her down the stairs and into the hall, where it already bustled with activity as the evening meal was being served. She hurried toward the raised dais, where Bowen already sat, and beamed at her brother as she directed Genevieve to take one of the empty places on either side of Bowen.

Rorie took the other one, her eyes dancing with excitement as she scooted the bench closer to the table.

Bowen reached underneath the table and curled his fingers around Genevieve's hand, squeezing in a silent message. The gesture comforted her and she squeezed back.

"Do your new accommodations fit your needs?" he asked. "And did Rorie manage to settle you in?"

" 'Tis perfect," Genevieve said in a sincere voice. "Rorie did far too much. I feel like a pampered princess. 'Twas not necessary to go to so much trouble."

Bowen shot Rorie a grateful look. "There was every reason. I want you to be comfortable and happy. You've suffered enough ill fortune. 'Tis time for someone to care for you as they should."

Her cheeks heated at the intimacy in his voice. She prayed that Rorie hadn't been paying attention to all that Bowen had said.

" 'Tis odd not to have Graeme, Teague, and Eveline at the evening meal," Rorie said. " 'Tis my hope that everyone will be returned soon. There is too much chaos of late. 'Twas much better when nothing ever happened and it was quiet around the keep."

Though her tone was teasing, Genevieve didn't miss the wistful note that crept into her voice. The lass obviously loved her family and missed them when they weren't near.

"Graeme and Eveline will be home on the morrow," Bowen supplied. "I know not when Teague will be returned. He is assuming my duties at McHugh Keep."

Rorie's face fell and she looked down at her plate, toying with the food in front of her.

"He'll not stay gone forever, sweeting," Bowen said in a gentle voice.

He leaned toward Genevieve. "Rorie is especially close to Teague. She's taking his absence hard."

Genevieve nodded, and then she paused, staring at Bowen.

"Do you know what I like best about Montgomery Keep so far?"

Bowen cocked his head, his lips curving into a delighted smile. "What's that?"

"The food," she exclaimed. "If I am never forced to eat another meal prepared by a McHugh, it will be too soon."

Bowen laughed, a deep, rich, throaty sound that was pleasurable to Genevieve's ears.

"I find I agree with you there, lass."

Rorie's nose wrinkled. "Was it so bad?"

"Yes!" Bowen and Genevieve answered in unison.

Rorie laughed. "'Tis little wonder, then, that you haven't fallen on the meal before you."

"I'm trying to exert a little control," Genevieve said with a grin.

Bowen and Rorie both chuckled.

What Genevieve noticed most was that the members of the Montgomery clan were open and friendly. Rorie had related that it hadn't always been so, and that the women of the clan, particularly, had shown a lot of animosity toward Eveline when Graeme had married her.

Genevieve had felt instant sympathy for Eveline, because she knew well what it was like to have such hatred directed at her.

But so far the women—and the men—had been nothing but courteous and warm toward Genevieve. She had no idea if 'twas their natural inclination or Bowen had issued a stern warning.

Bowen leaned over so his words would only be heard

by Genevieve. "When we've finished our meal, let's take a walk. I'll show you the outside of the keep."

There was more in his voice, a frustration that they hadn't spent any time together since their arrival. Her cheeks grew warm with pleasure, and she smiled back at him.

"I'd like that."

This time it was she who found his hand under the table and gave it a squeeze. He laced his fingers through hers and held tightly until they were forced to disentangle their hands in order to eat.

At the finish, Rorie looked expectantly in Genevieve's direction, but Bowen was quick to interject himself.

"I am taking Genevieve around the grounds outside the keep. I'll escort her to her chamber when we are finished. There's no need for you to wait on her."

Rorie pursed her lips and surveyed Bowen and Genevieve with a keen eye, which told Genevieve the lass wasn't fooled in the least. A grin curved her lips and a mischievous light entered her eyes.

"I think I shall go find Father Drummond, since we missed this morning's lessons. Perhaps he can fit in a few minutes this eve before he takes to his bed."

Bowen groaned. "Give the man some peace, Rorie. You'll drive him daft before long. The poor man will run screaming from Montgomery lands and swear an oath never to return."

Rorie glared at Bowen, then rose from the table, her chin thrust upward. She turned and stalked away, leaving Bowen and Genevieve alone at the table.

"So what think you of Rorie?" Bowen asked.

"She's fun," Genevieve said. "And she has a huge heart. I like her very much."

"She's a meddlesome, interfering brat," Bowen said in amusement. "But 'tis the truth we love her dearly and life would not be the same without her antics."

Genevieve grinned. "Isn't that the way with little sisters?"

Bowen rose and held out his hand to Genevieve. "Are you ready to take our walk?"

She slid her fingers over his, savoring the intimate contact. "I'd like that very much."

He assisted her down the dais and turned to walk out the back entrance, past the bathhouses.

"You're welcome to use the bathhouses or, if you prefer, you can have a tub and water brought up to your chamber if you require privacy. There is also the river, and Eveline often makes use of it, much to Graeme's dismay. But if 'tis your preference, let me know and I'll arrange it so you have complete privacy."

Her heart squeezed, fluttering wildly. He was so solicitous. So caring.

He took her hand and enfolded it in his as they moved past the stone skirt surrounding the keep and toward the hillsides that overlooked the river.

The river was larger and deeper than the one at McHugh Keep. There were areas that could be used for bathing or swimming without fear of being seen.

Bowen led her to a vast expanse of green rolling terrain where sheep and horses grazed. The river was not far away and it posed a magnificent backdrop to the setting sun.

She breathed in a contented sigh. 'Twas beautiful here, and so very peaceful. She was filled with hope and, at last, happiness.

"I think I will be very happy here," she said in a low voice.

Bowen looked away, unable to meet her gaze. She cocked her head, confused by his demeanor. Had she said something wrong? Did he plan to send her to the abbey after all?

" 'Tis my heart's wish for you to be happy," he said. " 'Tis all I want for you, Genevieve. You've suffered long enough. I would do whatever necessary to ensure that you are content."

She squeezed his hand. "I never thought to meet a man like you, Bowen Montgomery. My experience has taught me to fear men and not to trust their pretty words and lies. You've been naught but honest and sincere with me."

His face turned gray, and there was clear dismay in his eyes. He looked as though he'd swallowed something exceedingly unpleasant.

Worry plagued her, for his mood was different this night. He seemed distant, as if something bothered him.

"Bowen? Is aught amiss?"

He tugged her underneath the shelter of his arm as they continued their journey toward the river.

"Nay. That you are content is all that matters to me."

"I am ever grateful to you," she said earnestly. "Now that I am away from the McHughs, I cannot fathom ever going back. 'Tis something that haunts my sleep at night. I've dreamed for so long of being free of Ian and his clan that now that I am here 'tis hard to believe it's not a figment of my most ardent desires."

He kissed her tenderly, his mouth sweet on hers. "You'll not ever return, Genevieve. You have my word on it."

She touched his face, letting her fingers linger along his cheekbone. "You are a good man, Bowen. I'll not ever forget all that you have done for me."

He closed his eyes for a long moment, and when he opened them they were bleak and forlorn. She knew not what occupied his mind, but it worried her, for he was not his usual self this eve.

"Come," he said. "Let us go down by the riverside

and watch the sun set. 'Tis a beautiful place to watch the stars. There will be a chill, but I'll keep you warm, lass."

She smiled and nestled more firmly into his side. She had no doubt that he'd do just that. And an evening spent in his arms was the most perfect way to spend a night.

CHAPTER 41

The excitement of the past few days rapidly caught up to Genevieve and she slept the sleep of the dead. As soon as her head hit the pillow, she was sound asleep, and she didn't stir when the first strains of dawn began to lighten the room. Nor did she move when Rorie knocked on her door to invite her down to break her fast.

In fact, she was still sound asleep when Rorie and Eveline burst through her door close to the noon hour. Genevieve stirred when her bed bounced and she heard chatter ring in her ears.

She blearily opened her eyes to see Rorie and Eveline Montgomery in her chamber. She shook the veil of sleep from her head and attempted to push herself up.

"What's wrong?" Genevieve croaked.

The fact that Eveline was here in her chamber was cause for alarm for Genevieve. Had she been so angered by Genevieve's presence that she'd come straightaway to order her out? Or perhaps she wanted to voice her displeasure in person.

But nay, Eveline was smiling sweetly, her eyes sparkling with welcome. And Rorie was grinning like a fool, fairly dancing with excitement.

"That's what we came to find out from you. If something was amiss. 'Tis nearly noon and we saw no sign of you. I knocked at your door when it was time to break our fast but you never stirred," Rorie said patiently.

Genevieve sat straight up in bed. "Noon?" she squeaked. "I've slept until noon?"

"You were tired," Eveline said in a soft, sweet voice.

Her speech patterns were different. The sounds of the words were different, but Genevieve had no issue understanding her at all.

Genevieve glanced cautiously up at Eveline, gauging the other woman's reaction to her.

"I'm Genevieve," she said. "And you are Eveline. I saw you . . ." She winced at having to bring up the fact that Eveline had been imprisoned—as had she—by Ian McHugh. "I saw you at McHugh Keep when Ian imprisoned you."

Eveline pushed Rorie to the side and sat on the edge of the bed next to Genevieve.

"I owe you a great debt," Eveline said solemnly. "You did much to aid me, and for that you have my thanks. Ian is—was—an evil man. I'm not sad that he is dead."

Genevieve was overcome with guilt. She couldn't even look the other woman in the eye. But she forced herself to hold her mouth where Eveline could see the words that came forth.

"You owe me nothing," she said painfully. " 'Tis my doing that you were captured to begin with. 'Tis not something I can ever forget, and I would understand if you could never forgive me."

Eveline put her hand on Genevieve's and squeezed lightly. "I know of your situation, Genevieve. Graeme told me all. My heart aches for you. I can't imagine what I would have done in your position. I certainly don't blame you for doing what you had to in an effort to gain your freedom. 'Twas an ingenious plan, and the fact of the matter is you fought for me. You protected me at great risk and shame to yourself. How can I find fault with you when you did so much to spare me? You directed my husband to where I lay imprisoned. 'Tis possible he would never have found me without your aid."

Tears gathered in Genevieve's eyes. She couldn't hold them back. The kindness and understanding in Eveline's voice were her undoing.

"There now, don't cry," Eveline said gently. " 'Tis glad I am that you're here. We'll not allow such to ever happen to you again. Rorie and I are glad to have the companionship of another lass, especially one as brave and determined as you. Just think of all the mischief we'll get into."

"And 'tis why we've come to your chamber," Rorie said excitedly.

She all but pounced on Genevieve, plopping down on the bed at Genevieve's feet.

"We want to learn to use a bow, and we want you to teach us."

Genevieve looked at the lass in confusion.

"You told me the tale of how you killed four warriors in battle with your bow and arrows, and Graeme repeated it to Eveline just this morn. 'Tis an amazing feat. You are very skilled! Eveline and I would like you to instruct us in the shooting of a bow. It would be great fun! We can start today if you're willing."

Genevieve shook the confusion from her mind and focused on the conversation at hand. 'Twas a bizarre happening. Rorie and Eveline were in her chamber. Eveline acted as though Genevieve had never done her wrong, and both lasses wanted her to teach them how to use a bow. It was all too much to take in.

"It would be great fun," Eveline urged, her voice cajoling.

Genevieve finally shrugged. "Why not? 'Tis a useful skill for a lass to have. 'Tis a good thing to be able to defend yourself and those around you."

Rorie puffed up her chest. "I will be the best at it, and then I'll challenge Graeme and Bowen to a match. They'll be humiliated when a mere lass defeats them."

Genevieve broke into laughter. The truth of the matter was she absolutely believed Rorie. She seemed a determined lass, and one who excelled at every task she set her mind to. It wouldn't surprise Genevieve at all if she bested all her brothers with a bow and arrow.

"Let me dress and collect my bow and arrows, and we'll find a place to practice," Genevieve said.

Rorie clapped her hands in delight. "We'll wait for you at the bottom of the stairs. Don't be long, Genevieve! We have much to do this day."

Genevieve smiled. "I'll need only a few minutes to ready myself."

"What in God's name are they doing?" Graeme demanded.

Bowen and Graeme had gone in search of Genevieve, Rorie, and Eveline when no one could report where the lasses were and they had been conspicuously absent the entire afternoon.

When he and Graeme climbed the hill overlooking the river, there in the distance were the three of them, shooting arrows at a flimsily constructed target.

"Do we want to know?" Bowen asked dryly. "I think Rorie is quite infatuated with Genevieve. She was most impressed by the fact that Genevieve felled four warriors during battle. She's recounted the tale to anyone who will listen."

"The very last thing Eveline needs to learn is how to shoot a bow," Graeme said. "Think you I want her filling my hide with arrows when I anger her? I'm blaming you for this, Bowen. 'Tis your lass who is corrupting my wife. There's no hope for Rorie, so 'tis pointless to complain about her wayward habits."

Bowen sobered. "She isn't my lass. Not for long."

Graeme went silent, his expression full of regret. "Forgive me. I did not mean to bring up a painful topic. I know you dread the day when the McInnises arrive."

"I'll never love another woman as I do Genevieve," Bowen said simply. "And because I love her, I must be willing to do what is best for her. She is not fully happy, though she is well content to be away from the McHughs. She misses her family, and she'll never be complete unless she resolves things with her clan. She may well hate me for what I have done, but I know 'tis best. I can live with her hatred if I know she'll find happiness."

Graeme clasped Bowen's shoulder. "Come, let's see what the lasses are up to."

The two men strode down the hill toward the women. Bowen rolled his eyes, because the first rule of battle was to be aware of your surroundings at all times. He and Graeme could have sneaked up and deprived them of their weapons, for all the attention they paid.

The lasses were so focused on their task that they never saw or heard him and Graeme approach. Eveline had good reason, of course, but Rorie and Genevieve should be more alert.

When they were but a few feet away, Graeme cleared his throat.

Genevieve and Rorie immediately spun around, while Eveline continued to fiercely concentrate on her target. She let her arrow fly, and it fell just short of the kill spot Genevieve had marked.

She turned, excitement blooming on her face, and she jumped up and down, the bow falling to the ground.

"I did it! I did it!"

Graeme smiled indulgently at Eveline's joy, but then she took in the fact that Bowen and Graeme were present and clamped her lips shut, looking guiltily in Graeme's direction.

Genevieve bent to retrieve the bow, dusting it off and smoothing any marks made by the fall.

"I see you're quite busy this day," Graeme drawled. "Pray tell, what enemy are you slaying?"

Eveline rushed to greet her husband, leaning up as far on tiptoe as she could to offer him a kiss, then she patted him on the cheek, leaving him befuddled and speechless.

Bowen smothered his laughter. Eveline knew well how to handle her husband. A kiss, a few touches, and he was completely in her thrall.

Genevieve's eyes were full of worry as she glanced nervously at Bowen, as if she feared reprisal for instructing Eveline and Rorie on how to use a bow.

He held out his hand, not caring if the others saw. He had only a few days to be with her, and damn what anyone thought. He would take these days and savor them. Hold them close to his heart and remember them when he was old and gray.

He'd left her to rest the night before, knowing she was weary from her travels and from the anxiety of coming into a new clan where she was unsure of her welcome. But tonight she would spend in his chamber, in his arms, and every night until the McInnises arrived to bear her home.

He'd hold dear every single moment he had remaining with her, and those memories would sustain him his life through, because he knew he'd never love another as he loved Genevieve.

She shyly slid her hand into his, glancing nervously at the others for their reaction. He cared not. He pulled her into his arms and kissed her, his heart swelling with emotion. God, he did not want to let her go.

The selfish thing would be to keep her here with him. To never let her family know that she was alive. To keep her close and by his side and never share her with anyone.

He wanted so much. Love. Children. To wake every morn with her curled into his side. He couldn't imagine his life without her, but, above all else, he wanted her to be happy. She'd been denied so much, and she'd endured so much pain and humiliation.

He had to let her go so she could soar and be the woman she was meant to be. Even if it killed him. And it may well do just that.

Genevieve blushed when he pulled away and glanced hesitantly at the others to gauge their reactions, but Rorie was grinning like a fool and Eveline wore a soft smile as she took in the tenderness between Bowen and Genevieve.

"Genevieve is teaching us her skill at shooting a bow!" Rorie said.

"Aye, that much is evident," Graeme said in amusement. "How fare you?"

Eveline clutched Graeme's hand. "I can hit the target! 'Tis amazing!"

"So can I!" Rorie interjected. "I'm quite good," she boasted. "I aim to challenge you and Bowen to a match. I'll best the both of you."

Bowen chuckled. "It would not surprise me, sweeting. You're determined and stubborn, if nothing else."

" 'Tis not a bad skill to have," Graeme said in a more serious tone. "You have my gratitude for instructing them, Genevieve. I would have Eveline able to defend herself if I'm not within reach. She means everything to me. If knowing how to use a bow saves her life, I will be forever indebted to you. I'll set to work having bows fashioned for both Eveline and Rorie."

Rorie squealed her excitement and Eveline clapped her hands together in delight.

Genevieve glowed with happiness and pride. Bowen put his arm around her shoulders and held her close. His own pride knew no bounds. Genevieve was an extraordinary lass. She was a survivor. Even if she was to be here only a short time, he knew Rorie and Eveline would benefit from the time spent with her.

He kissed her again, because he couldn't help himself. He couldn't be near her without wanting to touch her and hold her close.

Eveline and Rorie exchanged smug smiles, but Bowen disregarded them.

It then occurred to him that Genevieve wasn't wearing her cape, nor was she attempting to hide her disfigurement. He squeezed her to him and pressed a kiss to the scar.

Maybe she was comfortable around Eveline and Rorie as well as him. She'd even shed some of the fear and nervousness that she'd exhibited every time she was in Graeme's presence.

She'd gained confidence, even if it was only around a select few, but it made him feel triumphant that she could hold her head up with no shame. In his eyes, she had nothing to feel shame over.

"Why don't you lasses show us what you've learned?" Graeme suggested.

"Oh yes, let's!" Rorie exclaimed. "I think there should be a prize for the one with the truest aim."

"Genevieve cannot participate," Eveline interjected. " 'Twould not be fair. You and I will try our hand."

Rorie's eyes gleamed with unholy glee. "And the prize?"

Eveline pondered a moment, then her face lit up. "If I win, you must do a reading after the evening meal. One of the stories Father Drummond has taught you. It would be a lovely end to the day."

"And if I win?" Rorie challenged.

"If you win, I'll send a missive to my father asking for scrolls from his personal library."

Rorie's eyes grew round and she clasped her hands together in excitement. "Oh, I must win, then!"

"Was there any doubt?" Graeme said dryly. "A more competitive lass I've never known. I'm still convinced you were born a lad and we just haven't discovered it yet."

Rorie stuck out her tongue at Graeme and turned to Genevieve.

"You set the target, Genevieve! 'Tis you who will be judge."

Bowen observed the glow in Genevieve's eyes. The shadows were gone, and there was not the haunted look he'd learned to associate with her. She looked happy, as if a great weight had been lifted from her shoulders.

He wanted nothing more than to bear her back to the keep and make love to her for the next three days, until neither of them had strength any longer.

The men stood patiently and watched as the two lasses took their turns aiming at the target. Considering the short while they'd been practicing, both displayed impressive skill.

But it was Rorie who won the day, not that Bowen or Graeme was surprised. She edged Eveline about by the barest of inches with her very last shot. At which point she thrust her arms in the air and let out a bellow of victory that rivaled that of any warrior on the battlefield.

"Send word to your father, Eveline!" Rorie crowed.

Eveline smiled. "I'll send a messenger on the morrow. My father's library is filled with manuscripts. I'm sure there is something that will interest you."

Rorie clapped her hands. "Anything he sends will be wonderful!" Then she threw her arms around Genevieve, and hugged her fiercely. "Thank you, Genevieve. 'Tis the most fun I've had in ages!"

Genevieve laughed and hugged her back. "You're very welcome. If you continue to practice, you'll be quite the marksman. Perhaps your brothers will seek to bring you into battle."

Graeme scowled. "Not bloody likely. The imp finds enough trouble within the walls of the keep."

The women laughed, and Eveline linked her arms through Genevieve's and Rorie's and they started back toward the keep. She turned and smiled sweetly at Bowen and Graeme.

"Be a dear and fetch Genevieve's bow and arrows for us. I find I'm famished after so much exercise. We're going to the kitchens to see what can be found to eat."

Graeme sighed as the women walked back toward the keep, their chatter rising and filling the air. He shook his head and bent to retrieve the bow and the quiver that housed the arrows.

"I think my life will be anything but dull as long as they are together," Graeme said in resignation.

But Bowen was staring after the women, his heart aching for what *could* be. Rorie and Eveline had welcomed Genevieve with open arms. This could be his future. Surrounded by his clan, the woman he loved, and a family so dear to him. This could be his life.

But Genevieve deserved to be with her own kin. He couldn't imagine thinking Rorie dead and losing her. If she was alive, he'd want her back, and he'd move mountains to make it so. Genevieve's family would be no different.

CHAPTER 42

Bowen held Genevieve close to him, nestled in the curve of his arm. He kissed her forehead and rubbed his hand up and down the silken skin of her arm as he lay contemplating the past few days.

They'd been idyllic. Borrowed time. Genevieve seemed so happy here. Her eyes were filled with a joy and light that he hadn't seen when they were at McHugh Keep.

He knew the decision to take her away and have her reunited with her family here had been the right one. She needed distance from the place that had brought her so much pain and suffering.

But with each passing day, and each passing night spent in each other's arms, he drew closer to the time when they would have to part, and a little piece of him died with every hour.

She stirred against him, whispered a sweet sigh of contentment, and then settled back into sleep.

The urgency with which he took her had increased with each stolen night. She'd barely settled into sleep before dawn had crept over the horizon, and he'd remained awake, watching her, soaking in every detail of her body, committing it to memory so that those images would sustain him through the coming years.

He knew he would never take a wife. He had no duty to fulfill or heirs to beget. There was no other woman for him than Genevieve. No other woman would ever fill the hole in his heart left empty by this brave, courageous lass who'd so captivated him.

A soft knock sounded at his door, and his pulse raced. He disentangled himself from Genevieve and carefully eased from the bed so as not to disturb her. When he opened his door, Graeme stood on the other side, his expression grim and regretful.

"I received word from our patrol. The McInnises come flying their banner. They move with great haste and, at their current pace, will arrive in an hour's time."

Bowen's heart sank. He knew that it was likely the McInnises would waste no time once they received word that Genevieve was alive, but he'd hoped for a few more days. Just one more night to hold her in his arms.

"I'll inform Genevieve and give her time to prepare," Bowen said quietly.

Graeme's face was a grimace of sympathy. "I'm sorry, Bowen. I know this is not easy for you."

"No, but 'tis what's best."

He turned, leaving his brother and shutting the door behind him.

Genevieve was awake, levered up on her elbow. Her hair was in disarray, and she gave him a sleepy look as she watched him approach.

"Is aught amiss?" she asked.

He couldn't even form the words. They stuck in his throat until he threatened to choke them.

He slid onto the bed, sitting on the edge, and gathered her hands in his. "There is something I must tell you."

Worry flooded her eyes and she sat up further. She attempted to pull her hands from his, but he refused to relinquish his hold.

He took a deep breath, expelling it slowly.

"When we departed McHugh Keep, I sent word to

your family that you were alive and that I was taking you to Montgomery Keep."

She went absolutely still, her eyes so wounded that it nearly slayed him.

"*Why?*" she whispered in a cracked voice. "Why would you do such? You knew I did not want them to know of my shame. Do you have *any* idea what this will do to them?"

He swallowed and pulled her hands higher to his chest. "Aye, I know it, Genevieve. But I see the sadness in your eyes when you speak of them. I know what it would do to me to think my sister dead. I know you'll never be truly happy—or free—unless you face this, face *them*."

"And so you made the decision for me," she choked out. "When I've had all my choices taken from me, you would do the same."

"I do this because I love you," he said, finally speaking the words he'd held so close to him. "And I want you, but, more than that, I want you to be happy. I want you to be whole again, and 'tis my feeling that you'll never be healed until you are reunited with your family—the people who love you. Almost as much as *I* love you."

Tears filled her eyes and slid unchecked down her cheeks. Then she flew into his arms and wrapped herself around him as tightly as she could.

"I'm so scared, Bowen," she said, her voice muffled by his shoulder. "What if they reject me? What if they look upon me in shame? I could not bear it. I would prefer they never knew I was alive than for them to suffer my presence, knowing they are shamed by my very existence."

"They'll not do such a thing," Bowen said, his heart breaking at the fear in her voice. "I won't allow it. I'll not send you into such a situation, Genevieve, I vow it."

Slowly she pulled away from him, vulnerability shadowed in her eyes. There was nothing he wanted more than to shut the door to the world and keep her locked to his side for the rest of their days. But he knew this was what she needed. Healing. The love and support of her family. She would never be whole, and he would only have part of her. He wanted her happiness and well-being above his own. Even if it tore his heart out of his chest to let her go.

"When do they arrive?" she asked in a small voice.

"Within the hour. Graeme brought word from a messenger that they were an hour away and riding swiftly. They must have come the moment they received my missive."

She hastily wiped at her tear-stained face. "I must make haste. I need to dress, and my hair is a mess."

Bowen leaned forward and kissed her slow and sweet. "I'll send Rorie and Eveline to attend you."

He reluctantly rose and started for the door.

"Bowen?"

He turned back and she launched herself into his arms once more, pressing her mouth to his. She kissed him hungrily and with quiet desperation. A farewell.

He held her close, crushing her in his arms, holding her as if he'd never let her go.

And then, because if he didn't leave her now he never would, he gently pulled himself from her grasp and walked away.

CHAPTER 43

Eveline and Rorie fussed and worried over Genevieve's appearance in between bouts of Rorie raging that Bowen had no right to interfere and send word to Genevieve's family.

" 'Tis because he wants what's best for Genevieve," Eveline said gently. " 'Tis what you should want as well."

Rorie's face crumbled as Eveline put the finishing touches on Genevieve's hair.

"But I shall miss her. 'Twas like having another sister, and a lass can *never* have too many sisters."

Genevieve hugged the younger woman and squeezed her tight. "We'll always be sisters. Of the heart, if nothing more. I'll not forget you, Rorie Montgomery. Or your kindness."

Rorie gave her a teary smile as she pulled away, and then Genevieve hugged Eveline, holding her fiercely. She waited until she'd stepped back before she spoke to Eveline, so that the other woman would understand her words.

"You've an understanding heart, Eveline. I was sore afraid to face you after all I'd done. I would not blame you if you'd insisted I leave your keep. But you welcomed me and you were kind. You've been a friend, even in the short time we've been acquainted. Thank you for that. I'll not forget you either."

"You must stop," Eveline choked out. "The three of us will all be weepy messes when you greet your family. You are a special woman, Genevieve McInnis. Never lose sight of that. What you endured would break a weaker woman, but you've become *stronger* for it."

"Promise me you'll visit," Rorie said fiercely. "I'll worry until I know you are happy and settled. And if you ever have need of anything, you've only to send word."

Genevieve hugged them both again, then took a step back to smooth the dress she'd dug from her trunk. It was one that her mother had lovingly sewn as part of her wedding dowry, and one of the few that remained of her trousseau.

"Do I look all right?" she asked anxiously.

Dread and fear crowded her heart at the thought of the upcoming reunion with her family. She could not bear to see disappointment in their eyes. It would kill her to bring shame to their name.

"You look beautiful," Eveline said softly.

Rorie leaned from the window and then ducked back in, her eyes wide, her voice hushed in awe. "'Tis time, Genevieve. Your clan approaches. They stretch as far as the eye can see. I vow they've brought the might of their entire army."

Genevieve hurried to the window and stared out, seeing, for the first time in a year, her father's banner, unfurled and flowing in the wind.

'Twas an impressive sight, and one that brought a lump to her throat.

He'd come for her.

Bowen and Graeme rode with a small contingent of Montgomery warriors to meet Laird McInnis just outside the walls of the courtyard. Laird McInnis called a halt to his men and shifted on his horse as he eyed the Montgomery brothers.

Beside him, an ornate litter pulled by two horses came to rest beside the laird and Bowen could see a woman sitting, but the moment the horses stopped she sat up, her expression anxious and expectant.

"Where is my daughter?" the laird demanded.

His features were drawn into a warrior's mask. 'Twas evident he did not know if he came to fight, but 'twas equally evident he was prepared for any outcome.

"Laird," Graeme said respectfully. "I am Graeme Montgomery, laird of the Montgomery clan."

"I know well who you are," Laird McInnis said impatiently. "I want to know where my daughter is and if she is well."

"Your daughter fares well," Bowen spoke up.

The laird's gaze fell on Bowen, his eyebrows drawing together.

"Are you Bowen Montgomery?"

"Aye, I am."

"You are the one who sent the missive."

Bowen nodded.

"Your missive was detailed enough, but there is still much I would know. The story was too fantastic to be true."

"I assure you that everything within the message I had delivered to you is true," Bowen said soberly. "Ian McHugh attacked Genevieve's escort on its way to her betrothed and slaughtered everyone save Genevieve. He was obsessed with her and kept her imprisoned at his keep until the Montgomerys and Armstrongs attacked and killed him."

The woman beside Laird McInnis gasped and put her hand to her mouth in horror.

"And you?" the laird asked, looking sharply at Bowen. "What role do you play in all of this?"

"I saw a woman sorely abused," Bowen said quietly. "I bore her back to Montgomery Keep, where I could be assured of her well-being and care, and I sent word to you so that you would know that she lives."

"Lachlan, 'tis enough talk," the woman said sharply. "I would see my daughter at once. It's been a year since I last held her, and I've spent the past year in hell thinking her dead. Surely you can converse with the Montgomerys once we've seen for ourselves the welfare of our daughter."

Lachlan sighed. "You are right. I am anxious to see her as well."

He glanced up at Graeme. "With your permission, Laird, I would enter your keep so that I may be reunited with my daughter. We've traveled hard these past days. We left the moment we received word that she was alive."

Graeme inclined his head. "Of course. I would extend an invitation to you and your lady wife for rest and refreshment."

Lady McInnis climbed from the litter, and Lachlan extended his arm to assist her. One of his men aided her and she was boosted into the saddle with the laird.

Graeme and Bowen turned and led the way through the gate into the courtyard, Laird McInnis and his wife close on their heels.

Graeme and Bowen dismounted, and Bowen went to assist Lady McInnis down from the horse. Laird McInnis's feet hit the ground, and the air practically vibrated with expectancy.

Bowen was about to send word to Genevieve that her parents had arrived when he looked up and saw her standing in the doorway to the keep.

Her face was deathly pale, and her eyes large in her

face. The scar was even more pronounced against such paleness, and it made her look even more fragile.

"Mama? Papa?" she whispered.

Lady McInnis and the laird whipped around at the sound of her voice. Lady McInnis went as white as Genevieve, and to Bowen's surprise, a look of anguish filled the laird's face and tears gathered in his eyes.

"Genevieve!" Lady McInnis exclaimed.

And then they were both running, Genevieve and her mother. They met at the bottom of the steps, and Lady McInnis enfolded Genevieve in her arms, holding her as if she'd never let go.

The laird joined them, folding them both in his beefy embrace. He held them so tightly that Bowen wondered if either could breathe. There was such joy that it permeated the air around them. No one could look upon them and not be deeply moved by the emotional reunion.

"You did a good thing, Bowen," Graeme murmured.

Bowen sucked in his breath and then turned his stare on his brother. "If I did such a good thing, why does it feel as though my heart has been torn from my chest?"

Graeme grimaced and put his hand on Bowen's shoulder, squeezing in silent sympathy.

Genevieve stood surrounded by her mother and father, her heart nearly bursting as they hugged and kissed her. Her mother openly wept, and the big gruff laird, her father, looked as though he battled his own tears.

She clung to her mother, soaking up the warmth that only a mother's embrace could provide. How long had she grieved for her mother? She thought never to see her again, or to see her smile. Or to simply enjoy the love and affection that flowed so freely within her clan.

"Oh Genevieve," her mother whispered brokenly. "My heart has been restored."

"Come here and give your papa a hug," her father said in a gruff voice thick with emotion.

She went into her father's embrace and he picked her up, just as he used to do when she was a child, and spun her around.

"My daughter is returned to us!" he shouted.

Just outside the walls, a roar went up from the assembled army and echoed across the hillside. It went on and on until Genevieve laughed as he spun her around again.

"My baby," her mother said, pulling her once more into her embrace when her father set her down.

Her father turned to where Bowen and Graeme stood, while her mother held her tightly, as if afraid Genevieve would disappear if she let go.

"I owe you a debt of gratitude," he said gruffly. " 'Tis one I can never hope to repay."

"Make her happy," Bowen said simply. " 'Tis all the debt you'll ever have to repay."

"Come," Graeme said. "You've journeyed long and you must be tired and hungry. A feast will be prepared this night to celebrate the return of Genevieve to your clan."

Genevieve's mother stroked her hair and tenderly patted her scarred cheek.

" 'Tis the most joyous moment of my life next to the day you were born. I'll long hold this day in my memory. The day my only child was returned to me."

Genevieve hugged her, burying her face in her mother's neck as she'd done so many times over the years. Her scent was the same, soothing and so much like home.

"I love you, Mama."

"And I love you, dearling. So very much."

CHAPTER 44

Genevieve hastened from the keep as the earth was bathed in the light of a new sun. She'd not slept the night before. Too much excitement. Her mother had slept in her chamber, not willing to be parted from her for even a moment. And today they would make the journey back home to McInnis land.

They'd feasted the night before, and Genevieve hadn't had one moment in which to speak to Bowen alone. She could not leave without seeing him one last time.

She'd searched his chamber, but found it barren. Nor was he within the keep.

She found him standing on the hillside, staring over the vast expanse of Montgomery land. She slowed her steps as she neared him, suddenly hesitant.

He heard her approach and turned, his eyes flickering as his gaze found her. Wordlessly, she flew into his arms, holding him tightly as they embraced.

"I would not go without saying farewell to you," she said.

"I'll be there when you ride out," Bowen assured.

Still, she hesitated. "I said terrible things to you, Bowen. I was angry and afraid. Mostly afraid. I was so fearful of facing my family after all that has happened. It was foolish of me to ever think they'd turn their back on me. I want to thank you for sending word to my father. 'Tis not something I would have had the courage to do, and that *shames* me."

He put his finger to her lips. "Shhh, lass. There is no reason to be sorry. What you endured is unthinkable. 'Tis understandable that you had fears."

"I'll never forget you, Bowen Montgomery," she said, her voice nearly breaking as she tried to say all that was in her heart. "I did not think a man such as you existed."

He smiled and lowered his mouth to hers. "And 'tis the truth I did not dream that a lass such as you existed. I do not want to let you go, but 'tis my selfish desires that fuel my reluctance. Your family has been deprived of you in a most horrible way. I cannot imagine the grief they've endured all this time."

She kissed him back, a kiss filled with heartbreak and desperation. She was torn between the impossible. A reunion with the family she loved above all else, and a man who had rescued her from the very depths of despair. A man who had looked beyond the scars on her face and soul to the very heart of her.

"Be happy, Genevieve," he whispered against her lips. "'Tis all I ask. I can live and die a content man as long as I know you are happy and well cared for."

She clung tightly to him, his arms wrapped around her as the sun rose higher in the sky. There was naught to say. Their hearts were heavy with the knowledge of what could not be—and of what was.

Finally, Bowen gently pulled her away and stroked a hand over her face. "'Tis time for you to go. Your father and mother will be looking for you."

He went blurry in her vision as her eyes swam with tears. "I love you, Bowen. I would not leave without telling you so. I will never love another. You will always hold a place in my heart and I'll think of you often, in my dreams and in the waking."

He palmed her face and kissed her fiercely, his lips moving with heated desperation over hers.

"And I love you, Genevieve. For all my days will I love only you."

No longer able to bear the look in his eyes, she turned and ran back toward the keep, leaving him on the hillside, a lone figure outlined by the rising sun.

Bowen watched as Rorie and Eveline noisily said farewell to Genevieve. They wept and clung to her as though they'd known her forever.

Graeme hovered close to Bowen, his expression worried and grim. 'Twas obvious he wanted to offer sympathy but had no idea what to say to his brother.

It was just as well, because Bowen had no desire to open the wound further. He offered his farewell to Laird and Lady McInnis and assisted Lady McInnis into the litter that would bear her and Genevieve back to McInnis Keep.

When it came time for Genevieve to take her leave, he stood stiffly to the side as she gave her farewell to Graeme. Then he offered her his hand to assist her into the litter.

She slid her fingers over his and lifted her gaze to his. They stared at each other for a long moment, their hearts in their eyes. Then she whispered her thanks and a farewell and climbed up beside her mother.

"Be well," Bowen said as he took a step back.

"And you," Genevieve murmured softly.

He took another step back. And then another. He had to put distance between them, else he'd haul her from the litter and never let her go.

Laird McInnis gave the order to move out, and the procession of horses began the journey from Montgomery Keep.

Bowen stood watching until the last of the horses disappeared in the distance. His heart was heavy, and a part of him died as Genevieve McInnis rode out of his life and back to her own.

"Be happy, my love," he whispered. "Be happy."

CHAPTER 45

"'Tis so good to have you home, Genevieve," Sybil exclaimed as she bounced onto Genevieve's bed.

Genevieve smiled. "'Tis all you've said these past weeks."

"It can never be said enough. I missed you so."

A look of sadness crossed her friend's face, and Genevieve reached to squeeze her hand.

So much had changed in the time Genevieve had been gone. Sybil had married and remained on McInnis land with her new husband, who acted as Laird McInnis's second-in-command.

Grief had altered her mother and father. They both looked older than Genevieve remembered. There were new lines on her father's beloved face, and wrinkles around her mother's eyes.

Not a day went by that her parents didn't cosset her endlessly. They worried over her comfort, her happiness, whether she was plagued by unpleasant dreams or memories of her time with Ian McHugh.

Genevieve didn't discuss the matter much, and her parents respected her wishes, not prying when she didn't volunteer information.

There was no point in their knowing all Ian had subjected her to. It would only make them grieve more, and there was naught to be done about it now. It was all in the past, and she was determined to leave it there. It was a part of her life best forgotten.

The only good that had come out of all of it was . . . Bowen.

She lay awake at night, aching for him. It carried over into her days. She wasn't herself. She was tired and lethargic, and she tried her best to exhibit enthusiasm, because she didn't want to worry her parents.

"Do you like being married?" Genevieve asked, knowing this would turn the conversation to Sybil's husband.

As expected, Sybil's face lit up and she fairly glowed. It filled Genevieve with jealousy and longing.

"I love him so," Sybil said wistfully. "He's strong and honorable. The perfect warrior. And he spoils me shamelessly."

Genevieve laughed. " 'Tis a good thing, that."

Sybil grinned. "Aye, it is."

A knock sounded at Genevieve's chamber door, and Sybil bounded up to answer. Genevieve's father stuck his head inside, his gaze seeking Genevieve.

"I thought you might want to go out hunting with me. Your mother has a taste for rabbit stew, and we make a good pair. Let's see if your archery skills are still up to par."

Genevieve smiled, warmed by the fact that he sought her out to spend time with her. Both her mother and her father had kept her close ever since their return. She couldn't walk for bumping into one of them.

"Aye, I'd like that. Give me but a moment to change into something suitable for hunting."

Pleasure lit her father's eyes and he smiled back. "I'll wait in the courtyard. I'll ready your mount while you dress."

"They grieved for you so," Sybil said in a quiet voice when the door had closed. "Your father was desolate for months, and not a day went by that your mother didn't weep for her loss. I thought never to see them smile again. When they received the missive stating you were alive, it was as if they were given new life. They were so afraid that it was false news and someone was playing a cruel jest. Your father packed up and they left in the dead of night to make haste to fetch you."

"I grieved for them too," Genevieve murmured. "I thought never to see them again."

Sybil patted Genevieve on the cheek. "You are their only child, beloved beyond measure. The entire clan rejoiced when they heard the news, for it was painful for all to see how broken they were over your disappearance."

Genevieve swung her legs over the side of the bed and went to her wardrobe to fetch the leggings and tunic her father had given her for their hunting excursions. No lass could properly hunt in a dress, according to him, so he'd outfitted her in men's garb.

She ran her hands lovingly over the worn clothing. Not a single thing had been changed in her chamber the entire time she'd been gone. Everything was as it had been when she'd left. Though she'd taken most of her clothing with her, she'd left the hunting apparel, since she couldn't be sure that her new husband would approve.

In the time since her return, her mother had worked feverishly to replenish Genevieve's wardrobe. She had a contingent of women working around the clock, sewing new dresses and undergarments.

Genevieve slipped out of her dress and pulled on the leggings and tunic, noting that they were larger on her than they had been before. She was thinner and didn't have as much flesh on her bones as she had a year ago.

It wasn't a surprise. She'd been treated little better than a dog, tossed a few scraps and the occasional meal during her imprisonment. But somehow seeing the clothing on her now brought home the realization of just how much she'd changed.

Her hand went to her face, and her fingers slid down the puckered flesh that marked the vivid scar. Her mother had been horrified and tearful when she learned how and why Genevieve had been disfigured so. Though Bowen had told her father of the event, his face had purpled with rage in the retelling of the story.

It was then that Genevieve had decided not to impart any further details of her captivity. She hated to see them so aggrieved.

She retrieved her bow and quiver of arrows and then motioned for Sybil to accompany her down the stairs. She met her father in the courtyard, where he stood beside two horses, holding their reins.

He smiled when he saw her, and then assisted her into the saddle. After mounting his horse, he took out in the direction of a section of dense forest on their lands.

Genevieve breathed deeply of the air, soaking in the feeling of home. She'd spent her entire childhood running wild over these hills. From a very early age, she'd tagged along on her father's hunts. He'd taught her skill with a bow and arrow, and she was adept with a knife as well.

They traveled a path well trod, a familiar trail into the wooded area where they'd hunted for years.

The first rabbit took her unaware and skittered across her path before she could react and draw her bow. Shaking off her sluggishness, she drew her bow and nocked an arrow. Her sharp gaze studied the bush for movement.

A moment later, one of the horses spooked a rabbit and it ran down the path. Genevieve took aim and pierced the rabbit with an arrow, pinning it to the ground.

Her father jumped down from his horse to retrieve the animal, grinning at her.

"Well done, lass. I see you've not lost your skill at all."

She smiled back, and then nocked another arrow.

By the time the sun began to sink in the sky, they had a dozen rabbits tied to her father's saddle and he turned them back toward the keep.

They rode into the courtyard, where their horses were taken by one of the McInnis men, and she followed her father around to where they skinned their bounty from hunts.

It wasn't an unusual thing for Genevieve to take part in the cleaning and preparation of the animals, but at the very first cut into the hide her stomach revolted and sweat broke out on her forehead.

Nausea coiled in her belly and she swallowed, desperately trying to control her reaction.

When her father peeled back the skin of a rabbit, Genevieve lost the battle and bent over, retching violently onto the ground. The smell offended her. The sight of blood made her stomach recoil. Her eyes watered from the force with which she heaved.

Her father's arm came around her, and he shouted an order to one of his men to take over the care of the rabbits. Then he led her inside the keep and to her mother.

"Elizabeth, do something," her father said in desperation. "The lass is sick."

"Hush now, Lachlan. I'll tend to her. You go on and finish with the rabbits. 'Tis woman's work to be done here."

"She's my daughter," he growled. " 'Tis nothing womanly about my concern."

Still, Lady McInnis waved her husband off and helped Genevieve up the stairs to her chamber.

"There now, lass, lie down a bit and catch your

breath," her mother said as soon as she'd tucked Genevieve into bed.

"Tired," Genevieve said faintly.

The bout of sickness had left her exhausted, and all she wanted to do was sleep.

Her mother ran a cool hand over her forehead. "I know, lass. Rest, now. I'll check in on you later."

"Love you, Mama," Genevieve said in a drowsy voice.

Her mother smiled and pressed a gentle kiss to her forehead. "And I love you, my darling. Sleep now."

CHAPTER 46

"How is the lass?" Lachlan asked when Elizabeth entered his chamber.

His expression was anxious and worried, and Elizabeth wished she could say something to ease him. But there was naught to do but tell the truth.

"She is with child. I'm sure of it," Elizabeth said bluntly.

Lachlan blanched, his face going white as he stared agape at his wife. His huge hands curled into fists, and he looked as though he wanted to strike the wall.

"The bastard!" Lachlan seethed. "Never have I wished for a man to be alive so that I could do the killing. May Ian McHugh rot in hell for what he has done to our lass."

"What are we to do, Lachlan?" Elizabeth asked in a worried voice.

Lachlan sent her a puzzled look. "Do? There's nothing to do, Elizabeth. Except what we've always done. Love her and offer her our support, no matter what may fall. 'Tis not the lass's doing that she is with child, and even if it were, I could never turn away from her."

"Oh nay!" Elizabeth cried. "I did not mean that! I only mean that my heart bleeds for her. Just when we think she can start anew and put the past behind her, 'tis evident she is carrying a bairn, and now she'll live with a constant reminder of all Ian McHugh made her suffer for the rest of her life."

"Talk to the lass," Lachlan said gruffly. "'Tis a matter for a mother to discuss with her daughter. A father has no place in such a conversation. But let her know that I love her and that she will always have a place here with us. As will her bairn. Do not let her think we are shamed by her. Indeed, I'm prouder of her than I could ever be of a son."

Elizabeth laid her hand on Lachlan's arm. "'Tis a wonderful thing you say. I am the most fortunate of women in her choice of husbands. I could never ask for a better protector for my only child, and yet you've never once held it against me that I could not bear you a son."

Lachlan pulled her close, his eyes tender as they gazed down at her.

"'Tis hard to complain when you provided me a daughter to rival any in all of Scotland. What other lass could survive all she did and then seek vengeance on the man who wronged her? 'Tis the truth I could not be prouder of my lass. I only wish I could have been present to see her fell Patrick McHugh in battle. Surely it was a sight to behold."

Elizabeth smiled and rubbed her cheek against his broad chest.

"Besides," he said gruffly. "'Tis I who am fortunate, for you could have chosen any husband. Many vied for your hand, and yet you chose me. A savage with no manners, and you helped me build one of the strongest clans in the whole of Scotland. Men still gawk at your beauty after all these years, and many would give their life for one chance to share your bed."

She grinned mischievously up at him. "Now, that would be awkward. 'Tis a hard enough fit with you in the bed, much less another braw lad."

"Cheeky wench," he said with no heat. "I love you, and you well know it, and I'd kill the man who ever dared touch the hem of your dress."

She gifted him with a kiss and then pulled back with a sigh. "I must tell Genevieve. She does not know."

Lachlan's expression sobered. "Do not let her think this changes how we feel. I have no words to describe the joy in my heart at having my daughter back where she belongs. There is nothing she could do that would ever make me regret that."

"You're a good man, Lachlan McInnis," Elizabeth whispered as she kissed him again. "I'll break the news to Genevieve in the morning. Right now, I wish you to take me to bed."

Lachlan's eyes gleamed and his hold became possessive.

"Bossy lass. You know I can deny you nothing."

When Genevieve woke the next morning, the first thing she did was make a run for the chamber pot and heaved the remaining contents of her stomach. For several long minutes, she leaned over, her body convulsing as she sought to gain control.

Cool hands rubbed up and down her back and then pulled her hair away from her face, holding it at her nape as she shuddered with the last of her illness.

"I was afraid you'd be sick this morning," her mother said when Genevieve finally lifted her head and staggered back toward the bed.

Her mother tucked her into bed and pulled the covers up around her, all the while rubbing her back in a soothing motion.

"It must have been something I ate," Genevieve croaked.

Her mother's smile was gentle, and her hand slid to her forehead as she smoothed the hair from her face.

"Nay, lass, 'tis not something you ate."

Genevieve frowned. "Then what's wrong with me?"

"You're carrying a bairn," her mother said gently.

Genevieve's jaw went slack. Her hand covered the flatness of her belly as she stared at her mother in denial. But her mother nodded in confirmation.

Joy exploded in Genevieve's soul until she nearly burst with it. She wanted to cry. She wanted to laugh and shout her happiness to the world, but her mother would think she'd gone mad. And so she lay there, savoring the knowledge that she carried Bowen's child. A tiny part of him that she'd always have.

Her mother grasped her hand and held tightly to it.

"Your father and I both want you to know that we fully support you and your bairn. You'll always have a place to live. We love you with all our hearts. We know this is difficult for you. To bear the child of a man who so abused you is unthinkable, but we'll help you in any way we can, and we'll never forsake you, Genevieve."

Genevieve stared dumbfounded at her mother, as it dawned on her what she was saying.

She leaned forward and put a hand out to staunch the flow of words from her mother.

"Mama, 'tis not Ian's child I carry," she said softly.

Confusion crowded her mother's gaze. "You don't mean . . . Genevieve, tell me it wasn't someone he . . ."

She broke off, too upset to continue, and Genevieve couldn't allow her to think the worst.

"I'm carrying Bowen's bairn, Mama. 'Tis his child, not Ian's."

Lady McInnis's eyes widened, and her mouth opened and closed. Then her lips thinned and she gazed sharply at Genevieve.

"I knew there was something between the two of you. I sensed it when we were at Montgomery Keep. The man looked positively distraught when you left."

"He loves me," Genevieve said softly. "He saved me. He let me go because he thought it would make me happy."

Her mother stared at her a long moment and then drew her legs onto the bed so she sat more comfortably next to Genevieve.

"I'm hearing a lot about what *he* feels and what *he's* done. But tell me, Genevieve, do *you* love him?"

"With all my heart," she said achingly.

Her mother sighed. "You've not been happy here, have you?"

Genevieve shook her head. "Nay. 'Tis not so! I wouldn't have traded this time with you and Papa for anything. Bowen was right. He risked my ire by contacting you. He did it for me, even though it meant letting me go. And he was right. I needed you—*both* of you—in order to be whole again."

Her mother's face crinkled in confusion. "He risked your ire? I do not understand."

Genevieve closed her eyes as shame crawled up her spine. "I did not want you to know that I was alive."

Her mother gasped and her eyes blazed with hurt. "Genevieve! Why ever not? Do you even know the hell we've endured thinking you dead all this time?"

" 'Twas selfish of me," Genevieve said quietly. "I was so focused on my shame, and I feared the disgrace I would bring to our name. I never wanted you to know what all I endured. I would have spared you that if at all possible."

"Oh, dearling," her mother said, her voice choked with tears. "Don't you know that nothing you could ever do would make us ashamed of you? We love you. You are the light of our lives—especially your father's. The sun rises and sets at your feet. When you were born, I feared he would be angry because I hadn't given him a son. But he was so taken with you 'twas obvious to anyone with eyes that he cared not if you were a lass. And then, when it became evident that I could bear no more children, I worried that he would be angry. And do you know what he said to me?"

Genevieve slowly shook her head.

Her mother smiled through her tears. "He told me that I'd given him the fiercest, smartest, most beautiful lass in all of Scotland, and what could he possibly want with a son when he had a lass as clever as you?"

Genevieve burst into tears and clung to her mother.

"I'm sorry, Mama. I was so afraid and ashamed. I didn't even feel like a person while Ian kept me prisoner. It was not until Bowen saved me and showed me how it could be between a man and a woman that I began to live again. He contacted you because he knew I would never be happy or whole without you. And he gave me up because he said he'd rather I be happy and with the people I loved than to remain with him and never truly heal."

"It would seem I owe this young man a great deal," her mother said. "I'm just glad one of you has sense!"

"Mama!"

"Well, 'tis true. It horrifies me to think that you would have gone on and never come home to us."

"I would have," Genevieve cried. "It would have taken me time, but I would have come home, Mama. I missed you and Papa so. I would not have been able to live long without you."

Her mother hugged her again and stroked her hair. "What is it that you want to do, Genevieve? Bowen deserves to know of his child. We cannot keep it from him."

Genevieve pulled back, her expression firm. "Nay, I'd never seek to do so. I—I love him, Mama. I love him so *much,* and I miss him every single day. I had to come home. I had to do this so I could be happy and whole. But I'll never be *completely* whole without him. He'll always hold a piece of my heart."

Her mother smiled that gentle, motherly smile that never failed to warm Genevieve's heart and soothe all her hurts.

"It would seem that we have another journey to make. Only this time the whole of our army will accompany you on the way to your betrothed. We'll not chance your being set upon as you were before."

"What if he does not want to marry me?" Genevieve asked hesitantly.

Her mother rolled her eyes. "Lass, the way that lad was looking at you when we departed, it was a wonder he didn't grab you from the cart and haul you into the keep over his shoulder. I'd wager he was sorely tempted! If he loves you as you say, and if he did all this for you even knowing he'd lose you, then he's a man above many. He'll likely have you before a priest before you can blink. Now, the hard part is going to be convincing your father to let his baby go after he's only had her back a month."

Genevieve's face fell. "I don't want to lose either of you."

Her mother smiled and kissed the top of her head. "We'll visit often, and I'll come for the birth of your child. As will your father, I'm certain. He'll not tolerate being left behind when his grandchild is being born. The Montgomerys will just have to become used to the presence of the McInnis clan."

Hope surged through Genevieve's veins and flooded her heart. A way for her to have her heart's desire *and* her family. 'Twas a dream come true.

"I'm afraid to hope," she admitted, her voice laced with fear.

"Don't you worry, lass," her mother chided. "I've never failed in a task I set my mind to. If I were you, I'd be packing my belongings for the return trip to Montgomery Keep. I wager I'll have your father talked around in less than a day."

CHAPTER 47

"Bowen, the McInnises approach!"

Bowen stopped in mid-swing and nearly lost his arm when the warrior with whom he was sparring nearly didn't halt his advance. The warrior blanched and hastily backed away, horrified at what he'd almost done. But Bowen wasn't paying him the least bit of attention.

He whirled to see Rorie standing a few paces away, her eyes dancing with glee. The lass was nearly beside herself.

"Do not jest with me," he warned.

"'Tis not a jest! The word was just delivered to Graeme. He comes to tell you himself, but I overheard and ran to tell you."

He pushed down his excitement. It might be nothing more than Genevieve's father paying a visit. But why? He couldn't allow himself to think that he would see Genevieve, because the disappointment would be crushing.

He'd only half existed in the time she had been gone from Montgomery Keep. The weeks had seemed like years, and he threw himself into training. His men avoided him. No one volunteered to spar with him, and his family despaired of him.

He was as a wounded wild animal seeking only to be left alone to nurse his injuries. He'd noticed the looks cast his way by Graeme and even Rorie. Eveline's gaze was filled with sympathy, but even she stayed out of his path.

He knew he was hard to live with and not fit company for anyone, but he couldn't pretend that he wasn't miserable.

He sheathed his sword and dismissed the warrior, who looked only too happy to take his leave. Then he turned to Rorie.

"Tell me all."

Rorie wiggled in her excitement, a broad smile on her face. "A messenger arrived just a few minutes past, bearing word that the McInnises will arrive within the hour. They're coming, Bowen!"

"'Tis possible Genevieve did not accompany them," Bowen said softly.

Rorie snorted. "What purpose would they have in coming here if Genevieve were not with them?"

Bowen remained silent, refusing to give voice to his hopes. Without a word, he strode toward the guard tower and climbed the steps to the top so he could have a bird's-eye view of their approach.

A moment later, Graeme arrived to stand beside him.

"I see Rorie found you first," he said dryly.

"She told me the McInnises approach. Have you any other information?"

Graeme shook his head. "The missive was short. They told of their arrival and requested our hospitality."

Bowen blew out his breath in frustration. What if she hadn't accompanied them? And why had they traveled to Montgomery Keep?

The questions burned in his mind, and he stood there, silent and brooding, as he waited for the first sign of their approach.

He stood there an hour, his gaze locked to the horizon. And then the first rider appeared, bearing the McInnis banner. His pulse kicked up and his breathing became more rapid. He leaned forward over the tower, straining to see each rider as they gradually came into sight.

His hands curled around the stone ledge and his jaw was locked. He was so tense that his muscles protested, but his entire being was on alert for that first sign of Genevieve.

"There is no litter," Graeme observed, as more McInnis warriors poured over the hillside.

Bowen's heart sank. He sagged, his body going slack as grief filled his heart all over again. He took a step back, prepared to descend the tower and retreat into the keep. Graeme could keep up the social niceties and discern the purpose of the visit.

As he started to turn away, one rider broke from the pack. The horse galloped forward at a faster clip than the others, and it was then he saw the long brown hair streaming behind her like a beacon.

His breath caught and he swayed and gripped the ledge to steady himself. His legs had gone so weak that he wasn't sure they would hold him up.

Genevieve.

Beside him Graeme grinned and slapped him on the back.

"What are you waiting for? Go and greet your lass."

Bowen bolted from the tower, nearly tripping in his haste to descend the stairs. He hit the courtyard at a dead run and bolted, racing across the rolling terrain as Genevieve bore down on him on horseback.

She pulled up a short distance away and slid from her saddle with a haste that nearly gave Bowen an attack of the heart. Her feet hit the ground, and then she was running just as swiftly as he did. Running to him, her smile so big it outshone the sun.

He held out his arms, and she hit him full force right in the chest. He lifted her, hugging her so close that he was sure he crushed her. He spun her round and round as he buried his face in her hair, absorbing the feel of having her in his arms again.

"Ah lass, I missed you so," he breathed.

"I missed you as well, Bowen. So very much."

He pulled her back so he could look upon her face. As she slid down his body and planted her feet back on the ground, he cupped her face and stroked her skin. He couldn't get enough of her.

"If this is a dream, I never want to wake up," he said hoarsely.

She smiled. " 'Tis no dream. I am here."

Unable to contain himself any longer, and uncaring that her father and hundreds of McInnis warriors now surrounded them, he fused his lips to hers.

He near devoured her mouth, so hungry for her that he ached. Her taste, her scent—just the feel of her, soft and willing in his arms. It was more than he could take in.

"Well, I suppose that answers one question," Lachlan McInnis said dryly.

Bowen reluctantly tore himself away from Genevieve and looked up to see Laird McInnis looming over them, still astride his horse.

Genevieve's cheeks were pink, but her eyes shone with happiness. Bowen didn't even dare consider the reason she was here.

"I must speak with you, Bowen," Genevieve whispered as she threaded her hand through his. "In private."

He squeezed her hand and then focused his attention temporarily on her father.

"I bid you welcome to Montgomery Keep," he said formally. "If you ride within the courtyard, your horses will be cared for and you'll be offered refreshment in the great hall."

Amusement crinkled the older man's eyes, and he shook his head. Then he looked at his daughter.

"Now, don't be long, lass. I have much to discuss with the lad."

"I won't, Papa," she said, ducking her head shyly.

Bowen waited until the procession of McInnis warriors had filed past toward the keep, and then he turned back to Genevieve, crushing her in his embrace just so he would know she was real, standing here in front of him.

He swept her into his arms and carried her back toward the keep.

"You do not have to carry me, Bowen," she teased.

"Lass, 'tis not likely I'll let you go anytime soon, so there's no sense arguing."

She smiled and relaxed into his hold, laying her head on his shoulder.

He bore her around the side of the keep and toward the river, where they'd once bid their farewells. When he was a distance from the keep, he lowered himself to the ground, still holding her tightly against him.

"I cannot believe you are here," he said in wonder. "*Why* are you here?"

'Twas a question he dreaded asking, for he wasn't certain he wanted to know the answer. But he hoped. God in heaven he hoped, with all his heart, that he knew her answer.

She regarded him solemnly, her gaze earnest. "I have something to tell you, Bowen. 'Tis of great import."

"Speak, lass. Whatever it is, it will make no difference in my feelings for you."

Her eyes sparkled with sudden light. "I certainly hope 'tis not true!"

He cocked his head to the side, curious as to her mood. She seemed so . . . different. Joyous and yet shy. There was a glow about her that radiated to everyone around her. She looked happy. And was that not what he wanted for her above all else?

She touched his face, and he couldn't help himself. He slid his hand over hers, trapping it against his jaw so her hand would linger there.

"I'm carrying your babe," she said softly.

At first he didn't think he'd heard her right. Then he worried that 'twas not welcome news. He studied her intently, but all he saw was deep contentment and a peace in her eyes he hadn't seen in all the time he'd known her.

"A babe?" he whispered.

His hands automatically went to her waist, but he could discern no evidence of a pregnancy. Her waist was still flat and narrow.

He rested his palm over her womb and stared up at her for confirmation.

She smiled and nodded. "Aye. 'Tis your bairn I carry."

He simply couldn't fathom it. Joy flooded his very soul, until he was dizzy with it. He tried to find the words to adequately convey his happiness, but nothing would come close to describing his elation.

He cupped her face, his fingers shaking against her cheeks. "You have to know that I'll never want to let you go."

Her eyes sparkled. "Aye, I know it."

He sobered. "I want you happy, Genevieve. I'll not force you to do anything you do not want. If you are content with your family, I would not take you away when they've only been reunited with you a month. I'll not force you into anything when your choices have long been taken from you."

Tears shone in her eyes and she put her hands to his face in a like manner. "I love you so, Bowen. Why think you I come with my father and the whole of our army? 'Tis not a short stay I plan. If you'll have me. My mother has grand plans of visiting often, and of coming when 'tis time to give birth to our child. She says the Montgomerys will just have to come to terms with the McInnises being frequent visitors."

"If I'll *have* you?" Bowen asked hoarsely. "Lass, there is no one in this world I'd rather spend my life with. *Have* you? I'd suffer visits from the Devil himself if it means you'll be by my side for the rest of my days."

"My father wishes to speak to you on the matter," she said in a more serious tone.

"Aye, I'm sure of it. He will want to make certain his only daughter is well cared for, and I cannot blame him. 'Tis certain I will be the same with the daughters you give me."

Her smile lit up the hillside. "You're so sure I'll give you lasses."

He covered her mouth with his own, savoring the joy of having her back in his arms. "I insist on it."

CHAPTER 48

It was difficult to relinquish Genevieve into Rorie's and Eveline's care even for a moment, but he settled the lass with his sisters and went in search of Genevieve's father.

He found him in the great hall enjoying a tankard of ale with Graeme.

Lachlan glanced up when Bowen entered the room, his face twitching with amusement.

"'Tis about time you pulled yourself away from my daughter."

Bowen inclined his head respectfully. "Genevieve says you have much to discuss with me."

"Aye, I do at that."

He gestured toward the seat in front of him. Graeme occupied the head of the table.

"Sit, lad. There needs be a serious discussion between us."

Bowen took a seat, prepared for the fight of his life. There was nothing he wouldn't do to prove himself worthy of Genevieve. And he'd move heaven and earth to have her as his wife.

"My daughter is carrying your bairn," Lachlan said bluntly.

Graeme nearly choked on his ale, coughing violently as he stared agape at Bowen.

Bowen nodded. "Genevieve told me."

"And? What say you to that?"

"'Tis most welcome news. I couldn't be more happy that she carries my child."

Laird McInnis stared shrewdly at Bowen. "She says you love her."

"With all my heart."

The laird looked satisfied with Bowen's response, his posture relaxing as he continued to stare at Bowen.

"And I take it that you're open to marrying the lass?"

"If 'tis what she wants, I'd marry her within the hour. However, I'll not force her to do anything she doesn't choose. She's been denied choices for too long."

Laird McInnis's eyes glinted with respect. "I like you, lad. I think you'd be a fine husband for my daughter, and don't think I'd accept just any man for her. She is my only child, and beloved by all her clan."

"I would love her and care for her all my days," Bowen said quietly. "There is no other man who will ever love her more."

"I believe you," the laird said in a sincere voice. "And 'tis obvious the lass loves you as well. Now, there are other matters—important matters—we must speak on before we settle things between us."

Bowen nodded. "I am listening."

"Genevieve is my only child, and my heir. When the lairdship falls to her, she will need a strong husband to stand beside her. Can you be content with that?"

Bowen sat straighter in his seat, his gaze narrowing. "If you're asking if I would seek to undermine her position or put her behind me so that I may assume leadership of your clan, the answer is no. All I want is Genevieve. She is enough. She'll *always* be enough."

The laird nodded again. "There's more I'm asking you, lad. Would you be willing to spend spring and summer within our clan instructing the men and training with them, so that when Genevieve does inherit the leadership role you will be an able taskmaster to assist her in her duties?"

Bowen let out his breath. It wasn't something he'd ever considered. Aye, he'd gone to the McHugh clan on behalf of his brother and he'd assumed leadership there, albeit for a short time. But it had never been on the assumption of anything more permanent.

What Laird McInnis proposed was no small thing, and it would mean leaving his own clan. His brother, to whom he owed his loyalty.

But to have Genevieve? To have her as his wife. To live and love and raise their children. Aye, he'd do anything.

He glanced at Graeme to gauge his reaction, but there was no disapproval on his face.

"If you are asking me my thoughts, I would say 'tis your choice. I'll support you in whatever you choose," Graeme said. "You'll be sorely missed, but 'tis also a great opportunity for you, and you'll have your heart's desire. If the positions were reversed and this was the way I could have Eveline, I would not even hesitate a moment."

"She would remain here until after the birth of the child. Through the winter," Laird McInnis continued. "But come spring, when she and the babe are able to make the journey, I would like for you both to come . . . home."

"Have you spoken on this with Genevieve?" Bowen asked. "Is she in agreement?"

Laird McInnis chuckled. "You truly do have my daughter's best interest and happiness at heart. A man can ask for no better when choosing a husband for his only child. Aye, I've spoken with Genevieve on the matter. She is of much the same mind as you. She is happy and content as long as you are together."

Bowen's shoulders sagged in relief. It was almost too

much to contemplate. When he'd said his farewell to Genevieve, he'd truly believed he would never see her again. That she was here, and he was being given an opportunity to marry her and that they were having a child together, was too much for him to take in. He was overcome and could not gather his thoughts enough to respond.

"It would appear we have a wedding to plan," Laird McInnis announced. "I would send word to my wife, who was not happy that I did not allow her to accompany us on our journey. She woke up ailing on the morning of our departure, and I feared the ride would prove too arduous for her. But she'll not miss her daughter's wedding, or I'll not be allowed back in my own keep. If 'tis agreeable to you, I'll remain until she's able to make the journey, and then you and Genevieve will be wed before both our clans. I'll not have some hasty affair, as though I'm shamed by the fact my daughter is with child. It will be a celebration unrivaled by any. I would give her a wedding worthy of a lass who has no equal in my eyes."

Graeme nodded. "I agree. Eveline will be delighted to plan such a grand event. It will truly be a joyous occasion. My brother has moped as a man half alive in this time that Genevieve has been away. I would see him happy and celebrate his good fortune."

Laird McInnis chuckled. "Between the lass ailing with the babe and her missing Bowen, it's been a dirge within my own keep."

"Sick?" Bowen asked sharply. "Genevieve has been ill?"

Laird McInnis waved his hand in a dismissive manner. "'Tis nothing more than the usual with a woman in her condition. I remember when my own wife was carrying Genevieve, we had to keep a chamber pot in every room. We never knew when the lass would take ill. Worry not.

Genevieve is hale and hearty, and now that she is returned to you she'll improve all the more."

Bowen took in a breath and leveled a stare at the man who would be his father by marriage.

"I know this is not easy for you, to let go of Genevieve so soon after being reunited with her. I can promise you that I will do everything in my power to make her happy and ensure she never wants for anything I can give her."

The laird smiled a little sadly. "Do you remember why you let her go?"

Bowen frowned. "I wanted what was best for her. I wanted her to be happy."

The laird nodded. "'Tis the same thing her mother and I want for her. She assures me she will be happy with you, so I am content to let her go. This time I know she'll be in a situation where she is provided for and not abused. I can be at ease regarding her welfare. 'Tis the not knowing that is agony."

"There will never be another woman more cherished," Bowen vowed.

The laird looked satisfied with Bowen's response. Then he picked up his goblet and toasted the air.

"I've kept you from my Genevieve long enough. I know you're itching to go back to her. There will be plenty of time to talk on matters in the coming days. I must send word to my wife, and we have a wedding to plan."

CHAPTER 49

Genevieve tried to concentrate on the excited chatter between Eveline and Rorie, but she kept glancing off to see when Bowen would reappear. After not seeing him for so long, she wanted only to sink into his arms and remain there for the next fortnight.

Eveline and Rorie had dragged her out to the make-shift target so they could show her how much they'd improved their archery skills. Genevieve was appropriately impressed, and she was warmed by their excitement at her return.

Things were so utterly perfect that she feared waking to find that she was back at McHugh Keep, under Ian's lock and key, and all of this was just a fanciful dream.

"Look, Genevieve, Bowen approaches," Rorie said as she looked over Genevieve's shoulder.

Genevieve whirled around and, without a word, took off at a brisk pace. Forgoing any sense of propriety, she broke into a run and flung herself into Bowen's arms as she'd done when they first greeted each other upon her arrival.

He caught her to him and kissed her soundly, until she was starved for air. Then he set her down and gave her a chiding look.

"You have to stop throwing yourself around thusly, lass. You have a bairn to consider now."

She smiled, wanting to squeeze him in her delight.

"Did you speak to my father?" she asked.

"I did."

She waited, and when he didn't offer anything further, she smacked him on the arm. "Well, tell me! I'm dying here. You cannot keep me in suspense any longer."

Brodie chuckled and pulled her into his arms, kissing her nose, her eyes, her forehead, and each cheek before finally claiming her lips once more.

"I love you, lass. I fear I'll never grow tired of saying so."

Her heart softened and she kissed him back, savoring the hard line of his lips.

"I'll never grow tired of hearing you say it. Now, tell me all. What did my father say?"

He turned, taking her hand in his as they walked away from where Rorie and Eveline practiced their aim.

"He told me of his desire for us to reside at McInnis Keep for half the year."

She glanced anxiously up at him. "Do you mind?"

He stopped and turned to face her, gathering her hands in his. "Genevieve, I would agree to six months in hell if it meant being with you."

Her cheeks warmed and she smiled, joy spreading like wildfire through her soul.

"Well, I hope you don't think six months at McInnis Keep is akin to hell," she teased.

"If I'm with you, anywhere is heaven."

"Oh, Bowen. You cannot keep saying such things. You'll keep me in tears, and I'm already an emotional mess with the babe. My mother tells me 'tis normal, but some days I feel as if I'm unraveling!"

He chuckled and kissed her on the nose again.

"The wedding will be here as soon as your mother is fit to travel the distance. We'll spend the winter at Montgomery Keep, and after you've delivered the babe, in the spring, when you're able to travel, we'll make the journey to McInnis Keep."

She bit her lip and stared hesitantly up at him. "Do you mind that my father intends me to be laird of our clan, and that he intends you to aid me in the role of leadership?"

"Are you asking if I'm threatened by the prospect?"

After a moment, she nodded. "Some men would not take it well."

Bowen threw back his head and laughed. "Lass, I wouldn't care if you were the queen of bloody England. As long as I have you as my wife, I care not if you are pauper or laird. You're a fierce and courageous lass. I cannot think of a better laird for your people when 'tis time for your father to pass on the mantle of leadership. If you think I'll stand back and sulk because my manhood is threatened, you're wrong. I'll allow you to take me into our chamber from time to time, so that you can show me that I'm still useful in some capacity."

Genevieve burst into laughter and hugged him fiercely, because otherwise she would cry. Not because she was unhappy but because joy crowded every inch of her heart and soul. She was about to burst with it.

"I love you, Bowen Montgomery. I love you so very much, and that will never change, even when we're old and gray. I thank God for you every single day, and that you came and lifted me from the depths of despair. You showed me how it can be with a man who loves me, and you've shined light on the darkest shadows of my memories."

He stroked her hair, tucking the wayward strands behind her ears. "We'll make new memories, lass. Every day for the rest of our lives. And when we're old we can recount the tale of how a lass overcame insurmountable odds and became one of the fiercest lairds in all of Scotland."

TELL THE WORLD THIS BOOK WAS		
GOOD	BAD	SO-SO
✗ ✗ ✗ ✗